ULTIMATE

SACRIFICE

ಲ☺ಲ

Laurie,
Happy reading!
Thank you for your support.

S. K. Lundberg

THE

ULTIMATE

SACRIFICE

∾

The Dead of Winter

S.K. LUNDBERG

Cedarside 🌿 Publishing

Published in the United States by Cedarside Publishing. The cedar branch logo is courtesy of openclipart.org.

Library of Congress Cataloging-in-Publication Data is available.
ISBN: 978-0-692-13934-9
eBook ISBN: 978-0-692-89477-4
Photography and Cover design: S.K. Lundberg

Printed in the United States of America

I dedicate this book to all the young men who have lost their lives, and to their families, friends, and loved ones who are left to endure an agonizing life without them.
Prayers and peace to you all.

May awareness bring you answers

▼

ACKNOWLEDGEMENTS

I would like to thank my family and friends for their grammar tips, technical support, and editing advice. Hugs go out to my special little editor. You know who you are. I really couldn't have done it without you. So grateful for the added support and the push to the finish line.

Nick, a special thanks to you for showing me how to organize and start my book. Your course is awesome.

An immense amount of gratitude to the researchers, bloggers, and believers for your insight and knowledge. May all of your hard work pay off one day. Keep on digging for the truth.

Librarians, you rock. Thanks for all of your help.

To those of you taking the time to post your wonderful online articles, tutorials, and writing software to help the rest of us jump the never ending hurdles. Thanks. You guys are great.

This goes out to the good guys; the police and the medical professionals who relentlessly protect and serve while tirelessly leaving no stone unturned. You truly are our heroes. Thank you so much for doing your job.

Thank you everyone for making my dream of becoming a writer possible. It has been a long, bumpy road filled with self-doubt and perseverance. I will forever be appreciative for your help and encouragement.

PREFACE

The year was 2006. I remember the first time I heard his name and saw his face on the news. After a night out with his friends—he vanished.

I found myself staring at the TV screen as the news anchor finished her story. My curiosity was definitely peaked. A red flag had just gone off in my head causing me to be forever drawn into this mystery. I remember saying to myself, "That's weird. The same darn thing happened last year."

What had happened to him? I knew I needed to find out the truth, so I dug in and started my research. His name has since been added to the long list of smart, popular, athletic, young men that had mysteriously disappeared and were later tragically found dead in the river, pond, or other water source. So far this list of drowning victims goes back to 1997. Sadly, new names are added every year. This strange phenomenon continues to this day and has become an urban legend.

The killer has been dubbed Smiley by the American media and The Pusher in the U.K. Where will they strike next? Honestly, no one seems to know. That is what makes this mystery almost impossible to solve. Therefore, for obvious reasons, in this book I chose to continue the mystery in the fictitious small town of River Bend. A cast of unforgettable characters are waiting for their fate to be revealed.

This fact-based tale with a fictional spin is my creative way of sharing this unsolved mystery with the world to bring awareness and justice for the boys.

CHAPTER ONE

IN THE MIND OF A MURDERER

I enter your world and soon you will leave this world, exactly as you came in, cold and screaming looking for comfort and compassion that never comes. The end is here for you. It is only the beginning for me. My game is just getting started.

When the time is right, I will hunt you from the shadows and steal the color from your eyes. To be perfectly clear, you will die an excruciating watery death. I will watch as your light fades and tell all.

The demented and the morally corrupt are already standing in line waiting for every juicy detail. Morbid curiosity will suck-in the rest while you are fighting for your last agonizing breath. I dare anyone to look away. You know you want to watch. Feeding your dark side and uncovering the truth is no longer an option. It is a necessity. But be absolutely positive that you can handle what I am about to show you. Once you see it, you cannot unknow it. There is no delete button in your brain. It is only a matter of time before I creep in and the nightmares begin. Shall we continue?

While I lurk in the darkness, my game unfolds. I watch as you desperately claw towards the surface searching for life. Gulps of icy water pour into your lungs. Panic sets in and you violently thrash in the water. You grab at everything, but touch nothing. Life is slipping through your fingers.

Your head briefly breaches the surface. You cough and then vomit. The attempt to clear the water from your lungs ends in failure, but nice try. Before you can catch your breath, the frigid water pricks at your skin like a thousand tiny needles causing your muscles to tighten, then spasm, dragging you back under.

The convulsions start as the freezing water circulates through your body. Pain twists your face. The fear that consumes you is rapidly evolving into acceptance. Any second, it will slither its way into your head. When it does, your eyes will give you away. The windows to your soul will speak to me and tell me what I already know. Your light is fading. That special spark is gone. Death is near.

For the last time, your hand slowly floats towards the surface. Calmly, you let go. Your body becomes weightless in the water. Blackness follows. The seal breaks. The dark, turbulent water returns to glass. Without remorse, I see you silently slip into your watery grave. Your death means everything to me and then nothing when your empty vessel floats away.

What am I? Some say monster, others say master. Does that make me the sick, twisted individual who walks among you freely, day or night? Or the genius who thrives on being the last person you would ever expect?

You can call me whatever you want. I know what I am. I am the most dangerous person, the most elusive murderer you will ever meet. I am charming on the outside, pure evil within. My darkness remains flawlessly concealed until you are chosen. Then I flip the switch and become a heartless bastard; a killing machine seeking out what I want, where I want, when I want.

What do I want? I want what you possess, my chosen prey. So when you hear a strange noise, always look over your shoulder. I am right behind you. Yes, it is me in your closet, under your bed, or in your back seat. I can wait patiently. So silent behind a tree or the stone arch of a bridge that you will never see me until it is too late.

If you are brave enough to be alone in the dark, you are stupid enough for me to kill. You are my perfect prey. That means I will be seeing you soon. You cannot hide from me. There will be no escape. There will be no mercy. I have a taste for it now, and I am never going to stop.

. . .

2

It is time for the new hunt to begin . . . I see you, my chosen prey. Following you is like a game for me. The hunt is almost as fulfilling as the kill. I have been two steps behind you most of the afternoon, watching and waiting for the perfect opportunity to strike.

You enter the grocery store, and I follow you inside. There is no need for me to hide from you because we have never met. I am just another face in the crowd. A stranger until we meet that last fatal time.

I watch you from a distance, just to be safe, while you pick out your last meal. You choose a frozen pizza and a Red Bull. Nice. At least you will get your wings before I send you to the depths of hell.

You round the corner and pause in the chip aisle. I move in closer. I see you trolling for that salty goodness that only crunchy, deep-fried corn chips can provide. You reach for your wallet. As you dig for dollars, you curse and set the Doritos back on the shelf. Excellent. I commend you on your chip choice, not your money management.

It is time for me to enter your world. I will count to three. Then I will run into you on purpose and start my demented game. This will be fun. Your reaction will tell me if I kill you quick or slow. It is my own personal version of heads or tails. Brilliant, is it not?

I feed my need to bond by accidentally ramming my cart into a towering display of mac & cheese. The tidal wave of tiny boxes knocks you and your dinner to the floor. I mentally pat myself on the back while I apologize and help you up.

The confrontation does not go well for you. To my witnesses, I come off as the Good Samaritan. You come off as the punk with the bad attitude and the eye roll. I was willing to give you the benefit of the doubt. Apparently, I am wasting my time thinking you could show me your good side. No need to flip a coin . . . slow it is then. More pain for you, more fun for me. You should really learn to smile more. You might live longer.

From the checkout lane, I spot the eye in the sky. Because someone is always watching, I stop at the door to tie my shoe. Creating space between us helps me build my alibi. No one must see us leave the store together, especially on the new surveillance camera overhead. With my head held high, I walk out guilty of nothing. The perception of innocence is crucial to my survival.

I get outside just in time to catch your red muscle car pulling out of the parking lot. From a distance, I follow you down Main Street. I decide

3

to speed up. My heart races and shifts into overdrive.

For kicks, I purposely ride next to you while eating handfuls of cheesy Doritos right out of the bag. My perfect peripherals catch your first glare. I annoy you by staring straight ahead at the road as I drive. I grin from ear-to-ear on the inside and shove another fist-full of Doritos into my mouth. When you glare over again, you speed up. Your engine rumbles with defiance as you shift gears to pass. Nice. I have gotten under your skin. We never make eye contact, but it was still a rush.

For now, I flip off the switch to avoid suspicion. I continue to head down Main Street. Out of the corner of my eye, I see you turn off onto Cedar Drive and head home to the college apartments. I could kill you there. Your roommates are gone. You are all alone. No one would miss you for days. Privately turning you into a puddle of rotting flesh would be too easy. I need a challenge to bring new life to my game.

Go into your apartment. Enjoy your last meal. I will be waiting for you and counting the minutes you have left to breathe. When you are ready, we will finish.

. . .

It is dark now. The snow is falling around me as I wait with anticipation in the bitter cold. After forty-five minutes, you appear as predicted on the jogging path. My pulse races with the sudden adrenaline surge pumping through my veins. I close my eyes, take a deep breath, and remember why I am here. I regain my composure.

I can hear your feet on the crisp, snow-covered path. You are close, dangerously close. I feel for my gun, brushing it lightly with my hand just to make sure that it is still there. The time is near. I hide behind a tree, holding my breath and my body perfectly still.

You jog past me, without seeing me, in the dim light of the New Moon. Now will you fall for my trap? Hidden beneath the dusting of new fallen snow is a sheet of ice that I prepared last night after your run.

Just as I predicted, your speed and agility work against you as you hit the ice. You find your wings and fly in the air like a cartoon character, landing hard on your back on the blacktopped path. Your hat-covered skull cracks down solidly on the ice, leaving you briefly unconscious. Maybe if I *am lucky, there will be blood. Blood will make your accident more believable. I look around to make sure that we are still alone. Then I step out of the shadows anxious to go to work. Much time has been spent learning how to make murder look like an accident, or better yet, a suicide. It is pure artistry, really, when Mother Nature and Father Science help me transform my game. However, the ancient secrets will have to remain with me for now. You must be patient if you want to learn the truth.*

My prey, you lay there so still on the path as if you are already dead. I stand over you now wondering what you could have done to deserve this. Maybe something . . . probably nothing. It is not up to me anymore. No one can save you now. Your coat of armor will suit you soon.

It is true what they say about the Northwoods. It is a perfect place to get away with murder. I should know. I am living, breathing proof. The killings have been going on for decades undetected. No one has a clue.

Sure, there are whispers around beauticians' chairs and morticians' tables, but nothing louder than whispers. The great motto of the North: "Everyone knows everything, and yet nobody knows nothing." Or for the simple folk: "Keep your damn mouth shut." Most of these people can keep secrets, deep dark secrets, except for this one bitch.

She has been poking around asking too many questions lately. This leaves me with no choice. I have to make a public example out of Payton Richardson. This time, it will not look like an accident. It will be a creative masterpiece. I will hold nothing back. When I am finished, there will be dead silence in the Northwoods forever. No one will dare speak of this without fearing my wrath.

I must go now. My prey is waiting. When I am done with him, all my attention will be focused on her. This game should be fun. Would you like to watch?

. . .

Ok, here's the short version. My name is Payton Marie Richardson. I'm standing on my parents' rooftop, in the dark, freezing to death, holding a Prada purse full of vomit. Why? Because someone is trying to kill me. Welcome to my ridiculously tragic, pathetic life.

It all started about ten minutes ago. I was in my bed, fast asleep, minding my own darn business, when out of nowhere, a loud noise downstairs woke me up from my Nyquil-induced coma.

Normally, I wouldn't give a tiny rat's ass, but I was home alone in the remote Northwoods of Wisconsin, so you can relate to my intense situation. I flew out of bed to investigate the strange noise.

As soon as my feet hit the floor, I blindly stumbled around my room in the dark. Before my eyes could adjust, I tripped over my garbage can and slammed into my dresser. After my entire CD collection dominoed to the floor, my room was dead silent. I heard the noise again. There was definitely someone else in the house.

From my doorway, I saw the faint glow of light downstairs. I was clueless to who could be rummaging around in my kitchen in the middle of the night. My parents, Stan and Janna, were in Texas on vacation. My slightly younger brother Luke was away at college. This was not a social call and definitely not a booty call. Currently, my Facebook status was single. To be completely honest, my status was more like undateable.

I stepped out into the hallway and quietly made my way to the staircase. When I looked over the railing to the first floor, a dark figure stepped out of the shadows. He flicked on the light at the bottom of the stairs. I darted back into the temporary safety of my bedroom before he saw me. My heart pumped on adrenaline overload as I quickly pushed my door closed.

I desperately needed to think of a quick survival plan. Who was I kidding? I had nothing and no escape route. It was time to panic and hide.

My room was still dark, lit only by the moonlight that came in the second story window. Turning on the light was not an option. It would give away my location. I nervously scanned my dark room for options. Where should I go? Where could I hide?

Their footsteps creaked on the stairs. Reality set in. The intruder had heard me. He was coming up to search the second floor.

I was frantically scampering around in the dark when my necessity suddenly crashed into my reality. My body chose this exact moment to remind me that I had the flu. My stomach stood up. It flipped over backwards as the acid rose in my throat. Heat raced across my forehead. Little beads of sweat ran down my face. The back of my throat tasted funky. The inevitable was coming. I hate the inevitable.

Under the circumstances, the only logical idea that popped into my head was to escape out the window. I quietly slid the window open. The Arctic, January air blasted me in the face. For a split second, it felt surprisingly refreshing. Then a shiver ran down to my toes. This had bad idea written all over it. But what choice did I have?

Before I climbed out onto the roof, I glanced over my shoulder at my bedroom door. The unmistakable shadow of feet appeared beneath it. My uninvited house guest was standing right on the other side of my unlocked door. He had me cornered with no time to change my mind. I needed to move fast.

Instinctively, I reached out and grabbed my favorite Prada handbag that hung on the chair next to the window. I swiftly crawled out, closing the window behind me. The cold of the icy shingles penetrated my fuzzy socks, then inched its way up my legs. I was trapped on my roof and quickly turning into a Popsicle.

I moved to the side of the window, shrinking back against the siding to hide. Both hands pressed against my mouth to postpone the inevitable and quiet my breathing. I tried to stay still in my hiding spot, but my body shook uncontrollably from the cold.

After only fifteen seconds of body shaking spasms and teeth chattering, I caved to curiosity. Who the heck was in my house? I needed to know who was on the other side of that door.

From my position alongside the window, I peered into my bedroom just in time to see the door swing open. My intruder stood in the doorway, backlit by the dim light from the hall. I couldn't see their face, just the outline of their body in the darkness. Why was he here? What did he want? Why was this happening to me?

When he stepped forward into my dark room, the light from the hallway glinted off something long, narrow, and shiny in his left hand. Seeing as how he just came from the kitchen, it was most likely a knife. This was not looking good for me.

My clammy hands continued to grip the windowsill as I stared into my room. I knew I should let go and hide again, but for some reason I couldn't take my eyes off of my knife-wielding friend. Then it dawned on me why. I realized that this person looked familiar to me. Could I possibly know my intruder? Could someone I know want me dead?

The light in my room flicked on. I jumped back into position alongside the window. When I let go of the frosty, metal windowsill a thin layer of skin peeled away from my hands. I cringed and did my best to quietly grimace in pain. When I looked down at my blistered palms, my stomach rolled again. The sight of the missing flesh made me sick. A flood of warmth filled my face. A dry heave rippled through my upper body. There was no escaping what was coming.

The inevitable happened at the worst possible time. Sadly, to muffle the noise I had to use my purse—my very new, very expensive, very roomy—Prada purse that was a gift from my mother.

The window flew open just as I finished abusing the Prada. I froze in position, clutching my open vomit-filled handbag with both hands. A shadowy head and torso suddenly jutted out from the opening. I still couldn't see their face, only the back of their head from where I was hiding. When he leaned out of the window to look around the roof, I saw the silvery blade of the knife. I knew I only had seconds before he found me. Maybe I only had seconds left to live.

Here we go. Life or death; I chose life. I did the only thing I could think of to save myself. The eighty-year-old woman deep down inside of me took over. I swung the Prada as hard as I could and hit my unwelcomed guest square in the face. After that, everything went south. We both lost our balance.

I'm not going to lie. It wasn't pretty. The disaster in my purse flew everywhere as we slid down the icy rooftop like Olympic lugers. There was screaming and the unavoidable thud when we both hit the snow-covered ground below.

CHAPTER TWO

What does not kill us, makes us stronger. We will just have to see about that. Smooth move with the purse. I did not see that one coming. Are you ready for round two?

. . .

My guest was out cold, face down in the snow bank. I fortunately landed on my mom's huge azalea bushes before I rolled to a stop next to my fellow luger. My natural instincts for survival took over. I jumped to my feet and ran as fast as I could towards the house.

I cut across the snowy yard to the driveway. Just before I reached the corner of the house, I awkwardly skidded to a stop on the icy pavement. For some reason I was drawn back to the front yard. I turned on my heels and headed back towards my attacker. Why would I do such a crazy thing? Maybe it was curiosity again. Who wants me dead? Or maybe it was just blind stupidity. I seriously don't know, but wish me luck. I'm going back anyway. Regrettably, I have done many stupid things in my life for very curious reasons.

I carefully moved back towards the body sprawled out on my parents' front lawn. The closer I got to it, the more familiar the person laying there seemed to me. Their short curly red hair, their apparent forty-something spare tire, their sweater my parents just bought her for Christmas. Oh, crap. The he is a she, and I know her. I think I just killed our housekeeper, Vivian Black.

This wasn't good. My mom was going to be really pissed at me. Vivian was an excellent housekeeper with reasonable rates. She was going to be hard to replace.

Wait a minute. Why would Vivian try to kill me? I am a fairly tidy person. Yesterday I might have left her a sink full of dried-on toothpaste and a glorious hair clog, but that doesn't give her the right to cut me into little pieces. Now I was pissed.

I stood motionless over Vivian, pondering my possibilities. Should I check her for a pulse or hit her with the Prada one more time? The Prada was stuck in the azalea bushes and didn't smell all that great, so I decided to go with checking her pulse.

When I bent down next to Viv, the wind blasted through my Victoria's Secret PINK sweat suit. A chill rippled through my entire body making me ponder the big question. Why the heck was I still out here? Honestly, at this point, it was a hundred percent curiosity. Did I really kill Vivian? Is she really dead?

I reached out with my hand and poked Viv with my finger. She didn't move. Just as I leaned in closer to feel her neck for a pulse, she screamed out in pain. I lost it. I fell backwards in the snow, screaming with her. Instantly, she was motionless again, and I was in serious need of a cocktail.

I figured I had maxed out my bravery and stupidity (B.S.) card for one day. It was time to run to the house and call 911. My frozen feet carried me around the left side of the house and up the driveway. As soon as I spotted Vivian's blue Honda parked up by the garage, I knew the back door must be unlocked. I climbed the wooden deck steps, raced to the door, and stumbled inside. The warmth of the house hit me. I fell to the kitchen floor completely exhausted.

SK LUNDBERG

After a few spastic deep breaths, I found the strength and motivation to move. The portable phone was next to its stand on the black, granite countertop. I crawled over to it and pulled myself up. I picked up the receiver and stared at the red low battery light. "Ugh!"

Now what? This was our only landline. Wait a minute. I'll just use my cell phone. Where was my cell phone? My head hurt as my brain shifted into memory mode. I felt the pockets of my clothing. It wasn't there. I glanced towards the front yard. Was it in the Prada? Nooooo . . . it was still sitting on the counter at work. Sonova . . . My finger immediately punched in 911 while I said a little prayer that sounded a lot like swearing. Please, please, please let me get through to someone before this bleeping battery goes dead.

As I impatiently waited for someone to greet me on the other end of the line, I limped towards the front of the house to see if Vivian was still where I left her. On my way through the kitchen, I noticed that my mom's Rikki Kay knife, from the Celebrity Cooking Network, was missing from the butcher's block on the counter. It had to be the knife Vivian used to try to kill me. Vivian was definitely on my shit list.

The frosted, etched glass of the front door made it impossible to see Vivian in the front yard, so I quickly moved into the dining room to look out the window. I let out a huge sigh of relief. Her short, stubby body was still face down in the wintry white stuff. Dead or alive, she was still there.

With the phone pressed firmly against my ear, I walked back through the kitchen. I could hear the phone ringing. Why wasn't the dispatcher answering?

Finally, there was a crackle in the line followed by a woman voice. "This is 911. What is your emergency?"

"Hi," I said frantically. "This is Payton Richardson. I live at 1321 Riverside Drive. I need help. My cleaning lady attacked me with a Rikki Kay butcher knife, and I think I might have killed her with my Prada handbag."

"Is this another one of those prank calls? I had two others tonight that turned out to be wild goose chases. The Chief is

12

pissed and the ambulance crew is more than a little cranky at me."

"No," I said completely exasperated. "I'm serious. I know it sounds crazy, but it's true."

"Ok, calm down. How did this happen?"

"That's not important right now. My phone's battery is about to die. Please send help!"

"Where are you right now? Are you somewhere safe?"

"Yes. I'm inside my house. Can you please get someone over here fast? My parents are out of town. I'm here all alone."

"Ok, Payton. Don't worry. The police and paramedics are en route. They should be at your location in five minutes."

"Thank you," I said with great relief.

"Would you like me to stay on the line until help arrives?"

"Yeah, that would be great. By the way, who else is on duty tonight besides the Chief?"

"Rex, Tim, and Brad are on duty tonight."

"Oh boy, this should be interesting," slipped out of my mouth.

"Is there a problem?"

"No," I lied, not wanting to elaborate. Not elaborating was no longer an issue. The phone went dead. "Hello! Hello!" I hit the redial button just in case. Nothing happened. "Dang it!"

My cold, wet socks squished on the floor while I nervously paced around the kitchen wondering what to do until help arrived. I glanced down at myself. Yikes. I was a mess. I set the phone on its stand and headed for the laundry room to look for some clean clothes.

On the way to the laundry room, I stopped in the hallway to inspect my sore ankle. When I bent over, the stench of my brown, shoulder-length hair overwhelmed me. As it fell across my face, I swore that I would never eat another cheeseburger as long as I lived.

I flipped my hair back with my hand. It was horrifying when I caught a glimpse of myself in the hall mirror. The dark circles under my eyes. The hamburger bits in my hair. My left-over mascara was the scariest part. It made me look like a rabid raccoon that had just finished dumpster diving. The regurgitated chocolate malt stains on my sized small sweat pants accessorized and pulled the disastrous ensemble together. Forget undateable. I had ratchet written all over me.

Inside the laundry room, I found a basket of clean clothes. Thank you, Vivian. Don't get me wrong. Vivian is an excellent housekeeper. She just sucks at the social interaction part where she doesn't try to kill other people.

My wet socks were the first thing that had to go. When I peeled them off, I discovered that the icy snow outside had scraped my feet. They weren't bleeding, but they throbbed as they thawed from the cold. To help warm them up, I put on two pairs of cozy socks. I paused for a minute to appreciate the feeling of warm, dry socks on my cold, shriveled feet.

A car door slammed shut outside interrupting my moment of Zen. Holy crap. She's still alive, and she's getting away. There was no time to change out of my rancid clothes. I jumped into my winter boots that were in the laundry room closet and ran to the back door.

From the window, I saw Vivian sitting in the driver's seat of her Honda. Hoping I still had one more punch left on my B.S. card, I ran out into the driveway behind her car to stop her. The engine turned over. The car's lights flicked on. The blue hatchback clunked into reverse. Vivian and her car were headed right for me, fast.

Ok, so maybe this time I was driven by pure stupidity. I barely had enough time to dive out of the way of her speeding vehicle. I landed on the hard-packed snow bank and then tumbled onto the icy blacktop driveway. My shoulder and hip throbbed with pain. Twice in one night Vivian had tried to kill me. I wasn't about to let her get away with that.

Her car was backing down our long driveway erratically fast when I heard the sirens and saw the lights. There were three police cars and an ambulance blocking her escape. Vivian wasn't going anywhere.

I picked myself off the blacktop, hobbling as fast as I could towards the end of the driveway. My bruised hip, sprained ankle, and sore feet slowed me down. I yelled out in pain and grabbed my shoulder, hoping they would throw the book at her. They all turned around to look at me. This was not my walk of shame. This was my Academy Award-winning performance. Everyone glared back at Vivian in unison. This was excellent.

By the time I made it to the end of the driveway, the Chief of Police, Richard J. Thomas, had Vivian sprawled out face down on the ground assuming the position. So far, this was better than any movie or episode of *Cops* I had ever seen.

The Chief looked like his overly macho self. His Snap-Fitness muscles flexed under his coat as he sat on top of Vivian's back. His anciently gray, almost fifty-something hair had recently been dyed a fake-looking shade of brown. It was obviously a feeble attempt to conceal his age. Normally, I would have given the Chief some crap about his sudden mid-life crisis, but I saw his loaded gun and decided to skip it.

The Chief still had Vivian face down on the ground beneath him. He grabbed her right arm to cuff it behind her back. She cried out in agony.

"Stop," she begged. "I think my arm is broken. Payton broke my arm."

The Chief and his son Brad, the Lieutenant, looked over at me simultaneously with the oh-so-familiar look. That look always meant deep shit for me.

I answered their look with a shoulder shrug and a head tilt that displayed my indifference to the situation. Here is my reality. Most people would be overwhelmed with joy to have Richard and Bradley Thomas come to their rescue. Me? . . . Not so much.

Well, to make an ugly story short, I kind of left Brad hanging at the altar. They are both still beyond angry about it. Apparently, they don't handle public humiliation all that well. But then again, who does?

Since that day last year, the two of them have enjoyed making my life a living hell. Today, I am sure will be no exception. For example, just to get even, Brad has deemed me undateable throughout the entire tri-county area. Every male from the age of eighteen to eighty is afraid to ask me out on a date in fear of being locked-up indefinitely. For this reason, my love life was on quarantine. Yep, strict isolation and free of disease pretty much sums up my dating profile.

Vivian looked over in my direction. She saw me standing near one of the squad cars. Vivian yelled, "There she is. Arrest her. Payton tried to kill me. She attacked me on the roof and then left me in the snow bank to die."

"What the—" was all that came out of my mouth before the charge of blue uniforms hit me. Brad and Rex jumped me, knocking me to the ground. They were trying to handcuff me before I could say anything in my defense. I could feel the weight of their bodies on mine. It was hard to breath and almost impossible to speak. I wasn't going to let Vivian win. I managed to squeak out a convincing, "But she tried to kill me first, with a knife."

They pulled me to my feet. I was gasping for air. Brad took a closer look at me. He started laughing. "Payton, you have really let yourself go downhill. Is that chunks of hamburger in your hair?"

"It is nice to see you too, Bradley," I said in an icy tone. "And yes, it is. It's kind of a long story."

"Oh, this should be good," said the Chief with a high amount of sarcasm.

I rolled my eyes at his comment.

Brad looked over at Vivian, wrinkling up his nose. "Is that—?"

"Yes," Vivian agreed. "Payton hit me with a purse filled with vomit."

"That's because you came at me with a knife. How was I supposed to know it was you?"

The police and ambulance crew made a poor attempt at holding back their laughter.

"This isn't funny," I protested. "Vivian chased me out on the roof with a knife."

"A knife?" Brad snapped. "What knife, Payton? We never found a knife. Did you have a knife, Vivian?"

"No. I have no idea what she is talking about," answered Vivian.

"I know what I saw Brad. She's obviously lying."

"You're delusional, Payton. Maybe you should talk to Dr. Parks again."

"I have an appointment tomorrow. I mean later on today. Like it's any of your business, jackass." I knew that last comment was going to cost me, but it felt fabulous.

"Ok, I've heard enough," shouted the Chief. "I am done standing in this damn snow bank. We are going to sort this out down at the station."

"What about my broken arm?" Vivian asked.

No one answered her. All the focus was on Brad and me.

"Wait a minute," said Brad, trying to hold back a laugh. "I just have to know one thing. Whose—?"

"That would be mine," I chimed in proudly.

"Well, Payton, I must say, you have never looked better. Were you out partying with your friends again?" asked Brad.

"Why do you even care, asshole? F—Y—I, I was not out partying. I have the F—L—U. Feel my forehead. I have a fever."

"Bullshit. You really expect me to believe that?" Brad grabbed me by the arm, swung me around, and led me to his squad car.

"Remind me again why I never married you."

There was silence, dead silence, except the sound of the wind howling through the trees. The world had stopped to wait for Brad's reply. Brad didn't say a word. He was speechless.

"So is this a bad time to ask you boys in blue about the missing college student? Any luck finding him yet?"

Brad remained silent. He and the rest of the officers and the ambulance crew stared at me with disbelief at the horrible timing of my inquisition.

My stomach flip-flopped again under the pressure of their guilty glares. "Wait," I called out in desperation. Brad continued to drag me towards his squad car. I felt my face get dangerously hot. Then the inevitable happened again on Brad's pants and shoes.

"I tried to tell you," I pleaded, when I saw the astonished look on his face. It was too late to say anything else in my defense. My head started to spin out of control. Everything went black.

CHAPTER THREE

When Vivian showed up, I was in your bedroom with you, Payton. Right now, you are scared of her, Payton. You should be scared of me. I am going to do despicable things. You can count on it. You got lucky when you went out the window. You could have hid with me in the closet. Maybe next time, I will be under your bed. That would be fun. Everyone's favorite childhood nightmare comes to life. Sweet dreams for now you nosy bitch.

. . .

When I came to, I found myself in the ambulance strapped to a gurney. An I.V. was in my arm. An oxygen mask was on my face. Vivian and Officer Tim Kline were sitting on the gurney across from me. This definitely was not my idea of a fun Thirsty Thursday, but things were looking up. Brad was nowhere in sight, and Tim the cute new deputy was here to serve and protect me.

I didn't know Tim as long as the other officers. He joined the police force shortly after the big break-up with Brad. Recently, our paths have crossed more often than not around our small town. Just the other day, Tim pulled me over for speeding.

19

He was nice and let me off with just a warning, instead of throwing the book at me. So in a weird roundabout way, we were kind of like BFFs.

The only disparaging comment I could make about him would have to be about his mustache. Tim had one of those ridiculous, macho, cop mustaches that looked pasted on his face. It made it hard to take him serious as an authority figure. I suppose he grew it to over-compensate for his younger, leaner body mass. I just hoped he was up for the challenge if Vivian tried to lunge at me.

We were just pulling up to the Emergency Entrance of the River Bend Medical Center when I heard Vivian complaining.

"My arm is killing me. When can I have something for the pain? Are we almost to the hospital? Can anyone hear me up there?" she said, directing her complaints to the EMTs riding upfront in the ambulance.

The sound of Vivian's nagging voice made my head hurt. "I wish I was still unconscious," I said from behind my mask.

"I wish Vivian was unconscious," Tim whispered with a smile. "She has done nothing but complain."

Weird mustache or not, I decided that I liked Tim a little bit more now. My mask made it almost impossible to talk, so I took it off.

"Are you here to protect me?" I asked Tim.

"No, the Chief sent me along to take your statements."

"Oh," I added, trying to decide if I was relieved or disappointed.

The ambulance crew unloaded us into the warmth of the hospital's Emergency Room and left. I was still on my gurney. Vivian was now in a wheelchair. Tim was hanging around to finish his report and keep the peace between us.

A tired and annoyed blonde-haired nurse greeted us at the front desk. Her name was Nancy Biggerton. On the night shift they call her Big Bad Nancy. I know this because she used to be my mother's supervisor. My mother used to work as an R.N. on the night shift with her until she took early retirement eight months ago.

Eight months ago, the craziest thing happened. My mother retired when my parents got lucky and accidentally won the big Power-Ball jackpot. By accidentally, I mean my mom bought a ticket as a gag gift for my dad's fiftieth birthday. How weird is it that they actually won, striking it rich. Imagine their delight and the jealous horror that ensued throughout our small community. Most of the town has calmed down now and moved on. I wonder if Nancy has done the same.

"Hi, Nancy. How are you?"

"Go to hell, Payton." Nancy threw down her pen. Then she scooped up her coffee cup and stormed off down the hall as impolite as she could without making a complete ass of herself.

I know what you're thinking. The Chief and Nancy should sign up for one of those online dating sites. They are obviously soul mates waiting for a connection. On the upside, that actually went better than I expected. At least she was talking to me now, so there's hope.

A young, dark-haired nurse with "Becky" on her name tag stepped out from behind the main desk with our charts in her hands.

"The on-call doctor just gave me the order for Vivian Black to be sent down to X-Ray. Payton Richardson, you will be placed in a room in Urgent Care until he has time to see you."

"What's the hold up?" asked Tim.

"Dr. Von Hohberg is tending to a critical patient in I.C.U. It might be a while."

"Ok," Tim sighed. "I will take Vivian down to X-Ray. Becky, you put Payton in a room down the hall."

Becky nodded in agreement. She was about to move me down the hall when the ER doors flew open. In came Brad and the Chief from the cold. The Chief looked agitated as always. Brad looked freshly showered and slightly frozen. His dark brown hair had crystallized from the cold night air.

"Hi, guys. What's up?"

"Don't push me, Payton," said the Chief with authority. He then turned his focus to Tim. It was obvious that the Chief made Tim nervous. The Chief made everyone nervous. "Tim, let me see your report on these two. Who's getting locked up?"

"I'm almost finished with Vivian's and well . . . sir . . . Payton was unconscious for most of the trip," Tim stammered.

The Chief was silent for a moment before he blew, and then he started barking orders. "Ok, people, this is how this is going to go. Tim, I want their statements done ASAP. I'll be expecting a call from you in half an hour."

Tim just nodded at the Chief with big, glazed over eyes.

The Chief turned his attention to Becky. He pointed his finger inches from her nose. "In the meantime, I want you to treat these two like frigging rock stars. Do whatever you have to do to get these two fixed up, so I can haul them off to jail. And if you don't, I'm gonna haul you off to jail." The Chief threw his hands up in the air. "I don't care who it is, but somebody is getting locked up tonight for annoying the hell out of me."

"Yes, sir," said the young nurse, clearly shaken.

After his outburst, Brad and the Chief disappeared down the hallway. Becky quickly pushed me to a room in Urgent Care, leaving me all alone. She either just quit or went outside for a cigarette. The Chief had that kind of effect on people.

Before Tim took Vivian to X-Ray, he stopped by my room long enough to slap a pair of handcuffs on me. "Don't go anywhere, Payton," he said as he hooked my left hand to the metal railing of the gurney.

"Even if I wanted to, where would I go?" I expected at least a smile out of Tim, but he'd momentarily lost his sense of humor. The Chief must have really embarrassed him. "Hey, Tim, before you leave can I ask you a quick question about the missing college student? Has anyone thought to look in the riv—?"

"Not now, Payton. The Chief just chewed my ass. I need to take Vivian down to X-Ray before he chews off the rest of it."

"Ok. Maybe later?" I struck out again. I made a mental note to pry people for information when they weren't pissed off.

He walked out of the room diligently pushing Vivian down the hall to the elevator.

The clock on the wall of my room said two thirty-three a.m. On a normal night, I would still be at my parents' restaurant, The Barbecue Shack, cleaning up and getting ready to punch out for the day. Tonight, I left early because I felt horrible. Maybe I should have just stayed at work. My night would have been far less dramatic.

I'm going to take a minute here to back up and finish the story about my parents. It's no big deal. I just thought a little back-story would help you understand me and my family better. So after my parents won the lottery, my dad had a heart attack and needed a quiet hobby. That is why they bought The Barbecue Shack. This happened to work out perfect for me, since I needed a job after I dropped out of college. I try to manage The Shack while they are away on their trips. I get to eat and drink all I want. My parents get to bask in the sun all they want. When they come home, my dad tinkers around in the kitchen. He also enjoys serving up his homemade microbrews in the bar. My mother spends most of her days shopping, donating time and money to worthy charities, and finding things to remodel. The world is a better place. Everyone is happy.

My eyelids felt extremely heavy. I decided to take a quick catnap until the doctor came in. My eyes closed. I drifted off.

My bladder woke me up at two forty-seven. All the I.V. fluid was looking for an exit. I pressed the call button repeatedly, but no one came to my rescue. The ER was deserted. The rest of the staff must still be up in ICU with the critical patient. I was getting desperate. It was time to take matters into my own hands.

"Hey, a little help," I yelled.

No one answered. The need for a bathroom consumed me. I sat up and slid off the gurney. My legs tangled in the blanket. I fell to the floor.

"Help!" I screamed.

From a distance, I heard a heavy metal door close. The echoing sound of footsteps intensified as they grew closer.

"Help!" I yelled out again in desperation.

Whoever was in the hall chose not to answer. Their

footsteps, however, continued until they stopped right outside my door. Not knowing what to expect, I frantically kicked my legs free from the tangled blanket. With a few more spastic maneuvers, I managed to pull myself back to my feet. After all of that, my bladder was absolutely bursting.

"Who's out there?" I shouted.

They still didn't answer me, but I saw their shadow. I could hear them breathing. What did they want?

. . .

Payton, you are in quite a predicament handcuffed to that gurney. Someone could come along and kill you quick. Your death should be slow and agonizing for all the trouble you have caused. Your cries for help, the panic in your voice, it is embarrassing. Do us both a favor and shut up. Hearing your fear should make me all warm and gushy, just like your insides. Instead, it makes me wish I could see the panic in your eyes before I close them forever.

. . .

"Brad, is that you? This isn't funny, you jerk."

This was getting old. Whoever was out in the hall wasn't answering me. It suddenly occurred to me that it might not be Brad out there. I crouched down next to my gurney, attempting to hide. This was probably my only option after I just finished yelling. I didn't move. I held my breath and listened for movement. The entire ER was eerily quiet. The only noise I could hear in the hallway was a scraping sound. Maybe it was the metal on metal sound of an old broken-down wheelchair. Or was it the sound of an ancient elevator struggling to pull its weight? I couldn't tell.

"By the way, I'm not scared of you." My trembling shout directed towards the hall.

. . .

I will have to do something about that. Do you hear that, Payton? That could be the sound of a knife scraping the door frame. It should be the sound of a knife tearing through your flesh until it hits the bone. That will have to wait. We have company. Soon, I can do whatever I want because no one will believe a single thing you say. That has been part of my plan all along.

. . .

The scraping sound suddenly stopped. The footsteps retreated down the hallway.

"Thanks a lot, asshole."

My bladder couldn't wait any longer. I looked around the room for a bedpan or a urinal. There wasn't one. I thought they were standard issue for every hospital room whether you wanted one, or not. There wasn't time for me to drag my gurney and I.V. pole down the hallway to find a bathroom. This was a full-on bladder emergency. I spotted a flip-top, biohazard garbage can in the corner of the room. Any port in a storm, right?

I dragged the gurney and the I.V. machine awkwardly behind me. The worst night of my life was just about to turn into years of therapy. I flipped up the lid of the biohazard can with the metal floor pedal. Then I carefully positioned myself over the can. Next, I pulled down my sweat pants with my one free hand. Luckily, my oversized sweatshirt stopped me from completely exposing myself. I am now permanently scarred for life by my act of public urination.

I heard a noise in my doorway and looked up. Standing in front of me was the most beautiful male specimen I had ever laid eyes on. My body became frozen in time over the garbage can. My mouth hung open. I stared at his perfect, flawless complexion. His wavy, brown hair framed his face setting off his warm, green eyes. I was positive that under his form-fitted, black leather jacket and pale, ragged blue jeans were the chiseled muscles of a God. Holy . . . Wow!

It was time for a reality check. I was not wearing my ready-to-flirt game face. I was still hovering over a garbage can, without pants, handcuffed to a gurney, with vomit and hamburger bits in my hair. My face heated up. I turned fifty shades of crimson.

A goofy smirk appeared on his face. "I must be in the wrong room," he said with a smooth, angelic voice.

As he turned to leave, all I could think of saying was, "It's not what it looks like."

Who was I trying to kid? It was exactly what it looked like, but I enjoyed the view of my perfect man as he walked away. I let out a blissful sigh when he was out of sight.

Well, if things couldn't get any worse, Tim showed up to take my statement. I was still in biohazard mode when he found me. My face felt like it turned from crimson to a nice shade of dark burgundy.

"I'm glad to see that you didn't go anywhere," said Tim in a joking manner. "Hey, did you just urinate in that garbage can? That's against the law, you know."

"How about I say no, and you give me a few minutes to redeem myself? Besides, this was your fault for handcuffing me to the stupid gurney in the first place."

"I'll be back in two minutes, not a second longer."

Lucky me, I got off with another warning. I took my foot off the pedal of the biohazard can. The lid slammed shut, closing this horrific chapter of my life. How symbolic. Forget needing therapy. I was going to need a strong prescription after this. I pushed the gurney back into the middle of the room, carefully climbing back on as if nothing ever happened.

Tim was a man of his word. He returned right on schedule to take my statement. I took a deep breath, composing myself for a long drawn-out tale about the events of this evening. When I finished, Tim had a confused look on his face.

"Oh boy. The Chief isn't going to like this."

"Why is that?" I was puzzled.

Before Tim could answer me, the ER doctor and Nurse Becky pushed their way into my room. Tim made a hasty retreat that made me more than a little curious.

Becky handed the doctor my chart. "Your call light was on. Did you need something?"

I gave her an exasperated look. "No, thanks. I'm good."

Becky, however, did not look so good. She looked like she had just spent the last twenty minutes crying. Her eye shadow was smudged. Remnants of her mascara ran down her face. Maybe the critical patient died. I knew better. It was most likely the effects from her run in with the Chief. Oddly enough, the Chief doesn't make me cry. I try my best to annoy him, and he returns the favor by scaring the crap out of me. What can I say? It works for us.

The forty-something ER doctor stepped towards me. He cordially held out his hand. He seemed remarkably wide-awake and overly energetic for this early in the morning. "Hi, I'm Doctor Von Hohberg." He greeted me with a smile. His smile faded as he got a closer look at my hair and clothing. "What brings you to the Emergency Room this morning, Ms. Richardson?"

"Well, Doc, to make a long story short, I threw up in my new purse. My maid tried to kill me with a knife. I threw up again on my jerkface, cop head, dingle fritz of an ex-boyfriend because he spun me around and wouldn't listen to me. Then, out of nowhere, I blacked out in my driveway. You know . . . I'm still not sure why I blacked out in my driveway. That's kind of weird, right? The next thing I remember, I am in an ambulance, which is way better than going to jail. So I'm not complaining. But I think someone tried to kill me again, here in the ER, just before I urinated in a biohazard can. And now, here I am talking to you."

"Are you serious?" he asked.

"Very." It is sad that people think I am joking about the tragic events of my pathetic life.

"Have you been drinking tonight, Ms. Richardson?"

"No, but I wish." I am totally telling him the truth on that.

"What about the handcuffs?"

"They're just a mere technicality. The police officer thought I might try to run away, but I didn't."

"Oh, I see," he nodded. "What would you like us to do for you?" he asked slowly with great curiosity.

"I do feel better since they started the I.V. Maybe I was just a smidge dehydrated. But my ankle still hurts from when I luged off my second story roof earlier tonight. And my hip still hurts from when my maid tried to run me over with her car."

"Is that so? I think we can take care of that. I am sending you down to X-ray and then up to the floor to be admitted. Then later this morning, I think you should talk to our resident Psychologist. You have been through quite an experience."

"Do you mean Doctor Parks?" I asked. "I already have an appointment with her later on today."

"That's great, Payton. It looks like my work here is finished. The attending Physician will check on your progress on her morning rounds." He directed his attention to Becky who stood silently next to him. "I'm going for a run. Call me on my cell phone if you need me." The doctor handed her my chart and walked out of my room.

"Ok, Doctor," she replied quietly.

Finally, I was making some headway. I would take a warm hospital bed over a cold cot in the jailhouse any day. Becky put my chart on my lap. She pushed my gurney to the elevator. When the elevator stopped, the door opened on the basement level. Becky pushed me out into the hall.

"Any idea why hospital basements are so creepy? I asked.

"I think it is because they keep all the dead bodies down here."

"They do? That's so gross. I always thought it was the lack of windows, the stark white cement walls, and the long dimly lit hallways. But your answer is better."

Becky's small stature and slim build made the trip down the long, windowless, stark white, dimly lit hallway take forever. When we reached the doorway to the X-ray department, she stopped.

"What's the matter?" I asked.

She motioned with a nod to the gurney down the hall covered with a white sheet.

"Is that what I think it is?" I sat up to get a better look.

"Yes, the morgue is down there. They're not supposed to leave them out."

"Is that the person from ICU?"

"No. Mr. Saunders pulled through. I have no idea who is under that sheet."

I was officially creeped out. Then the body beneath the sheet twitched. I instantly jerked backward and sucked in air. I would like to take this time to correct myself. Now, I was officially creeped out. "Do they always do that?"

"Sometimes that happens when rigor sets in. The body should really be in a drawer in the morgue before it stinks up the place. I'll have to find someone to put it away."

"You are not leaving me down here all alone with it." I tried to give her my best don't you dare leave me, I'm terrified look.

"Ok, I will wait until we are done with your X-rays."

Becky pushed me into the Radiology department.

"I hope that is the last dead body I ever see."

"Don't worry. You get used to it after a while."

I gave her a weird look. "That's just not possible in my book."

The female X-ray technician must have been waiting for us. She seemed impatient and in a big hurry to get home and go back to bed. She took two quick pictures. One shot of my left ankle and one shot of my right hip.

"Ok, I'm finished," said the bed-headed technician. "You can take her back upstairs."

Becky pushed me back out into the hallway. She came to an abrupt stop. We both immediately noticed that the body was gone, but the sheet and the gurney were still there.

"Where did the body go?" I asked.

"Someone must have put it away."

I don't think she believed that any more than I did because she pushed me back to the elevator with record speed. On my way upstairs, I had a disturbing thought. I wondered if a dead body had ever been on my gurney. I pushed that thought out of my head by thinking about a nice hot shower and some serious rack time. Oh yeah, and a toothbrush would be kind of handy.

. . .

It seems we have ourselves a practical joker. Nice. Riddle: Who is on the gurney outside the morgue? Is it a fabulous prankster, an advisory, a nemesis, all of the above, or none of the above? Could it be me? Answer: Seriously, I would love to tell you, but there is no fun in that for me. It is too early in the game for you to know that little piece of information. It might slip out later on. For now, just know that I am watching. I am always watching.

CHAPTER FOUR

The elevator door opened. Nurse Becky pushed me out onto the fifth floor. The good news: I don't have any broken bones. The bad news: I was just admitted to the fifth floor with all the crazy people. Or to be more politically correct, the mentally challenged. Crap. I have just been dubbed the Queen of the Strait Jackets.

I was barely off the elevator when I spotted the Chief and Tim having an intense argument by the Nurses Station. Becky noticed them too. All it took was one quick look at the Chief for her to decide to ditch me. She abruptly vacated the fifth floor out of the fear of impending jail time.

"Sorry, Payton, every man for himself," said Becky, just before the elevator door closed.

Sensing my arrival like some superhuman radar, the Chief turned and glared at me. This was nothing new for me. I could see the anger building in his face. He took a few steps towards me. I automatically cringed.

He pointed his finger at me. Just short of waking the dead, he proclaimed to the universe, "I better not see you or your housekeeper anytime soon, or I will lock you both up!" He

31

stormed off, cussing and swearing. "God damn, wild goose chasing, waste of my time."

"Wow, that was kind of embarrassing," I said to break the awkward silence on the floor.

After a few moments of feeling completely uncomfortable, a gray-haired nurse who was pushing the limits of her longevity brought me down the hall towards my room.

I took a look at my surroundings. The atmosphere on the fifth floor was amazingly sterile and void of color. I know that earth tones can be soothing. This was downright depressing. A tiny splash of color mixed in with the beige and taupe would help out a whole bunch.

As Helen and I passed by Tim in the hall I asked, "So are you going to tell me what that was all about?"

Tim walked along side my gurney, following me to my room. "Apparently, you and Vivian are free to go."

"That doesn't make any sense," I said in disbelief. "She tried to kill me."

"Chief Thomas told me to tell you that you and Vivian can sort it out."

"That's just crazy. I know that the Chief hates me, but this is ridiculous."

We reached the doorway to my room. I motioned to Tim by clanking my handcuffs against the metal railing that I was ready to be set free. He got the message and removed the cuffs. Despite her age, Helen skillfully pushed my gurney into the room without banging it against the door frame. Tim tried to follow, but Helen slammed the door in his face. I think the door must have smashed Tim's nose a bit because he uttered a few choice words from the other side.

"Hey," I said with disapproval. "I was talking to him."

"No boys allowed. You need a shower. You smell like an old bar whore who passed out in her own vomit."

"Thank you for your honesty, Helen. But sometimes the truth can be over rated.

. . .

After my shower, I felt squeaky-clean. I tucked myself into my bed with damp hair, sore muscles, and multiple scrapes and bruises. My hospital issued blue fuzzy socks with the little floor grippers cheered me up; at the same time, my oversized hospital gown depressed me because it was three sizes too big. Good grief, this place was making me unstable. I hope they let me out of here before I start talking to myself.

After the wild events of the evening, I was beyond tired. I turned on my television and patiently waited for sleep. There was nothing on but the local news. The monotone drone of the news anchor was putting me into a coma until I heard him mention the missing student from the River Bend Campus.

My eyes snapped open wide with curiosity. I had been following the story since it broke a few days ago. ". . . His lifeless body was discovered Wednesday floating in the river behind the college. No foul play is suspected."

"I knew they would find him there," I commented to the TV and myself. I must have been too busy staring at the TV when Tim came in. He was invisible to me until he spoke.

"I snuck by the old bat, so I could finish talking to you," he whispered. "Chief Thomas told me that I couldn't go home until I talked to you both."

The news anchor started with the weather forecast. I turned my full attention to Tim who was standing just inside my doorway. He seemed like he was in a better mood. I decided to try to pry him for info.

"Hey, do you know anything about the case of the missing UW-RB student that they found in the river?" I asked Tim.

"There isn't any case or ongoing investigation."

"Why not? They were just talking about it on the news."

"They have already ruled it as an accidental death due to drowning. He slipped on some ice while jogging, hit his head, choked on a chip, then he stumbled into the river and drowned."

"That sounds a little too neat and methodical, don't you think? And who jogs while eating chips?"

"They found blood where he hit his head, a chip lodged in his throat, and a bag of *Doritos* near the body, Payton. The case sounds closed to me. There are no loose ends."

"Really?"

"Yes. The Chief thinks he stumbled into the river trying to get a drink of water to dislodge the chip."

"That's about the stupidest thing I have ever heard."

"I talked to the kid's family, Payton. His mom told me that he loved those chips. They were his favorite snack. Too bad he choked on one of those tasty triangles."

"Yeah, I agree. They are tasty. But I still don't buy it, Tim. Why do all these boys keep ending up dead in the river?"

"What boys, Payton? What are you talking about?" Tim walked over to my bed. He took a seat in a gray office-looking chair.

"Well, last winter there was one from Mill Prairie, Wisconsin. The year before that, boys went missing from Illinois, Massachusetts, Michigan, and Wisconsin. The three from Wisconsin were from Menoshko Bay, Delton's Pointe, and again Mill Prairie. The winter before that, there was one from Michigan and one from Clearwater Falls, Wisconsin. The winter before that was the mother lode of drowning victims: three in January, three in February, and three in March."

Tim pulled his chair closer to the bed. "That does seem like an excessive amount of dead teenagers."

"Do ya think?" I said sarcastically. "In January, the three boys went missing in six days. It started north of here in North Beach, Wisconsin; then Appleton Lake, Minnesota; and after that in Amuxley, Iowa. It was like someone was driving down Hwy 35 up to no good."

"That is an interesting theory, but I am sure it is just a coincidence."

"You can be skeptical if you want. I think I'm onto something." I looked at Tim for support on my theory. I didn't get it. "In March, boys went missing from Indiana, Rhode Island, and Illinois. The three in February, however, were all from Wisconsin. The first one was from Eagle Ridge, the second from Clearwater Falls, and the last one from Algon Springs."

"Actually, Payton, the one from Algon Springs doesn't

legitimately count because he was stabbed."

"Yeah, stabbed to death and left on the river bank," I said raising my voice.

"Payton, calm down. They caught the guy. He confessed."

"I know. He said, 'the devil made him do it, and he was supposed to kill six more that year.' "

Tim sighed. "Payton, the guy was obviously crazy, on drugs, or both. That case is not related to the others."

I gave Tim a frustrated look. "Maybe? Maybe not? I am not ruling anything out yet."

Tim leaned back in his chair, folding his arms across his chest. "Just out of curiosity, where did you get your information? You seem to know more than you should. Do you have an inside source on the police force?"

"No, just the internet and an insatiable need for the truth. Did you know that this has been going on since at least 1997? Maybe even longer. Boys have gone missing from Oregon to Maine just to be found later drown in a river, pond, or other water source. Some boys are never found at all. I think all the families deserve justice, don't you?"

"Payton, I'm sure that they were all accidents or suicides. There has been no proof of foul play and nothing to link the cases together. If there were, someone would have done it by now."

"You don't think it's odd that they are all male college students of roughly the same age?"

"No, actually it has been proven that adolescent females can handle stress better than adolescent males."

"Yeah, look at me. I'm not in a strait jacket yet. I'm the poster child for good mental health." I laughed at my own situation. "Actually, I think it is because females can multitask better than males."

"There is probably some truth to that. And the fact that girls travel in packs everywhere they go, even to the bathroom. At least the smart ones don't travel alone."

"Hey, that's not fair. I am very capable of finding my own way to the potty and back, thank you."

"Sorry," said Tim, trying not to offend my loner mentality.

"So all jokes aside, you seriously don't think there is anything sinister going on?" I asked Tim.

"Absolutely not. Boys get drunk, they get depressed, maybe they jump, or they fall into the river. Accidents happen."

"I don't buy it. Maybe you and I should investigate?"

"Are you crazy? The Chief goes nuts whenever anyone goes behind his back and bucks his authority. Anyway, can I tell you what I found out from Vivian? I want to go home. It has been a long day."

"Oh yeah, why is the Chief letting Vivian go?" I asked.

"Vivian claims that she came to your house to look for her lost bracelet. You were supposed to be at work. She didn't think you would mind if she went in to look for it. She heard a noise upstairs and went to go investigate. Well, you know the rest of the story. It was all a huge misunderstanding."

"Wow, not good. No wonder why the Chief was mad."

"No, he is pissed. You and Vivian had better stay clear of him for a while. I would consider moving."

"It's that bad?"

"Yes. I think it would be a good idea if you had a heart to heart with Vivian ASAP to clear this whole thing up."

"Wait, what did Vivian say about the knife?"

"She claims that she never had a knife. We never found one."

"Shit, maybe I was delirious from my fever. Maybe I really do belong up here on the fifth floor."

"All I know is that you need to work it out with Vivian, so she doesn't press charges against you for assault."

"She can do that? But she was in my house."

"Yes, she can. My advice to you is to suck up to her. Offer her a raise or a paid vacation."

"Ok, I promise to go talk to her as soon as they let me out of here."

Tim smiled back at me. He stood up, moving slowly towards the door.

"Before you go, can I ask you a question? I really need an

honest answer from you. Please tell me the truth."

"Ok," he agreed without hesitating.

"Do you think I'm crazy? I'm just asking because I can't tell anymore."

Before Tim answered, he took a deep breath and smiled. His steel blue eyes looked deep into mine. "No, Payton. I don't think you're crazy."

I blew out a huge sigh. "Well, that's a relief."

"You do, however, have the worst luck of anyone I have ever met."

"Thank you for noticing."

We both chuckled. It was nice to know I had someone on my side. I decided that Tim was an ok guy as long as he kept his handcuffs to himself.

"Get some sleep, Payton. Everything will look better in the morning."

After Tim left my room, I closed my eyes hoping for a long peaceful sleep.

. . .

A woman's high-pitched shriek of agony jerked me out of my REM sleep. Thank goodness she was standing next to my bed or I might have missed it. I rubbed my tired, swollen eyes hoping that I might be dreaming. I wasn't.

A stunningly beautiful woman in her sixties stood in the glowing light from my television. For some unknown reason, she continued to shriek at the top of her lungs without stopping to consider my daily tolerance for bullshit. I tried my best to hide the fact that it was at an all-time low. Good grief, I have owned alarm clocks less annoying than this woman.

For a complete whack-job, she appeared impeccably groomed. She wore a dark green, taffeta evening gown. Fancy, silver, high-heeled shoes decorated her feet. A plastic jeweled crown sat upon her well-groomed, gray-haired up-do. In her arms, she carried a bouquet of decayed flowers. They were roses. I think. When she took a few steps closer to me, I was motionless in my bed, too shocked and tired to move.

Before I could do anything to protect myself, she struck me repeatedly in the head with her bouquet. Yep, they were definitely roses. I felt every thorny blow. Like a flash, she suddenly pinned me to my bed. Her face now inches from mine. Her eyes enraged as she chanted her insane nonsense.

"Boy froze, red nose. Boy froze, red nose. Boy froze, red nose."

This time, I let out a high-pitched shriek of my own that made two large male orderlies run to my rescue.

The two orderlies grabbed the old woman. They dragged her kicking and shrieking from my room. I jumped up, quickly shutting the door behind them.

"This place is a flipping nightmare."

I, Payton Marie Richardson, perhaps of sound mind and body, relinquish the title of Queen of the Strait Jackets to the crazy-lady down the hall. She clearly deserves the title more than I do.

I glanced at the clock on the wall. It was five minutes after five o'clock in the morning. My hard-lumpy bed and flat pillow were calling my name. I meant that figuratively, not literally. I'm not that crazy.

. . .

Get some sleep, Payton. We have a big day tomorrow.

CHAPTER FIVE

I am the monster in your head. Can you feel me under your skin? Can you feel me creeping into your every thought? Soon, I will consume you.

. . .

I was in a deep, deep sleep in a faraway land. Somewhere in my subconscious, I was lost at sea, stuck on a deserted island, helpless and happy in my dream world. Nothing could bring me back from my paradise except for the sound of his voice.

"Payton, Payton, what the hell happened to your face?" asked my ex fiancée Brad.

"Oh my God," I mumbled, still completely comatose. "Shut up and go away, Brad."

"I'm not joking. What did you do to your face?"

I bolted out of bed and ran to the bathroom mirror. I was awake in my very own nightmare. Brad was here, and I had scratches all over my face from the crazy beauty queen.

Brad came over to the bathroom to check on me, totally intending to gloat. He leaned his shoulder against the door jam and crossed his arms in front of his chest. Brad let out a drawn-out sigh. "Start talking. Tell me what happened to you this time."

"If you must know, the crazy rhyming lady from down the hall came into my room last night. She woke me up with her screams. Then she beat me in the head with her dead flowers."

"Sorry I asked," he said with a snicker.

"Don't you dare laugh. This place is a nightmare. Please tell me you are here to take me to jail. I cannot stand to be here another minute. I will be in a strait jacket by noon. I swear."

"Actually, I am getting you out of here. You have your appointment with Dr. Parks in fifteen minutes. My dad told me that I was to personally escort you to Dr. Parks' office and give her a copy of the police report."

"That bastard!"

"Now, Payton, if you don't go to your appointment, you will never get out of here. And more important, you won't get your weekly allowance from daddy."

"You know about my allowance?" I said with disgust. "Do you guys just sit around the bakery all day eating doughnuts and talk about me?"

"Of course not, the bakery is closed. Remember? Now we go down to Max's for breakfast and talk about you like everyone else."

"Haha, very funny."

"Grab your clothes and change. We're late."

I opened my closet. "Crap, all I have are my boots. Everything else is in the laundry."

"Put on your boots. You can wear my coat over your hospital gown for now. Let's go."

I put on my knee-high Sorels and quickly slid on his navy blue police jacket. Brad and I left my room, walking in stride to the elevator.

We rounded the corner. It was her again. The crazy lady was between my freedom and me. She was still in her full-length green gown, guarding the elevator door. I tried to hide behind Brad's muscular, six-foot frame. She spotted me and started chanting her rhyme.

"Dark moon, gone soon. Dark moon, gone soon. Dark moon, gone soon."

"Is she talking to you?" asked Brad.

"Apparently." I pushed the elevator button frantically.

"Do you know her?"

"Brad, meet my face mangler. Face mangler, this is Brad."

"Be nice, Payton," said Brad, in a scolding tone. "She is a harmless old woman."

I pointed at my face. "Does this look harmless to you?" I asked in a rapid, super stressed tone.

The elevator door opened, Brad stepped inside. Before he turned around, the crazy-lady grabbed my arm and pulled me to her. She whispered, "The Little King dies tonight," in my ear. Then she let me go. I got in the elevator unsure of what just happened. Did the queen of the fifth floor just have a moment of clarity? She quickly sank back into her own universe. She began chanting about the moon again as the elevator door closed. I guess not.

"That woman is three quarters of a turn passed crazy," Brad mumbled under his breath.

"Oh, I think she's made it all the way around the block, if you ask me."

"What does she want with you?"

"I don't know. I just bring out the crazy in people, I guess. Hey, I need to stop off on Vivian's floor, so I can talk to her quick." I pushed the second floor button before Brad could say no.

I hopped out of the elevator on the second floor.

"Make it fast. We're already running late," he ordered. "I'll wait by the Nurses Station."

"You're not going to come along to make sure that Vivian doesn't try to kill me again?"

"Nope. I think I would actually pay money to see the next round."

The face I made at him was not attractive. I hobbled down the hall to find Vivian. What was I going to say to her?

Vivian was awake, sitting up in her bed when I entered her

room. When I saw the cast on her arm, I knew I needed to kiss some serious butt. She smiled at me, which I took as a good sign. She could, however, be smiling about my mangled face.

"I just stopped by to say that I am sooooo sorry for knocking you off the roof and breaking your arm, which I plan to pay for, by the way. You can take as much time as you need before coming back to work, with pay of course. If there is anything I can do for you, just name it." I groveled like an idiot.

There was a pause. I could see Vivian mentally weighing out her options.

"Well, my stepson just moved back to town. He needs a job to help pay for college."

"Ok, what did you have in mind?"

"He's a chef. I heard you could use some help in the kitchen since your parents are out of town."

"That would be awesome. What kind of food can he make?"

"Dylan can make anything. After culinary school, he studied in France for a while. Right now, he just needs money for some business classes. Dylan wants to open his own restaurant someday."

"Great. I will take all the help I can get. Tell him to come to the restaurant at three o'clock today. I will show him around the kitchen."

"Thank you, Payton. I will tell Dylan the good news."

Brad interrupted us. He grabbed me by the arm, pulling me towards the door. "We're late," he insisted.

"Ok, I'm coming," I said with great annoyance. "Bye Vivian." I tried to wave politely as Brad pulled me out of her room.

"Good-bye, Payton."

. . .

Brad and I were in his police cruiser on our way to Dr. Parks' office. We were traveling from North Main Street to South Main Street in complete awkward silence. Brad was actually letting me ride in the front seat next to him, instead of in the back seat behind the metal cage. He hadn't done that since we were dating. This made me very suspicious of his motives.

We rode in absolute silence without looking at each other or talking for the remaining two minutes it took to get to Dr. Parks' office. He pulled in the parking lot, parked, and then shut off the engine. I turned to say thank you, so I could quickly escape the weird tension in the car.

Before I could, he said, "Stop stalling and go. Give this report to your doctor. I'll be out here when you are done."

Brad was being nice to me, painfully nice to me. What did he want? What was his angle? I took the report and climbed out of the police cruiser.

The wind caught my hospital gown. It blew the back of it up, exposing my underwear. With lightning speed, I quickly pushed it back down with my hand, but not before it caught Brad's attention. He flashed a familiar smile at me. I knew what it meant. Trouble was brewing.

Dr. Evelyn Parks was calmly sitting at her desk when I walked in the door. She was wearing one of her usual dark colored, curve-hugging pantsuits. The one today was a nice black pinstripe that matched her long, silky, straight, black hair. Her jewelry and reading glasses always perfectly coordinated with her outfits. She always looked so sophisticated. Doctor Evelyn Parks was definitely the picture of good mental health. I, on the other hand, looked like a cross between a natural disaster and a terrorist attack.

"Payton, you are a half an hour late," she said, looking up from her paperwork. "Oh my, what happened to your face and your clothes?"

I handed her the police report. "This should explain everything except my face." I took my usual seat in the expensive, high-backed, brown, leather chair next to her desk.

She read the report in silence. To kill time, I stared at the new shelf Dr. Parks had just put up behind her desk. She had replaced her family photos with a variety of sports trophies. Great, Dr. Parks was not just graceful and well dressed. She was coordinated and highly competitive. I sighed and eyerolled.

When she was finished, she looked up at me with understanding and sympathy. "Bad things seem to keep happening to you, don't they?"

"Yes. I totally agree."

"And how does that make you feel?" Dr. Parks looked at me with empathy.

"Terrible. Just look at me. I'm a walking disaster."

"I see," the doctor said with a smile. "Do you still think Vivian was trying to kill you?"

Seeing as how I was late, Dr. Parks wasn't going to waste any time getting down to business. "No, that was all just a stupid misunderstanding that I feel horrible about."

Dr. Parks looked down at the report, reading it again. "What about the knife that you claimed you saw?" She asked.

"I must have been delirious with fever," I explained, trying to be as convincing as I could.

"Ok, that is good. You seem to be grounded to reality."

"What does that mean, exactly?"

"It is just a fancy way of saying that I do not think you are crazy."

"Good to know. What if I told you that I feel like someone is watching me."

"Go on." Dr. Parks leaned towards me. She shifted her weight in her chair. Her curiosity obviously peaked.

"You know how you feel like someone is in the room with you. Or you swear someone is right behind you."

"Yes." She briefly stopped taking notes. Dr. Parks put her pen down, resting her left hand on her desk to listen more intently.

"Well, when I turn around, no one is there. And I keep hearing creaking noises in the house."

"Oh, I understand."

"You do?"

"I am sure that large rambling house of your parents feels pretty empty with them gone."

"I don't think missing my parents is my problem. The other

44

day, I heard a noise in the living room. I went to go see what it was. When I came back to the kitchen, the other half of my sandwich was missing. How freaky is that?"

"Payton, we all get forgetful from time to time. You suffered a traumatic experience eight months ago. A little amnesia is very common."

"Ok, Dr. Parks, if you say so."

"How are your nightmares and your anxiety?"

"To be perfectly honest, I'm too tired to be anxious about anything."

"That is good. I guess."

"As far as the nightmares go, I keep having that same dream over and over again. I keep reliving what happened that day at school."

"Have you remembered anything new from that day last May?"

"No, I haven't remembered anything new, yet. In my dream, I open the door to the sorority house and find Lyle, my landlord, dead in the entryway. I keep saying, 'Lyle what are you doing on the floor? Get up.' In my dream, I see him lying on the floor staring up at me with his glassy, gray, fixed eyes. The next thing I remember, I am waking up on the floor next to Lyle, his bile and urine stains on the rug. When I look up, my roommates and the paramedics are standing over me. This is the point in my dream when I always wake up."

That day at school, eight months ago, it didn't end there. My emotions and my breathing were out of control. I couldn't catch my breath. I actually thought I was going to die. I ran outside to get some fresh air. My roommates told me that they weren't sure which one of us was paler, me or Lyle. This was my first panic attack.

Something else happened to me that day, something horrible. I just can't remember. The memory of Lyle dead on the rug was too much for me to handle. I quit school and moved back home. Eight months ago, buying a new rug for the entryway was not going to help the demons in my head go away.

"Have you had any more panic attacks?" asked Dr. Parks.

"No, and seeing how my life is a complete disaster, I think that is a good sign, right?"

"I agree. Do you think you would like to try going back to school sometime soon?"

"Do you think I am ready?"

"You have been off your medication for a month and seem to be doing fine without it. As far as I am concerned, you can go back anytime you want."

"I can't go back after Winter Break next week because my parents are still in Texas. They need me to run the restaurant. I could go back to UW-Clearwater Falls for the fall semester."

"Great. Do you think you will move back in with your sorority sisters?"

"Definitely, we are sisters for life. Maybe it will jog my memory. I've also been thinking about changing my major to Criminal Justice with a minor in Psychology."

"You want to be a police officer?" Her voice skipped an octave. Dr. Parks seemed a little shocked. "Does Brad or the Chief know about this decision?"

"No, not yet. I want it to be a surprise. I was thinking more along the lines of a FBI agent. How cool would that be?"

"That sounds like a good idea, Payton. I feel that you are making great progress."

The buzzer rang ending our session. I got up and headed for the door. I turned to ask the dreaded question. Dr. Parks was a step ahead of me.

"Yes, Payton, you are free to go." She signed her name at the bottom of a document and handed it to me. "Give this to Brad."

I walked back to her desk. "What is this?"

"Your discharge papers from the fifth floor. I am not sure why Dr. Von Hohberg admitted you in the first place."

"Thanks." I blew out a sigh of relief. I wasn't about to tell her that even I was doubting my own sanity earlier this morning.

"You are welcome. By the way, what happened to your face?"

"The crazy, rhyming lady from the fifth floor attacked me

with her dead flowers. What is wrong with her?"

"Miss Gilbert attacked you?"

"Yes, she came into my room early this morning, spouting off her rhymes. Then she hit me in the face with her dead flowers."

"Miss Gilbert suffers from severe dementia. She is relatively harmless."

"She didn't seem that harmless to me. She seemed very agitated about something."

"Thank you, Payton, for letting me know. I will check on her today. That is all. I will see you the same time next week." Dr. Parks looked down, focusing on the paperwork on her desk.

"Bye, Dr. Parks."

I bounded out the door happy to be free. Then I saw Brad sitting in the cruiser. He was still waiting for me. Yikes.

. . .

We hardly spoke on the eight-mile trip to my parents' house. I could feel the sexual tension building between us. It made me nervous. Brad pulled up the driveway. He parked close to the back door of my parents' massive, white, two-story, Victorian mansion.

"This is a far cry from your old starter-home you used to live in," commented Brad.

"This is my parents' idea of a house, not mine. My mom fell in love with the huge kitchen and the pool in the backyard, so my dad bought it for her. Now I get crap for it 24/7."

"Sorry I brought it up."

"Thanks for the ride home and the get out of jail free card." I got out of the cruiser. I made a fast dash for the house. Brad followed me into the kitchen. I turned to look at him. "What do you want, Brad?"

"My coat," he said. He grabbed the collar of his jacket with both hands. Brad pulled my lips to his.

His mouth was warm, wet, and familiar. I found myself kissing him back. This was odd. Normally, even the mere thought of Brad repulsed me. I put my arms around his neck and kissed him back with greater intensity. It had been a long time for me, a long time for the both of us.

His hands moved from the collar of his jacket to under my hospital gown. Brad didn't waste any time. He went right for my underwear, pulling them down until they slid down to the floor on their own. I let out a small moan of approval. He answered me back with one of his own. Our hurried breaths were equally passionate. His hands slid back to my waist. He lifted me onto the cold, granite countertop.

He pulled me closer, as if that was even possible. I could feel that he was just as ready as I was. I reached for his zipper. His hands moved past my waist and grabbed my ass. He pulled his lips away from mine for just a second. Brad looked into my eyes smiling, he said, "Someone's joined the clean plate society."

All of my hormones came to a screeching halt. "What?" I said in disbelief as I took my hand off his zipper. "Did you just insult me?"

"No!" he pleaded.

"Yes, you did. You could have said, I still love you, Payton. Or I missed you, Payton. But nooooo . . . I get, you have a fat ass, Payton. Are you out of your mind?"

Pushing him away, I jumped down from the counter. "You want your coat?" I took it off and threw it at him. He just stood in the middle of my kitchen laughing at me. "Brad you are such a, such a, such a wiener sometimes." I was so angry, I thought about throwing a few small kitchen appliances at his head. I had it with him. "Get out." I pointed at the door.

I turned, stomped up the stairs, bare-assed in my Sorel boots. I slammed my bedroom door behind me. What a mistake. What a jackass. What was I thinking?

. . .

By the way, your sandwich was delicious.

CHAPTER SIX

I am here in the bathroom with you, Payton. The steam is thick. You cannot see me, but you know I am here with you. You can feel me. I know that you can.

The floor creaks outside the shower door. You pause briefly. What a rush. This game just keeps getting better. I am going to disappear for now with the steam.

I will be back Payton, watching, and waiting. Tonight, I am going to kill the Little King, and you are going to watch.

. . .

I stopped and listened. "Brad is that you? Is anyone there?" No one answered. I turned the shower to cold, to clear my head. I must be hearing things.

The short blast of freezing water worked. It kicked out any impure thoughts that Brad had started. After my shower, I put on my favorite Wisconsin Badger hoodie and my favorite pair of distressed American Eagle jeans. My hair was perfect. My makeup darn near flawless. I even managed to cover up the scratches on my face, but not the dark circles under my eyes from lack of sleep.

I took one last look in the full-length mirror. From the front, I was downright adorable, almost dateable. As I turned, I caught the image of my butt in the mirror. Yikes, Brad was right. It looked like I was trying to fit ten pounds of shit in a five-pound bag. When the heck did this happen? Well, that settles it. No more deep-fried food from The Shack for me. I was on a hunger strike.

On the way out the door, I grabbed a low-fat yogurt from the fridge. I jumped into my black Ford Escape. As I motored down the road, I cranked up the volume of my stereo until I could feel the bass in my chest. Nothing puts me in a good mood like kick-ass rock and roll.

When I came to the stop sign at the intersection, I paused longer than usual. I could be good, turn to the right, and get to work early. Or . . . I could be bad, turn to the left, and go snoop around where they found the dead kid's body. What can I say? I was born to be bad. I just can't be caught at it this time.

I drove past the college apartments to the dead end. I parked my little SUV by the metal barricade on the east side of the campus. It occurred to me that maybe the killer had done the same thing. So I looked around for clues just in case something was overlooked. I didn't see anything. The rescue vehicles, paramedics, and police officers had trampled down the snow. It was impossible to find a clear tire track or foot print.

I climbed over the barricade and walked down the small hill. Below the hill was the walking path along the river's edge. In the summertime, the path was lush, green, and full of life. Now, it was desolate and disturbingly creepy.

The beginning of the path curved between rows of barren, lifeless trees. A short ways ahead, there was a clearing where the riverbank was void of trees and lined with rocks. The path veered close to the river there. This had to be the spot I was looking for.

My curiosity kicked into high gear. I jogged to the clearing. Suddenly, both feet flew out from underneath me. I landed on my back. I must have looked like a cartoon character flying through the air. This was definitely the place. I remembered what Tim had told me. The dead boy had slipped on the ice while jogging and hit his head.

The sheer grossness of lying in the exact spot as the dead kid made me spring back to my feet with record speed. I realized that I had come dangerously close to the same accidental fate.

Next in my investigation was to determine where the boy had fallen into the water. I attempted to recreate the crime scene. I pretended to choke. I stumbled forward to mimic his actions. This led me to the riverbank lined with large rocks. The rocks were snow covered and slippery. It was easy to see how someone could trip on them and fall in. Maybe it was just an accident.

I was about to turn around and walk away when I saw a shiny object in the water. Kneeling down on the rocky edge, I stretched out my arm to grab it. It was just beyond my reach. I used a broken branch from a nearby bush to hook it and pull it out of the water. It turned out to be a gold crucifix on a heavy gold chain. Maybe it belonged to the dead kid. I put the necklace in my coat pocket for safekeeping while I finished looking around.

When I turned around from the riverbank, I noticed a water faucet on the edge of the path. I walked over to it, turning it on to see if it worked. Cold water tricked from the faucet and ran onto the path where I had fallen. Did someone deliberately make an icy spot on the path? Did the killer set a trap and wait for someone to literally, fall for it? The little voice in my head said yes.

I looked at the surrounding trees and bushes for a good place to hide and wait for someone. On the far side of the path, away from the water, was the perfect line of trees. In the drifted snow, I could see a faint set of tracks that led from the trees back to the path. How could the police have missed this? What a bunch of idiots.

Because I wasn't wearing boots, I stepped carefully in each footprint. I walked in stride until they ended by a grove of trees. The tracks stopped next to a big oak. It was the perfect place to hide. I could see the path, but the line of trees concealed me from view. If someone jogged by, they would never see me. It was brilliant. I clearly stood in the footprints of a killer.

An owl hooted in the tree above my head. When I looked up, I noticed something much more interesting than my feathered friend. It was a smiley face etched into the tree trunk just above eye level. It looked freshly carved. The wood was a fresh cut beige color, not a weathered gray. I removed my glove and ran my index finger around the four-inch circle. That was a stupid thing for me to do. A splinter of wood from the jagged edge of the bark jammed into my finger. It immediately drew blood.

When I looked down at my finger, I spotted something orange in the snow. I bent down to pick it up. It was a half-eaten *Dorito*. I looked over at the path and then back to the tree. Birds? I don't think so.

My finger was still bleeding. Instinctively, I put my finger in my mouth to cleanse the wound. It tasted cheesy and salty from the chip.

When I glanced up through the trees, I saw him for the first time. A Bald-headed Man stood on the cement balcony of the Commons Building of the college. He was watching me. The man was wearing a dark suit and dark sunglasses. His eyes were covered, but it was obvious that he was glaring at me from behind the dark lenses. He was ridiculously tall and remarkably thick. He certainly was not the janitor. The Bald-headed Man looked more like someone's hired muscle.

I didn't know how long he had been watching me, but I figured he had seen enough. The chip slipped from my fingers, landing back in the snow. I ran as fast as I could across the snow to the path. When I reached the path, I paused for a split second to see if he was coming after me. The Bald-headed Man remained motionless. His gloved hands still fixed to the black metal railing of the balcony. His eyes undoubtedly followed my every movement from behind his blackened shades. I continued running until I reached my car on the top of the hill.

My car was moving down the road before I could breathe normally. I checked my rearview mirror all the way to the restaurant to make sure that I wasn't being followed. I decided that being bad wasn't such a good idea for me. I promise to be good the rest of the night. Yeah right, like that's gonna happen.

. . .

I pulled up to The Barbecue Shack, my parents' newly remodeled, log-sided, wonder bar on the lake. It was just before three in the afternoon. Vivian's reject of a son would be here soon to help me. I guess that is not a fair assumption. I had never met Dylan. I just assumed that dealing with Dylan would be my penance for his stepmother's broken arm. He will undoubtedly be a geeky, French speaking, nerd-boy with a bad complexion, that can't boil water, and won't do the dishes. With my luck, he will be even more undateable than I am.

I jumped out of my car and headed right inside the restaurant to see if I could locate my missing cell phone. Never thought I would miss my lifeline to the world quite this much. I found it right where I had left it. It was on the counter in the kitchen. It still had half of its battery life left and showed five missed calls from my mother. I blew out a deep, breathy sigh. Definitely not in the mood for my mother and her twenty questions. Maybe later, or better yet, next week worked for me.

I was busy in the kitchen chopping veggies for the salad bar, downing my second Red Bull, when I heard the front door open. When the door to the kitchen opened, I didn't look up. I was in mid-chop when he introduced himself.

"Hi, I'm Dylan Slayter. Are you Payton?" he asked with a smooth angelic voice.

I knew that voice. I looked up, continuing to chop. My perfect man stood before me in my kitchen.

"Ow," I yelled, as the knife sliced though the flesh of my index finger. I must have been in shock. The blood poured out of my finger. I just stood there and stared at it.

Dylan rushed over. He guided me to the sink, washing out my wound. When he touched me, it was as if the planets collided. The Earth moved or some stupid, sappy, love-struck crap you read in books. I never in my life felt anything like this. I wondered if he felt it too.

"Are you all right?" Dylan asked me with a silly smirk on his face.

"Uh huh," I answered, staring into his emerald green eyes.

"Your cut is really deep. You should go to the hospital. You probably need stitches."

"Oh, no! I'm not going anywhere near the Emergency Room. I'll just have to bleed to death." I grabbed a towel and applied pressure to stop the bleeding."

"That's where I know you from. You're that girl I saw handcuffed to the gurney this morning."

"Guilty," I said, feeling my face turn as red as my hoodie. "I was having a bad day." I desperately needed to change the subject. "How about I show you around the kitchen, then you can get started?"

He smiled at me the entire time I gave him the tour. Maybe he was into me, too. Or maybe he just remembered me in my biohazard mode. I left him in the kitchen alone while I went out to restock the bar. It was going to be a long night of impure thoughts and hopefully sexual tension.

I poured myself a double shot of tequila. Maybe a liquid courage diet was just what I needed to have the guts to make a move on Dylan. I downed my shot. Then I examined my finger. The bleeding had stopped. I found a few Band-Aids behind the bar and carefully placed them on my finger. I was staying clear of the ER tonight. My next step was coming up with a plan to seduce my future boyfriend.

The TV was on channel four out of the big metropolis across the border. As I took inventory of what I needed from the storeroom, I listened to the recap of the day's breaking stories. News Anchor and Reporter Crystal Pierce had covered the story that instantly peaked my interest.

"The missing twenty year old male from Twin Valley, Minnesota was found dead in the Mississippi River around eleven o'clock this morning. The university student had been missing since last Saturday. His partially nude body was discovered face down near the shore. Two elderly women happened upon him today while walking their dogs along the river. A smiley face made out of rocks was found on the water's edge near his body. It was the young man's final farewell message."

The two smiley faces were not merely a coincidence. This was the clue that linked the cases together. This was so big. I poured myself a celebratory shot of tequila for being a fabulous detective. Now I needed to call Crystal Pierce. She could know more than she was reporting.

I used the pay phone on the wall of the bar to keep the call anonymous. I dialed the number that information gave me for the Channel Four News Station.

"This is Channel Four News. How may I direct your call?" asked a sweet young receptionist.

"Can I speak with Crystal Pierce please?"

"She isn't available at the moment. Would you like her voice mail?"

"This is an emergency. I need to talk to her about the body that was found in the river this morning."

"Please hold while I patch you through to her cell phone."

It was the longest three minutes of my life waiting for Crystal to answer her phone.

"Hello, this is Crystal Pierce. Hello? Is anyone there?"

This is when I should have hung up the phone and minded my own business, but the liquid courage was starting to work. "Hi, Crystal, this is Pay . . . lula." God, I am a horrible liar. "I just have a few questions for you about the young man's body that was found today."

"Sure," she said, sounding eager to help.

"Did they ever find any carvings in the trees by the body?"

"No, not that I know of. What kind of carvings?"

"A smiley face," I asked.

"No, the only smiley face we found was made out of stones. Why do you ask?"

"Because I found one today carved into a tree by where a boy drowned earlier this week."

"Really? Where was the body found?"

"In the river behind our college. The police seem to think it was an accident. I don't think that it was."

"That's interesting. Can you tell me more?" She was genuinely intrigued.

"No, not really." I didn't want to say too much. "If you don't mind, I just have a quick question for you."

"Sure. Ask away."

"Was the boy that was found today missing anything?"

"Maybe," Crystal answered, trolling for more information.

I could tell by the tone of Crystal's voice that I was definitely onto something. "Was he missing some sort of jewelry?"

"Maybe." Wherever Crystal was, she was definitely on the edge of her seat.

"Was he missing a cross necklace?" I asked.

"How do you know that?" She insisted. "That wasn't in the police report. Only the family and I know that it is missing."

Bingo. Now it was definitely time to hang up. So I did. I had gotten the information that I wanted from Crystal. Man, I hate it when I am right. Now what do I do with this information and the crucifix I found?

. . .

Eeny, meeny, miny, moe, Catch a Little King by the toe. If he hollers, make him pay, for now he is my chosen prey. Which of Payton's friends needs to go? Eeny, meeny, miny, moe. My mother—told me—to pick—the very—best one—and that—is you.

CHAPTER SEVEN

When I turned around from the pay phone, I found two teenage gamers at the counter. Stocking the bar and solving a murder would have to wait until later. I had customers.

To help pay the bills, my dad rents out the small apartment upstairs above the bar to the local X-Box junkies that live in the area. Their parents don't mind getting them out of their basements. My dad doesn't mind the insane amount of food the teenagers consume when they have their tournaments.

I don't know their real names, just their gamer tags. The two boys at the counter go by Streak and Chameleon. Both boys have shoulder-length dark hair. They're both dressed in their Army fatigues today ready for battle, but they have very different demeanors.

Streak is a happy, somewhat twitchy kid with fast thumbs. He has an impressive Halo and Call of Duty winning streak going. They also call him Streak because for some reason the boy cannot keep his clothes on while he plays.

Chameleon, on the other hand, is dark and funky around the fringe. I find him harmless and often highly entertaining with his quick wit and constant need to reinvent himself. He is one of the newcomers, a noob, but fairs well with his smoothness and chameleon-like ability to adapt. This one leaves his clothes on while he plays. However, proceed with caution. He might spontaneously hug you or make you wrestle him without warning.

"What's up guys? You're early today," I said.

"It's Tourney Time," they replied in unison.

"What can I get for you?"

"A couple orders of chicken wings to go," said Streak.

"Yeah, the good kind," Chameleon insisted. "Deep-fried with hot sauce, the hotter the better."

I went into the kitchen just so I could look into Dylan's eyes and say, "Order up."

When I got back to the counter, I had twelve more boys waiting to place their orders. Apparently, they were all trying to beat the 4:20 rush. Most of the boys were regulars. The rest I had never seen before. Obviously, they were Wolfman's new recruits.

Wolfman is the leader of the pack. He is the gatekeeper who holds the lease to the apartment and organizes the X-Box tourneys. Wolfman collects the entry fees and sets up the brackets. If there is any question about cheating, he alone decides who is in and who is out.

He appears to be the responsible one of the group. When he barks, the others listen. He has a knack of keeping the other boys under control by using his wit and good sense of humor, rather than brute force.

Wolfman got his tag name from either his unbelievable thick head of sandy brown hair, or from the fact that he can eat his weight in chicken wings. As far as his gaming skills go, he is at the top of the food chain giving Streak some tough competition.

Blond Ambition is Wolfman's right hand man in organizing the tournaments. His tag comes from the natural color of his hair and his loud, smart-ass attitude. He can always be heard yelling over the other boys when the games get heated.

The only time he is quiet is when he has a bad case of heartburn, or when he is passed out somewhere. Obviously, he is slightly high maintenance like most blond-haired people. He often requires Tums, a barf bag, and sometimes a mop. Hey, I'm not judging. I just serve them food. His gaming skills are fair, but he shouldn't put his money where his mouth is.

The Bag Brothers are a unique trio. The older two, T-Bag and D-Bag are troublemakers. Their tags are self-explanatory. They just come to party and have little-to-no gaming skills whatsoever. They are worse than noobs. These two just hang out, pick fights, and cause problems.

The youngest Bag Brother is Feed Bag. His tag is also self-explanatory. He eats anything and everything except onions. I had to start ordering extra wings from my supplier when he became a regular.

Feed Bag has a silly sense of humor. I think that his gaming skills would improve if he would concentrate on the game he was playing and didn't spontaneously burst into goofy made up songs. He can't add and often forgets things he's told. I guess that would put his gaming skills slightly above noob status. On the up side, he is well mannered and very polite, unlike his two brothers.

There is one other regular blond gamer in the pack. He isn't naturally blond, just naturally loud. His TV is always the loudest and he refuses to turn it down. So I think he might be naturally deaf. He goes by the tag Pump up the Volume or P.U.T.V. for short. His tag is self-explanatory. The color of his hair is not. It is an odd iridescent yellow. The only way to describe the color is to say it looks like a dog peed on his head. I would say his gaming skills are fair. You might be able to trust him around your X-Box, just not around your girlfriend. How was that for a burn?

The Singe and his brother Fourteen are the last of the regulars. The Singe is a tall, wiry, very loud redhead who tends to misplace things, a lot. It's a well-known fact that his parents often buy him two of everything he owns because he loses at least one of them. Rumor has it that the only thing he hasn't lost yet is his virginity. When he does, maybe his parents will just buy him another. Once again, I'm not judging.

As for his gamer tag, when there is smoke, there is The

Singe. As you've already guessed, he has a habit of accidentally setting things on fire. We all try to keep an eye on him and his stuff. I'm not sure about his gaming ability. He spends most of the time looking for misplaced backpacks, TVs, and controllers.

Fourteen is The Singe's older brother, so his tag has nothing to do with his age. I think it has something to do with how many times he has gotten lost on the way to the bathroom. Or perhaps it has something to do with how many times he has reorganized his sock drawer. Obviously, he has a slight case of O.C.D.

I am not sure about his gaming skills. From what the boys tell me, he spends most of his time rearranging the video game cases instead of actually playing the video games. Both brothers are great to have around because they always clean up after the other boys. When they order food, they always leave me a huge tip. I hope it's not prepayment for fire damage.

Dylan was busy in the kitchen with twelve more orders for chicken wings. Apparently, wings are a gamer friendly food.

"Can we get our wings with extra ranch delivered upstairs ASAP?" asked Feed Bag. "Streak is battling Warlock in a rematch dual of COD. We don't want to miss it."

"Ok," I said, rolling my eyes. "I'll send Callae up with your orders when she gets here. Remember delivery charges are extra, so please tip your waitress this time."

"Will do. Thank you, Payton," said Feed Bag.

"Which one of you guys is Warlock?" I asked, pretending to care.

"Warlock isn't one of us," added Blond Ambition.

"He's this guy we started playing against online last week. He's got an unbelievable high KD (Kill/Death ratio) and hates to lose," said The Singe.

"Yeah, he gets really mad and says he's going to kill us little bastards," added Feed Bag.

"It's frickin' hilarious!" laughed D-Bag, which turned contagious.

"Ok, sounds like fun," I said sarcastically. It must be a guy thing.

"Hurry up. The Tourney starts in five minutes," said one of the younger unknown gamers.

The boys funneled out the door and up the outside staircase to their adolescent man cave.

CHAPTER EIGHT

I see you. My nose prints on the window. My hot breath fogs the glass. You do not see me watching. You will not see me . . . until I want you to. Soon. It will be soon.

. . .

Business was steady with regulars until around eight o'clock. Just after eight, I had two unexpected visitors. It was Rod Huntley and his creepy, much younger business partner Kurt Meriwether.

Rod owns the bar and restaurant down the road called Your Last Chance. It is really more of a strip club than a restaurant. Rumor has it that Rod is in bed with the mob. I know you can't believe anything you hear and only half of what you see. But right now, I am staring at two crooked scumbags that look like they could have just whacked someone. So I'm going with my gut on this. They were certainly guilty of something. I will try my best to stay clean and clear of their baseball bats and anything accidentally falling off a truck.

They both took a seat up at the bar. Rod started looking at a menu. What the hell were these two up to? Maybe they were just scoping out their competition. I caught them looking around at my dad's expensive remodeling job. They visually inspected the two new floor-to-ceiling fieldstone fireplaces, the warm rich pine log siding on the walls, and the huge new eight-foot high windows that overlooked the lake for perfect views of the sunset.

"Looks like your dad put at least half a mill into this place," Rod said spitefully.

"Yeah, I think he spent a hundred grand just on the stuffed animals," I added. "The cougar in the back by the conversation pit is my favorite."

"Too bad he's never going to see any of that money again," said Kurt the pervert, eyeing me up and down like a piece of meat.

Gross. I did a mental shiver. "What do you mean by that?"

"There is no way your dad will ever sell enough crappy chicken wings and crusty corn dogs to stay in business."

I wanted to hit him. I should have hit him. Instead, my mouth took over. I dug myself a big hole that I couldn't crawl out of. "For your information, we just hired a new chef. We are working on a whole new menu." I grabbed the old menu out of Rod's hand and threw it into the garbage. "I'll be right back with my chef's recommendations for this evening."

As I walked to the kitchen, I was positive I was turning blue from the lack of oxygen to my brain. I went into the kitchen, dramatically leaning on the counter next to Dylan. He looked at me with inquiring eyes. He sensed my panic and noticed my paleness.

"Please tell me you're a Master Chef," I blurted out. "I kind of got cocky with the restaurant owner down the road and bragged that I had this great new chef and a fabulous new menu."

"Did you say new menu?" asked Dylan.

"Yeah, I know. I'm a big moron, right?"

"Are you kidding? This is awesome." He was so excited. Dylan could hardly contain himself. "I have all new appetizer recipes I wanted to show you. My buffalo chicken cheese balls, deep-fried green beans with ranch, apricot glazed baby back ribs, teriyaki chicken wings, and wonton chicken tacos."

"Can you make all that stuff right now, tonight?"

"Yes, just stall them for thirty minutes while I work my magic. I brought my secret spices, sauces, and herbs with me. If I can't find something in the pantry, do I have your permission to send one of the waitresses after it?"

"Absolutely. You are a lifesaver. I could kiss you right now."

He smiled. I turned a ridiculous shade of red. It was true. I wanted to kiss him. Why was I such a chicken? I backed out of the kitchen grinning from ear-to-ear at Dylan.

I stopped in the doorway. "Ok, here's the plan. I will go suck up and play nice with them. That should give you the extra time you need. When you are finished, deliver the tray to the fat, balding man and his skinny, creepy sidekick. They are sitting at the bar near the front door."

"Consider it done."

"Thanks, Dylan. You really saved my ass."

"No problem. That is what I am here for."

I left the kitchen with a newfound confidence. I was messing with the mob and getting away with it. I walked up to Rod and Kurt with a mile-wide smile on my face. "Can I buy you boys a round of drinks while my chef prepares you a special sample platter?" I said, trying not to be too smug.

"As long as you are buying, I will have a Jameson and Coke," said Rod.

"I'll have a double Cognac," said Kurt, jumping on the opportunity for an expensive free-bee.

I made their drinks, and then I sat down on a stool behind the bar. I poured myself my celebratory liquid supper: a glass of light beer. No more food until my butt shrinks two sizes. I took my first sip when I heard a familiar voice behind me.

"Drinking on the job again, I see," she laughed.

I swung around in my barstool. My three old roommates and best friends from college Amber Reynolds, Lisa Wilson, and Teagan Green stood just inside the front door. We all screamed. I ran and hugged them causing a scene in the bar. After about five seconds of silence, everyone went back to their food, drinks, and conversations.

The kitchen door flew open. Dylan stuck his head out. "Is everything ok out here?" he asked in his velvety voice. "I heard screaming."

I had almost forgotten how cute the man was. His shoulder and chest muscles bulged under his dark green, Hollister t-shirt. My friends and I stood breathless for a moment to take in his male beauty.

"Everything is fine, Dylan," I finally answered. "Amber, Lisa, and Teagan are my friends from school. We were just excited to see each other."

He waved, giving them a shy smile. Then he went back into the kitchen.

"First dibs on the hottie," said Teagan in her usual man-hungry demeanor. She was on her way to the kitchen for a second look when I stopped her.

"Don't even think about it, Teagan. Hands off, he's mine," I insisted. Wow, I'm not exactly sure where that came from. I obviously didn't want Teagan anywhere near Dylan. Which could only mean one thing, I've got it bad.

Teagan has a bad habit of flirting with anything with a pulse. She throws her long, fake blond hair around constantly trolling for the opposite sex. Nothing shocking about how she always gets what she wants from men. Her tight, slightly skanky clothes and provocative walk just seals the deal. Don't get me wrong. Teagan is my friend, my slutty friend. Like it or not, everyone has one. If you don't, I suggest taking a close look in the mirror assessing your own personal situation with men. You could be the slutty friend and not even know it. It has been my experience that sluts, rarely know they're sluts.

"Sorry, I didn't know you already had your claws in him," said Teagan, attempting to apologize. "But, Payton, do you really think it's a good idea to get involved with 'the help'?" she added with seemingly jealous, spoiled rotten undertones.

Meow. Scratch. Scratch. I shot a daggered glare in her

direction. Teagan can be a real condescending bitch when she wants to be.

"Really, ladies? I thought we were here to partay and have some fun," remarked Amber in a calming yet humorous tone.

Amber is great. I'd have to say that she is my favorite of the three. She is an incredibly smart pre-med student who is surprisingly mellow and very logical for a fiery redhead.

"Well then, let's get this party started," said Lisa, my spunky, sporty friend.

Lisa went behind the bar to mix a pitcher of margaritas. Lisa is normally well-disciplined. She exercises all the time and eats ridiculously healthy. Her strict lifestyle has earned her a place on two college sports teams, basketball and soccer. She is also a Sports Medicine major. So to sum Lisa up, she is the complete opposite of me. This is why we get along so well. We complement each other's personalities. She lets me eat all the macaroni and cheese I can handle, and I let her run around the block as many times as she wants.

"You girls help yourselves to drinks. Don't forget to pour me a glass."

"You got it," answered Lisa. "Hey, Payton, do you have any organic limes we can use for the margaritas?"

Leave it to Lisa to put a healthy spin on binge drinking.

"Sorry, we are all out," I said, humoring her. "You'll just have to slum it with regular limes."

"Did Payton say slum it or slam it?" asked Teagan. She attempted to be funny instead of bitchy.

The other two laughed at Teagan's awful joke. It made me wonder how much they had to drink before they got here.

I looked over at Rod and Kurt. They both looked bored, ready to leave at any moment. I poured the mobsters another free round, which seemed to pacify them for now. "I'll be right back," I said to my friends. "I need to check on something in the kitchen."

"Something? Or someone?" asked Teagan laughing. "Oh, Dylan," she said, raising her voice. "Will you make Payton breakfast in bed tomorrow morning?"

I looked at my three friends. "Don't you dare embarrass me tonight. I mean it. I really like him."

"Does Brad know?" Amber started.

"Does Brad know what?" Brad inquired as he walked through the door. He took a seat on the other side of the bar.

"That he is an overbearing ass." I walked away, going into the safe refuge of the kitchen with Dylan.

CHAPTER NINE

The moon has risen. The river runs fast. My prey I have chosen. This meal—his last.

. . .

Dylan was busy preparing a rack of baby back ribs on the grill when I entered. He smiled at me. I melted back at him. While I walked over to the grill, I tried to devise a plan to make a move on him before Teagan did. I could toss my hair around. No, that was too cheesy. I could try to walk sexy. No, I would just twist my ankle and hurt myself. I could give him a seductive stare. No, I would just look constipated and scare him off. I will just give up on this stupid fantasy. I'm pathetically out of practice.

"Is my special order almost ready?" I asked.

"Almost," he said, looking up from the grill. "Payton, your hand is bleeding again."

He took me by the hand, leading me over to the sink. He removed my band-aids. Then he applied pressure with a clean towel. "I still think you need stitches," he said in an overprotective manner.

I felt the same electricity when he touched me. My heart raced when our eyes met. I got a weird feeling that he might kiss me. So much for needing a plan, I just needed to be my pathetic self. It was like a moth to a flame. We were both leaning in for the big moment when the kitchen door flew open.

It was Brad. Ugh! He stood in the doorway, glaring at the two of us.

"Go have a beer, Brad," I said. "I'll be back out there in a minute."

Brad managed to slam a double swinging door as he huffed out of the kitchen.

I gazed back into Dylan's twinkling green eyes and sighed. The moment was over. Thanks, Bradley.

"I need to go back out to the bar before you burn something," I said reluctantly.

"Boyfriend?" Dylan asked carefully.

"Definitely not," I assured him.

"Good," he said with a huge grin. Dylan applied fresh band-aids to my wound.

I left the kitchen all googly-eyed and very much smitten.

When I returned to the bar area, I found Brad brooding. He sat at the bar sipping on his beer. My friends were laughing and being silly. They were obviously feeling no pain, working on their second pitcher of margaritas. This seemed to infuriate Brad even more. He never liked my friends, and they never liked him.

As I approached the bar, I saw what was making Brad squirm in his seat. The same person made my friends cheer and giggle. It was Streak. He was behind the bar in his boxers, bent over looking for something.

My friends and a few drunken middle-aged women around the horseshoe shaped bar were throwing quarters at him as he bent over.

Dylan walked out of the kitchen shortly after me. He set the platter of appetizers in front of Rod and Kurt. "Enjoy," Dylan said to them. He couldn't help but notice the intense situation brewing in the bar. He immediately disappeared back into the kitchen to avoid being caught in the crossfire.

"Streak," I said, raising my voice. "You can't be down here in your underwear. This is a family restaurant."

"I had to come down for a victory lap 'cause I totally slaughtered Warlock tonight. I am the champion of the online gaming universe."

"That is so cool," said Amber. "Can I sign your shorts? I've never met an online champ before."

I looked over at Brad while Amber signed Streak's shorts right across the fly with a Sharpie. Brad looked like he was going to have an aneurism. His nostrils flared, and his upper lip twitched. I found myself hovering in a state of shock, or stroke, wondering what else could possibly happen tonight. I had never seen Amber act like a community bicycle before. That was normally Teagan's job.

Amber signed: *Great Job Streak! Hugs and Stuff, Luv Amber*. Brad slammed his beer and then his glass down on the bar. He ordered another beer. I don't know why he didn't just leave. He obviously wasn't having a good time.

"That's great, Streak," I said. "But next time can you do your victory lap with your pants on?"

"No can do, Payton. I am a free spirit. I cannot be confined by earthly garments. I need to let my energy out."

"I think you need to cut down on the Mountain Dew. What are you doing behind my bar?"

"The boys sent me down here for five more double baskets of wings. They told me to tell you that they are the best wings they ever had."

"That's fabulous." I looked at Rod and Kurt. "Business will be booming because of Dylan."

"Yah, no doubt. He is the wing master. My friends also told me that the winner has to buy," said Streak.

"Bummer. Sucks for you. But you still haven't told me what you are doing behind the bar?"

"Blond Ambition asked me to get him some Tums, and Feed Bag needs a toothpick 'cause he has a chicken bone caught in his teeth."

"Sorry, I asked." I found him some antacid tablets from under the bar. Then I gave him a box of umbrella toothpicks to take upstairs. "I will put in your order for the wings. All of my servers have left for the night. Can you please send someone down here, who is wearing pants, to pick up your order?"

"Ok. Got it," he said, throwing a hundred on the bar. He hurdled the bar top like an Olympic gymnast on the horse, nearly knocking over Kurt's Cognac.

"Watch it, you little naked freak," said Kurt.

Streak stopped by the sample platter in front of Rod and Kurt. He grabbed a buffalo chicken cheese ball and popped it into his mouth. "That's the best damn thing I have ever eaten," he mumbled as he chewed. He pulled another hundred from somewhere in his underwear and put it on the bar. "I'll take five double baskets of those too, with ketchup." He did a cartwheel and ran out the door.

Wow. If I knew what that kid was on, I would order a round of it for everyone.

I headed for the kitchen to put in Streak's order. Brad caught me by the arm. "I need to talk to you," he said.

"I have nothing to say to you. We are sooooo past over."

I turned away from Brad. I walked to the kitchen door. He stopped me. Brad pushed me up against the wall just to the right of the doorway.

"What about today in your kitchen? You wanted me, and I wanted you."

He had me trapped. His hands were on the wall with his forearms on either side of my shoulders. He leaned in to kiss me. I slid down the wall, quickly escaping by ducking into the kitchen. I heard Brad pound the wall outside the door as I sought refuge with Dylan.

I looked out the windows along the back wall of the kitchen. The snow was really coming down. There was easily six inches of new fallen snow on the ground. I gave Dylan Streak's order.

"After you fill this order, you can shut down the grill and the deep fryers. It is almost eleven. There are only a few people

71

left out there at the bar. We should probably close soon."

I stood around not saying anything else. It was obvious that I was stalling. I had to say something fast before it became awkward. "Thanks for doing such a great job tonight," I said nervously. "Everyone loved your food."

He smiled at me. Not just with his mouth, but with his eyes as well. "I'm glad I could live up to your expectations. I'll work up some new main menu ideas before I come in tomorrow."

"That would be great." I looked out the window again. "It is really snowing hard out there. We should probably close soon so everyone can make it home safe."

"That is a good idea. If you want, I can plow the parking lot before work tomorrow?"

"That would be really helpful. Thank you."

"I could come by your house early in the morning and plow you out too," he said with a mischievous grin. "Vivian tells me you can use all the help you can get."

"Isn't that the truth," I said back with the same intense focus.

Amber stuck her head in the door. "Payton, we have a little problem out here."

"Be right back," I said, but Dylan followed me out to the bar anyway.

It was Dennis, AKA Dennis the Pennis. He was one of the local drunks from the neighborhood. Dennis spent most of the winter fishing in the ice-shack village located on the frozen lake near the restaurant. He received this nickname for manhandling women while he's intoxicated. He was up at the bar demanding to be served. The girls, my peeps, held their ground.

"We are getting ready to close, Dennis," I told him.

"I just want a beer, Payton," he pleaded. "Just one beer and then I'll leave."

"Fine. Just one," I said, giving in, knowing that he didn't have far to go to pass out in his ice shack.

I motioned to Teagan that it was ok to serve him. She poured him a beer from the tap. He took one drink of his beer and fell off his barstool.

I rushed over to make sure that he was ok. Stupid me, I should have known better. He helped himself up by grabbing onto the back pocket of my ragged jeans. I heard the rip and then the gasps as Dennis tore the ass right out of my favorite pair of jeans. Note to self: always wear underwear to work.

. . .

Bad things keep happening to you, Payton. You have not seen anything yet. This is like foreplay for me. I am heating things up slowly for your big wet dream, or should I say nightmare.

CHAPTER TEN

When the door opened, a draft of cold air hit the big hole in my jeans. A woman appeared in the doorway. I recognized her immediately. Her expensive monochromatic pantsuit and the typical news anchor shade of blond. It was her all right. It was Crystal Pierce. Crap. What was she doing here? I literally did not want my ass on the Five O'clock News.

Dylan ran over to me, taking off his apron. He tied it around my waist to conceal my wardrobe malfunction. No doubt about it, he was my prince. I hugged him without thinking about the PDA aftermath. It was the best hug ever. From behind me, I heard the sound of someone clearing his throat. It was Brad and he looked pissed. He had witnessed the whole thing from outside the men's bathroom door. I thought he had left. I guess not.

Crystal scanned the bar as if she was looking for someone. She stood in the entryway for a moment and then she finally spoke. "Is there a Paylula here?"

"Goddamn caller ID," I mumbled under my breath.

"Paylula?" asked Teagan. "You must mean Payton. She is right there," she said, pointing at me.

"Thanks for all your help, Teag. I really appreciate it," I

said sarcastically, giving her a closed mouth grin that wrinkled up my nose.

"Anytime," she said, raising her glass in the universal cheer motion.

Crystal walked over to me. In the meantime, Dylan made a fast beeline to the kitchen. He wasn't about to be on the news or deal with Brad's insane jealousy. Crystal and I walked over to an unoccupied spot on the end of the bar, so we could talk in private.

"Are you the one that called me?"

I reluctantly agreed, nodding my head yes. "I have a deal for you. I will tell you what I know, if you tell me what you know."

Crystal agreed. "How do you know about the missing necklace? It was never in my news report."

"It was a hunch," I told her. "I found a gold cross necklace in the river by where a young man drowned this week. Why would the killer take it?"

"So you think someone is killing these young boys?"

"Yes, I do. I think I saw the killer today. And what is worse, I know he saw me too."

Crystal's nose for the news kicked in. "Where and when did this happen?"

"This is strictly off the record, right?" I asked, trying to stay anonymous.

"Of course, Payton. Tell me everything you know. I am on your side."

I decided to trust her. "Before I came to work today, I went behind the college to look around the crime scene. I was down by the river next to the jogging path when I found a smiley face carved into a tree. When I looked up the hill, I noticed a big Bald-headed Man watching me from the balcony of the Commons Building."

Crystal was clearly intrigued. "What did you do then?"

"Being the huge chicken that I am, I ran."

"Did the man follow you?" she asked, eager for more information.

"No, thank God. I think I lost him. I haven't seen him since."

"What makes you think that he is involved?"

"It was the way he looked at me from behind his dark sunglasses."

Crystal seemed skeptical about my theory. "There's no proof that he is involved. Maybe he was glaring at you because you were trespassing."

"Ok, so it's a hunch. You have to admit that my hunch was right about the necklace. I know that I am right about this, too."

"What did you do with the necklace? You didn't turn it over to the police, did you?"

"No. I still have it," I said. "I think it is best if the police are not involved until we know more."

"I agree. Do you have the necklace with you?"

"Yes. I do. Let me go get it." I left the bar area to retrieve the necklace from my jacket. When I went into the kitchen, Dylan was nowhere in sight. Maybe he was taking out the garbage or in one of the walk-in coolers taking inventory for tomorrow's new menu. I didn't have time to dwell on where he went. I was eager to pry Chrystal for more info. I grabbed the necklace from my jacket and went directly back to the bar.

I showed the gold crucifix to Crystal. She took it from me, admiring it for a moment. "It is really beautiful," she said. "I will make sure this gets back to the family when I go talk to them." She opened her periwinkle purse that sat on top of the bar and placed the necklace inside.

I didn't know what to say. When I went to get the crucifix, I never intend to give it to her. It was the proof that something dastardly was going on. There was a moment of brief awkward silence on my part. What do I do? Should I grab it out of her purse or demand she give it back?

I looked over at Brad. He was watching us with a scowl on his face. I decided it was best to let Crystal deal with it and not create a scene in front of him. Besides, the boy's family had the right to have it back. I certainly didn't want to be caught with it. The last thing I needed was to be chased around by someone who wanted that necklace. The image of the big, bald guy popped into my head confirming my fear. I decided it was best to let it go.

To put an end to the awkward silence that was brewing, I decided it was her turn to dish out some secrets. "Ok, Crystal. Spill. What do you know?"

She took out a small notebook from her purse. "This morning, I found these four symbols carved into the trees by the Mississippi River. They were near where they found the dead boy." She showed me a piece of paper with four triangles. Two of the equilateral triangles were right side up and two were upside down. One of each had a horizontal line running through it.

"I thought you told me you didn't find any carvings."

"Look, Payton, I am a reporter working on the scoop of a lifetime here. I couldn't just tell you everything over the phone. I didn't know who you were. You could have been another reporter or the killer. After you hung up on me, I knew I needed to find you. Seriously, I am trying to work with you on this."

I decided to believe her explanation. "So what are they? What do the carvings mean?" I asked her.

"I don't know yet, but I am going to find out. They were carved into four separate trees in a circle, marking North, South, East, and West."

"That's weird. Are you sure the carvings are related to the boy's death."

"I am positive. The carvings were fresh. Did you see any carvings like these by the river today?"

"No. The Bald-headed Man scared me away before I could finish looking around."

"That's too bad. Maybe I should go check it out before I leave town."

"Crystal, have you looked outside lately? There is a blizzard raging out there. You aren't exactly dressed for exploration." She was dressed more like my therapist than a Private Investigator. Her black, double-breasted pea coat and periwinkle, high-heeled pumps that matched her purse and pantsuit were not practical for the weather. "It could be dangerous."

"Don't worry. I am a big girl. I will be fine."

"Ok, suit yourself. Just watch out for my Bald-headed Friend," I warned her.

"I'm always up for meeting a new bald-headed friend," said Teagan with a ridiculous amount of sexual innuendo.

I closed my rolling eyes at her, sighing at her stupidity. For once, I wished she would shut up and stop embarrassing me. But like it or not, Teagan had been eavesdropping on our conversation. I hoped she didn't hear much. If things weren't already bad enough, Brad walked over to us with a caustic look on his face. My life continued to spiral downward out of my control.

"Hey, Brad," said Teagan with a huge flirtatious smile. "Trolling hard for the ladies tonight?" She winked at him as he approached.

I was horrified.

"Is that your gun or something else in your pocket?" Teagan flipped her hair.

Seriously, she did not just say that. I slapped my hands over my eyes when she started her come-hither stagger for attention. I found myself peeking through my fingers. There was a huge vortex of disaster swirling around me, and I was in the eye of the storm. Was she really trying to come on to Brad? I was appalled.

"Yes. It is a gun, Teagan, so stay the hell away from me," Brad said angrily.

Teagan returned the sour look. She staggered back over to Lisa and Amber at the other end of the bar to escape Brad's feisty demeanor.

Crystal took this as her cue to leave. "I will be in touch, Payton." Crystal slipped me one of her cards as she shook my hand. I stuck it in my pocket without anyone noticing. She grabbed her purse from the bar and left.

As Crystal was going out the door, in came a stunningly beautiful dark-haired girl with a TV tight exercise body. I thought she must be lost. This girl had never eaten deep-fried food in her life. She clearly had another motive to be in the bar.

"Is Dylan here?" she asked impatiently. "Vivian told me that I could find him here."

My heart sank. What did she want with my Dylan? "I think he is in the kitchen." I pointed to the door on her right. She disappeared when the kitchen door closed behind her. My friends looked at me with mystified sympathy, but said nothing.

Brad pulled me aside. "What the hell was Crystal Pierce doing here? What the hell are you up to, Payton?"

"It is none of your damn business, Bradley?"

"I can't babysit you, Payton. Whatever you and Crystal are up to, knock it off."

"I don't need you to babysit me, Brad. I think you should leave." I pointed at the door.

"Are you serious? You can't throw me out, again."

"Leave," I demanded. My friends chanted, "Leave," repeatedly pounding their fists on the bar.

"Whatever mess you've gotten yourself into, Payton. Don't expect me to help you out of it this time. I am done."

"Fine by me," I snapped back at him.

"I better not see you on the news." Brad pushed past me, almost knocking me over. He grabbed his coat from the barstool and walked out the door.

My friends cheered. I walked over to the three girls. They had poured me a margarita from the pitcher. I could really use a drink. What a night. The ice had melted from sitting out on the bar. I picked up the glass. "Hey, you forgot to salt the rim."

"Salt is bad for you," said Lisa, my health conscious friend.

"And tequila is not?" I answered back. "To healthy intoxication," I cheered, raising my margarita. The girls and I toasted. We emptied our glasses.

"What are you going to do about Little Miss Tight Ass?" Amber asked me.

"What can I do?"

"I could go beat her up for you?" volunteered Teagan. She staggered towards the kitchen.

Lisa and Amber grabbed her and their belongings, pushing

Teagan towards the front door. "We should probably get Teagan out of here before she throws up."

"Good idea. But are you ok to drive?" I asked Lisa.

"Payton, statistics show that you are more likely to survive a crash if you are hammered," slurred Lisa.

"That's comforting," I replied. "Just drive carefully please."

"Okie dokie," said Lisa.

"Call me," said Amber. "Good luck." Amber gave me a hug.

"Jump his bones," added Teagan. "Don't let that skinny little bitch get in your way." Teagan turned to Lisa and Amber. "Hey, can we bar hop on our way home?"

Out the door they went, leaving me all alone in the bar area.

Dylan was still alone with the mystery girl in the kitchen. Maybe Lisa was right. The best way to survive a crash was to be hammered. I could see the crash with Dylan ahead. I poured the leftover margarita from the pitcher into my glass. I drank it while I cleaned up the bar.

. . .

Just because you cannot see me right now, does not mean that I am not still here. It also does not mean that you have seen me at all tonight. Think about that. Do not let it drive you crazy. Do not let me in your head. Once I get in, good luck getting me out.

. . .

I tried to stay busy cleaning the bar area, but my thoughts kept drifting to what was going on in my kitchen. As I washed the glasses and wiped off the bar, my head went crazy with random thoughts of Dylan and that girl doing unspeakable things with my kitchen utensils. Good grief, calm down. I was just being irrational. She was probably his aerobics instructor, or his dietitian, or better yet, his sister. Seriously, I'm not that stupid. She was his booty call, plain and simple.

To pass the time and make myself feel better, I made up a new drinking game. I call it Mystery Shot Mania. Did you know if you close your eyes, pick three random bottles of liquor and mix them together in a shot, it actually tastes delish. I tested my theory out three or four times to make sure that it wasn't just beginner's luck.

My favorite mystery shot was Rum Chata, whipped cream favored vodka, and cherry flavored Dr. McGillicuddy's. It tastes like a bowl of Cinnamon Toast Crunch topped with whipped cream and a cherry. I think I will call it a Breakfast Sundae. No. Sunday Breakfast is better. The recipe was so good, I had two more. The shots were starting to hit me. I had just the right amount of liquid courage in me, on an empty stomach, to go into my kitchen and pull out a chunk of her hair.

It had been quiet in the kitchen until I heard the dark-haired girl raise her voice. She yelled at Dylan. I couldn't make out exactly what she said, but it was obvious she wasn't happy. Joy to me! Things were looking up.

The kitchen door flew open. She walked past me without acknowledging my existence. Then out the front door she went. It was impossible to read her by her emotionless expression. I couldn't tell if this meant good news or bad news for me. Before I went into the kitchen, I waited a few minutes for the tension to subside.

I took several deep breaths and headed to find Dylan. When I was at the kitchen door, I heard the front door open. From where I stood, I couldn't see who was at the other door. "Sorry. We're closed," I yelled. The front door creaked and then closed shut.

. . .

We are finally alone. Patience is a virtue for me. It is a bitch for you. Stop whining. It is almost time to play. What do you know? Now, I am in your head, controlling your thoughts. Nice.

. . .

I pushed the kitchen door open, stepping inside. The kitchen was empty. Where was Dylan? I checked both walk-in coolers. There was no sign of him. He had disappeared.

"Dylan, where are you?"

"I'm right here," he said in his usual angelic voice. "I had to take the garbage out."

I turned around. Dylan was standing just inside the back door of the kitchen. Our eyes met, but not like before. Something had changed. Dylan started cleaning the deep fryer. I moved over next to him, leaning against the counter. When I popped the question, I wanted to see it in his eyes.

"Girlfriend?" I asked.

He looked down at the ground before answering me. "It's complicated." Dylan seemed perplexed, not knowing what to say.

I couldn't tell what he was thinking. "It's ok. I understand," I said, lying my ass off. I should be used to being undateable. "Here is a key to the front door. Can you lock up when you are done? I need to go home and get some sleep."

"Sure. No problem." He took my hands in his. "Are you ok?"

"I'm just really tired and kind of drunk. I just want to go home. Things didn't turn out exactly as I planned tonight."

"Was there something wrong with the food?"

"No. That's not what I meant. The food was great. You were great. You are a great guy, Dylan . . . you know, with the whole food thing." Yikes. I tried to cover up my steaming crush.

He looked at me awkwardly. Then he smiled when he finally figured out that I was talking about him and me. I pulled my hands away. I was so embarrassed.

"See you tomorrow, then?" he asked, hoping he still had a job.

"Yep. See you at three."

"I'll be by early to plow you out."

"Ok," I agreed. "See you." Dylan went back to cleaning the deep fryer. I was sure he didn't mean it the same way as he did earlier. I was seriously bummed. My driveway could use a good plowing.

When I turned to grab my coat, purse, and phone, I wobbled. I grabbed onto the counter with both hands to steady myself. The shots were hitting me hard. I needed to get out of here fast. Maybe the fresh, cold air outside would help clear my head.

I dropped Dylan's apron on the desk. This left my back pocket flapping behind me as I exited the kitchen. Once again, I was a walking disaster. Nothing ever goes right for me. This was why I needed therapy. I was bare-assed (well almost) bare-assed and emotionally compromised by two different men, twice in one day. That was a new personal best, even for me.

The kitchen door closed behind me. I was now in the dimly lit bar area. This was weird. I didn't remember turning off the lights. It was spooky with my dad's dead stuffed animals staring at me. From behind me, the jukebox kicked on. I jumped, frantically spinning around. A Taylor Swift love song blared from the speakers in the darkness. It was mine and Brad's song.

"Hello? Is anyone there?" No one answered. "Brad is this some sick joke to get back at me for . . . everything?" Still no one answered. No one ever answers me. I should really quit asking. I blew out a sigh of relief. It must have been a leftover credit on the machine. I slowly and carefully walked over to the jukebox and pulled the plug from the wall.

By the time I reached the front door, my head was woozy. It was spinning out of control. I staggered slightly, catching myself on the door jam. My knees felt weak. They almost buckled beneath me. I plopped myself down on the bench in the entryway. It was a horrible idea to think I could drive. This was a good spot for me to ride out the perfect storm that was brewing in my head. If I wasn't feeling better by the time Dylan finished in the kitchen, I would catch a ride home. I laid my head down on the hard, wooden surface of the bench and closed my eyes just for a second.

. . .

It is time for my game, Payton. Ready to play? I picked someone special to join us. You are really going to hate me after this.

You frolic in the snow with him. You are laughing and having a good time, but all good things must come to an end.

CHAPTER ELEVEN

My eyes opened. I was cold and wet, lying on top of my own bed. I had no idea how I had gotten here. It was as if I had blinked and lost hours of my life.

All my clothes were on, which I found to be a good sign that I hadn't done anything too stupid and regretful. I felt something cold and wet next to my left hand on the bed. I sat up to see what it was. Wrapped around my hand was a necklace, a silver crucifix on a heavy silver chain. Shit, so much for the theory of nothing-bad happening. That theory just flew out the window. Or maybe it just floated down the river.

I jumped out of bed, driven by my sudden adrenaline rush. The necklace looked familiar to me. Where had I seen it before? Whose was it? And why did I have it now? I thought about finding the golden crucifix yesterday. As an ice-cold shiver shook my body, I noticed the blood on my clothes. Automatically, I feared the worst.

The what ifs and oh shits bounced around inside my brain. Before I could come up with any answers, I heard a noise downstairs. I had a shocking sense of déjà vu. It was probably because the same damn thing happened to me yesterday. The banging quickly turned into pounding on the walls and then a loud stampede of footsteps on the stairs.

I went out the window again to avoid being trapped in my room. It was cold outside, absolutely bone chilling. Maybe I should have hidden under my bed. Well, too late for that. At least I wasn't throwing up in my purse this time. Instead, I was in bloody clothes with my ass hanging out of my pants. How about we just call it even? Good grief my life sucks.

As my wet socks became permanently adhered to the icy shingles, my thoughts oddly shifted to Dylan. It wasn't because I had cold feet where he was concerned, but because he should have been here by now to plow. I looked over my shoulder at the driveway. It was still snow covered except for a fresh set of vehicle tracks. My eyes followed the tracks down the driveway to the road.

A dark sedan was parked down there behind the bushes. The vehicle slowly pulled away. Behind the wheel was the Bald-headed Man. He had found me and was watching me. My day just maxed out on the creepy scale. I was already at a ten and the sun wasn't even up yet.

My focus shifted back to my room and who was about to enter it. I peered around the window frame in anticipation. I held onto it as tight as I could with frozen hands. My whole body shuttered from the cold. When I finally saw their faces, I was extremely grateful, but confused. It was Amber, Teagan, and Lisa.

I threw the window open and flung myself into the warmth of my room. My natural grace didn't fail me. I face-planted my-self onto my beige shag carpet, leaving behind my poor frozen socks stuck to the rooftop.

My three friends were laughing hysterically. Obviously, they were still under the influence of alcohol. Maybe I was too. My brain could barely comprehend what was happening to me.

"Payton, I give that move a 6.5," laughed Amber as she closed the window. "What were you doing on the roof?"

"Did we scare you?" asked Teagan, mocking me.

My teeth were chattering too hard to answer her right away.

"Yes," I said finally. "You guys got me good."

"Why didn't you hide in the closet or under your bed like a normal person?" laughed Lisa.

"Because I'm a moron," I added with a laugh. This sadly was the truth. I was positive I could be a fabulous moron if I set my mind to it.

"Why is there blood on your clothes?" asked Teagan.

I didn't know what to say. I hadn't had time to come up with a good cover story. "I have no idea. I don't remember what happened."

"Payton, are you wasted?" asked Amber. "The blood clearly came from the cut on your finger."

I looked down at the dried blood on my hand and hoped to God that she was right. Could all the blood smeared on my pants be my own? "I know. I was just joking." Before my friends could grill me for more information, I disappeared into my walk-in-closet to change. I quickly threw on a blue River Bend hooded sweatshirt and matching sweatpants. I replaced my missing socks with a clean, dry pair. I shoved the bloody clothes and the crucifix into the hidden access panel in the back of my closet. Hopefully, this would all make sense soon.

I stepped out of my closet. "So who wants breakfast?" I tried my best to act as if nothing was wrong. "I'm starving. Let's go raid the refrigerator."

My three friends stared at me with quiet conviction before one of them spoke.

I stared back at them nervously. "What?"

"We know what happened, Payton," said Amber with pity in her eyes. "We know everything."

"How do you know what happened to me?" I didn't know what was going on.

"We heard the whole thing last night," said Lisa.

"That's why we came back to help you," explained Teagan.

"Help me?" I asked. I was completely confused.

"After we left the Barbecue Shack, we stopped at Hannigan's for one last margarita," said Amber.

"A couple of the nurses from the hospital were in the bar.

They were talking trash about what happened between you and Vivian," said Lisa.

"That nurse Nancy isn't a very nice person, so I let the air out of her tire," explained Teagan proudly.

"Oh, you were talking about the thing with Vivian," I said, no longer confused.

"What did you think we were talking about?" asked Teagan.

I wasn't about to answer that. "Gee, I don't know."

"Payton, what did you do?" asked Amber. "You have a guilty look on your face."

"I do?" That isn't a good thing. I needed to cover up my emotions better.

Teagan reached into her bag, pulling out a green lacy thong. She threw it on the floor at my feet. "Did you think we were talking about this? We found it on the kitchen floor."

"Spill it, Payton. Dish us the dirty details," added Lisa.

"Oh God," I said, completely disgusted with myself. My eyes rolled back in my head until I was almost blind. With everything that happened, I completely forgot that my underwear was still in the kitchen.

"What are you hiding from us, Payton?" demanded Amber.

"Did you and Dylan do the nasty in your mom's kitchen?" Teagan asked laughing.

"Ok, I will tell you what happened if you promise not to judge me. I had a temporary moment of weakness. It wasn't last night, and it wasn't with Dylan. It was yesterday afternoon." I paused debating if I should really tell them. This secret wasn't as bad as the other one. So I just blurted it out. "I almost had sex with Brad in the kitchen." I held my breath waiting for their reaction.

My friends were silent. They just stared at me with wrinkled up noses. Finally Teagan spoke, "That is just gross, Payton. What were you thinking?"

"Well, we are not going to let that happen again," stated Lisa in a protective tone.

"Oh, so that's why Brad went crazy when you and Dylan

were getting chummy last night," said Amber as she put it all together.

"Hey, so did you hook up with Dylan last night, or not?" asked Teagan. "You didn't let that skinny little bitch have him, did you?"

Teagan once again struck a nerve. Before I could answer, we heard a car pull up outside. The kitchen door opened and then closed.

"Doesn't anyone ever knock anymore?" I was angry. I headed downstairs to see who it was. The girls were right on my heels.

I flew down the stairs without thinking about any impending doom. Considering my life in general lately, it wasn't such a smart idea. There was a fine line between bravery and stupidity, and I was walking it without a safety net. My visitor could be my Bald-headed Friend. Or worse, it could be Brad. On the other hand, it could be Dylan and all would be right with the world.

. . .

You wish it were Dylan. Do not worry, Payton. You made a lingering impression last night that he will never forget.

CHAPTER TWELVE

The girls and I cautiously walked into the kitchen. There, sitting at the kitchen table, was my old friend Julie Pederson. We had grown up together in one of the starter-home neighborhoods in town. She had been my maid of honor last year when I almost married Brad. I hadn't seen her much lately since we moved out here along the river. Her once short, dark hair was now shoulder length. Julie even looked like she had lost twenty pounds.

When we walked across the kitchen, she looked up and smiled. She was wearing more makeup than normal. Whatever the reason was for her makeover, she looked great.

Julie stood up, walked over to me, and gave me a hug. "I heard about what happened to you from my mom," she said. "I thought you might need to go for a walk and talk like we used to."

"Sure," I said, happy to see her. "Can it wait until after we eat breakfast?"

"I suppose" she said.

Julie seemed uneasy and nervous. Maybe it was because we had lost touch lately. Maybe it was because she didn't feel comfortable around my friends. They can be intimidating and bossy at times. What can I say? They live up to the Delta Omega Zeta stereotype of being obnoxiously bitchy.

"Are you guys crazy?" asked Teagan. She threw her arms up, displaying her disgust. "Why would you want to go for a walk? The sun is barely up and it's freezing cold outside."

Julie and I ignored Teagan's mini tantrum and continued planning our walk. Teagan took a seat at the table. She brooded while she flipped through a fashion magazine.

Lisa walked over to the refrigerator and opened the door. "I'm making breakfast," she announced. "Is egg white omelets and whole wheat toast ok with everyone?"

"That's too healthy, I'm hungry," I protested.

"Payton, why don't you give Julie the tour, and I will help Lisa make breakfast," suggested Amber.

"Ok," I agreed. "But there better be some fat and grease on my plate when I come back in here."

"Don't count on it," said Lisa.

Julie took off her coat. She placed it on the back of a chair at the table. "It's kind of cold in here, Payton. Did you forget to pay your heat bill?" she said in a joking manner.

"No," said Teagan. "Payton was so wasted last night that she forgot to close the door when she got home. We found it hanging wide open when we got here."

"It was?" I asked with disbelief, not remembering that I had done such a stupid thing.

"How do you think we got in?" asked Lisa.

"What time did you get here?" I asked, trying to piece together my missing memories of last night.

"We got here and went right upstairs to your room," said Amber.

Julie walked over by the kitchen window, looking out over the backyard. "Wow," she said.

"I know," I replied. "The pool was my mom's idea."

"No," said Julie. "I wasn't talking about that. What is that awful smell?"

I looked over at the granite countertop. There sat The Prada. One of the police officers must have found it in the front yard and brought it inside.

"Sorry. My bad," I explained. I took the purse from the counter. I went to the back door off the laundry room and chucked The Prada onto the deck.

After we all enjoyed our fat-free breakfast, I finished giving Julie the tour of the downstairs while the girls went upstairs to crash out. When Julie and I finished our tour, we found the girls upstairs in my parents' master suite looking through my dad's telescope.

"Payton, did you know that this telescope was pointed right at your neighbor's house across the river?" asked Amber.

"Hey, isn't that the creepy guy from the restaurant last night?" asked Teagan. "What is he doing down by the river?"

"Let me take a look," I said, not believing that Teagan could remember much of anything about last night. I peered into the telescope. It was Rod all right. He was down on the edge of the riverbank. He repeatedly poked at something in the water with a long stick. I couldn't tell what it was because it was behind a large log and thick brush. He suddenly looked directly at me as if he knew we were watching him. I backed away from the telescope.

"What's the matter?" asked Julie. "Is there something wrong?"

"Rod saw me. He knows we were watching him."

"Cool," said Teagan as she sprawled out on my parents' huge king-sized bed.

"No. It's not cool. Rod and his partner are bad news. Stay away from them," I told the girls. I walked out of my parents' bedroom. Julie followed me down the stairs.

"Are you ready for our walk?" asked Julie.

"Almost. Can you wait for me in the kitchen? I need to make a quick phone call before we go."

"Ok, Payton. I'll go clean up the kitchen while I wait for you."

I went into my dad's wood paneled den, closing the door for privacy. I sat down in his brown leather chair behind his massive, solid oak desk. I needed to make the call. I needed to find out if Dylan was ok. He seemed like a responsible person that wouldn't just blow me off. I found the courage to dial. The phone rang several times before a woman answered.

"Is Dylan there?" I asked Vivian, who sounded like she had just crawled out of bed.

"Payton, is that you?" She asked.

"Yes, it's me, Vivian. Is Dylan there? He was supposed to come by early this morning and plow my driveway."

"Let me go get him," she said. "He probably overslept. I'll be right back."

Vivian set the phone down. My heart sped up with anticipation while I waited. Vivian came back a minute later.

"Payton, Dylan didn't come home last night. His bed hasn't been slept in."

I felt faint. It was a good thing I was already sitting down. "Is there another number where I could reach him?"

She gave me his cell phone number and hung up. Vivian didn't seem concerned. Maybe he was just with Little Miss Tight Ass. At this point, that would be a relief.

I snuck out of the den without Julie seeing me. My cell phone should be in my purse in my room. I wanted to use my cell phone to call his. If Dylan didn't answer me right away, he could call me back wherever I was at.

I headed upstairs quietly without anyone noticing. Just as I had thought, my purse was next to my bed. I didn't expect to find my cell phone and the contents of my purse strewn out on the floor. This was weird. I didn't remember digging through my purse. Crap, who was I kidding? I didn't even remember how I got home.

I sat down on my bed, frantically punching Dylan's number into my cell phone. A few seconds later, I heard a phone ring. It rang twice before I realized that the ringtone was coming from underneath my bed.

My fight-or-flight reflex propelled me off the bed. My phone fell out of my hand, hitting the floor. I quickly moved across my room towards the door. My instincts told me to run, but I had to know for sure. Was just Dylan's phone under my bed or was Dylan under there too? After waking up soaking wet with a crucifix in my hand, anything was possible.

I slowly inched my way closer. Every step carefully mastered until I reached the side of my bed. I took a deep breath and bent down next to it. By now, the phone had stopped ringing. It had gone into voicemail mode. I was down on all fours ready to find out the truth. I was going to be either ecstatically relieved or living a horrible nightmare.

Cautiously, I lifted the bedskirt with a plastic hanger I found on the floor. My hand started to shake. The tiny hairs on the back of my neck were standing at attention. I leaned over craning my neck. There was no turning back. I was now at eye level with the opening under my bed. Holy crap! This was intense. I was about to find out if someone was lurking in the darkness.

"What's under your bed?" Julie asked from the doorway.

I jumped to my feet. "Nobody," I said and sighed with relief.

Julie gave me a weird look. "Are you ready to go?"

We bundled up and went outside. I was still reeling from my second adrenaline rush of the day. Who needs coffee when you have a pathetically tragic life like mine?

On the outside, I tried to appear to be in control, but on the inside, I was an emotional basket case. I still didn't know where Dylan was, or how his phone got under my bed. Did he give me a ride home last night? Did he come up to my bedroom with me?

I looked over and saw my Escape parked in the opened garage next to Lisa's Land Rover. Well, that shot down that theory. I must have driven myself home. Yikes.

Julie and I stood in the middle of the driveway. A thick blanket of snow covered everything. I turned to her, "So which way do you want to go? We can walk down the road or take the scenic tour by the river. Last fall, my dad cut a path through the trees down there. It's nice."

"Why don't we go down by the river? The view will be better down there," suggested Julie. We headed across the lawn towards the river in the knee-deep snow. "How much land do your parents own out here? It's pretty secluded."

"They own about three hundred acres along the river."

"Wow, no wonder you don't have any neighbors close by."

"I know. I could scream for help and no one would ever come." I laughed and then stopped after I realized that was probably going to happen someday.

"That's not true. Your creepy neighbor across the river would probably hear you and come to your rescue."

"No, thanks. I'll pass. Besides, after I steal all of his business with my fabulous new chef, he would probably rather see me dead."

Julie stopped walking. She stood still in her tracks staring at his house through the trees. "You were watching him today. Do you think that he ever watches you? You can see across the river, right into each other's houses."

"That is a gross thought. Next subject, please," I begged.

Julie turned towards me. "Hey, did you guys get a dog?"

"No. Why?" I asked, adjusting my hat, pulling it down to cover my ears.

"Look at all the dog tracks down here by the river."

I looked around us. Julie was right. There were tracks everywhere.

Julie started to act nervous again. She frantically scanned the woods around us. "Payton, there is something I should—"

"Oh my God," I screamed, when I spotted the bluish flesh of a body in the river. Without hesitating to consider my options, I ran down the bank and into the black, bitterly cold water. Within seconds, the frigid water penetrated my clothes, reaching my skin. I inhaled sharply. My breaths remained quick and shallow as the surge of adrenaline pushed me forward.

As I moved through the water, Julie paced back and forth impatiently on the riverbank. "What are you doing, Payton? We have to call the police."

I ignored her. My waterlogged body pushed through the cold, chest-deep liquid. Please don't let it be Dylan, echoed over and over in my head. As I drew closer to the body, I could see the bare skin of their back protruding out of the water. It was most likely a male because of the muscular definition. Shit. This was so bad. My prayers for Dylan echoed again in my head.

I hit a drop off. Part of my head bobbed under. I gagged and spat out a mouthful of water. Shit. Shit. Shit! The struggle was real on my tiptoes in the chin-deep water. I tipped my head back slightly to avoid swallowing more water and pressed on.

The icy river continued to rob my body of heat to the point of numbness. My quick, hysterical breaths made me lightheaded. For a split second, I thought about giving up. Then I remembered something my father used to say to me when he coached my little league team. 'Stop your whining, Payton, and hit the damn ball.' Not exactly inspirational, but it was enough to keep me focused.

I fought the current the last few yards in my heavy, wet clothes until I was next to the face down body. I stood still in the water. His dark brown hair floated with the current. I couldn't see his face, but everything else about him was familiar.

Tears formed in my eyes. I took off my soggy gloves and dropped them in the water. I reached out, rolling him over by grabbing his bare left shoulder with my left hand. His pale blue skin was icy to the touch. I didn't feel the spark. His body rolled towards me in the water. He touched me. A scream left my body as his gray, fixed, lifeless eyes met mine. I recognized them immediately. I backed away from the body still in shock. It wasn't Dylan. It was Streak.

Confusion, relief, and anger topped off my emotional profile. I grabbed Streak's arm and pulled him through the icy water.

"Payton, what are you doing?" asked Julie.

"We need to do CPR," I said, pulling Streak to the edge of the riverbank.

"Payton, he's dead. He's bluer than your hat," replied Julie.

"Julie, help me pull him onto the shore."

"Payton, I'm not touching him. Let it go. He's dead."

"Fine. I'll do it myself."

Somewhere, somehow, I found the strength and the footing to pull Streak out of the water and onto the snow-covered riverbank. I knelt by his right shoulder and tipped his head back with the palm of my left hand. Next, I pinched his nose closed with my thumb and index finger. Without considering the consequences, I filled my lungs with a deep breath. I put my warm lips against his stone cold mouth and blew as hard as I could. It was like kissing a Cullen until the river water mixed with his wretched stomach contents blew back in my mouth. It was totally gross and kind of tasted like chicken. The thought of buffalo chicken cheese balls briefly entered my mind. Those glorified cheese curds just got added to my never eating that again list.

I had let go of his head and started doing chest compressions when Julie pushed me off Streak's lifeless body. I fell backwards, landing in the snow.

"Payton, he's gone. He's dead. You have to stop. You can't save him sweetie. He's a frickin' ice cube."

I looked at Streak. Julie was right. There was no sign of life, or hope, or . . . his underwear. I must have been in shock before not to notice that Streak was in full-on Streak mode.

It was time to go get help. We both ran up the riverbank to the house screaming. Julie and I made it as far as my backyard when we came to a dead stop. We looked at each other. I could see the terror in her eyes. They had not been dog tracks in the snow. They were wolf tracks.

A pack of five large gray wolves stood between us and the safety of my house. Four of the animals had thick grayish-brown fur. The dominant male in the middle was pure black. The black wolf took a few steps towards us, which left the other four evenly flanked on each side.

His muzzle curled back, exposing his perfectly white carcass polished teeth. He released a deep thundering growl. Just as I thought my life couldn't possibly get any worse, the other four wolves growled and formed a circle around us.

"Stand perfectly still," said Julie. "Maybe they will go away."

"I think . . . that works . . . on bees . . . not wolves." I stuttered and convulsed from the cold. We might as well have rung the dinner bell and yelled come and get it. There was no possible solution out of this mess. We were both going to die an agonizing death.

Out of nowhere, Amber appeared on the back deck. "Get ready to run." The sound of her voice drew the wolves' attention from us, to her. She threw the vomit filled Prada as hard as she could over the wolves' heads.

The pack chased after it as if it was a juicy, venison tenderloin steak. Oh boy, were they in for a big surprise. Julie, Amber, and I bolted for the house. We ran inside. Amber slammed the patio door shut. Behind the safety of a pane of glass, we watched the pack of hungry wolves devour what was left of The Prada. I was sorry to see it go. It had saved my life twice.

. . .

How do you like me now, Payton? Are you pissed yet? Do you hate my guts? Well good! Now you know how I really feel about you.

Do you think it was an accident that you found the body? I think not. I will always be one-step ahead of you dangling the string, kitty cat. Too bad for you, I am a dog person. God, I love this game.

CHAPTER THIRTEEN

I made Amber call 911. The dispatcher might actually believe her and send help until they hear the Richardson address. While Amber was on the phone, I went upstairs to thaw out in a hot, steamy shower. Not to sound disrespectful to Streak, but I could not wait to gargle and wash the death cooties off me. Deep down I felt horrible. Even though I cannot remember, I just know this is somehow my fault.

You would be surprised at how much scalding hot water and soap it takes to remove the death cootie. My skin was raw and dermabrased by the time I was finished. I shampooed, rinsed, and repeated until I could no longer repeat. I went through a whole bottle of Scope and threw my toothbrush and toothpaste right into the garbage can when I was done. Now, my body was clean and clear, but my brain was not.

I still had too many unanswered questions and blacked out memories rummaging about in my brain. If I could hit myself in the head hard enough to regain my memories, I would gladly do it. Dr. Parks assured me that my memories could come back at any time. I just hoped that they didn't all come flooding back at once. Maybe under the circumstances, it would be best if they never came back at all.

By the time I finished with my beauty regimen, the crime scene crew had arrived. Even though I had layered myself up in clean dry clothes, I still felt frozen on the inside. Wearing my best brave face, I slowly made my way downstairs to discover my fate.

The girls were in the back living room with Tim. He was busy taking their statements. I took a seat in the big green recliner next to the fireplace. I wrapped myself up in my favorite, fleecy, Biederlack blanket and patiently waited for my turn. As I sat there, I suddenly realized that I didn't have an alibi for last night. I couldn't just declare that 'I do not recall' the events of last evening. Only the slyest of politicians could ever get away with that excuse. I began to perspire at the thought of my impending persecution.

I was deep in thought down alibi alley when I heard Amber say, "Right, Payton?"

"What? Sorry, I wasn't listening."

"After the bar closed, we came back here with you," Amber repeated.

"Yes, they did," I said, lying to protect us all. "And then in the morning, Julie came over and we went for a walk. During that walk, Julie and I found Streak's body in the river. On our way back to the house to call the police, we were almost eaten by a pack of hungry wolves. Amber saved us by throwing my vomit-filled purse at them."

I smiled at Tim when I finished my story. I knew how farfetched it sounded.

He smiled back and asked, "Was that the same vomit purse that broke Vivian's arm or a different vomit purse?"

"Oh, it was the same vomit purse. I only have the one."

"I'm afraid to ask," said Tim. "But for the report, where is the purse now?"

"It's gone. The wolves ate it."

"Oh brother," sighed Tim. "You girls are all going to have to sign this report or the Chief will never believe a word of it."

"You can ask Julie too. She was right there with me when it all happened," I said, looking around the room for her.

"She left before the cops came," commented Lisa.

"Don't worry. I will track her down," said Tim. "So none of you girls heard or saw anything last night?"

We looked at each other. We all shook our heads no.

"I just have one more question and then we are done. Payton, at any time did you or anyone else touch the dead boy?"

"Why does that matter?" asked Amber, obviously thinking about her misguided sharpie incident.

"Just in case we find your DNA or other evidence on the boy," stated Tim.

Amber looked over at me. She had helped me out with an alibi. Now it was time for me to return the favor. Besides, any trace of Amber should have washed away in the water.

"I was the only one to touch Streak," I said. "I rolled him over in the water to see who he was. Then I dragged him to shore and attempted to revive him by performing CPR."

"You did?" Tim said, surprised by my heroism.

"Yes. My DNA is definitely all over him."

"If the coroner discovers there are any signs of foul play, you know that won't look good."

I hadn't thought about the consequences of trying to save his life. I turned pale at the thought of myself on death row in a bright orange jumpsuit.

"Just out of curiosity," asked Tim. "did you girls happen to find any of his belongings? Clothes, socks, underwear, anything?"

Before we could answer Tim, someone crashed through the kitchen door stomping their boots. Before I saw his face, I knew who it was. I would know that stomp anywhere. I almost married that stomp. It was Brad. His stomp sounded pissed. Out of impulse, I braced myself for impact.

Brad blew by Tim and the girls. He gave me a big ole bear hug, which I was not expecting after his performance last night.

"Are you ok?" asked Brad with honest concern in his voice.

I hugged him back. Does that make me a bad person? I was having an extremely crappy day and clinging to any chance of not ending up in the electric chair.

"No, I am not ok," I answered back. His hug was warm and strong. I melted into it. For a few moments, it was like we were the only two people in the room. Amber abruptly broke up our little party. She took me by the arm, pulling me away from Brad.

"If you boys in blue are finished with Payton, she needs to get something to eat and take a nap before work," ordered Amber in a stern gingified voice.

Amber pulled me to the kitchen. We passed by a window that overlooked the backyard. My backyard that was once a beautiful paradise was now a jungle of yellow crime scene tape. I saw the coroner and his crew carrying a big, black, zippered bag past the window. The sight of Streak like that made me nauseous. My appetite vanished.

"I'm not hungry," I informed everyone. I headed for the stairs. Brad tried to follow me. The girls stopped him. They transformed themselves into a human barricade. I didn't look back. I could tell he was angry. I crashed on my bed with my blanket. The last thought I had before drifting off was about Dylan. Where was he? I barely knew him. Why did I care so much?

. . .

Rough morning, Payton? Could you look any guiltier? One anonymous call from me, and the police could link you to the other crime scene. Your fingerprints are all over the faucet handle. Your DNA is on that chip and the smiley face carved into the tree. Your footprints concealed mine perfectly. It is as if I was never there, only you.

But if they lock you up now, my game and my fun will be over. We cannot have that. The game must continue. You can count on me raising the stakes and the KD.

. . .

I woke from my nap hoping that it was all a dream. It wasn't. It was a nightmare. I could write a book. "My Life is a Nightmare" by Payton M. Richardson. It would be a best seller.

I stared at the bumps on my ceiling looking for answers to

so many questions. The bumps weren't talking, so I decided to get up and write a new, happy, fun-filled chapter to my life. The refrigerator was a good place to start. I'm thinking pudding, chocolate pudding.

When I got down to the kitchen, I found a note from the girls: *We went to grab the necessities of life. Be back soon. Luv Amber.* I was glad they were sticking around. I didn't want to be alone after what happened.

The clock on the microwave said noonish. My stomach said it was lunchtime. I opened up the refrigerator. There, on the second shelf, was my chocolate pudding. I ate two and chased them down with a Miller Lite. Don't judge me. It was a pudding and beer kind of day.

After I finished my beer, I was still restless and needed a change of scenery. There wasn't enough beer or chocolate pudding in the refrigerator to make my demons go away. I was faced with too many unanswered questions and too much crime scene tape. I was on my way upstairs to grab my purse and phone, when I had a brainstorm. Which knowing how I am, will certainly translate into trouble.

First, I retrieved the card with Crystal's cell phone number on it. It was in the pocket of my bloody jeans I hid in my closet. I punched the numbers into my phone. Her phone didn't even ring once. It went straight to voicemail.

Next, I tried her office number. Her receptionist answered.

"Hi, this is Payton Richardson. Can I please speak with Crystal Pierce?"

"Crystal hasn't come in yet today," replied her receptionist. "No one has been able to reach her. She was supposed to be on the air thirty minutes ago."

"When she comes in, have her call me. It's an emergency."

I gave her my number and hung up. Now I had a bad feeling about Crystal, too.

For my next brilliant idea, I retrieved Dylan's phone from under my bed. Huh, it was the exact make, model, and color blue as my phone. Maybe I grabbed it by mistake last night. It could have happened, right? Sure. Let's go with that.

I stared at the screen of his phone wondering if I should violate his privacy to try to save his life. Yeah, right. It took me two seconds and I was on "A" of his contact list. Like an inquisitive stalker, I began dialing. In a calm voice, I managed to ask everyone who was willing to answer, if they had seen Dylan. I got a lot of 'hell no' from his hung-over friends. 'Who are you, again?' from his casual acquaintances. And the secret family banana bread recipe from his Grandma Eleanor. The recipe kind of helped, but I still felt disappointed. Nobody had seen Dylan last night or this morning. Where was he?

I had crept through and called everyone on his entire contact list except for one number. The last contact person on his list was not a name just "S". I was about to dial when his phone rang. How freaky. It was "S". Should I answer it? Abso-flippin-lutely! Desperation to find Dylan made me do it. I answered it on the third ring, but remained silent.

"Hey, asshole!" said a women's voice. "I want it back. I know you have it."

Hang up, said the little voice in my head. I hate that little voice because it is always right. Instead, I said, "Hello, do you know where Dylan is?"

"Payton?" asked the mystery girl.

I'm not going to lie. I should have hung up and stayed out of whatever this was, but now I was intrigued. She knew my name.

"Yes, this is she."

"Payton, this is Stephani Waters. Give Dylan a message for me. Tell Dylan that he is a dead man. I will get even."

"What is going on?" I was already worried that he might be a dead man.

Her end of the line was silent.

"Wait. Don't hang up." I pleaded. "Where is Dylan?"

I heard the click. She was gone.

I redialed her five times. She wouldn't answer. I sent her a text. "Where is Dylan?"

She sent back, "Drop dead."

Wow, I am not a Stephani fan. She was obviously not a

happy camper or a decent human being. Wait a minute, her voice sounded familiar. Did I just have a conversation with Little Miss Tight Ass? If Dylan wasn't with her, at home, or with any of his friends. Where the heck was he? This was not good. So far my new chapter in my life was not a happy tale. I've decided, no more brilliant ideas today. My ideas stink and make me want to drink more beer.

I tossed Dylan's phone in my purse, then dug around for my car keys. They weren't in my purse. They weren't in the kitchen. Hopefully, they were in my Escape. Out the kitchen door I went, literally running into Tim on the steps.

"Whoa," said Tim. "Slow down, Payton. What's the rush?"

"Sorry. I just need to get out of here. It has been a bad morning."

"I just stopped by to give you the update on the Italian kid."

"Who?" Tim caught me off guard.

"I believe they called him Streak. His real name is Dominic Delcavotti."

"Oh yeah. Sorry. Come on in."

Tim came inside. We went into the kitchen to talk. Tim sat down at the table. He carefully placed a brown paper bag on the table in front of him as if its contents were of great importance. I remained standing. I wondered what he was about to let out of the bag.

"So what did you find out?" I was extremely curious to see if anything sparked my memory.

"We found Dominic's truck with a flat tire on Eagles Point Bridge. That bridge crosses the river about a quarter mile west of here. It looks like he stopped there to change his flat tire."

"Then how did he get in the river?"

"Dom's tire iron was found down below the bridge on the ice. The Chief thinks he crawled down there to get it and was chased into open water by the wolves."

"Seriously?" So far this was good news for me, but I didn't believe a word of it.

"Yes. We found shreds of his underwear on the ice and

wolf tracks all around where you found his body. A conclusion was reached that the boy froze to death waiting for the wolves to go away."

"Do you agree with the Chief's conclusion?"

"I did, and then I found this down below the bridge." He pulled a periwinkle pump out of the brown crime scene bag.

I believe I turned whiter than a new pair of socks. "I need to sit down," I told Tim. I collapsed onto one of the chairs at the kitchen table.

"Is there anything you would like to tell me, Payton?"

"No, not really," I said, trying not to hyperventilate.

"Payton, who does this shoe belong to?" Tim insisted.

"I have no idea," I said, lying epically.

Tim pulled his chair closer to me. "Look, Payton, I am on your side. Whose shoe is this?" asked Tim in a calm convincing tone.

"You won't tell Brad or his dad, will you?" I pleaded.

"No, of course not. Those two are idiots. Tell me what you know."

I was running out of options and allies, so I spilled everything, well, almost everything. I skipped the part about completely blacking out, waking up wet and bloody holding a cross necklace. I am desperate, not stupid.

Tim pondered the information for a few minutes. "Ok, so let's just say that I agree with your theory on the drowning boys. What is the motive?"

"I'm sure if we knew the why, then it would be easy to figure out the who."

"If we knew the who, then we would know the why?"

"Good point," I said. "So far none of it makes a whole lot of sense."

"I don't mean to change the subject," said Tim. "But before I forget, I was talking to the Italian kid's family this morning. They asked me if we recovered a silver cross necklace with his body. The family mentioned that he always wore it. They would like to bury him with it. Could you look around the restaurant and the apartment where the kids hang out? Let me know if you find it. If it's not too much trouble."

I was trying my best to keep my hyperventilation to a minimum. I managed to say, "Sure, I'll look around for it and let you know if I find it." The trouble was . . . I knew exactly where to look . . . in my closet. Once again, I knew way more than I should and a hell of a lot more than I wanted to. I was deep in it now. There was no turning back. I was in it until the end.

"What do you want me to do about Crystal?" asked Tim. "Should I put an A.P.B. out on her car? We can't officially report her missing for seventy-two hours."

"We can't wait that long. She could be dead by then."

"Or maybe she is involved somehow. Don't dismiss that theory."

"I hadn't thought of that." At this point, anything was possible. "Can you put out a quiet A.P.B., so Brad and the Chief don't find out? Brad knows she was with me last night. The shit will hit the fan."

"Payton, there is no such thing as a quiet All Points Bulletin. Here is what I can do. I will look around town for her car. I will contact the news station where she works and see if anyone has seen her or knows where she is."

"That would be great, Tim. Thanks for all your help."

"That is what I am here for, to protect and serve."

"Good one," I laughed. I don't think Tim meant that to be funny. I noticed a sour look on his face. Apparently, he takes his job seriously.

"Payton, should I call the DNR today and have them relocate the pack of wolves, or would you like me to leave them here with you?"

Ok, he made his point. Do not dis the badge. "If you could call the DNR for me that would be greatly appreciated." I smiled big for added effect.

"Consider it done," he said, smiling back. "Payton, try to stay out of trouble today."

"I wish," I said, trying to be completely serious.

"And, Payton, stay away from the river. The wolves are

still out there. It's not safe for you to be wandering around."

"Ok, will do." I said it, but not sure if I meant it. I could be relentlessly inquisitive when I wanted to be.

"It probably wouldn't be a bad idea if you had your locks changed. The guy on the south end of town comes highly recommended."

"That is an excellent idea, Tim. I will do that pronto. Anything else?"

"No more beer today. You should probably try to keep a level head."

"Wow. You are a good detective. Why don't you follow me around today? You could be my bodyguard."

"I would, but I need to go check out a B& E. Last night, someone broke into one of the ice shacks on the lake across from your parents' restaurant."

"What is the crime spree this time? Is somebody stealing tip ups again?"

"No, that's the weird thing. Someone broke into one of the shacks and used the owner's ice agar to drill a hole big enough to fit a truck through and then they left. Now I have to go out there and put up open water signs before some bozo falls in. You didn't see or hear anything last night?"

"No. That is weird. Maybe someone was bored because the fish weren't biting. You should talk to Dennis. He was out and about last night. Maybe he will remember seeing something if he wasn't too wasted."

Tim got up from the table and walked to the door. I followed to show him out. "Thanks for the tip, Payton. I will let you know if I hear anything on Crystal. Don't worry about Dylan either. I am sure he will turn up soon."

"Thank you. I hope you are right. See you later."

After Tim climbed into his police car and left, I figured that it was safe for me to go upstairs and retrieve the dreaded necklace from my bedroom. I wasn't sure what I was going to do with it yet. Maybe I should plant it at the restaurant for someone else to find. I really was not proud of the diabolical turn in my personality. I couldn't help it. I was in survival mode.

I was on my way out the door again when my phone rang. I took one look at the screen and sighed. Oh crap, it's my mother. From thousands of miles away, Janna Richardson somehow felt my diabolical shift off the path of righteousness. Yes, my mother is that good.

CHAPTER FOURTEEN

Yes, it is a sad day when your own mother scares you more than a dead body and a pack of wolves. I decided to pick up. If I didn't, she would just keep calling me until I did. My mother can be downright relentless when it comes to getting what she wants.

"Hi, Mom. What's up? How is the weather in Texas?" I asked, trying to sound breezy and casual. Not to toot my own horn, but that was pretty darn good under the circumstances.

"Payton Marie Richardson, don't you dare pretend with me," insisted my mother. "I know that you were almost eaten by a pack of wolves this morning."

Wow. It is creepy when she is almost psychic. Could it be mother's intuition? I think not. It is more like the small town gossip hounds sold me out. "Who ratted me out this time? Was it Betty, your golf partner? Or was it Cindy, your tennis instructor?"

"No. It was Wanda, my hairdresser."

"Yeah, the girls at the beauty shop do get all the good gossip."

"This morning, I called Wanda to make an appointment for a cut and color. She had the nerve to ask me if my daughter had any teeth marks in her. Teeth marks. The nerve of some people. You don't, do you?"

"No, Mom. The last time I checked, I didn't have any bite marks. Really Mom, I'm fine," I lied.

"Should your father and I come home?"

"No, the police are having the wolves relocated and I think all the crime scene tape would just freak Dad out right now."

"Crime scene tape," said my mother, raising her voice. "What crime scene tape?" My mother demanded an answer.

I thought Wanda had completely clued her in. I guess not. "A boy accidentally drowned in the river by our house last night. Rumor has it that he was chased into the river by the wolves." A rumor isn't technically a lie if people actually believe it, right?

"That is horrible. Do we know the family?"

"No, I don't think you know the Delcavotti family."

"Delcavotti? Delcavotti? Oh, I think the father, Vinnie, works down the road from our restaurant," said my mother.

"Really? Which place?" Sometimes my mother can be a fountain of knowledge when it comes to idle town gossip.

"He works at that sleazy dive, The Last Chance Saloon. I've heard stories of what goes on there. If you ask me, the place should be condemned."

I just got a shiver. Rod Huntley's name came up again. "What does Delcavotti do for Huntley?"

"He does deliveries."

That was mob code for 'don't ask, don't tell.' I wasn't going to ask my mother any more. I didn't want to know. I was doing my best to mind my own business. It was time to change the subject. "So when are you and Dad coming home?"

"We'll be home right before Easter weekend. Are you and your brother still coming down for Spring Break in March?"

"I hope so. I have Vivian's stepson helping me in the kitchen. Maybe I can get away for a few days." I held my breath for a moment, wondering if my mom had heard about our roof top adventure.

"That's nice dear. I'm glad you have some help while we are gone."

Exhale. That was close. It was just a matter of time before she found out that I broke Vivian's arm. That was a disastrous topic for another day.

"Is Vivian's son good looking? I am just asking because you really need to move on from Brad, my dear. Payton, it has been almost a year since you have been out on a date."

"Gotta go, Mom. Say hi to Dad for me." I hung up before she could push me down the aisle with her golf partner's son. Who, by the way, was recently divorced and has two-point-five children. Oddly enough, the half-a-kid doesn't scare me as much as the other two. That is probably because I have no maternal instincts whatsoever and half-a-kid sounds like less work.

The clock on my cell phone said one thirty. I had just enough time to do something incredibly stupid before I had to be at the restaurant. I know what I said about minding my own business, but my mother pushed me over the edge with her dating comment. I could get a date if I really wanted one. I don't need Brad. I was sure there was a great guy out there somewhere just dying to go out with me. I just hoped his name wasn't Dylan, and he wasn't already dead.

I pondered my incredibly stupid options for a minute. It didn't take me long to come up with a fabulously stupid plan that involved me, my dad's binoculars, and a backyard filled with crime scene tape. Somewhere in my plan, I was sure to discover a troublesome glitch. I always do.

My dad always kept his binoculars in his den. I found them on top of his locked gun cabinet. Too bad he always kept it locked. A loaded gun neatly tucked into the waistband of my pants would have come in handy this week. Wait. Who am I kidding? I would have probably shot Vivian for breaking and entering, Brad for pissing me off, and my left butt cheek just because I have no idea where the darn safety is located. For me, and everyone around me, thanks Dad for always keeping the gun cabinet locked.

I grabbed the binocs and headed for the backyard. When I

reached the first set of crime scene tape, I paused for a moment of silence for Streak. I also paused and thought about why I was about to do this dangerously stupid thing. This wasn't just for Streak. It was for Crystal and Dylan who were still missing. Most of all, it was for all the other boys who had mysteriously ended up dead in the icy waters of winter. It was time to find out some answers and bring awareness to the problem.

I crawled under the tape, making my way down the hill. I trudged through the snow to the riverbank where I found Streak's lifeless body. The vision of his bluish skin and fixed opaque eyes crept back into my memory. It upset me. I wanted to run for the house. I stopped and pulled myself together. Thinking of my dad again, 'Keep your eye on the ball, Payton.' If I was going to make it through this mission of stupidity, I needed to develop thicker skin, nerves of steel, and a set of female cohunes would be really helpful.

For fifteen minutes, I searched the riverbank. I came up empty handed. There was not one single clue. My symbol theory had fallen short. I was sadly disappointed. I should be relieved that some weird serial killic murder didn't take place in my backyard.

Maybe it was just a tragic accident, a horrible series of unfortunate events ending another young life. How was that for news anchor B.S.? I almost bought the shit I was shoveling and then it hit me. I never checked the trees on Rod's side of the river for symbols. I pushed on. I needed to find out why I had Streak's necklace.

I put the binoculars up to my eyes and scanned the riverbank filled with trees. A sudden flash of movement drew my eyes from the riverbank to Rod's house. I watched the windows until I saw Kurt walk by eating a sandwich. He sat down in the living room and turned on a ball game. That should keep Kurt out of my hair for a while. So far there was no sign of Rod. Maybe he wasn't home.

I turned my attention back to the trees. There were hundreds of trees to scan for carvings. This could take all afternoon. Movement drew my attention again. This time it was a shadow on the treetops. It was a young eagle or maybe a hawk soaring overhead. The bird was so graceful. I got lost in its peaceful flight.

The bird glided from the treetops to the water's surface. It snatched up a small fish from the river in its talons. The large bird soared upward to the treetops, landing in its nest. I followed the tree trunk down towards the ground. Bingo. Ten feet from the ground, I found what I was looking for. There was another symbol carved into the bark. The eagle had shown me the way.

My persistence paid off. My hunch was correct. It felt gloriously unsettling to be right again. The evidence was stacking up against Rod. I needed to turn my hunch into cold, hard facts.

This symbol carved into the tree was different from the four triangles and the smiley face. It looked like a stick man. I needed a closer look, which meant sneaking onto Rod's property. What a seriously stupid idea. I'll do it.

Five minutes later, my car was parked at the end of Rod's driveway. I hid behind trees half my size with military precision. I am such an idiot. It took me little effort to reach the symbolized tree and climb to my destination. I have to say, I was feeling darn good about my newfound stealthiness.

My cell phone was in my pocket. I pulled it out to snap a quick picture of my fabulous find. This picture would be evidence to prove my theory. The symbol of the horned stick man was in the center on my screen when a familiar voice boomed up at me from the ground below.

"What the hell are you doing in my tree?"

"Shit," slipped out of my mouth as my phone slipped out of my hand. I looked down to find Rod and the Chief staring up at me.

"Payton, what the hell are you doing?" asked the Chief.

"Bird watching," I replied, without hesitation. Which I had to admit was a pretty good freaking lie. I was definitely impressed with myself and no doubt going straight to hell for doing so. "See the eagle's nest?" I pointed up into the tree.

"Get your ass out of Rod's tree, Payton," ordered the Chief.

"Okie dokie." I skillfully made my way down to the ground.

Once I reached the ground, two scowling middle-aged men greeted me. My eyes bounced from Rod, to the Chief, then back to Rod. They just looked at me with loathing and disdain.

I decided to break the ice with some clever banter. "What brings you boys out here on a fine day such as this?"

"Cut the crap, Payton," said the Chief. "Rod called me because you were trespassing on his private property."

"I was bird watching," I insisted, pointing at the binoculars that hung around my neck.

"She was spying on me," Rod blurted out.

"No I wasn't. I didn't even know you were home."

"That is a lie," said Rod. "She was spying on me last night too."

"What the heck are you talking about? You came into my restaurant, ordered food, and left without paying for it."

"I'm not talking about that. I saw you down by the river last night."

"No, I wasn't," I protested.

"Ok, people, break it up," declared the Chief. "I don't care about any of this crap." The Chief pointed at me. "You stay the hell off Rod's property." The Chief pointed at Rod. "And you stay the hell out of her restaurant. Let's go." The Chief grabbed my arm, pulling me towards the driveway.

"Wait! My phone." I pulled away from the Chief to retrieve it. The Chief kept walking down the driveway without me. I bent down and grabbed my phone from the ground by the tree.

As I was walking away, Rod added one more verbal jab loud enough for the Chief to hear. "I saw you, Payton—you and your little friends. I know what you did."

I looked back at him with a puzzled glare. "You are such a liar, Rod. You are just making shit up, trying to get me in trouble."

Rod stood there with his hands on his hips. He had a huge

smile on his face. Rod was playing some sort of evil game with me. He had underestimated my wit and willingness to save my own ass. I was about to pull my trump card and beat this mobster at his own game.

I walked back just enough to make good eye contact with Rod. My voice intensified as I spoke. I wanted Rod and whoever else was in the area to hear what I was about to say. "My friends and I saw what you did down by the river this morning. What were you poking at?" I asked with a sassy tone. "I think we both know the answer to that," I said, bluffing my butt off. Then I laughed in his face.

This wiped his smile clean off. My plan had worked. He was a mobster with many skeletons in his closet. He did not like the thought of someone witnessing something incriminating. For a few brief moments, I had Rod by the seeds and my swag was back on.

I walked back to my car feeling very proud of myself for standing up to him. Then my swag was gone when I saw the Chief's scowling face. He was waiting for me by my Escape.

"Payton, what the hell are you really doing here?"

"I told you. I was bird watching."

"That is your story?"

"Yep, and I'm sticking to it."

"You are just damn lucky that I hate Rod Huntley more than I hate you, or I would lock you up and throw away the key."

"That's comforting, Chief."

"You watch yourself, Payton. I better not see you again for a very long time."

He turned and climbed into his squad car. I climbed into my Escape. The Chief was mad enough that he burned a layer of rubber off his new tires as he left. I don't know about you, but it made my day.

Now that I was all alone, I was dying to check out my phone to see if I had gotten a decent photo of the carving. My photo gallery popped up. Dang it, I didn't get it. The picture was blurry. I will just have to sneak back up into the tree and take another one. The door handle was in my hand. I was about to get out when I looked up and saw Rod standing next to the driver's door of my car. Maybe I should come back another day. Rod didn't move. He stared at me through the glass with serious mobster mentality. This is the part in the movie when the bad guy usually pulls out a gun and threatens the young heroine.

Rod reached into his jacket and pulled out a nine millimeter. I hate it when my instincts are spot on. With lightning fast reflexes, I locked the doors to my car and made a mental note to check into bulletproof glass.

Rod tapped on the glass with the barrel of his gun. He motioned for me to roll down my window. My mother didn't raise a daughter with horrible self-preservation instincts. Well, maybe she did, but even I knew better than to roll down my window. I shook my head no. If you hadn't already guessed, this is the spot in the movie where the heroine almost wets herself.

Rod leaned in close to my driver's side window. His hot breath fogged the glass. "Stay the hell out of my business and off my property. If you don't, you and your little friends will be floating in the river like the dead kid."

I believed that Rod actually meant every word by the look I saw in his eyes. I slammed my car into reverse and sped off to the restaurant. Holy crap! That was close.

117

CHAPTER FIFTEEN

Did you find your boyfriend yet, Payton? Do you know where Dylan is?
Do you think he is dead? Or is he alive? You will find him soon.

. . .

When I pulled up to the parking lot of my parents' restaurant, it was only half plowed. It was obvious that Dylan had been here, but where did he go? Why would he leave without finishing the job? I hope nothing bad happened. I maneuvered the Escape into my usual parking spot and got out to look around.

Nothing in the parking lot seemed strange. The only thing I found that was remotely unsettling and out of place, were random sets of butt prints in the snow bank next to the front door. What is wrong with people when they drink too much? Don't they have any common decency? This is a family restaurant. I used my mitten to wipe away the evidence of booze gone bad from the front doorstep. It was time to go inside and look for clues to what happened to me. More important, I needed to check in the kitchen for any sign of Dylan.

Once I was inside the restaurant, I looked around for

something to spark my memory of last night. Everything in the dining room and the bar was in its place. Nothing was out of the ordinary. I was as clueless as ever.

When I went into the kitchen, it was unmistakable that Dylan had been here. All the lights were still on. When I walked further inside, I noticed the knocked-over desk chair and an unfinished menu plan on the desktop. A can of pop sat next to the menu. I felt the can. It was almost full. Something or someone had interrupted Dylan causing him to leave unexpectedly.

"Dylan, are you here?" I called out, hoping he would miraculously step out of one of the walk-in coolers. He didn't. Maybe he just ran to the store to pick up some items for the new menu. I was still too apprehensive to feel any relief. I knew I wouldn't feel better until I saw Dylan walk through the door.

I looked up at the clock. I was already behind schedule. Hungry customers would be here soon to dine and hear my tale of the big bad wolves and the floating boy. I let out an enormous sigh knowing the intense night of storytelling that I had ahead of me. I went to the meat locker to figure out what I could prepare just in case I had to fly solo in the kitchen tonight.

I had my hand on the lever that opened the freezer when I heard movement inside. It had to be Dylan. Maybe he accidentally locked himself in. I threw the door open happy to have finally found him. Instead of being greeted by his smiling face, I was unexpectedly sideswiped. Two boxes of chicken wings greeted me as I walked into the freezer. They tumbled from the overstocked shelf and hit me in the head, knocking me to the floor. That was not what I needed today. Now, I had a bump on my head and there was still no sign of Dylan. I picked myself off the floor and got back to work.

It was my lucky day. Well, as far as my luck goes, anyway. There were still plenty of the staples: corn dogs, hamburger patties, BBQ ribs, French fries, and chicken wings. Nothing wonderfully gourmet like last night, but doable.

An obnoxious bunch of racket came from the upstairs apartment interrupting my train of thought. I could hear the stampede of footsteps on the stairs. It was clear to me that the boys were back in town and would be looking for food soon. With a box of chicken wings under each arm, I emerged from the walk-in freezer prepared for the ambush.

I closed the freezer door with my hip and let out a scream. Standing before me wielding a huge butcher knife was my friend Julie. She had an odd look in her eyes. A look I had never seen before. My sweet neighborhood friend was harboring a wicked passenger today. I'm not going to lie. I was more than a little troubled by her behavior. I tried to stay calm. Maybe it was just that time of the month.

"I thought you could use some help," she said anxiously as she ran her index finger down the full length of the blade, admiring its razor sharp edge.

"Sorry that I screamed. I didn't hear you come in the kitchen." I was desperately trying to tremble in a calm, cool manner.

Julie started laughing. "I'm sorry, Payton. You should see the look on your face. It's priceless."

I didn't find her joke all that funny, but I laughed anyway. In the last year or so, I have learned not to intentionally hurt someone's feelings, especially when they are holding a sharp kitchen utensil. "That was a good one," I said, humoring her. "So, Jules, what brings you out here to the restaurant?"

Julie walked over to the butcher's block countertop. "Seriously, I came to help." She stuck the knife into the countertop with determined precision.

I hadn't quite figured out her angle yet. "Sure, I can use all the help I can get right now."

"Yeah, I heard about your chef."

"What did you hear?" I asked frantically.

Muffled screams interrupted our conversation. Intensely loud pounding noises from the upstairs apartment held our attention. Our eyes followed the sudden stampede of frenzied footsteps thumping across the ceiling above our heads. Then the thumping ran down the stairs. This sent me into panic mode. Within seconds, there was the distinct sound of the upstairs fire alarm. Without saying a word, we both rolled our eyes with exasperation and ran for the front door.

Once we were both safely out in the parking lot, I looked up at the second story to assess the damage. A steady stream of smoke billowed from one of the upstairs windows. The good news: I couldn't see any actual flames. Perhaps the fire was out already. When I focused my eyes back down to the ground, I discovered the bad news.

This was mind-blowing. For some unknown reason, as far as my eyes could see, boys were frantically running around the snow-covered yard and parking lot in nothing but their boxers. Some were carrying their controllers. Some were carrying their flat-screen TVs. Some were carrying their X-Boxes. All of the boys were carrying a candle except one, The Singe.

This seemed like a logical place to start. I walked over to him and put my hands on my hips, waiting for him to spill his guts.

"Hey guys, has anyone seen my TV? I don't remember where I left it," announced The Singe, AKA the boy who loses everything.

I cleared my throat and continued to stare at him. Then I folded my arms firmly across my chest to show my impatience with the situation.

"Oh. Hi, Payton. I have a funny story to tell you," said The Singe, standing before me in a random pair of red, white, and blue plaid boxers.

"I bet you do. Let's hear it."

"We, meaning me, and all my fellow X-Boxers here decided to have a candle light vigil for Streak, you know, in our underwear. That is the way Streak would have wanted it."

"Of course," I said, trying to understand their logic. "Yes, I am aware of Streak's philosophy: no earthly garments, blah, blah, blah."

"Exactly. So after my fifth can of soda, I had to use the bathroom and drain off some Dew. That is when the toilet paper roll accidentally caught on fire from the candle."

"Naturally," I said with a sigh.

"I tried to put out the fire by smothering it with a twelve pack of toilet paper. That didn't work so well, so I threw the rolls of burning toilet paper into the bath tub and opened the window."

"Because everyone knows that oxygen and kindling will help put out a fire?" I asked with great skepticism.

"Duh. No. I opened the window to let out the smoke. But then the wind blew the shower curtain into the flames, and the whole bathroom went up like a frickin' inferno."

I smacked myself in the forehead with the palm of my hand. It hurt both physically and mentally. "Please tell me that you turned on the showerhead to put out the fire?"

"No, we couldn't reach the knob on account of the raging flamage. Some of the boys and me were quick on our feet. We were thinking outside the X-Box." He stopped briefly, chuckling like Beavis or Butt-head at his joke. "We sprayed two cases of Dew on what was left of the shower curtain and the wallpaper. It might be a little sticky in there, but all the plumbing still works."

A group of boys behind us yelled, "Stickies." At that point, they did a hand gesture to each other where their fingers touched and wiggled. I seriously didn't want to know anymore. I turned, walking away to spare my sanity and The Singe's life.

As I walked through the endless sea of boys, the crowd parted. I could feel the warmth of the fire. Someone had earned their fire badge using charcoal starter, firewood, and my dad's new fire pit. I should have been appalled that someone would dare start another fire, but I was freezing and expected the big, red, fire truck to roll up any second.

Chameleon and Blond Ambition approached me. Blond Ambition was wearing one of those beverage dispensing hard hats. Today his beverage of choice was non-alcoholic, but not sugar-free. On his lower half, he donned a pair of American Eagle boxers covered in a dill pickle design.

Chameleon stood barefoot in the snow wearing a space helmet and a black cape. He was sporting a pair of pink boxers while carrying a pink controller and a light saber. Most people would find their behavior odd. I find it quite hilarious knowing the smart-ass nature of the offenders.

"Is it true that you found Streak's body this morning in the river behind your house?" asked Chameleon.

"Yes, unfortunately, it is true," I said regretfully.

"Is it true that he was half eaten by the wolves?" asked Blond Ambition.

"No, that is definitely not true. Where did you hear that?"

"On Facebook, where else?" answered Blond Ambition.

"That figures. You know you can't believe all the idle adolescent gossip, right? You can't even believe the idle adult gossip."

"You mean the Zombie Apocalypse isn't really going to happen?" asked Blond Ambition.

We ignored his idiotic comment. I turned the conversation back to Streak. "Did either of you talk to Streak last night before he left?"

"After the tournament was done, I hung around for a while. I got bored. I left to go find some girls." Chameleon lowered his voice. He didn't want anyone else to hear what he was about to say. "I did get a weird message from him around 12:30 this morning."

"Did he send you a text?" I whispered back.

"No, he left me a voicemail. No one ever sends me texts."

"Why is that?" I asked.

"Because I can't read it." He held up the completely demolished glass of his iPhone screen.

"Wow, you are not Mac compatible."

"Tell me about it. You should see the screen of my laptop. The Bag brothers accidentally sat on it."

I was anxious for answers. "What did Streak say to you in his voice mail?"

"I could barely understand him. He wasn't making any sense. He said, 'the plants were coming alive and were trying to eat him.' "

"Was Streak drunk or on something? He seemed pretty wound up last night."

"No, Streak doesn't drink or do drugs," responded Blond Ambition, taking a slurp from his straw. "Streak is always wound up after a tournament because he doesn't take his ADHD medicine. His hyperactive twitchiness gives him the edge over his competition. That's why he wins all the time."

"Oh, that explains his cartwheels through the bar last night."

"Yeah, he was cool like that," said Chameleon with a sad look on his face.

"Can I listen to the voicemail? Maybe I will understand what he was trying to say."

"Sorry, I deleted it from my mailbox."

"Dang it! Do you remember anything else about his message?"

"Yeah, Streak kept saying, 'he was on fire.' No wait, that's not what he said. He said, 'he was burning up.' I don't think he was talking about his gaming skills. Maybe he meant he was hot."

"That is weird because I found him in the freezing river without any clothes on."

"That's not weird, that is normal for Streak to run around in his underwear," said Blond Ambition.

"I know. But when I found him, he was commando. The police found pieces of his underwear shredded on the ice. Any idea what could have happened to them? Normally, people from the Midwest don't take their clothes or their underwear off outdoors in the middle of winter." I looked around me and realized that comment was futile. Thirty-five teenagers that stood before me in their boxers would disagree with that statement.

"Those were his lucky smiley face underwear, too," said Chameleon. "He wore them for every tourney. He wouldn't just rip them to pieces like the Incredible Hulk."

I caught the smiley face comment. This case was definitely linked to the others. For now, I decided not to share this fact with the two boys.

"Maybe Streak really was the Incredible Hulk," commented

Blond Ambition. "Or maybe some random hot chicks ripped them off his body."

"In the middle of a blizzard? Really?" I began to rethink my non-alcoholic beverage comment. "The police seem to think that the wolves ate his underwear."

"The best the cops can come up with is the dogs ate his homework?" asked Chameleon.

"What can I say? They just disappeared except for a few shreds they found on the ice. It really isn't important," I said reluctantly. "Can we change the subject back to his bizarre message? Maybe he was acting strangely because someone drugged him. Could he have been given something that would cause him to hallucinate or have some weird reaction?"

"There are drugs like GHB and Rohypnol that can cause side effects like hot and cold flashes," said Chameleon. "That would explain the hot theory. The drugs are traceable in the hair follicles for up to five weeks. Ethylene glycol, AKA anti-freeze, is another possibility. This sweet liquid can cause slurred speech, but it is a slow poisoning. It causes kidney failure and then death. So it probably wasn't that. However, there is Rocuronium. If injected, it paralyzes the muscles, immobilizing the victim causing an agonizing death by suffocation. It could look like a drowning, I suppose. All though, it is more logical that someone slipped something into his food or drink."

Blond Ambition and I looked at him strangely. "How do you even know this stuff?" I asked.

"My father is a Science teacher," he said, waving his light saber around like he was ready for battle.

We both continued to stare. I still wasn't getting the correlation.

"I have read all of his Science books and magazines. I have also read a multitudinous amount of books on a multitude of different subjects. I even know everything there is to know about dairy. Ask me a question about cows."

"No, thanks. Maybe later." It was hard to take him serious while he was holding his light saber. "Did either of you see anyone suspicious hanging around after the tournament?"

"When I left, Streak was in the parking lot talking to three really drunk girls and a guy in an apron," said Chameleon.

"Those were just my friends and my chef. Don't worry about them. They are harmless. Blond Ambition did you see anything suspicious last night?"

"No, I didn't see anything. As soon as I got rid of my heartburn, I passed out until five o' clock this morning."

All the rest of the boys started to crowd around us. They were either interested in what we were talking about, or they were trying to stay warm. I looked towards the road when I heard the sirens. Rod and Kurt were driving by slowly in Rod's red pickup truck. They were both laughing hysterically at my dilemma.

"I seriously hate those guys," I said.

"Streak hated them, too," said Chameleon. "They beat the hell out of his dad last week for being fifteen minutes late with a delivery. They beat him so bad that they put him in the hospital. Streak said that he was going to get even with them. I guess that will never happen now that he's dead. Maybe they will still get what is coming to them. Karma can be an evil savage bitch."

"God I hope so. That would be fabulous," I said in agreement.

The fire trucks and the three police cars squeezed their way through the crowded street. Then they turned into the parking lot. Great, the cavalry and the firing squad were here. This should be interesting.

. . .

I rode to work with you today. You should always check your back seat.

CHAPTER SIXTEEN

I pointed the firefighters in the direction of the upstairs bathroom. Then I calmly waited to be put to death by Brad and his anal-retentive father. I realized that I had a shit storm coming my way. That storm was about to go splat and get real messy because Julie and I were surrounded by a bunch of high school boys in their boxers. Wait a minute. Where the heck did Julie go? I can't believe she bailed on me again. It was too late to make a run for it. The Chief had me in his crosshairs.

"Payton Marie Richardson, what the hell is going on here? Why are all these boys in their underwear?" asked the Chief at a decibel level that could surely shatter glass.

"Chief, I think we should let Payton explain what happened before we jump to any conclusions," added Tim, fearlessly.

The Chief turned pink, and then red, skipped blue, going straight to purple before he exploded. "Tim, who's the Chief in this town, you or me?" asked Richard J. Thomas. His thundering voice made a few neighboring squirrels and most of the half-naked boys scatter to save their nuts.

"You are sir," answered Tim in a meeker voice.

"Ok, then never question my authority again, or I will have your badge, Deputy. Is that understood?"

"Yes, sir. Sorry, sir," came out of Tim's mouth. The comment seemed honest and sincere until I saw the unbound hatred that came across his face as soon as the Chief turned his back. He was undoubtedly my new ally.

Before the Chief walked to his squad car, he ordered Tim and Brad to find out what the hell was going on. Tim casually approached the remaining boys in boxers and started asking them questions. Brad unfortunately headed straight in my direction.

"You really did it this time, Payton. You almost burned down your parents' restaurant."

"What? No hug before you insult me?"

"Trust me. That moment has passed. What are you doing with all these naked boys?"

"This is not my fault." I shot him a hateful leer.

He glared back with a double eyeball shot of scornful loathing. "That would be a first."

"Look, Brad, I don't want to fight with you. I'm kinda having a bad day."

"So what else is new? You're always having a bad day."

"Thank you, Captain Obvious. Can I please tell you what happened, so you will leave me alone?"

"Fine. Let's hear it." He took out a small pad of paper and a pen from his jacket pocket. Brad was actually going to write down what I had to say or write me a ticket.

I gave him the semi-short version that included thirty–four boys in their boxers, a shit load of vigilating candles, the red-headed fire starter, and my burnt candy-coated bathroom.

Brad was silent for a moment. "This could only happen to you, Payton. No wonder you need therapy." He shook his head, laughing.

"Well, I'm glad we both agree that my life is like a nuclear disaster. Beware of the fallout. It could be hazardous to your health."

Brad looked up at the small billows of smoke escaping from the charred, second story window. "You've got that right. I can see the radiation burn from here."

The Fire Chief, Bob Woodworth, walked out of the front door of the restaurant and into the parking lot. He was your stereotypical Fire Chief. Bob was in his mid-fifties. He was slightly overweight, but still able to save a baby from a burning building. Bob was my dad's fishing buddy, which meant good news for me. He would treat me fairly. Unfortunately, this also meant that my parents would hear about the fire before the Mountain Dew had time to dry.

Bob signaled Brad over for a conversation, so I took this opportunity to find Tim and pry him for information. When I found him, he was talking to a small group of boys with whom I was not familiar. As I approached the group, I heard one of the boys say, "That's her." He was pointing at me. Tim turned around. He greeted me with a puzzled look on his face. I had a bad feeling. This was not going to end well for me.

"Payton, you didn't tell me that you were one of the last people to see Dominic alive," said Tim.

"It must have slipped my mind," I added. Wasn't that the truth. I was a blank slate.

"According to Josh, he saw you around midnight making ass angels in the snow bank with the dead kid."

I wasn't sure how to make ass angels, but apparently, I did last night. Wait. Oh hell. The butt prints I found by the front door must have been his and mine. Good grief, no more Mystery Shot Mania for me. Let me pause here to take a few moments to pluck the crow that I am about to eat. That would explain why my pants were all wet when I woke up this morning. Another piece of the puzzle fell into place. I just didn't like the scene that was being created.

"Which one of you is Josh?" I asked.

A tall, dark-haired, stoner-looking kid gave me the customary head nod greeting. "I prefer to be called by my gamer tag, #Faded," he said with a slow smile that narrowed his eyes.

Great, my eyewitness was a human rain delay. "Do you remember seeing anything else, Hash Tag?"

"No. I was outside on the balcony having a smoky treat when I saw you two playing in the snow. Man, were you wasted."

I gave him my best evil glare. He was not helping my plea of innocence. "Does anyone remember seeing anything else last night?" I asked the remaining boys in a pleading tone. "We need to find out what happened to Streak."

"Sorry," said Hash Tag. "My X-Box was like calling my name, so I went back inside to chillax and 'be one' with the gaming universe."

I let out a huge I'm disappointed sigh.

"It's probably not important," said a quiet little voice from the back of the group. "Last night I saw a big, bald man lurking around outside."

The small, quiet kid tagged Cricket had my full attention. "What time was that?"

"The first time I saw him was around eight. Then I saw him again around ten thirty. The second time, he was talking to two guys in a red pickup truck."

"Really," I said, looking at Tim to see if he caught the connection. "Did anyone else see the Bald-headed Man last night?" All the boys shook their heads no to my question.

Cricket leaned in and whispered in my ear. "The policeman was here too last night."

I looked over at Brad. "Thanks, but I already knew that," I whispered back.

Brad and the Fire Chief walked over to the group. The remaining boys scattered into the wind. Tim walked to his squad car to finish his report.

"I have good news and bad news, Payton," said the Fire Chief.

"Give me the good news first." I could live with my glass being half-full.

"The fire is out and the damage seems to be contained to the second floor apartment."

"The bad news?" I held my breath waiting for my glass to become half-empty.

"The upstairs has extensive smoke damage. I'm afraid the bathroom up there has to be gutted. All the sheet rock in there was 'Singed' beyond repair. There is a crusty, golden, candied substance covering the entire bathroom. I've never seen anything like it."

"That would be Mountain Dew," I said. "Don't ask. You are better off not knowing any more than that."

"Interesting," said the Fire Chief. "I also recommend that you close the restaurant for a few days to clean up the upstairs apartment. I need to have an inspector come out for insurance purposes before you can reopen."

"Sounds like good news to me. I could really use a few days off."

"Payton, I will let you know when the inspector makes his evaluation," said the Fire Chief.

"Ok, Bob. Thanks for all your help and speedy service."

"You're welcome, Payton." Bob and the rest of his crew climbed into the fire truck. They pulled out of the parking lot, leaving Brad and I alone.

"Well, that went better than expected," I said.

"The little bastards almost burned down your parents' restaurant and you're happy?"

"No, Brad. I am far from happy. My parents are going to be pissed about this. And if that wasn't bad enough, a boy is dead." Crying was not an option in front of Brad. I turned and walked away.

"Maybe he shouldn't have been hanging out with you in the snow bank."

I turned and looked at Brad strangely. "What the hell is that supposed to mean?" I walked back to confront him.

"It means trouble follows you. Bad things happen to people around you."

"That kid is not dead because of me, Brad. Don't even go there."

"Hanging out with you didn't help his luck any. Look what happened to your boyfriend."

"Boyfriend? I don't have a boyfriend." I paused mentally to comprehend what Brad was trying to tell me. "Omigosh, do you mean Dylan? You found Dylan?"

"Yep, I know exactly where he is," Brad said with a laugh.

SK LUNDBERG

"Brad, where is he? I've been worried about him all day, you jerk."

"Don't worry, Payton. He isn't going anywhere." Brad stood there smiling at me.

"What is that supposed to mean?" I gave Brad a shove. "Tell me where he is right now," I demanded.

"Geez, take it easy. I should book you for police brutality, but since you are already having a shitty day, I will give you a pass. Dylan is down at the police station. I booked him this morning."

"What did you arrest him for? Did you make up some bogus trumped up charges?"

"Go see for yourself. I hope you two will be very happy together." Brad stood before me with an extra large smirk on his face.

"You are such an ass, Brad." Because of him, my blood was close to reaching 212 degrees Fahrenheit.

"But you still love me anyway."

I wrinkled up my nose in disgust and sneered at him. "In your dreams," I answered back before I abruptly turned my back to Brad and walked away.

Tim was still sitting in his squad car at the edge of the parking lot. I got in and slammed the car door. "Brad just told me that Dylan is down at the station."

Tim looked up from his paperwork. "That's great. I knew he would turn up."

"No, it's not great. Brad arrested Dylan this morning. Do you know why he arrested him? He won't tell me."

Tim could tell I was upset. He put his hand on my shoulder. "No. I do not. I haven't been back to the station since early this morning."

I leaned over, putting my hands over my face.

"Everything will be ok, Payton. I am sure that Dylan is fine. Wait, did you say Brad arrested Dylan?"

I looked up at Tim. "Why does that matter?"

"Brad wasn't on duty this morning. Why would he arrest Dylan?"

132

"Brad would do it just so he could rub it in my face."

"That's not right. He shouldn't abuse his power like that."

"Well, I guess that is what ex fiancées are for."

Tim sat quiet for a moment. "Oh, that explains all of the hostility between you two. If there is anything I can do for you, just ask me."

I debated if I should take him up on his offer so soon. What did I have to lose? He was offering, so I jumped on it. "Actually, I have a tiny police related favor to ask."

"Sure, what is it?"

"Can you run an off the record toxicology screen on Streak's hair for me?"

Tim narrowed his eyes at me. "Why? What's up?"

"This is just a hunch. A couple of Streak's friends and I were wondering if Streak's odd behavior last night could be drug related."

"Which drugs in particular are you looking for? Was Dominic a drug addict?"

"No, I am not talking about narcotics. We are wondering if somebody could have drugged him. Could you test for GHB, Rohypnol, and Rocuronium?"

"Whoa, those are some pretty hardcore drugs that are not easy to come by."

"Can you do it, or not?" I asked Tim, giving him an ultimatum.

"Yeah, I can pull some strings and secretly have it done. You would be surprised at what you can accomplish if you have the right paperwork."

"Thank you, Tim. I really appreciate you helping us figure out what happened to Streak, even though everyone else thinks it was just an accident."

"Too bad you didn't ask me earlier before they embalmed him. We could have gotten blood, urine, and stomach contents to test."

"I don't know about his blood or urine, but his stomach contents tasted like chicken and had a faint herbal flavor that I can't quite put my finger on. Does that help?"

Tim narrowed his eyes at me and shifted his jaw.

"I gave him CPR, remember?"

Tim nodded his head, realizing how I had obtained my knowledge. I was about to hop out of Tim's squad car when Tim grabbed my forearm. "You really should be careful. It is a known fact that criminals usually return to the scene of the crime to bask in the glory of what they have done. They often attend wakes, funerals, and even candle light vigils, so keep your eyes open. The person could even integrate themselves into your life."

"Wow, good to know. I will be careful." I made a mental note of everyone I had seen in the last two days, logging it into my memory for future reference. I opened the car door and slid out. I had many possibilities to ponder. I went back inside the restaurant to shut off the lights and lock the door. I was not looking forward to my next stop in Thomas Town, AKA the River Bend Police Station. Wish me luck.

. . .

Everything in your life happens for a reason, Payton. I am that reason. There are no accidents in your life. All it took to start that fire was a few strategically placed drops of lighter fluid. It was child's play. I control you and everyone around you by my actions. You are nothing but a puppet on a string. I enjoy watching you dance for me.

CHAPTER SEVENTEEN

By the time I reached the Police Station, they could have thrown the book at me. I should have gotten a ticket for speeding, following too close, failure to yield at a stop sign, and my personal favorite, driving under the influence. FYI, I grabbed a Miller Lite roadie before I locked up the restaurant.

My beer can was empty when I pulled up in front of the station, but my adrenaline was overflowing. I parked my Escape in the nearest space I could find and ran inside the front door of the one-story brick Police Station. My luck continued to go right in the crapper. I ran right into the Chief in the hallway scattering his file all over the tile floor.

"Payton, you're just begging to get locked up."

"No doubt." I quickly bent over to help him pick up the file. "I am here on official police business."

"Don't tell me. Let me guess. You are here to confess to a crime?"

"No," I snapped. "I am here to bail my boyfriend out of jail."

He rolled his eyes at me while he continued to shove papers into the file folder. I could tell he was getting even more annoyed at me, but my mouth kept flapping anyway.

"Well, he's not really my boyfriend. He's my new chef."

The vein in the Chief's forehead was expanding with each spoken word. "Payton, I don't really give a rat's ass. You are wasting my time."

I handed him the final piece of paper from the floor. As the page left my hand, I recognized the person in the mug shot. It was a much younger version of Rod Huntley. "Hey, what are you doing with Rod's file? Are you going to arrest him?"

His eyes blazed a look at me as we both rose to our feet. I instantly knew that I had overstepped my need to know basis. That had never stopped me before, so I pressed on. "What if I told you some juicy tidbits about your buddy Rod?"

"What could you possibly tell me about that slimeball that I don't already know?"

"After you left this afternoon, he pulled a gun on me and threatened me."

"Payton, I'm about to pull a gun on you and threaten you for being a pain in my ass."

My jaw dropped on that one. "Hey, that was totally uncalled for, you know?" I continued to plead my case as the Chief stared at me in disbelief at my tenacity. He was shocked that I wasn't backing down. "Rod also said, 'my friends and I better stay out of his business, or we will end up in the river like the dead kid.'"

The Chief pulled me into the closest room and closed the door. "Are you suggesting that Rod had something to do with that boy's death?"

"Rod and Kurt were at my parents' bar last night. The dead kid stole a buffalo chicken cheese ball from Rod's plate. Then he ate it right in front of them."

"I'll make sure Rod gets the electric chair." His comment oozed sarcasm. "You think he killed him for eating food from his plate?"

I shrugged. "I am sure the mob has killed for less."

The Chief was still skeptical. He crossed his arms in front of his chest. "Is that all you've got?"

"No, that's not all. A few days ago, Rod and Kurt beat up

the dead kid's dad. They put him in the hospital."

"So? Nobody's pressed charges. It is not police business." The Chief had heard enough. He walked to the door and opened it.

This was obviously my cue to leave. As you've probably guessed, I don't follow directions all that well. "The dead kid told his friends, 'he was going to get even with Rod and Kurt.' Maybe the dead kid was snooping around on Rod's property. Maybe Rod caught him." I gave the Chief an exasperated look of desperation. "The dead kid's car was found on the bridge by Rod's house."

The Chief stood in the doorway with his hands on his hips. His forehead vein was turning purple. He was definitely frustrated with me. "Why are you so dead set on pinning his death on Rod?"

The question caught me off guard. Did I really think that Rod did it or was it just self-preservation? I was speechless. He had me doubting my own motives.

"The way I see it, Payton, the dead kid's car was found on the bridge by your house, too," said the Chief. "The last report I read stated, 'you were the last person to be seen with the boy.'"

"So?" I asked.

"So—stay out of police business or there will be trouble for you."

"But I never got a chance to tell you about the mysterious Bald-headed Man I saw or the weird symbols I found."

The Chief approached me. He was so far inside my personal space bubble that he made me extremely uncomfortable. "Walk away, Payton, and keep your damn mouth shut. The wolves and the freezing river killed that boy."

"You don't think there is a serial murderer in the North-woods preying on young men?"

"The only serial murderer around here is alcohol mixed with stupidity."

Why was the Chief being so stubborn? Why wouldn't the Chief believe me? What was he hiding, or better yet, who was he protecting? These were all fabulous questions for another time. Should I remind him that this morning I saw Rod down at the river just before I found the dead kid's body? Should I tell him his alcohol theory was dead wrong? Streak doesn't even drink. It was probably not a good time to tell him anything but good-bye.

The Chief was so far up in my grill, I could count the wrinkles on his face and the blackheads on his nose. It was definitely time to take his advice and walk away. I had seen and asked enough for now. I slowly backed away from him until his face was no longer in high definition. Then I turned and made a speedy retreat down the hallway.

When I found Tim, he was at his desk diligently working on his report. He looked up from his paperwork when he noticed me standing in front of him. "Payton, you're so pale. You look like you've just seen a ghost."

I plopped down in the chair in front of his desk. "Not a ghost, just the Chief. We just had an intense run in." I did a few deep breathing exercises to relieve my stress.

Tim nodded. He knew how the Chief could be. "Is there something I can do for you?"

"Actually, I was wondering if you heard any information on Dylan? Do you know why he was arrested?"

"Yes, I do. I talked to Brad a few minutes ago."

"Why is Dylan here? Does he have too many unpaid parking tickets?" I nervously began playing with the three paperweights on his desk.

"I'm afraid it is more serious than that, Payton. Brad arrested him this morning for breaking and entering and grand theft auto."

"What?" I said, completely bewildered. "There has to be a mistake or a misunderstanding. He's too hot to be crooked."

"Look, Payton, you can't always judge a book by its cover."

I gave Tim a strange look. "What are you, like eighty? You sound like my grandpa."

"I'm just saying to be careful. You can't always tell what is going on in someone's head. Especially someone you just met."

"I know. I'm sorry. You are right. I just need to go talk to

Dylan right now and clear this mess up. I will feel better once I hear it all from him. How do I find him?"

"Go down the hall to the right and then take a left at the pop machine. You will see a counter down the hall on your right."

I stood up from my chair. "Thanks," I said. I started to walk away.

"Payton, I almost forgot. I followed up on your missing news anchor. I talked to Crystal's news station this afternoon."

I instantly came back and took a seat. "You did? What did they say?"

"They told me that she called in this morning. She is taking a leave of absence to work on an important story."

"That is odd. I wonder why she didn't call me about it."

"Maybe she is going undercover and cannot be reached. News anchors and journalists do that just like police officers."

"I am glad to hear that she is ok. Maybe she hasn't had time to call me back because she is shopping for another periwinkle pump." I said, trying to make light of the situation. I was obviously relieved that she was ok.

"Are you sure that shoe I found is hers?"

"No, I am not one hundred percent sure. Who else would wear an expensive pair of periwinkle pumps in a blizzard?"

"True. But maybe the shoe was planted to throw us off track, and by us, I mean the police."

"Wow, Tim. I never thought of that. You are good." I was impressed with his reasoning skills. Tim had great instincts for a deputy.

"That is why I think I would make a great detective. You have to be able to think of all the angles," said Tim.

I could tell that Tim was mighty proud of himself. "Being a detective would be ok. I would rather work for the FBI. That would be my dream job. So here is an interesting angle to consider, Tim. What if you planted the shoe to throw me off track?"

"Good point," said Tim. "Payton, maybe you planted the shoe to throw me off track."

"Good point," I agreed. "Or better yet, maybe Rod Huntley planted the shoe to throw us both off his scent."

"Rod Huntley? Isn't he the owner of the Last Chance Saloon?"

"Yep, and his name keeps popping up in my investigation. Unfortunately, he is also my neighbor across the river. I am not proud of the fact that Rod and the Chief actually caught me snooping around on Rod's property this afternoon."

"Payton, I thought I told you to stay out of trouble and no more beer today."

I gave Tim a weird look, and he gave me a mint. He was a better detective than I thought. "Well, I attempted to stay out of trouble. I have concluded that it is impossible for me. Therefore, it is ridiculous for me to try."

Tim took a moment of silence trying to decipher my logic.

I filled Tim in on my run in with Rod and my recent run in with the Chief. "Do you have any ideas who the Chief would be trying to protect with his wolf theory?"

"I have a few theories on that. The first, he is saving his own ass for not investigating. The second, he is protecting the whole department from scandal. The third, he is protecting someone he knows."

"Who do you think that is? The Chief knows a lot of people."

"Yes, he does. So watch who you share this theory with." Tim started to squirm. He looked uncomfortable in his chair.

"I almost forgot a juicy part of my story about Rod. I saw him this morning down by the river before we found Streak. He was looking at something in the water. Then he poked at it with a stick. Maybe it was Streak's body. Maybe he put the body in the water and pushed it to my side of the river, so I would find it."

Tim restlessly worked on his report in silence.

"Any ideas on why the Chief would be looking at Rod's file? Is there something wrong? You don't look so good, Tim."

A dark shadowy cloud by the name of Richard J. Thomas had moved in behind me. He was about to rain on our tea party.

I needed to do something fast to take the heat off Tim.

I stood up and pretended not to notice the Chief directly behind me. "Thank you for helping me relocate the wolves. I wouldn't want anyone else to get hurt by them. Then I reached in my purse, pulling out the silver cross necklace. "I found this. I believe it belonged to Streak. Can you see that his family gets this back for his burial?"

Tim looked at me with great gratitude for saving his butt and his job. "Yes, I will drop it off at the funeral home." He gave me a wink.

By the wink, I knew he meant that he would take care of my toxicology screening favor for me. When he took the necklace to the funeral home, he would obtain the samples that he needed.

When I turned around, the Chief was giving me the look. "Hi, Chief. The Bond Office is down the hall to the right, isn't it?" I didn't expect an answer, and I didn't get one. I left before Tim or the Chief could ask me any questions about where I had found the necklace. I was already going to hell for lying today. There was no sense of actually setting myself a blaze.

. . .

Liar, liar, pants on fire. Who will be the next victim I desire? If you believe everything you hear and see, you will never catch me.

CHAPTER EIGHTEEN

While I was at the counter waiting to see Dylan and pay his bail, Brad was kind enough to stop by and grace me with his never-ending charm. He greeted me with a "How's it goin'?" followed by a slap on the ass. "Somebody's been working out," he said with a gleam in his eye.

"Nice try. And by the way, I'm not talking to you. You have crossed the line this time."

"Here to bail out your boyfriend?"

I gave him my best 'Really?' stare. "Brad, you know I don't have a boyfriend any more than you have a girlfriend."

"What do you mean? I have a girlfriend."

"Yeah, right. After the way you've pawed at me lately, I seriously doubt it."

"Actually, she's not really my girlfriend anymore. She is more like my fiancée."

I decided to play along. "Sure, Brad. Anyone I know?" I was remotely curious.

"You will find out soon enough." He smiled. "It was time for me to move on."

"You are so full of shit, Brad, and you know it." He was lying, right? I was the only woman stupid enough to want to be

Mrs. Bradley Thomas. That was a definite no-brainer.

Brad backed away from me smiling. He actually looked happy. He did a little shuffle dance down the hall before he rounded the corner. It almost looked like a victory dance. What was he up to?

Rex, one of the Chief's loyal minions, appeared from behind mystery door number two. He summoned me over to his spot at the counter with a wave of his hand. Rex explained the paperwork and showed me how many zeros it was going to take. Wow. It was almost painful.

Next, Rex escorted me back to see Dylan before I signed the paperwork. That was ok by me. I needed to hear his side of the story before I signed on the dotted line and forked over the cash.

"You've got five minutes, Payton," said Rex.

"Ok, thanks." He left me alone outside Dylan's cell. The jailhouse was ridiculously sterile with no warmth or personality whatsoever. Just lots of gray cement and iron bars. It reminded me a lot of the fifth floor. You would have to be crazy to want to stay here too.

When I first caught his attention, Dylan was sitting on his cot in his orange jumpsuit. He gave me a half smile and walked over to the bars. Was it wrong for me to think he was even hotter now that he was a bad boy? The answer is yes. I seriously need help.

"Payton, what are you doing here?" He had a sad look on his face. "I'm embarrassed to have you see me like this."

I gave him an empathic look. I totally understood. He had seen me at my worst in the Emergency Room. "I am here to bail you out."

"Why would you do that for me? We hardly know each other."

"Because . . . I need you to help me with the restaurant."

He smiled. "Vivian told me about the fire."

That's just great. Now he knows I'm lying. I could feel my face getting hot. "So you talked to Vivian?"

"Yeah, she was my one phone call. Vivian won't bail me

out. I guess she's trying to teach me a lesson. Great, huh?"

"That's crappy."

He shrugged. "That's Vivian."

I decided to come clean with Dylan. He needed to know that he could trust me. Rex would be back soon, and I didn't have any answers yet. "Look, Dylan, I am not here to judge you for what you've done. I am here to bail you out if you can answer some questions and tell me the truth about last night."

"Ok. Where do you want me to start?"

"How about you start from when I left the kitchen."

"All right. I was busy cleaning up the kitchen when I realized something of mine was missing. Remember that girl that came to see me last night?"

"Yeah," I said with a sigh and a daggered heart.

"It was right after Stephani left the kitchen that I noticed my recipe book was missing. I figured she must have taken it. I hustled to finish the dishes and left to go after her."

"Did you see me when you left?" I asked, holding my breath.

"Yes. You were passed out on the bench by the front door. You were snoring and drooling in your sleep."

"Now I'm embarrassed. One minute I was feeling fine. The next minute, I needed to lie down. Can you help me and tell me everything you remember about last night?"

"You seriously can't remember?"

"I'm trying to piece it all together. I shouldn't have been drinking on an empty stomach."

"When I saw you in the kitchen you seemed ok, maybe a little buzzed. A few minutes later, you were on the bench passed out. Sounds more like you were drugged."

"Wow, I never thought of that. That totally makes sense."

"Who would want to drug you?"

I thought of a short list of possible Payton haters, cross-referencing them with the people who were at the restaurant last night. One name stood out to me—Rod Huntley. I kept this information to myself. I didn't want to scare Dylan off with my possible hit list. It comes with the territory of being a smart-ass.

Eventually, you are going to rub the wrong person the wrong way. If you're lucky, that person won't try to rub you out.

"I wish I knew." Was the best answer I could come up with without lying my ass off to my future husband. "Do you remember seeing anyone hanging around last night when you left?"

"When I went out to my truck, I saw a few of the kids from upstairs. They were leaving too. I really wasn't paying much attention to them. I got in my truck and went after Stephani and my book."

"Why is that book so important to you?"

"The book belongs to my great, great grandmother. It contains old family recipes handed down through many generations. I have added my own recipes to it while I've studied and traveled the world. It means a lot to me. I can't lose it. It belongs in my family."

"Why would she take it?"

"She is mad at me. She took it to piss me off."

I stared at him through the bars. I wondered if she was mad at him because of me. "Did you get it away from her?"

"You bet I did. I went to Stephani's place last night. Her car was parked outside, so I waited for her to go to bed. As soon as I saw her turn off the lights, I snuck in the back door. It should have been an easy in and out. She had left the book on the kitchen table. I was about to grab it and leave when she caught me red-handed. We struggled. I ended up with the book. She ended up with my keys."

"Stephani ran into the bathroom. She locked the door before I could stop her. I pleaded with her to give me back my damn keys. All I wanted was my book and to leave, nothing more. Instead, she tried to play a stupid game of keep-away with me. I was in no mood for her crap. When I turned away from the bathroom door, I spotted her car keys in the living room on the end table. I grabbed them and left. I just wanted to get away from her. I never thought she would report her car stolen and have me arrested. I guess she got even with me."

"Yeah, she did. I talked to her this morning. She was pissed."

Dylan stared at me through the metal bars. "Stephani called you?"

"She actually was calling you, but I answered your phone."

"Ok, I am still confused. How did you get my phone?"

"This might sound strange. I found your phone under my bed this morning."

Dylan's eyes widened. "How did it get there? I figured it dropped out of my pocket at Stephani's."

"Beats me. I'm just glad I didn't find you under my bed this morning."

"What?" Dylan was baffled and a few shades paler. He narrowed his eyes and furrowed his brow at my comment.

"Never mind," I said, trying to lighten the creepy mood I created. "Sorry, that sounded funnier in my head. By the way, your grandma seems nice. A lovely woman, salt of the earth."

He stared at me again with a puzzled look. "You spoke to my grandmother?"

I put on my best apologetic face. "Yes. I was looking for you. I was worried. Sorry?"

His face went back to normal.

It was time to stop freaking him out. "You look hungry. How about we get the heck out of here? We could go find food somewhere. That is . . . if you want to?" I reached in my purse and handed him his phone. "I hope you don't mind. I put my contact info in your phone. You know, just in case you ever need to call me about work or something."

Dylan smiled.

Bingo. Houston, we have lift off. I blushed and smiled back. Our bonding process was definitely improving. Rex marched back in, spoiling the moment. I went to go sign the papers. I ponied up the dough for Dylan's release. Dylan met me out front of the station after he changed back into his street clothes and collected his belongings. This had to be the most expensive first date ever. I'd better at least get to first base for the load of cash I just dished out.

We jumped into my Escape. "Where to?" I asked as I buckled up for safety.

"How about I cook you dinner? I can at least do that for you."

"Sure, but the restaurant is closed. The Fire Chief has it on lockdown until the repairs are finished, and the inspector gives his seal of approval."

"We could go to your house?" He suggested, with a raised eyebrow.

"Cool, but I'm not sure what's in my fridge." I did a quick mental inventory. "I hope you are good with leftovers. I think I have tortillas, ham, beer, and chocolate pudding."

"Don't worry. I prefer a challenge."

"Good. Because with me, that is exactly what you are getting."

He laughed.

I was serious.

"You know, I'm probably going to raid your pantry," he said with a mischievous grin. "I'm going to need eggs, cinnamon, butter, and of course, whipping cream. I thought I would make you a nice quiche and a chocolate mousse Napoleon for dessert."

I hoped he hadn't notice that I was swerving all over the road. The thought of Dylan and whipping cream was too much for me to handle. I wasn't sure if he was serious or trying to flirt with me. I flirted back anyway. "Sounds like fun. No one has raided my pantry in months."

"I will even let you drink a beer while you watch me cook."

Oops, I just went over the centerline.

We were still in town when my phone rang. It was the hospital. They still had my clothes I left on the fifth floor. "Do you mind if we stop by the hospital first? I need to pick up something."

"Sure, but make it quick. I'm hungry," he said with a wink.

I had just finished running a red light when I realized I hadn't asked Dylan about Brad arresting him. If I asked him, would it spoil the mood? Maybe my erratic driving had done that already. I had a couple blocks to work out everything. I smiled back. "Sorry to change the subject, but I have a quick question. Then we can talk about food all night if you want."

"Sure, you can ask me anything."

"I have been trying to figure out something that has been bothering me. I wanted to hear it from you first. Was it Brad that arrested you?"

"Yeah, he found me at the restaurant this morning. It must have been right after Stephani called the police station."

"I thought so. When I got to The Shack around three o'clock, I could tell that you had been there. The lot was only half plowed, and the lights were still on in the kitchen. I found a chair knocked over by your unfinished menu plan on the desk. At first, I thought that someone might have kidnapped you, or possibly worse."

Dylan sat silent for a long time. "I don't want to talk about Brad or Stephani anymore."

"Sorry. You are right. Let's not talk about them." I could tell he was thinking about what I had said. Maybe I should have waited to ask him until after dinner. I pulled up in front of the hospital. "I'll be right back." I parked my Escape close to the front door and hit the ground running. Dylan sat anxiously in the passenger seat while I dashed inside.

The middle-aged receptionist at the front desk was enthusiastically friendly. She immediately pointed me in the direction of the fifth floor. I just assumed I was going to the laundry department to pick up my clothes. This trip to the fifth floor better be short and sweet. I had a big night planned for Dylan and me.

The elevator was empty. I stepped inside and pushed the button. The elevator door opened on the fifth floor. I cautiously stepped out, finding myself very much alone. Apparently, you can check in anytime you like, but you can never leave.

The Nurses Station was completely deserted. All of the nurses must be with the patients. I checked the time and made a mental note: six-thirty pm. was an excellent time to sneak in or out of the fifth floor. I was behaving myself, patiently waiting by the main desk, when I spotted Miss Gilbert's chart.

I set my new Prada purse down on the counter. I walked

around the desk to take a closer look. Why? Morbid curiosity, I guess. Who is she? Why is she crazy? Why does she think we are besties? These were all very good questions, and I wanted some damn answers.

I flipped her chart open to the patient information page. Her full name was Rose Mary Gilbert. Rose, that figures. She beat me in the face with a dozen of her thorny beauties. Her maiden name was Gilbert. There was no mention of another last name. I guess she was never married. Her date of birth was April 1, 1847. I guess the jokes on me. April Fools. Wait a minute . . . 1847. That would make her . . . I paused to do mental math. She was like . . . one hundred and seventy years old. That had to be a mistake.

There was a noise behind me. I jumped, dropping her chart on the desk. When I turned around, I found Rhyming Rose rummaging through my purse. "Hey, give me back my purse," I shouted.

"Mine," she said. Rose continued to rummage through it. I ran around the counter. With both hands, I grabbed one of the straps. My phone rang. I tugged harder on the leather strap. "Let go," I protested. "I need to answer my phone."

She defiantly tugged back as she dug around in my purse. Rose completely ignored my pleas.

It was time to get tough with her. "Rose Mary Gilbert, give me back my purse this instant," I demanded.

The old woman finally made eye contact with me. She let go of my purse and said, "The light will reveal the darkness. Use your reflection to discover the truth."

"What are you talking about, Rose?"

"What is going on here?" ordered Dr. Parks.

When I looked up, I saw my doctor standing at the Nurses Station by Rose's open chart.

"Rose, I mean Miss Gilbert, had my purse. She wouldn't give it back to me." I looked in Rose's direction. She had vanished, leaving me holding the bag.

"Payton, how did you get up here? It is not visiting hours." She looked down at Rose's open chart and closed it.

Dang it! I was busted. "I came up the elevator," I said nervously, hoping my visit to the fifth floor was still only temporary.

"The elevator should be locked at six o'clock for security reasons. Someone could escape."

"Sorry. The receptionist at the front desk sent me up here to pick up my clothes." It was time to turn on the charm or pick out a room. "Hey, cool shoes. Are those Via Spiga?" I asked, admiring her very expensive pink pumps. "They match your outfit perfectly."

Dr. Parks' demeanor seemed to change to a lighter tone. "No. They are Badgley Mischka."

"Size seven?"

"No, I'm a six." She said proudly.

"They look fabulously expensive. My mom would love a pair for her birthday. Where on earth did you find them?"

"Bloomingdale's. Last week I had to run to a psychiatric consultation. Afterwards, I did a little shopping."

"Was it the Bloomingdale's store downtown or the one by the airport in the mall?"

"This style is sold exclusively at the mall, never downtown, and certainly not online. Their limited edition status ensures their demand stays high. Last week I was extremely fortunate to have come across a rare red pair as well."

"I bet they look amazing in red," I said. "Too bad I was just by the mall last week when I took my parents to the airport. I don't know when I will get a chance to make it back over there before they're sold out."

"Payton, I actually have to go back to the area in a few days for another consultation. I will have to drive right by the mall. Would you like me to pick her up a pair?"

"That would be great, Dr. Parks. I think she would like a red pair. If not, whatever colors you can find in a size nine."

"Oh my, your mother has large feet."

"I guess. I never thought about it before since I wear an eight and a half."

"Sorry, Payton. I didn't mean to offend you or your mother."

"Don't worry about it. My foot size is the least of my problems. But seriously, whatever color you can find is ok with me."

"This style only comes in red and pink. I will see what they have in stock. Actually, the larger size might be easier to find."

"Great. Thanks, Dr. Parks. I really appreciate you doing this for my mother."

She smiled. "I will locate one of the nurses to help you find your clothes." She picked up Rose's chart and exited the Nurses Station.

I blew out a huge sigh. That was close. You'd think I would learn not to be such a nosy bitch, but I actually learned some interesting information.

After about ten minutes of complete impatience on my part, I had my belongings. I anxiously headed back downstairs to Dylan in the parking lot.

On my way down to the lobby, I checked my phone to see whose call I had missed. Yikes. It was my mother again. It was no doubt a call about the fire. That didn't take long for Bob to rat me out. I turned off my ringtone. I will be a good daughter and call her back next week. Or whenever they remove the crystallized Mountain Dew. After the restaurant was open again, I could have a nice civilized conversation with her.

In the parking lot, I saw Dylan climb out of my Escape. He was walking over to a beat up black Camaro. "Dylan, wait," I yelled across the parking lot. I ran over to him. When he looked at me, I saw the depressed look on his face. "What's up? Why are you leaving?"

"This is so embarrassing," he said. "Vivian called me when you were in the hospital. She told me about the dead kid you found today."

"Yeah . . . And?"

"She won't let me hang out with you." He looked at me with sad eyes.

"Do you guys really think I—?"

"No. I don't," he said abruptly. "That's not it. Vivian told me that I'm grounded. And she doesn't want me sucked into your wake of destruction right now. Those were her words, not mine."

"That is crazy. Is she going to let you come back to the restaurant after it reopens?"

"I don't know, Payton. I'm so sorry." He looked down at the ground. "I am so sorry about everything. I really . . . need to go."

I thought for sure he was going to say something else. He climbed into the black Camaro. The unknown driver maneuvered the car out of the parking lot.

I stood in the lot and let out a scream to release my anger. I'm sure there were witnesses. I didn't care. My anger consumed me. Then I stomped back to my car and slammed the door shut. I screamed again, beating the steering wheel with my fists. "This frickin' sucks." I was so close. Now I know how a guy feels after he springs for dinner and a movie and doesn't get any. I need a shower, a cold shower.

. . .

Do you miss me, Payton? I bet you do. Maybe it is time for another visit. To feel your heart race, your short panic breaths, the fear of impending doom. What a wild ride. Giddy-up!

Riddle: Just out of curiosity, do you think I want Payton for her mind or her body? That is a good one. Answer: I will never tell. That is up to you to figure out. She has something of mine. That is all I will say for now.

CHAPTER NINETEEN

The icy water from my shower ran over my head while the ice-cold beer ran down my throat. I no longer had impure thoughts of Dylan's hot, naked, chiseled, god like— Crap! So I stood under the frigid water until I had a terminal case of brain freeze where I could no longer remember my name, let alone his. I chased away any other lingering thoughts of him with the last chug of my beer.

I shut off the water and wrapped myself in a towel. I slid the shower door open, stepping out onto the rug. This just got disturbing. I was not alone. Sitting on the lid of the toilet was my oldest friend Julie.

"Hi," randomly flowed from my mouth in a nervous, squeaky, high-pitched tone.

"I need to talk to you, Payton," sprang out of her mouth.

"It must be urgent, otherwise you probably would have just texted me, right?" I asked, trying to lighten the creepy mood in the room.

Julie stood up abruptly. "Why do you always have to do that? You always have to be so funny, cute, and likeable."

That is when I saw the reflective flash of her left hand. I was stunned. "No way," I said. "Is that my diamond ring on your finger? Why are you wearing my old engagement ring?"

Julie was silent. My brain was still frozen. I couldn't comprehend what was going on. Out of the corner of my eye, I saw movement by my walk-in-closet. I turned and spotted Brad emerging from the shadows. The Titanic just struck my brain, knocking a big chunk of the iceberg loose. All the pieces from earlier today fell into place. "Sonovabitch!"

Maybe it was my lack of sleep or sex. Maybe it was all that cold water making me cranky. Maybe I shouldn't give a tiny rat's ass, but I did. I lunged at Julie and tried to take my ring back. Before doing so, I clearly should have thought through my clothing predicament. For the most part, I was winning the fight until I almost lost my towel. Brad finally jumped in. He pulled us apart and off the floor. I caught my towel and secured it before we were all scarred for life.

If I wasn't embarrassed enough over my actions, I heard applause coming from the doorway. It was my younger brother Luke and his girlfriend Lily Boman. I looked at Brad and Julie. "You two are free to go." I pointed the way out of my bathroom and my life.

After Julie and Brad left the room, Luke started with "What the—?"

"Apparently, those two are getting married. I don't want to talk about it."

"Why do you even care?" asked Lily. "I thought you were over Brad."

"The sonovabitch gave her my ring. My ring! I'm still not talking about it." I slammed the bathroom door in their faces. I took a deep breath, and then I slammed the toilet lid five times. "There I feel better," I yelled through the door.

"Good to know," Luke yelled back. "Don't come out until you are a sane person."

"There is no guarantee of that ever happening. I might need a few moments alone with my thoughts."

"Ok," said Lily. "We will wait."

I took a seat on the toilet lid. On the bright side, I was no longer concentrating my every thought on Dylan, who was plan A.

THE ULTIMATE SACRIFICE

Now Brad, who was my plan B, was off the table. This also meant so was my friendship with Julie. I needed a plan C. Maybe I should join the convent. I could find God. Who was I kidding? When I found him, he would just tell me that he wanted nothing to do with me. Even I know that I'm a piece of work.

"Payton, you are awfully quiet. Is everything ok in there?" asked Lily.

"I'm still thinking."

"Ok," said Luke. "We are still waiting."

I was actually surprised to see Luke. He hates coming back home to River Bend. He would rather fade into the background on the University of Clearwater Falls campus, than shine in the limelight as one of River Bend's elite. Something important must have dragged him back here.

As far as Lily goes, there is no blending or fading into any normal background anywhere. She is a Goth chick to epic proportions. She wears all black, all of the time. She has even dyed her hair black. I know this because every four to six weeks she tries to hide her blondish roots under a hat. Lily also has piercings, lots of piercings. Rumor has it that some are visible and some are not. Trust me. I would rather not know this, but the frat boys talk too much when they're intoxicated.

Lily accessorizes her style with black leather collars, extra black eyeliner, rosaries, and black fishnet stockings. If it is black and borderline creepy, she wears it. At least everything she owns goes together. Unfortunately, Lily's idea of a little black dress has skulls and cross bones on it. Her black army boots and black, eight-legged, fuzzy, spider purse pushes her fashion statement over the top. Over the top of what, I have no idea.

Don't get me wrong. I actually like her. She has a cool personality and is not as dark as you might think. She is always fun to play beer pong with. To sum her up, Lily is like a piece of Gothic candy. She has this hard, black, candy-coated shell filled with sweet caramel and lots of nougat. But be very careful. That nougat can on occasion turn sour without warning. I have personally seen it happen.

I am going to let you in on a little secret of mine. I think my

155

brother dates her just to piss off my mother. When my mom bought the winning lottery ticket, she wrecked his quiet, sublime existence. Furthermore, Lily doesn't exactly fit The Richardson's new high-society profile, but then, neither do I. I am like the rebellious black sheep boil on the back of humanity that everyone loves to talk about.

Well, I am finished feeling sorry for myself. It is time to forge ahead, falling flat on my face in a puddle of my very own liquor-induced vomit. Besides, I am cold and bored in here. If I stay in here any longer, I might attempt to make origami animals out of the toilet paper. That would not paint a good picture of mental health. My family doesn't need to find me half-naked talking to paper animals.

I went into my walk-in-closet and found something fabulous to throw on. It needed to be comfy chic because I was more than likely going to pass out in it later. A pink Liz Claiborne sweater and a pair of American Eagle jeans fit the evening I had in store perfectly. When I was finished with my hair and makeup, I opened the door to find Luke and Lily standing impatiently before me with their arms crossed.

"Ok, what gives? Why are you guys still here?" I asked.

Luke uncrossed his arms and brushed his sandy brown bangs out of his eyes. "Mom sent me, all right? She called me at school and made me promise to come and check on you because you won't answer your damn phone."

"Sorry. My bad. I've been busy," I said in my defense. I was now calm enough to fill Luke and Lily in on my perils of the last few days. They got to hear about Vivian, Brad and the Chief, Dylan, the dead body under the sheet, Rose and the fifth floor, Brad and the sex thing, the Bald Guy, Crystal, Streak, the fire, Rose again, Dylan again, Brad and Julie, which they already knew about, and last but not least, my homicidal, mobster of a neighbor that would love to bust a cap in my ass and turn me into a frozen floatation device. Yes, I told them everything. Well, almost everything. A girl needs a little mystery.

"Jeez, Payton!" said Luke. "How in the hell are you still a sane, sober person?"

"Seriously, I have no idea."

A unanimous decision was made to find me copious amounts of liquor pronto. We were down in the kitchen, on our way out, when the door flew open. It was Amber, Lisa, and Teagan.

"We are back to party," announced Teagan.

"Well then, you have come to the right place," I said, cracking open a beer.

"I don't think we should stay here," said Amber. "Your creepy neighbor is parked down at the end of your driveway."

"Road trip?" asked Lisa.

"My roommate, Levi, turned twenty-one today," said Luke. "Let's go get wasted with him and the rest of my frat bros."

"Sounds like a plan." I looked out the window towards the driveway. There was no sign of Rod or the Bald Guy. I sent Luke and Lily on their way. I told them I would see them at the birthday party at the frat house.

Now that we were alone, I could finally ask my friends something that had been bugging me all afternoon. "Can you guys sit down for a minute? I need to ask you a serious question."

"God, Payton, way to wreck the party mood," Teagan said sourly.

The girls all took a seat at the table. I remained standing. "This will just take a minute. There has been some weird stuff happening lately. I really need an honest answer from all of you."

"Sure, we are sorority sisters. Anything for you, Payton," insisted Amber.

"Ok, great," I said. "Last night when you left Hannigan's, where did you go?"

"Why is that so important?" asked Lisa.

"Just answer the question," I said, raising the tone of my voice.

The three girls looked at each other for a moment and then Amber finally spoke, "We came back here."

"But you didn't get here until around five this morning.

Where were you for nearly four hours?"

My longtime friends stared at each other again in silence.

"Well, should we just tell her?" asked Lisa.

"Please tell me," I begged.

"Lisa was so wasted last night, she drove off the road. We were stuck in a snow bank," said Amber.

"For four hours?" I asked. "How did you get out?"

"This is embarrassing," said Teagan. "If we tell you, do you promise not to tell anyone?"

"Ok, I promise. Now spill it."

"We had to call a tow truck," said Lisa.

"That's it?" I protested.

"Well, there is one other little thing, but Teagan has to tell you," said Amber.

There was more silence and then Teagan blurted, "Fine. I took one for the team. Ok? I totally saved Lisa's ass. The tow truck driver was going to call the cops and have Lisa arrested for DUI."

"Oh my God. What did you do, Teag?"

"I am not proud of this, by the way. The tow truck driver wasn't even cute."

"Ok, I've heard enough. For the good of all mankind, stop talking. Spare me the gory details," I said horrified. This was bad, even for Teagan.

"Now that you know my deep dark secret, can we go party?" asked Teagan, moving towards the door.

"Sure. Everyone grab a roadie," I said.

"Wait a second," said Amber. "Why was it so important that we tell you where we were?"

"Yeah, why do we need an alibi?" asked Lisa.

"It doesn't matter. Let's just go have fun," I said.

"No, now it is your turn to spill, Payton," insisted Amber.

"Ok," I finally agreed. "This afternoon, my creepy neighbor Rod told me that he saw us down by the river last night."

"What? Are you serious?" asked Amber. "We should go over to his house and let him have it."

"Yeah, we should go yell at him," said Teagan.

"No, we definitely are not. He is crazy and he has a gun. After I told him that we saw him down by the river this morning, he showed it to me and threatened me."

"What a jerk. Did you tell the police?" asked Amber.

"Yes, I told the Chief. He doesn't seem to care."

"That's insane. We have to do something," said Amber.

"No, we're going to the party." I pushed Amber towards the door. "I think the best thing for us to do is to get out of town. We will let Rod cool off."

The girls piled into Lisa's SUV. I jumped into my Escape. We headed to Clearwater Falls for a much-needed night of fun. About a mile down the road, I spotted head lights in my rear view mirror. I think someone was following us.

. . .

We are going to play another game because you have what I want. Who has to die this time? The hunt for my perfect prey is on. Ready or not, here I come.

CHAPTER TWENTY

The life, or should I say, death of the party has arrived. Think whatever you want. I am comfortable in my own skin. For me, murder is second nature; an acquired habit deeply imbedded in my soul. It is stuck there like nail biting or riding a bike. I cannot stop myself from doing it or forget how to do it. It just happens, so I go with it.

Lately, killing people has become as automatic as breathing. Before I can exhale, murder has me on another involuntary journey. I jump on and go for a ride to see where it takes me. Tonight, the wheel takes me to fraternity row in Clearwater Falls to search for my perfect prey. I plan to kick it up a notch. Pushing myself to the next level is 'the new black.' The training wheels are coming off tonight. Look at me, Ma, no hands. Shall we get started?

Automatically, I scan the area around the two-story frat house looking for obstacles and ways to complete my plan flawlessly. Empty cars line both sides of the narrow street. This means many possible witnesses and many possible victims. Toying with the idea of a hit-and-run puts a smile on my face. Low visibility and split-second timing would be crucial. I could cream one of the little bastards, but then I would have to buy new tires and have my ride detailed. Dents and DNA could take me down. As tempting as it is, I will have to pass and stay one-step ahead of the prosecution.

Through the glass, I examine the houses across the street with a critical eye. Older, two-story houses crammed so close together they should really be apartment complexes. They are mostly college rentals randomly scattered amongst a few single-family homes. Soon, college kids will wander from house-to-house in the dark, hitting up every party in the three-block radius. I would be lying if I said I was not mentally aroused at the thought. This could be my playground. This could be better than Halloween. As sick and twisted as I am, I will not go completely fratricidal tonight. I promise to be diligent with my choices.

From a secure place on the front porch, I see my first real problem. We have a nosy neighbor across the street; an old lady with nothing better to do. She tends her front curtains like the Gestapo of the neighborhood watch. Great, a nosy bitch being a pain in my ass. I should give her a new hobby, one that includes a cane and a Seeing Eye dog.

As I wait in the shadows, I clear my head and focus on a clever alternative to gouging her eyes out. As judge, jury, and executioner, I hereby request a change of venue. It is time to pull the plug on this party. The frat house is not public enough for me to get to work with the old bitch hovering. I will force everyone to play my game by my rules. Never forget. I am in control.

The old lady finally gives her blinds a break and walks away from the window. I take this as my one chance to make a dash to the back of the frat house before she returns to her post. Well, what have we here? Someone left the back door unlocked. Nice. This is too easy, almost criminal. I find the fuse box in the basement. It is lights out—for all of you. The screams get my heart racing. I cannot breathe. What a rush. I briefly bask in the glory of a job well done and then slowly make my ascent up the stairs.

Just as I predicted, I hear plans to move the party to Water Street. The bar scene. Excellent. I sneak out of the basement and follow the crowd. Through the neighbor's hedge, I spot the old lady getting into her car with a suitcase. Her overnight escape plan to avoid the party noise just made my life easier.

The old lady roars down her driveway in reverse. Seconds later, she slams on the brakes almost taking out two frat boys when her car enters the street. Screeching tires and yelling pedestrians cause a scene. She shakes her fist at the two boys lying in the street. The rebellious old woman honks her horn non-stop until they get up. Both boys flip her off in response to their near-death experience. The alpha of the two boys, pounds on the trunk of her Lincoln Town Car as it passes by. They both yell obscenities. She stops just long enough to glare out her back window. If looks could kill, this one would certainly melt glass or burn through metal.

The corners of my mouth curl up with unmitigated joy. The old lady's hit-and-run attempt just made my night. For now, there is no need for Miss Buckley to have an unfortunate accident. She and I are kindred spirits on the same path. You stay out of my world tonight, Miss Buckley, and I will stay out of yours.

Despite the freezing temperature, most of you decide to walk to the bar. I am guessing, impaired motor skills caused by too many bong hits and keg stands are to blame. I stay far enough back from the pack to observe and pick out the weakest link. Already a few staggering numbskulls are standing out from the crowd. Once again, faking a drunken accidental death will be child's play. I was so looking forward to a challenge.

A group of boys stop to take a leak. One actually tries to write his name in the snow. Dave, you have no originality . . . and now you have piss on your pants. Good luck with that, Dave. You had better dig deep and find your "A" game pal. Chicks like their dicks housebroken.

The pack of boys is on the move again. They slowly wander closer to Water Street. These drunken losers are boring as hell and annoying me with their stupid immature comments about the Zombie Apocalypse, the Kardashians, and chicks with three boobs. I am a big fan of the number three, but this shit makes me want to run out into oncoming traffic. I should just kill them all, take every last one of the little retards out of the gene pool. I could spare all future generations from their idiotic nonsense.

I regain my composer with the thrill of the hunt and the quest for inspiration. It is time to make up a new game to push the chase to a new level. I am going to call the game Your Number is Up. Yeah, I like it. Want to play along? Here are the rules. Match the town number, the location number, the date number, and the name number of one unlucky bastard. Here is a clue for you dumb asses who have no idea what day it is. It is January 29 (1-29). What time is it? It is time for someone to die. Confused? I will throw you a bone. Figure out the chart. Use it wisely. Here is a gift. Hint: Replace the letters with numbers. Add to reach the smallest number.

1	2	3	4	5	6	7	8	9
A	B	C	D	E	F	G	H	I
J	K	L	M	N	O	P	Q	R
S	T	U	V	W	X	Y	Z	

Scratch Paper for Math

Everyone makes it to Water Street alive. There were six flesh-freezing blocks for me to get pumped for my game. I scan the street north and south adding the names of the bars in my head. A group of hot girls enters Smiley's and a group of frat boys enters Stables. Quick quiz brainiac, which group do I follow? Even without the math, there should be no question.

Before I enter the bar, I press my nose to the icy glass and look inside. What do you know? The gang is all here. It must be fate. This time fate is

163

written in the stars, guided by my mother. Did you catch that? If you did, you get one of three apples. And if you caught that, we need to talk.

Back by the dance floor, the music surrounds my head, filling my body with its bass. My heart beats in tune with the music as I carefully make my way through the crowd. I blend in, mixing with the pack in the back of the bar. The chitchat is mundane as I gather my information that I need to complete my game.

The first contestant's name is Bryce. He is a Leo. Bryce enjoys Texas Hold'em, long jogs in the park, large mugs of Leinies, and he is a champion La Crosse player. What can I say? Been there, done that.

Contestant number two's name is Todd. He is a Taurus that is a complete narcissist. When he is not checking out his own reflection in the mirror behind the bar, he digs beer, belching the alphabet, chicks with blond hair, and billiards. Seriously, I would be doing the world a favor.

Next is Caleb. Caleb is a bad boy. He is here with his girlfriend, but prefers to spend his spare time looking at other guys' asses. He wears turtlenecks and drinks chardonnay. Caleb thinks that no one has a clue because he smokes cigars and is cultured. He is most likely a Gemini standing at the closet door.

Last, but not least, is Bob. His friends call him Tap-Out. He is a Virgo that just got dumped by his girlfriend. Boo-Hoo. These are my personal favorites because they are easily transmutable. They also tend to cry in their beer before they guzzle it. Which makes my job that much easier. Bob revels in acting like a macho idiot. Despite his Ivy League IQ, he likes to party until he pukes and picks fights with complete strangers when intoxicated. For that reason, I bought him a beer. My bad.

Who is it going to be? Who is the chosen one?

Ah, it all falls into place. I see you, my chosen prey. You were right in front of me all along. Hello, birthday boy. Sorry, Levi, but there is no greater day than one's own birthday, especially your twenty-first birthday. I hope the correct answer added up for everyone.

I glide in closer, my prey, to make my move, gain your trust, and take your life. Wait. What is he doing here? Interesting? It is time to shift gears. Do not worry. I am not going to sit around until my ass gets numb trying to figure out what to do. I am moving ahead with a modified plan. I will deal with my Payton problem in my own special way.

. . .

"Payton, do you have any gum in your purse?" asked Lily. "My breath is all funky from that last Jagerbomb."

"I think so. Let me look." I fumbled around in my new Prada Bag. By the way, it was an emergency replacement gift from my mother. What can I say? She felt the negative shift in my Prada collection when the other one was put on life-support. My mother replaced my green bag with a fabulous bright red one.

I was in the middle of bobbing for gum in my purse when a huge drunken jock named Bob rammed into me. He caused the contents of my purse and me to hit the sticky, wooden floor. "Thanks a lot," I yelled at the muscle-bound jerk. He ignored me. Bob moved on, plowing people over as he moved through the crowd.

Lily joined me on the floor. She helped me gather up my stuff. "Wow, Payton, nice necklace. Is it a family heirloom? It looks really old."

I looked at Lily with surprise and confusion. "Why do you think that's mine?"

"But I saw it fall out of your purse along with this small mirror and pocket flashlight."

Lily handed me the flashlight and the mirror so I could inspect them.

"Those are definitely not mine." I tried turning on the flashlight. It was broken. I looked at my reflection in the small, cracked mirror. Yikes. My distorted image was horrifying. "I hope I look better to some hot guy at closing time." I handed them back to Lily. "Here, get rid of these. I don't know where they came from."

Lily handed me the necklace so I could take a closer look at it. She was right. It did look old, almost ancient. The two-toned, key-shaped pendant was made of a combination of a dull gray and a shiny metal. The pendant hung majestically on a sturdy silver chain.

"Is that white gold?" asked Lily.

"No, I think it's made of silver and lead. What an odd combination."

"Maybe your mom put it in the purse as a surprise," suggested Lily.

"Maybe? But that's not really her style. She likes to brag about the cool stuff she finds for me." We both sat on the floor staring at its old-world, antique beauty. There was something mysterious and magical about the jeweled piece. We couldn't take our eyes off of it.

The key itself was made of a matte-finished lead that was approximately three inches long. The shaft of the key was smooth with three flat square-shaped teeth at the end. The bow, or head of the key, was round with scalloped edges. The bow also had a fancy, solid silver, diamond-shaped overlay. Each corner of the overlay contained a different colored round gemstone.

At the top corner, closest to the chain was a purple stone. To the right of the purple stone was a golden-yellow stone. In the bottom corner was a light-green stone. Up to the left corner was a dark-green stone. In the center of the overlay, a hand carved blooming rose with a diamond in the middle. Around the rose there were seven vines each with seven leaves.

"It is so beautiful in a creepy sort of way," I said.

"Yeah, I am picking up the creepy vibe too. Do the gem stones look like birthstones to you?"

"Yes, they do. I think you're right." I stopped talking the minute I noticed the four triangular symbols carved into the lead around the silver overlay. They were the same as the ones Crystal had shown me. I flipped the key over. I sucked in air because of what was on the back. In the middle of an ancient form of writing was the same horned stick figure I found in Rod's tree. Even though it didn't have eyes, I felt it staring back at me. There was no question in my mind. It was up to me to expose the connection between the pendent and the trees.

"You look like you've just seen a ghost. What's the matter?" asked Lily.

Before I could answer her, someone behind me unwillingly pulled me to my feet. I shoved the pendant into my purse and turned to face my assailant. "Ugh! Seriously?"

"Isn't it a little early for The Pub Crawl, Payton?"

"You are such an ass, Brad. What are you doing here? Did you follow me?"

"Relax. I am here for your protection."

"I don't need a babysitter, Brad."

"Well, with your track record, I think ya do."

"Look, Brad," I said, carefully pointing out each person in the group. "I'm here with my brother Luke, his girlfriend Lily, Amber, Teagan, and Lisa." Then I waved my arms in circles to include the rest of the gang. "And a whole frat house full of boys. I'll be fine."

"You're not fine. I can tell you're drunk already because you are talking with your hands again."

"So do you understand what I am saying to you now?" I asked Brad, while giving him the finger.

"I am done being nice to you, Payton."

I turned away from Brad, walking towards the dance floor. Someone in the crowd grabbed my arm. I assumed that it was Brad. It had his M. O. written all over it. "Let go of me you jerk," I said in extreme protest. I swung around fully intending to land a punch on Brad's chin. Instead, I found myself staring into his dreamy, green eyes. It wasn't Brad. It was Dylan.

Dylan ducked my flailing punch. He chuckled at me. "Having a bad night?" he asked.

"Not anymore." I answered back. "Things are definitely looking up." I wasn't interested in why he was here. I was just glad that he was.

"Wanna dance?" he asked.

It was a slow song. Things just got interesting. I blurted out "Yes" like a stupid middle schooler.

He smiled.

I turned red.

Dylan took me by the hand. He led me to the dance floor. I was floating on air and margaritas. We put our arms around each other. It felt like we melted into one person. I closed my eyes and got lost in the beat of the music. For once in a really long time my life didn't suck.

I felt a nudge on my arm. My eyes slowly opened. It was Lily dancing with Luke. She gave me the thumbs up. I smiled back at her approval rating.

As we slowly turned in a circle, I scanned the crowd for Brad's angry face. I didn't see him anywhere. He was gone. I was glad. Dylan sensed my tension. He pulled me even closer. Our eyes met. He kissed me. I swear that fireworks went off in my head. Pop! Crackle! Zoom!

The slow set ended, but our kiss did not. There were some obnoxious cheers from the drunken crowd of bystanders. I looked up to see Amber, Lisa, and Teagan leading the cheering squad.

"Do you want to go grab a drink?" Dylan asked me.

I said yes to the drink. To be perfectly honest, right now, I would have said yes to almost anything he would have asked me. We met up with the birthday party at the bar. It was a typical Saturday night. The place was packed with people. Dylan and I walked over to Lily and Luke who were lucky enough to have found two stools up at the bar.

I introduced Dylan to the gang. They all gave him a drunken enthusiastic welcome.

"What do you guys want to drink?" asked Luke.

Dylan looked at me for a suggestion.

"We'll have two margaritas," I said with confidence.

"A tequila girl. I like you more already," he said with a sexy grin.

"Hey, Lily," I said. "Can you put my purse on the bar by yours?" My new Prada bag was overloaded. It was killing my shoulder.

"Sure," she said. Lily took it from me, setting it next to hers on the glossy, shellacked, wooden bar top.

"What about—?" Lily started.

"Where is the birthday boy?" I cut her off the instant I noticed that Levi wasn't with the rests of frat boys. "Is he passed out in the bathroom?"

168

"No," said Logan. "Levi said, 'he needed some air'. He's over by the front door talking to some bald guy."

"Shit." I ran to the front of the bar to find him. He was nowhere in sight. The front door was packed with people. I pushed my way outside. I scanned up and down the street looking for him. There was no sign of either of them.

Dylan met me in the doorway. "What is going on?" he asked.

"It is a long story, but whenever I see this big, Bald Guy, bad shit happens to someone I know."

"You're joking, right?"

"I wish I were. Help me look for them."

"Maybe we should split up," Dylan suggested. "I could look around out here. And you could look around inside the bar."

"Good idea. We will find them faster. Call me if you see either one of them. I mean it, Dylan. Don't be a hero. This guy is dangerous."

"Ok, I promise," he said. Our eyes met and held for a moment. Without saying a word our connection grew deeper.

I turned away from him and ran inside the bar. When I was back inside it hit me. Wow, I am so stupid. I should have kissed him good-bye.

The bar seemed more crammed with drunken hooligans than before. I pushed my way through the crowd looking for Levi, my Bald Friend, or a familiar face. As I pushed people, they pushed back. My space bubble was seriously invaded. I felt someone in the crowd grab my ass. I turned around ready to take on my attacker, half expecting it to be Brad. There was no one there to claim their victory. Gross. I was just anonymously violated.

I looked across the crowd. By the dance floor, I saw a familiar face. She too was searching for someone. It was Stephani disguised in a blond wig. What was she doing here? Our eyes met. She bolted. I tried to follow her through the mob of people. I lost her somewhere in the back of the bar by the bathrooms.

Shit, now what? Do I go into the women's bathroom to see if she is cowering in one of the stalls? The door to the guy's bathroom burst open. My brother Luke and Levi stumbled out. I was relieved to say the least.

"Hey, Payton baby," said Levi. "How about a birthday smooch?"

He and my brother were obviously wasted. Neither one of them could stand without the assistance of the other.

"No, thanks, Levi. I am all smooched out at the moment. I need to ask you about the bald guy you were talking to."

"That's too bad, 'cause I am an excellent kisser." He tried to lean in and plant one on me. He lost his balance, pulling Luke to the floor with him.

"Dude, that's my sister," said Luke, from underneath Levi.

"But she is so hot," replied Levi, which caused my brother to begin pummeling Levi's head with his fist.

I had no choice but to jump in and try to stop the fight before someone called the cops. Once I pulled them apart, I yelled at them impatiently. "Guys, knock it off. I need you to focus."

"Ok, jeez, we were just messing around," said Luke, slowly pulling himself to his feet.

"Levi, the Bald Guy, what did he say to you?"

"Give me a kiss, and I'll tell you."

My temper and desperate need for answers took over. I grabbed Levi by the shirt. With superhuman adrenaline skills, I threw him up against the wall. "Just tell me what he said," I demanded. My intensity had reached an unhealthy level. The adrenaline had pushed my eyeballs to the edge of their sockets. They felt like they were about to pop out of my skull.

"Ok. God, Payton, you don't have to be such a bitch," said Levi. "He just asked me about one of your friends."

"Which one?" I asked, banging Levi's head against the wall.

"Payton, stop PMSing and let Levi go," shouted Luke. "It's his birthday for crissake."

I turned to rage some witty remark at my brother when I realized I had an audience. A small group of bar patrons stopped to watch me go ballistic on Levi. I immediately let go of him. "Sorry," I muttered. "Who was he looking for?" I asked in a much calmer voice.

Levi gave me a bewildered look while smoothing out the wrinkles I had caused in his t-shirt. He had no idea why I was so spastic. "The Bald Guy was looking for your friend Dylan."

. . .

Game on. Bitch!

CHAPTER TWENTY-ONE

Needless to say, I was beyond freaked out. I sent Dylan outside by himself. How stupid was that? The adrenaline in my veins surged out of control. I shoved people out of my way like a lunatic on crack as I made my way towards the front door. My phone fumbled around in my hand. Dylan's number popped up. I tapped the screen. "Come on answer." His phone went straight to voicemail. "Damn it."

I stopped just short of my friends at the bar. Something was wrong. It suddenly became hard to breath. Lily walked up from behind me. She couldn't help but notice. My flailing, spastic attempts to catch my breath were a dead giveaway. The look of extreme anguish showed across my face.

"What is going on, Payton? You look terrified," said Lily.

My brain was trying to send a message to my mouth, but only weird inaudible sounds came out.

"You need to calm down," said Lily. "I think you are having a panic attack. Here drink this." She handed me one of the watered-down margarita.

It could have been my margarita or maybe it was Dylan's. I didn't care. I drank the whole thing and took a deep breath. "The Bald Guy is after Dylan. You gotta help me find him."

"Where did you last see Dylan?"

"I left him outside," I said regretfully.

"I'll check out front. You check out back in the alley," ordered Lily.

"Ok," I agreed. I grabbed my coat and purse. I followed Lily towards the front of the bar.

"Payton, use the smoker's exit in the back by the bathrooms. It will take you directly to the alley out back."

I gave her a funny look. "When did you start smoking?"

"Look at me, Payton. I'm a Goth chick. It was bound to happen. Just don't tell your brother, ok?"

I nodded in agreement. Then I pushed my way through the crowd to the back of the bar. The back door was oddly unmanned. Smokers could come and go as they pleased. Seriously, the honor system. This was an underage drinkers' dream come true. Anyone could easily sneak in and out without detection. I bet that was how Stephani was able to disappear earlier.

The back alley was dark, cold, and abandoned. Yet the smell of smoke still lingered in the air. "Dylan? Dylan? Are you out here?" He didn't answer. I took my phone out of my back pocket, immediately dialing Dylan's number again.

My focus was on my phone, so I wasn't watching where I was walking. By the time I realized there was something hard, round, and slippery under my right boot, it was too late. My foot slid across the icy ground. I came down hard on my back. My head hit the pavement. I was down and out for the count.

When I opened my eyes, I was staring up at the night sky. My backside chilled. My tailbone and ego definitely bruised from being a klutz. I sat up and looked around. I must have tripped on one of the many beer bottles next to me on the ground. There were no obvious eyewitnesses to my blunder. Just me and a tipped over garbage can. Good lord, what is it with me and garbage cans lately?

I grabbed my phone from the pavement and got to my feet. I dialed Dylan again. A phone rang down the alley.

"Dylan," I called out as I ran down the alley towards the ringing phone. The ringing stopped. I froze in my tracks and dialed his number again. The phone started to ring. It had to be Dylan's phone. The ringtone sounded like it was coming from the dumpster. I ran over to it, threw the lid open, and looked inside. All I found were bags of rancid garbage. What a relief.

I dialed his number again, so I could hone in on its location. I knew I was close, and I wasn't about to go dumpster diving unless I had to. The ringing started. I bent down and found the phone under the dumpster. It was definitely Dylan's phone all right, but where the hell was he? How was he separated from his phone again? I had a bad feeling.

When I was almost to my feet, I sensed the presence of someone behind me. My fight-or-flight mechanism in my brain kicked in. I pasted my creeper right in the nose. My fist had already made contact with his face before I realized it was Dylan. I watched him fall backward to the ground in what seemed like slow motion. All I could say was, "Oh my God. I am so sorry."

I sprang to his side as he laid on the cold, hard pavement of the alley. He had a fat lip, along with other bumps and bruises on his face. "What happened to you?"

He stayed on his back, silent for a moment. I think my punch must have dazed him a bit. "You hit me in the face."

"I know. I'm sorry. There's good news. I found your phone again." I tucked his phone into his jacket pocket. "Do you remember what happened to you?"

Dylan sat up. He attempted to get to his feet, but fell backward obviously still woozy. I took hold of his arm, helping him up.

"Someone jumped me from behind. They knocked me out. When I was unconscious, they did this to my face."

"Stephani was here. She left out the back door a short time ago. Maybe it was her?"

"Maybe? I didn't see their face. It could have been anyone." Dylan's knees buckled. I could barely hold him up.

"We need to get you to the hospital. You could have internal injuries."

"No. I'm fine," he winced. "Let's just get out of here. I've had all the fun I can handle."

I agreed. It was time to call it a night. My wake of destruction was still at high tide. I was lucky that I had Dylan safe in my arms. "I'll take you back to the frat house. We will have to walk five or six blocks. Can you make it that far?"

"I borrowed Vivian's car. It's parked around the corner."

"That works for me. Does Vivian know that you borrowed it?"

"Nope. It will be our little secret."

"Is she going to be mad when she finds out?"

"Hell, yeah. I'm supposed to be grounded. Remember? We better make the best of our time together because she is going to be pissed."

"Oh, brother. I don't think I want to see her pissed. She already scares me."

Dylan laughed. Then he reached up feeling the side of his face by his eye. He was obviously in pain. "Do you think you can find me some aspirin for my head, some ice for my face, and a place to lie down? If you can, I will let you drive The Viv Mobile."

"I think that can be arranged," I said with a flirtatious smile. I was holding on to Dylan for dear life as we walked slowly to Viv's blue Honda. It seemed like only yesterday that she tried to run me over with it. Wait. Maybe that was yesterday. Lately, the days have been blurring together.

We came to the end of the alley when my phone rang. It was Lily. Crap. I had forgotten about Lily. I answered it with my one free hand.

"Any sign of Dylan?" she asked.

"Yes. I found him in the alley. Someone jumped him. He is beat up pretty bad."

"That is terrible. Is he ok?"

"I think so. We are on our way back to the frat house. Keep an eye on Luke and Levi for me. They are really wasted."

"Ok. I will."

"See you back at the frat house."

"Have fun," she said with a giggle before she hung up.

I tucked my phone away and put both arms around Dylan.

He was radiating a tremendous amount of heat through his cold, crinkly leather jacket. "Are you sure you're ok? You are really hot."

"Thank you," he slurred. "You are really hot too."

I laughed. "Are you sure you don't have a head injury? Maybe a concussion?"

"No, thanks. I'm good. I just need to take off some clothes. It is getting really hot out here." He paused in the alley, pawing at his jacket with his hands, attempting to take it off.

"Come on, Dylan." I pulled him forward. "It's freezing out here. Are you sure you're ok?"

"Not really. I'm feelin' kinda funky. Where are we? Are we lost? Holy crap, is that zebra talking to you, or me?"

Good grief. He's worse than I thought. "That ugly striped couch next to the building is not a zebra, and it is not talking to you." I could see Vivian's car ahead. I found the car keys in his jacket pocket. "I need to take you to the hospital ASAP. I think someone drugged you. You're hallucinating."

"I'm fine. I like the zoo. Let's go find Shamu. Whales are awesome."

Wow, that's some good shit. I put Dylan in the passenger seat. I slid behind the wheel. It was a sure bet that neither one of us should be driving. I was willing to chance getting a DUI to get Dylan the help he needed.

The Honda clunked into gear. We were off. I looked over at Dylan. His eyes were closed. I nudged him back awake. He gradually opened his eyes. I needed to make sure he was still breathing.

I drove about a block down Water Street towards the hospital. Dylan's eyes were closed again. He looked so sexy. The things I wanted to do to Dylan to wake him up were making me hot. I turned down the heat in the car and turned on the radio. Music blared from the speakers of Vivian's Honda. Good, the noise will keep me alert and focused. I nudged him awake again. "Hey, Dylan, are you ok over there?"

"Payton?" he asked, with his eyes closed.

"Yeah?" I answered back.

"You still have it, right?" he mumbled in his sleep.

"Do I still have what, Dylan?" I had no idea what he meant. He was still delirious.

Another wave of heat hit me. I rolled down the window. The frigid air from outside the car wasn't cold enough. Now I was burning up. Shit! It's contagious. Sensing what was to come, I unzipped my coat. I turned off Water Street and headed towards the frat house. I hoped I could get us close before I tried to buy a ticket to the zoo or lost consciousness. I prayed that my brother and his friends would find us on their way home before it was too late.

I dug out my phone as a last-ditch effort to save us. My eyesight blurred. It was hard to read the screen. I squinted as I scrolled. As far as I could tell, I was in the "L"s of my contact list. I desperately needed Luke and Lily's help. I was afraid we weren't going to make the last four blocks to the frat house.

Before I could hit send, the muscles in my hands became weak. The phone slipped out of hand, dropping to the floor of the Honda. I pulled the car over before I lost complete control of my limbs. I managed to paw around on the floor to retrieve my phone. I slapped at the screen with my malfunctioning hand. I heard it ring. Soon help would be here.

Lisa answered. I could hear her. "Hello? Hello? Is anyone there?"

I tried to answer her. She couldn't hear me. When I tried to yell, nothing came out. My voice wouldn't work.

"Payton?" asked Lisa, "Did you just butt dial me? Whatever." Click.

I panicked. I knew it was a stupid thing to do, but I put the car back in drive. The frat house was on Seventh Avenue. It was only a few blocks away. I had to do this. If I didn't get us closer, my wasted friends would never find us.

I drove only three more blocks when I had to pull the car over again. I couldn't help myself. My skin was on fire. I got out of the car. Desperately, I tugged and pawed at my jacket. It wasn't coming off. I was burning up. The muscles in my hands started to spasm. It was incredibly painful as my muscles tightened.

In my head, I screamed in agony as I peeled off my jacket. It didn't help. The heat rising from inside of me was unbearable. Dear God. Is this what menopause was going to be like?

Fists full of cold snow were my only relief. I painfully rubbed the icy, wet snow all over my body. I was freezing and sweating at the same time. I tried to scream for help again. Nothing came out. My mouth was as dry as a desert. I was thirsty beyond my wildest imagination. I found myself eating the dirty snow along the street trying to quench my thirst.

Dizziness filled my head. My knees weakened. They buckled beneath me. I was down on all fours in the street. I tried to crawl uncontrollably to the nearest water source, completely driven by my insatiable need for copious amounts of cold liquid. My arms grew heavy. My muscles continued to cramp and seize up. My vision became intensely impaired. I could no longer crawl. I collapsed in the gutter. Was this where I was going to die like a dog in the street? The last thought before I lost consciousness was of Dylan. I am so sorry my love. I could not deliver us from evil.

. . .

Your boyfriend is still alive for the second time. Do you think you will be that lucky, Payton? Maybe the third time will be the charm for him. Unfortunately, it is do or die for you both. It is all up to you, Payton. Which will it be?

CHAPTER TWENTY-TWO

The steamy rays of the sun felt great on my bare skin as I lay on the warm sand in my favorite thong bikini. Hunky god-like waiters continued to bring me an endless supply of umbrella drinks, while hordes of virile strapping lads rubbed fragrant oils into my skin. I was about to roll over and tan my backside when one of my loyal subjects poked me in the arm and then licked my face. Had I died and gone to heaven?

"Payton—Payton," said a familiar voice.

I opened my eyes. Crap. I had passed out in front of the space heater with a wedgie, and the Frat Cat was licking my face.

"Payton," said Lily in a stern voice. "What happened to you last night?"

I sat up immediately, zapped back to reality by Lily's question. My brain hit the inside of my forehead leaving a painful mark. "I don't know. How did I get here?"

"We found you in the snow bank outside. The boys threw you in front of the space heater to thaw you out."

I looked around me. There was no sign of my beloved. "Is Dylan here?"

"No. We only found you outside."

I jumped to my feet. Bits and pieces of last night flood-ed into my brain. My muscles ached. My palms and knees were raw. My mouth tasted a lot like a dirty margarita, which I could only speculate to be road salt mixed with tiny bits of gravel. It was very unsettling. "Did you happen to see a blue Honda outside?" I asked Lily.

"No, I didn't see it. Whose car is that?"

"Dylan borrowed Vivian's car last night. I think I tried to drive us both back here."

"Maybe he sobered up and went home."

"I don't think so. I can't remember much." I found my phone in my pocket. I dialed Dylan's number. He didn't answer. I needed to make the dreaded call to Vivian before I went into full panic mode. I tapped her name. She answered.

"Hi, Vivian. Is Dylan there?"

"No—he's—not! The little bastard took my car without permission, and now I can't get to work. He is more than just grounded this time." She hung up. I couldn't hold back the tears. He could be more than just grounded. He could be dead.

"Come on, Lily. We need to go to the Campus Police and report Dylan missing. Maybe they can help us find him."

. . .

If you hurry, Payton, your boyfriend might still have a pulse.

. . .

Lily and I sat impatiently in the makeshift office of the UW-CF Campus Rent-a-Cop. The portable, beige, fabric walls and the molded plastic office chairs didn't exactly install my confidence in Officer Todd's abilities. As he sat at his desk, I noticed his gray hair, gold watch, and donut induced belly. They were all the true tattletale signs of a good veteran cop recently put out to pasture. I hoped for Dylan's sake that Officer Todd was still on top of his game.

Officer Todd stayed at his desk making phone calls. After about the tenth call, he turned his attention back to Lily and me. It was about time. My butt was going numb from the cheap plastic seats.

"Well, ladies, I have some good news and some bad news," said Officer Todd.

My heart rose up in my throat and sank back down again at the good news, bad news scenario. It had been the story of my life lately. I just hoped that the good outweighed the bad for once.

"First of all, there has been no one admitted to the hospitals or the morgue fitting Dylan's description," said Officer Todd.

That had to be the good news, right?

"Secondly, the Clearwater Falls Police Department has not arrested anyone fitting his description."

"That's great," I said. This was more good news, seeing as how I bailed him out of jail yesterday.

"However, the Clearwater Falls Police Department has located Dylan's missing vehicle," said Officer Todd with a disheartened look on his face. "The good news is that there seems to be no sign of a struggle."

Lily and I held our breath waiting for it. By the look on his face, I knew the bad news was just around the corner.

"Payton, I hate to have to tell you this—"

My heart stopped.

"But we have no idea where Dylan is. We found the abandoned car on the side of the road with the driver's door hanging open. It is as if he just walked away and disappeared. There is one other thing. They found his wallet containing his driver's license at the Grey Hound Bus Terminal downtown."

I sat perfectly still, frozen in time. Doing my best to process what Officer Todd had just told me. Dylan wouldn't just walk away and leave Vivian's car. He wouldn't just skip town either. I was sure of that. We needed to find him.

Lily being of sounder mind and body started asking the appropriate questions. "Where did the police find his car?"

"A police officer spotted the car while making his routine inspection of the area around Larson Park. Would Dylan have any reason to go there?"

"No. Not that I know of." I chimed in, finally able to join in on the conversation. "So it's just a park with swings and ball fields?"

"Yes," said Officer Todd. "It is a very popular place for families in the summer time. It isn't very popular during the winter. I am not sure why your boyfriend would go there. This time of year the park is closed. As soon as it warms up again, all the kids will flock to the park to go swimming in Half Moon Lake."

When I opened my eyes, I was staring up at the ceiling tiles of the Campus Police Office. I was still woozy and unsure of how I ended up on the floor. I must have passed out.

"Are you ok?" asked Officer Todd. "You fainted." He held out a paper cup of water. "Here drink this. You will feel better."

The truth: I was not ok. I wasn't sure if hitting my head on the tile floor, or the need for water jogged my memory of last night. Now I knew why Dylan would go to the park. He had the same uncontrollable need for water that I had last night. His dying thirst might have just killed him.

The phone rang. Officer Todd answered it by the second ring. He put his hand over the mouthpiece. "Payton, I have good news. They pinged Dylan's phone. They traced it to the Ash Wood Mall. He is probably shopping."

Officer Todd thought this was good news. This was horrible news. The mall wasn't even open yet, and he didn't have his wallet. "Tell whoever is on the other end of that line to bring every available officer and an ambulance to Half Moon Lake. This is a rescue mission, people."

Officer Todd and Lily were shocked at my behavior.

They stood wide-eyed and opened mouth at my tenacity.

"Do it. Do it now," I ordered him. "Trust me, Officer Todd. I am right about this."

While Officer Todd was giving instructions to whoever he was talking to, Lily and I were out the door. We were on our way to my car.

"I think I should drive," suggested Lily.

"Why is that?"

"Because, I know where I am going."

"What do you mean?"

"Relax, Payton. Before all the piercings and black nail polish, I was a happy kid with pigtails that hung out with my parents and my brother at the park. Trust me. I know my way around the park."

"What happened to that happy kid?"

"I don't want to talk about it. Just give me the stupid keys and get in the damn car, so we can go save your frickin' boyfriend." She paused for a second and smiled at me.

"Ok." I handed her the keys. I made a mental note that Lily's former life as a happy child was a big frickin' secret. I jumped in the passenger seat and buckled up. I wasn't taking any chances. "Come on, Lily. Let's haul ass to the frickin' park."

"Payton, I don't want to freak you out more than you already are, but Larson Park has a history of mysterious unexplained drownings."

"Oh dear God, Lily, drive faster."

. . .

We crossed the bridge over Half Moon Lake and pulled up to the east gated entrance to Larson Park. I knew we were in the right place when I saw Vivian's blue Honda hooked up to a tow truck. My feet hit the ground before Lily came to a complete stop. I ran over to the tow truck driver.

"Where are you taking this car?"

"To the impound lot next to the police station."

"I'll give you five hundred dollars not to tow it," I said, trying to spare Dylan any further trouble from Vivian.

"Sorry, toots. I have my orders."

"Seven fifty?"

The pudgy, middle-aged man went about his business without acknowledging my comment.

It was time to up the ante. "Two grand?"

The man stopped in his tracks. "The car is barely worth that."

"Sentimental value," I told him.

"Bullshit, sweetie. Try again. This car isn't stolen, is it?"

"Three grand? Cash."

"I hope you and your car will be very happy together," he said, as he released the Honda from the tow truck.

I ran back to my Escape to grab the money. This was the first time I realized that my purse was missing. After last night, it could be anywhere. So much for my new Prada bag, it was gone.

"What's the hold up?" asked the tow truck driver as he walked to my car. "Do you have my money, or not?"

"You're not going to believe this, but I don't have my purse with me. Can I send you a check?"

"Are you trying to pull a fast one on me, young lady?"

"Absolutely not," I replied. I looked at Lily. She was pointing to her watch. I was wasting precious time. "Lily, do you have any money?"

"Not three grand. I think I have like twenty-seven dollars in my wallet."

"You bitches better not be trying to scam me."

"Seriously, we will figure something out," I assured him.

"So . . ." he said, looking at me. "How bad do you want that Honda?"

I had a flash of Teagan and her misguided tow truck driver experience. It made me shutter. I gave him a not on your life sour look.

"Take it easy, toots. I am a happily married man. I was just wondering if you were sentimentally attached to those diamond earrings you are wearing?"

"Are you joking? They are worth six grand, and they're my mother's."

"I have a big anniversary coming up next week. My wife would really love those earrings."

Lily and I looked at each other. We were running out of time and options. I needed that car to look for clues just in case Dylan wasn't in the park. I let out a huge sigh. "Ok, you have a deal." I handed over the diamond studs, making a mental note to think of a darn good story to tell my mother.

"It was a pleasure doing business with you ladies," he said, with a big smile before he drove away.

Lily and I quickly looked through Vivian's car for any clues. We found the keys still in the ignition and Dylan's coat in the front seat. This was not a good sign. He was outside somewhere without protection from the elements.

"Maybe we should split up and look for Dylan," suggested Lily. "I could take your car, go to the south entrance, and work my way back up here to you."

"Good idea. You know the park. I will take Vivian's Honda and head north."

"Payton, even you shouldn't have any problem getting lost. The park is a peninsula surrounded by a crescent shaped lake. Just follow Larson Park Drive. It runs in a circle along the lakeshore. Call me if you find him."

"You do the same, ok?" I asked, just before she drove off.

. . .

Where is Payton's boyfriend? Is he at Ash Wood Mall, at The Grey Hound Bus Terminal, on Larson Park Drive, or in the nearby Algon River next to the campus? Let me know when you eager beavers have the correct answer. Tick-tock. I am still waiting. This is life or death. Give up yet?

1	2	3	4	5	6	7	8	9
A	B	C	D	E	F	G	H	I
J	K	L	M	N	O	P	Q	R
S	T	U	V	W	X	Y	Z	

Scratch Paper for Math

CHAPTER TWENTY-THREE

Now that everyone is done crunching numbers. Let us see if we are all on the same page. Is Payton looking for her boyfriend in the right place? Are . . . you . . . sure? I like to play a game I call Sink or Swim. The Italian Kid thought he could play—I guess not. Did you catch the clue? I will give you a second. Did I make any of you idiots scrabble to recheck your math? Nice. I still control you.

Fine. I have had my fun. I will stop the bleeding in your brains. Sink or Swim has nothing to do with the math. It should be obvious. It has to do with water and the art of survival. And no, Payton's boyfriend is not in the fountain at Ash Wood Mall. But I like the way some of you think.

For those of you who are still trying to apply a tourniquet. Let me stop any further hemorrhaging. The magical answer to Your Number is Up game is three. Any wizards out there get it right? If any of you wannabe wizards are still struggling, do not have a mental meltdown. Let me throw you another bone. The month of January is always a one, not a nine. Yesterday's date was 1-29. All the numbers add up to three. 1+2+9=12, 1+2=3 or 1+29=30, 3+0=3 Smiley's is 1+4+9+3+5+7+1=30, 3+0=3 Get it now, brainiacs?

We need to get back to more important business. Our game is still liquid. Payton has a fluid situation on her hands. Obviously, you think you know where he is, but is he still breathing? Today is a new day, with new possibilities. I suggest you hurry.

. . .

There was fifteen wasted minutes of my life that I'll never get back. I wasted too much time on Vivian's car. I was sure it held a clue to Dylan's whereabouts. Right now, my focus must urgently change to searching for Dylan. He was out there somewhere freezing to death. It was time for me to put on my superhero cape and soar to his rescue.

I was fresh out of spandex, so I hopped in Vivian's car and started it up. The radio blasted one of the oldies stations. I turned off the radio and blasted the heat instead. The east gate was chained shut with heavy metal links, held in place by a sturdy padlock. For six grand, I should have had the tow truck driver bust the gate open for me. At least I would have gotten my money's worth.

The gate wasn't that tall. Maybe eight to ten feet max. I could probably climb over it. I got out of the car and climbed the chain-linked gate. Half way from the top, I spotted footprints on the other side. They lead away from the gate, heading down Larson Park Drive. They had to be Dylan's footprints.

I jumped down from the gate and climbed back into the Honda. There was no time to wait for the police and EMTs. It was up to me to save him. Vivian's car clunked into reverse. I backed up far enough to make a run at the gate. I pushed the gas pedal to the floor and closed my eyes. This was not a good combination. I wouldn't suggest trying this at home.

When I heard the car crash through the gate, I opened my eyes. Just as I expected, hitting the gate mangled the front end of Viv's car. So much for paying six grand to keep Vivian from being pissed. Now she can be angry with me instead of Dylan. I have a feeling that I might be sending her on a cruise to the Bahamas while her broken arm heals.

I followed the footprints down the road past the ball fields.

After about a quarter mile, the tracks veered off Larson Park Drive to my right. The tracks headed towards the water. My foot slammed on the brakes. This caused the back end of the Honda to swing around. The driver's side of the car smashed into the Paul Bunyan statue.

The driver's door felt cemented shut from the crash. I rammed my shoulder against it until the latch finally gave way. I fell to the ground. My cat-like, adrenaline surging reflexes kicked in. I did a gymnastic ninja roll that landed me upright in the snow. Without hesitation, my feet miraculously hit the ground running. I followed the tracks through the trees to the water's edge. I slid to a stop when I found Dylan's motionless body face down in the snow.

I ran to his side. Did I get here in time? Was Dylan still alive? The water of Half Moon Lake was frozen solid, so he couldn't have drowned. However, that didn't mean he couldn't have died from hypothermia.

I rolled Dylan over, bracing myself for the possibility of seeing gray, lifeless eyes. A huge sigh of relief left my body when I saw his closed eyes and pale lips. Yes! He could still be alive.

While I reached for Dylan's neck to feel for a pulse, the sound of the sirens wailed in the distance. "Help is on the way." I assured him. There was no electricity this time when I touched Dylan. His skin felt icy. I tried, but I couldn't feel a pulse. My heart was pounding out of my chest. I took a deep breath trying to calm myself down. I had to try again. I felt his neck. Nothing.

Lily ran up behind me. "Is he still alive?"

"I can't tell," I said. My eyes were welling up with tears. I was shaking and hyperventilating. I was useless.

Lily pushed me out of the way. She placed her index and middle finger on his neck. Then she bent down close to Dylan's face. She looked at his chest. While I sat motionless in the snow, she dug in her purse. Lily pulled out the small mirror we found last night and a tiny glass vile. She poured the liquid from the vile between his lips and then stuck the mirror under his nose.

"What is that?" I asked.

"It's a homemade energy shot."

"Ok? So what's in it?"

"It's made of mostly ginger root and guarana."

"Isn't that bat poop?"

"No. You are thinking of guano. Guarana is a natural nerve stimulant. I am trying to wake him up."

"So he is still alive?" Lily didn't answer me. "Oh God, Lily, say something."

"Yes. He is still alive. Dylan's pulse is weak, but he appears to be breathing on his own."

"You are sure he is still breathing?"

"I know he is still breathing because he is fogging up the mirror."

Our serious mood turned to joy and relief.

"We need to keep him warm," instructed Lily.

I placed my coat on Dylan's chest. Then I wrapped my arms around him trying to keep him warm. Lily covered us with her long black cape coat. I tried to be the superhero. Instead, I am giving all the credit to Lily and her black cape.

I held Dylan tight and whispered in his ear, "Please hang on. Help is almost here."

"Payton," he whispered back, breathing my name. He was letting me know that he had heard me.

Lily ran up to the road when she heard the sirens approaching. She directed the ambulance crew down to us. I moved out of the way to let them work on Dylan. After the crew checked his vitals, they loaded him on a gurney. They covered him with several layers of heated blankets before they loaded him in the ambulance. One of the EMTs was in the process of starting an IV when I tried to climb on board.

"Is he going to be ok?" I asked.

"It is hard to say, but it looks as if we arrived just in time."

The other male EMT grabbed my arm, pulling me back. "Excuse me ma'am. I need to close the door. We need to get him to the hospital ASAP."

"But I am riding with Dylan."

"No, ma'am. You're not. The police need to speak with you." The EMT closed the back door. Then he jogged to the cab of the ambulance.

"Where are you taking him?"

"Sacred Heart Hospital." He jumped into the driver's seat. The siren and the red flashing lights started as the ambulance pulled away.

Two police officers cornered Lily and me for our statements. We gave them the edited for TV version of what happened last night. They gave us a stern talking to about the destruction of public property, breaking and entering, and the evils of drugs and alcohol. We got lucky. They let us off with a warning because my boyfriend almost died. How about that? I officially have a boyfriend. I am no longer undateable. Woo Hoo! I am going to see my boyfriend at the hospital now. How exhilaratingly depressing is that?

. . .

Do not break your arm patting yourself of the back, Payton. Dylan is not alive solely because of you. Believe whatever helps you sleep at night.

. . .

I sat with Lily in silence at Dylan's bedside. I waited impatiently for him to wake up. Lily had called my brother Luke. He was on his way to join us. My brother and I fight about random crap, but he can be cool and supportive when he wants to be.

When we arrived at the hospital, I reluctantly gave the nursing staff Vivian's phone number. I'm not looking forward to seeing her. After our last conversation, I am not so sure she will be happy that Dylan is still alive. When she sees her car in the parking lot, I pity anyone within earshot of her ranting. It is going to be epic and explosive.

My mind trolled for ideas to soften the blow of Vivian's wrath. I was already down six grand, plus loads of bail money.

After she gets back from a cruise, she might enjoy driving around in a new car. Seeing as how her arm is still in a cast, I'm thinking a hatchback isn't going to cut it. She is going to want a nice sedan or a convertible. There goes a few months' worth of my allowance. But I have a boyfriend now, so I don't care about the money.

Luke and Logan showed up on the fourth floor at Dylan's door. They looked like crap. Neither one of them looked like they felt much better than Dylan did. They were both still green from last night's cocktails.

"How is he?" Logan asked.

"No change," said Lily. "They say he has an excellent chance of surviving."

"How is she holding up?" asked Luke, making a head nod in my direction.

"She can hear you and would like you to go find her something to eat." I said to my brother with a smirk. "I'm feeling carnivorous."

"I think you mean cavernous," said Lily. "Us three will run down to the kitchen and grab something for you." Before she left the room, she leaned over and whispered in my ear. "When we get back, I need to talk to you about something."

I peered at her with a puzzled look. "Ok?" I agreed. I had no idea what that subject was going to be. After Logan, Luke, and Lily left the room, I moved from the recliner to a spot next to Dylan on his bed. I picked up his right hand and held it in mine. I stroked it slowly with my fingers. That's when I noticed it. Someone had tried to carve a smiley face into the palm of Dylan's hand. I was sure that was there to get my attention. I looked away, trying to hold myself together for Dylan.

After a few minutes of blinking away tears, I felt like I was able to tell Dylan the things I needed him to hear before it was too late. "Dylan, I don't know if you can hear me. I hope that you can. I have never met anyone like you before or had the instant chemistry that we share. I feel completely comfortable with you even though I have only known you for what . . . two days?"

"This is all happening so fast. Is this what true love feels like? Is this the kind of love that lasts forever? I don't know because I have never experienced anything like this before. You have to wake up. You have to get better. If I lose you now, I feel like my life will never be the same. I will never know if this was it. You know . . . the real deal. God, this is so crazy. I don't really know anything about you. I don't even know your middle name. So please wake up and be all right. We need to continue what we started, ok?" I tried to keep it together, but I could feel the tears start to roll down my cheeks as I stared out the window.

"It's Jacob," he whispered back at me.

I turned and looked at Dylan. His eyes were closed. "Oh God, Dylan, you heard me. Oh God . . . how much did you hear?"

"Don't worry. You had me the first time we met." He whispered back.

"But the first time we met, I was—"

"I know. That's what I dig about you. You keep life interesting."

"You are so demented," I said with a smile. "I'll go get your nurse." But first, I leaned in and kissed him. After last night, I wasn't taking any opportunity for granted. "Don't go anywhere," I told him.

"Even if I did, I have a feeling you would find me . . ." He was unconscious again, sleeping like a baby. We were so meant to be. I could feel it. I was definitely psyched.

. . .

Did anyone notice that today's magic number, and the location of where Payton's boyfriend is comfortably resting now, matches something else?

. . .

1	2	3	4	5	6	7	8	9
A	B	C	D	E	F	G	H	I
J	K	L	M	N	O	P	Q	R
S	T	U	V	W	X	Y	Z	

Scratch Paper for Math

CHAPTER TWENTY-FOUR

Payton's boyfriend is floating on a cloud. He is sleeping like a baby at Sacred Heart Hospital. He could be floating in the frigid waters of Algon River sleeping like the dead. Correct? The choice was his. He passed my test. He knows what he needs to do to survive.

I know I said it had nothing to do with the math. Surprise! I lied. I am a serial killer, not a saint. And it never hurts to have a back-up plan. Pay close attention. I am a stickler for details.

This should get your hearts and your calculators thumping. Today's magic number matches some of Payton's friends. Who will be my next contestant? Who wants to play a game? The day is still young. Just about anything can happen, and it will. I see you, my chosen prey. Which of Payton's friends did I pick? This will be Payton's greatest challenge.

. . .

Dylan's doctor and nurse came into his room to examine him. The doctor gave him an upgrade from serious to stable. I was ecstatic. His doctor couldn't tell me anything specific yet, but it looked as if Dylan was going to be ok. They were still running a few tests. So far, everything was coming back normal. This was all great news.

Luke, Lily, and Logan were not back with my food yet. What could be taking so long? I was so hungry, I could have eaten the couch in the waiting area. The trio showed up with a sub just in time. Carbohydrates, seasoned meat, and veggies stopped me from going over to the darker side of the culinary world.

While I was eating my sub, Dylan woke up again. He tried to climb out of bed.

"Dylan, you need to lie down."

He sat up regardless of what I said, pulling out his I.V. "I feel fine. I want to get the hell out of here."

I couldn't argue with him. Hospitals were not my favorite place to hang out. They gave me the creeps. Maybe we should get the hell out of here before I do something incredibly stupid. Getting the grand tour of Sacred Heart's fifth floor was not on my bucket list for the day.

Luke, Lily, and Logan stepped out of his room, but I hung around just in case Dylan needed help getting dressed. Yeah, I know. My mind was in the gutter. Dylan seemed to be doing fine behind the curtain until he tried putting on his pants.

"What the hell?" Dylan asked from behind the curtain.

"What's the matter?" I asked.

"I don't think these are my pants."

"What are you talking about? How is that even possible?"

"They look like my pants, but they aren't the ones I was wearing last night."

Out of curiosity, I peeked around the curtain. "Why? Don't they fit?"

"Yeah, they fit. But the pair I was wearing last night had a hole, right here," he said, pointing to his right knee. He put his hands in his front pockets and pulled out a black braided cord. It looked like a hood string to a sweatshirt. "I know that's not mine," he said, throwing it in the nearby garbage can in his room.

I was confused because he was confused. Was this a clue, or a mixed up memory from last night? "You look upset. Why don't I give you a minute alone to collect yourself? I will be out in the hallway."

Luke was sitting on the couch in the waiting area listening to music on his iPod. Logan was on the other end of the couch slumped over, sleeping with his mouth hanging open. Lily was busy reading a magazine while nervously chewing on the hood string of her cape coat.

"Dylan seems to be fine, so you guys can go if you want," I said.

"Are you sure?" asked Lily.

"Yeah, thanks for all of your help and support today."

"Sure," said Luke. "I am assuming that we are not telling Mom or Dad about this."

"You have assumed correctly," I said to Luke. "I am still hoping to find my new purse, so I don't have that awkward conversation with them either. Let me know if you find it at the frat house."

"Will do," said Luke. He slapped Logan on the chest to wake him up.

"I will look for it too," said Lily.

Logan didn't move. Luke slapped him again. "Dude, wake the "f" up. Let's go." Logan still didn't move, his complexion a shade paler then before.

Lily walked over to Logan. "This normally works when he passes out in the bathroom." She grabbed a hold of his left nibble and twisted. Logan yelped. He jumped to his feet. "The purple nurple works every time," she said, with an evil grin.

. . .

Did you really think it was going to be that easy? Dead frat boy on the couch? So unoriginal. So overdone. I have something else in mind.

. . .

After I said good-bye to Luke, Lily, and Logan, I headed

back to Dylan's room. When I got there, Dylan was in the bathroom. I took a seat in the recliner. While I was waiting, I found myself staring at the garbage can wondering if the string Dylan found in his pants had any significance. Obviously, the string didn't belong to him. Maybe it belonged to the person who abducted him. Hey, I should have it analyzed. If I was lucky, maybe the killer left some of their DNA on the string.

Before Dylan came out of the bathroom, I quickly snagged the small plastic bag and string from his wastebasket. The small plastic bag fit neatly in the pocket of my jacket. I just hoped Tim was willing to help me out with another favor.

My next move would have made Nancy Drew proud. I spotted a plastic cup containing Dylan's urine. It was sitting on a small table next to the bathroom door. I know it's gross, but I snagged the sample. The screw-topped cup barely fit into my other pocket. Clearly, someone had drugged us. Maybe Tim could have the lab run a toxicology screen on the sample. It just made sense. If I knew which drug they used, it would help me figure out who was messing with me. I had just finished my crime scene investigation when I heard Dylan yell from the bathroom.

"What the—?" Then he flushed the toilet.

"Is everything ok in there?" I asked.

Dylan came out of the bathroom with a very unhappy look on his face. "What happened last night?" he asked, holding up the smiley face on his palm. "I don't remember anything after the alley."

I carefully brought him up to speed from what I could recall. There were bits and pieces missing from the story and my memory. There were things even I couldn't remember. Dylan had no idea how his wallet had gotten to the bus station, or how his cell phone had gotten to the mall. I think it was all a wild goose chase to waste time and throw the police off track.

He seemed ok until I told him the part of the story where the Bald-headed Man was looking for him. When I told him that Lily revived him with an herbal energy shot, he was more than a little agitated. I don't think that he understood until then that he could have died. He was clearly distraught.

"I wasn't going to show you this, but I have no choice." Dylan unbuttoned and unzipped his pants, exposing a patch of skin below and to the left of his belly button. Someone had raggedly scratched the number three into his skin. "What does this mean?"

"It means that someone is playing a sick game and unfortunately you are right in the middle of it now. Vivian was right. You needed to stay clear of my wake of destruction."

Dylan hoisted his pants back up. Before he could zip and button them, a piece of paper fell out of his back pocket. He bent down and picked it up off the floor. He handed it to me. "It's for you," he said slowly with disbelief.

"Wow, that's creepy." He was right. My name was on the front of the folded piece of paper written in all capital letters. I opened it. The note read: "GIVE ME WHAT I WANT OR NUMBER FOUR DIES."

"That's not creepy. That's twisted," said Dylan.

"Well, at least we know what the number three means."

Dylan gave me a horrified glare. He was clearly not happy to be number three. "What do they want?" he asked.

"I don't know. I don't have anything. I don't even have my purse. That's it. My purse, I need to find my purse."

"Why would a deranged psychopath want your purse?"

"They don't want my purse. They want what's in my purse."

"Is this sick game about money?"

"No. Lily and I found an old antique key last night. The last time I saw it, the key was in my purse. That is the only thing that I have that the killer could want. I need to find my purse ASAP."

"I'm coming with you."

"It is too dangerous for you to be around me right now, Dylan. I don't want anything else to happen to you. Vivian should be here soon. Go home with her, lock your doors, and stay put."

"Oh great, Vivian is coming here? You don't have to worry

about me going anywhere ever again. I will be grounded for life when she sees her car."

"Just tell her that I crashed her car through the gate trying to save your life. It is romantic. She can't be mad."

Dylan's face turned red with anger. "I can't do that. I'll catch hell for hanging out with you. I will tell her that I got drunk and crashed it into a tree at the park."

"Good luck with that excuse. How about I just buy her a new car?"

"I am serious. Our relationship has to stay a secret from her. She can't know that we were together last night. I promise that I will tell her when the time is right."

"That is so cute." I leaned in and gave him a kiss. "Then I should probably go before she gets here." I kissed him again. "Seriously, I could do this all day." This time he kissed me.

"Before you go, I need to ask you a favor."

"Sure, anything for you, Dylan."

"I hid a book under the dash of your car. Find it and hide it somewhere safe."

"Why would you hide a book in my car?"

"It's the book that Stephanie took from me. Promise me that you will hide it. Never tell anyone where it is."

"Ok, I promise." I leaned in. This time I gave him a kiss he would not soon forget. It would have lasted longer, but we heard a commotion at the Nurses Station.

"Vivian," we said in unison.

I peeked out Dylan's door. The coast was clear. There was no sign of Vivian yet. I ran down the hall, practically diving into the stairwell. From behind the closed stairwell door, I could hear Vivian's voice.

"Did you know that I had to take two buses and a taxi to get here?"

Yikes. Epic and explosive. Good luck with that, sweetheart.

. . .

Just to keep things interesting, I added a twist to the game. This is for all the golf fanatics out there. Do not try to play dumb with me. I know who you are. You are just like me. You will do anything to improve your game. You will do anything to win. You will do anything as long as it does not break the rules. The integrity of the game must be maintained at all cost.

I recently found a new foursome to play a round with. This new game will be hazardous to their health. A few of them are already in the deep rough, chipping to save their lives. Obviously, some of them will not be making the cut. Who will make it back to the clubhouse? Grab your sticks and play or stay the hell on the practice green. I need to run. I am late for my tee time. Has anyone seen my caddy?

CHAPTER TWENTY-FIVE

From the stairwell, I dialed Lily. She didn't answer. I left her a call me, it's an emergency, voicemail. Then I dialed Luke. He picked up on the second ring.

"What do you want, Payton? You are interrupting a serious game of beer pong."

"Did you find my purse?"

"Nope. Sorry. We looked everywhere. There's no sign of it."

"Shit, where can it be?"

"Mom's gonna be pissed if you don't find it."

"She's not the only one." I couldn't help but think how pissed my pen pal was going to be if I didn't find that necklace. "Hey, is Lily with you? I need to talk to her."

"No, she's not here. Lily had to go to the store. She was out of eyeliner."

We both chuckled briefly at the thought of Lily without her makeup induced, blacker than black, raccoon eyes.

"When she gets back, don't let her leave."

"Why? What's going on?"

"It's too long to explain. No one I know is safe right now. Do me a huge favor. You and the rest of your frat mates stay in tonight and lock the doors. Make sure it's all of the doors and the window too."

"Don't you think you are being a little overly dramatic with your post-traumatic stress disorder?"

"Damn it, Luke, just do what I say for once. I don't have time to argue with you."

"Ok, jeez, we will stay home as long as we don't run out of beer. That is the best I can promise."

"Just do it, ok? I've got to go." I walked across the lobby of the hospital and out the front door. I was on my way to my car when my phone rang. It was Lily.

"Thank God. Are you all right?" I asked.

"No, I'm not. Someone is following me," she whispered.

"Where are you?"

"I am hiding in the bushes by Wal-Mart."

"Stay put, I'll be right there."

"No, you don't need to come. I can see my car from here. I am about to make a run for it. I am just making sure that someone knows where to look for me, just in case I don't make it."

After Lily said that, I was creeped out. I ran across the lot to my car and climbed inside. "Did you get a good look at who is following you?"

"Yeah, he followed me from Larson Park to Wal-Mart in his dark sedan. Payton, it's the big Bald-headed Man. I think he is after me."

"Lily, what were you doing at Larson Park by yourself? You know it's not safe."

"Remember in Dylan's room when I said I needed to tell you something?"

"Yeah, I remember." I said, while I double-checked my door locks on my car. "You kind of left me hanging."

"I know. I needed to go back to the park and make sure before I said anything to you."

"Just tell me. What it is, Lily?"

"When I went back to the park, I couldn't find any symbols. They weren't in the trees or on the ground."

"What does that mean?"

"I'm not sure, but it doesn't fit the pattern. You are not going to like what I am thinking."

"Are you seriously trying to suggest that Dylan is involved somehow? Lily, he almost died."

"Yeah, I know. I'm sorry. But I still can't help the way I feel about Dylan."

I stopped talking to her because I was pissed.

"Payton, are you still there?"

I sat in silence wanting to hang up on her. I didn't. My brother would be irate, and I couldn't live with myself if anything bad happened to Lily. I sighed. "Yeah, I'm still here. Is there any sign of the Bald-headed Man?"

"No, I think I lost him. I am going to make a run for my car now."

"Ok, Lily. Be careful. Drive straight to the frat house, go inside, and lock the doors. Do not let anyone leave until you hear from me."

"Where are you going, Payton?"

Lily was now on the need to know basis with me. She no longer needed to know my every move. "I need to find something. Talk to you later." I hung up.

That was a good question. Where was I going? My purse wasn't at the frat house or in Vivian's car. Maybe it was still at the bar, but I doubt it. If a starving college student jacked my cash and maxed out my credit cards buying pizza for the entire campus, I would hope someone would have called me by now.

I guess I could start at the bar and check the back alley. Then I could go to the police station to see if the most honest person on the face of the Earth found it and turned it in. At least I had a plan. I was on my way down the State Street Hill when my phone rang. It was Brad. I let it go to voicemail. He called back four times. I finally answered. He wasn't going to give up.

"What!" I answered in a tone, so he knew I was not happy to be talking to him.

"Guess what I have?"

"A scorching venereal disease."

"Ha Ha. Very funny, Payton. I don't have V.D., but I do have your purse."

"Why do you have it?"

"Someone dropped it off at the station this morning."

"Did you see them? What did they look like?" I asked spastically.

"Calm down, Payton. I don't know. I wasn't there because it's my day off. My dad told me to give it to you. If you want it, stop by my house. I will be here all day."

"I'll be there in about an hour. Brad, don't you dare go through my purse."

"I wouldn't dream of it." He laughed and hung up on me.

"Ugh!"

. . .

Payton, I am about to raise your handicap.

CHAPTER TWENTY-SIX

Before I went to Brad's, I needed to keep my promise to Dylan. The perfect place for me to hide the book was in the floor safe at the restaurant. I was pulling into the parking lot of the Barbecue Shack when my phone rang again. This time it was Teagan.

"Hi, Teagan. What's up?"

Without even saying hello first, she blurted out, "Amber is missing."

"When is the last time you saw her or spoke to her?"

"The last time I remember seeing her was shortly after you left the bar last night. She told me that she saw your creepy neighbor watching us through the window of the bar. Amber went outside to tell him off. I don't know if she came back in."

"What do you mean you don't know?" I raised my voice at Teagan.

"I'm sorry. I was really drunk. Levi and I were dancing. We started making out. He was a good kisser. I got distracted and forgot about her."

Before I went into my panic mode, I needed to ask the big question. "So you are absolutely positive that she didn't go home with someone last night?"

"Hello, we are talking about Amber. The girl probably still has her V card."

Teagan was right. Amber kept her shit on lockdown. Except for the way she was acting with Streak, Amber was the unsluttiest girl I had ever met. She was the responsible one of the group. She wouldn't just leave without telling someone where she was going.

"It gets worse," said Teagan. "I wasn't that worried until Smiley's called the sorority house a few minutes ago. Payton, they have Amber's coat and purse at the bar."

"That's not good." It was time to panic. No coat was bad. No purse was worse. Our entire lives are in our purses. We will do just about anything to get them back if we lose them. This includes seeing ex fiancées.

"I know it's not. That is why I called you. Do you think your neighbor could have done something to her?"

"God, I hope not. I will go talk to Rod and Kurt."

"You shouldn't go by yourself. Maybe you should get Brad to go with you."

"I will figure something out. I will check it out and get back to you soon. In the meantime, you should call the Clearwater Falls Police Station and the local hospitals to see if anyone fitting her description has turned up."

"Good idea, Payton. I will do that. Call me as soon as you know anything. Bye."

I ran into the restaurant and put Dylan's book in the hidden safe. It would be secure there until I could think of a better place for it. Now that I fulfilled my promise to Dylan, I could concentrate on finding Amber.

When I got back in my car, I sent Tim a quick SOS text. I was about to back out of my parking space when a crowd of bald-headed, but fully clothed, teenagers jumped on the hood of my car. Don't get me wrong. I was genuinely concerned for Amber. My curiosity about their lack of hair got the best of me. Besides, I needed to warn them to go home and lock their doors. A killer was still on the loose. After what happened to Streak, none of the boys were safe.

I rolled down my window. "Hey guys, what's up?"

"Are you here to make us chicken wings?" asked Feed Bag. "I'm hungry."

"No. Sorry, boys. We had to close the restaurant because of the fire. Remember?"

"That's why we're here," said The Singe. "We're fixing the apartment."

"Yeah, my dad volunteered to be the contractor for the project," said Blond Ambition. "My dad said, 'he would rather fix the apartment than have us little assholes in his basement.'"

"That's great . . . I think. Tell your dad thank you, but we have insurance."

"The Singe's dad is paying for the supplies, and my dad is helping us with the labor. It's all good. Don't worry, Payton. The place will be good as new in no time."

"Cool. Thanks, guys. Once we reopen, I'm sure Dylan can cook you guys up some free rounds of food for all of your hard work."

"Awesome. Dylan is the King of the Chicken Wing," said Chameleon, doing the best impersonation of a chicken I had ever seen.

We all laughed. He was such a goof.

It was time to switch to a more solemn mood. I put my car in park and hopped out of the driver's seat. "Guys, I need you to be serious for a minute. You need to listen to what I have to say." The boys quieted down and gathered around me. "This might come as a shock to most of you." I took a deep breath and exhaled. "A pack of wolves didn't kill Streak. There is someone out there doing bad things to good people, people that I know. I need you boys to go home now before someone else gets hurt."

"But we are in the middle of a 'Shoot Your Bro For His Fro Tournament,'" said Feed Bag.

Well, that explained their lack of hair. I had to be talking to the loser's bracket. The one thing I didn't have an explanation for was their lack of concern for their own safety. I guess they all thought they were young and invincible. We've all been there.

"Seriously guys, I'm not kidding. You have to go home."

Tim pulled up next to us in his squad car. He must have gotten my SOS. Tim rolled down his window. "Boys, listen up. I've gotten several complaints about noise from the neighbors. I need you to break it up and go home."

"Aw, ok," they said, hanging their bald heads as they walked away.

"How did you do that?" I asked. "They wouldn't listen to me."

"The power of the badge is always mightier."

I learned my lesson. I wasn't about to dis the badge again. "Thank God you're here," I said as I hopped in the front seat of his squad car. "I need a huge favor."

"I am still working on your last huge favor. I returned the necklace to Streak's family, but I don't have the results back yet on his hair sample."

"Well, now I have a few more samples for you." I pulled the plastic bag containing the sweatshirt string, Dylan's urine sample, and my fresh urine sample that was in a zip lock baggie from my pockets.

"Someone's been busy playing CSI."

"Someone's been busy trying to kill me. Can you run a toxicology screen on the two urine samples? The one in the baggie is mine. The one in the cup belongs to Dylan. Can you also run a DNA analysis on this sweatshirt string Dylan found in the pocket of his pants?"

"Payton, what is going on? Did I miss something?"

"Dylan almost became victim number three last night, and now Amber is missing."

"Don't you mean victim number four?" Tim asked.

I looked at him strangely. I thought about what he had said. Tim was right. If I included the boy from Twin Valley, Dylan should have been number four. What did that mean? I decided to ask his opinion. "How does the boy from Twin Valley fit in with the other three?"

"That is a good question," said Tim. "He really doesn't. You didn't know him, right?"

"No, I have no idea who he was. To be completely honest, I'm not sure if I ever heard his name on the news."

"I'll have to check that out and get back to you," said Tim. "It could be the missing piece of the puzzle. The clue that makes everything fall into place."

"Great. You could be right. Let me know ASAP."

"I will add it to your list of demands," he said in a smart-ass tone.

"Hey, do you think there could be two separate killers? That would explain why the first one doesn't fit in with the others."

"Or maybe it is two people working together," suggested Tim.

"I think it would have to be two people working together because of the similar M.O."

"I totally agree," said Tim. "If we could connect one of the other boys to Dylan or the Italian kid, it all might make more sense. Well, we could talk about the psychological theories of a serial killer all day, but didn't you say that Amber was missing?"

"Oh, shit! What is wrong with me? I completely forgot about Amber. I have been so forgetful lately." Whatever they drugged me with last night was still seriously messing up my head.

Tim put his hand on my shoulder. "Payton, don't be so hard on yourself. You have been through a lot lately."

"No offense, but you sound like my shrink. I need you to be a tough badass and help me find her, not patronize me." I shrugged Tim's hand from my shoulder.

"Ok, sorry. Tell me what you know about Amber's disappearance."

"The last time anyone saw her was around 11:30 last night. She was outside the bar with Rod Huntley and Kurt Meriwether."

"What the heck was she doing with those two degenerates?" asked Tim.

"Amber saw them outside watching us through the window. She went out there to yell at them for following us and threatening me."

"That was a stupid thing for her to do."

"No shit. Amber is one of the smartest people I know, but she gets incredibly brave when she drinks. What can I say? She gets beer muscles. Do you think you could go over to Rod's house and arrest them?"

"Payton, men of the law can't just harass whoever they want. You need to have probable cause."

"You are kidding, right? They were the last people to be seen with Amber."

"Ok. I hear what you are saying. As of five minutes ago, I was officially off duty. I will call the station to see who would be willing to go talk to them."

"Thank you, Tim. That would mean a lot to me."

Before Tim could pick up his radio and call the station, Blond Ambition and Chameleon appeared at Tim's window of the squad car.

"Do you have any leads on who might have killed Streak?" asked Chameleon.

"We are currently working on it," answered Tim.

"That means you cops don't have a clue," snipped Blond Ambition.

"That's not true. We have some leads that we are following up on," explained Tim.

"Like what?" Chameleon asked. He casually leaned against Tim's car.

"You guys know that I can't discuss anything about an ongoing investigation with you boys."

"Do the cops still think the death of Hood Rat—the kid they found behind the college—was just an accident?" asked Blond Ambition.

"That is what the police report says. It was an accident. He slipped on the ice, hit his head, choked on a chip, and drowned," said Tim, lacking the conviction to believe it any longer. He was doing his best to not let on to the boys that he

thought otherwise, but I could tell. There was something different in his voice.

"Hood Rat?" I asked. "That sounds like a gamer tag. Did
you boys know him?"

"Not really," replied Blond Ambition. "He came to a
couple of the tourneys."

"He was a real douche," said Chameleon. "So we gave
him the boot."

Tim raised an eyebrow. "Do you boys have something
that you would like to tell me?"

"We're not snitches," stated Blond Ambition.

"Cuz they get stitches," finished Chameleon.

"Guys, you can tell us. No one will get stitches. I
promise."

The boys looked at each other. They made a nonverbal
agreement with their eyes and a head nod. "Ok, we will talk if
it helps catch Streak's killer," said Blond Ambition. "We heard
around that Streak and Hood Rat were working for that
sleazeball down the road."

"Do you mean Rod Huntley from the Last Chance
Saloon?" I asked.

"Yeah, that's him," said Chameleon.

"We don't know what they did for him, but Streak always
had a lot of cash," said Blond Ambition.

His comment brought back an image from the night Streak
died. Streak pulled hundred dollar bills from his underwear to
pay for all the food. And then, there was the altercation with
Rod and Kurt over a chicken cheese ball. I had no idea that
Streak knew those two. I looked at Tim. It was obvious that he
was thinking the same thing. We now had our link between two
of the victims. It all pointed right at Rod.

"Thanks guys, you've been very helpful," said Tim. "I will
personally see that this lead is checked out."

"No, thank you!" said Chameleon. "I hope it helps catch
Streak's killer." Without warning, he leaned in the car window,
enthusiastically hugging both of us.

"I am sure it will," said Tim.

"No one deserves to die cold and alone screaming for help," said Chameleon.

"Yeah, help that never comes," finished Blond Ambition.

The boys walked to their cars to leave.

I rolled down the passenger window. "Hey, you guys left the lights on upstairs."

"Wolfman and Pump Up the Volume are still up there," said Blond Ambition."

"Wolfman just beat Warlock to win the championship. He gets to keep his fro," said Chameleon.

I had to admit . . . that was a lot of fro. "That's super," I said sarcastically.

The boys pulled out of the parking lot. I looked at Tim. I could tell that he was connecting the dots in his head. "What do you think about what the boys said?" I asked.

"It looks like we have more evidence against Rod."

"Yes, we do. Do you think that Rod and his creepy partner could be involved somehow?"

"Now, I actually do. I saw Kurt at the police station this morning. He was acting odd. For the life of me, I couldn't figure out why a grown man would be carrying a woman's red hand bag."

"Was it a red Prada hand bag?"

"Do I look like I could tell the difference? It was a large red purse with straps and silver buckles. Why does it matter?"

"Because it's my purse. I had that purse with me when Dylan and I left the bar last night. The only way Kurt could have gotten my purse is if he was the one that tried to kill Dylan."

"You are absolutely positive?"

"Yes. You have to do something right now before it is too late."

"The Chief won't like it. He has to be the one to give the order for the arrest warrant."

I grabbed Tim by the shoulders and looked him straight in the eyes. "Tim, you know how the Chief feels about this whole investigation. You don't need to arrest them, just talk to them and look around for Amber. You can do this, Tim."

"I don't know, Payton. If we are wrong, the Chief will take my badge."

"And if we're right, you will save lives and get a promotion. Heck, maybe they will even make you chief. Tim, you need to go over to Rod's and shake the tree to see what falls out."

Tim was silent, weighing out his options.

"Look, Tim, we have connected what happened to Dylan, to Rod and Kurt. That is three out of the four victims connected to them. They could very well be the two people/killers working together. And they were the last to be seen with Amber last night."

"You are right," said Tim finally. "I am sure if we keep digging, we will be able to connect the mysterious bald man to them also."

"The bald man was there at the bar last night. He was looking for Dylan."

"He was?"

"Yes, he was. He was there outside the restaurant on the night Streak died too. He was seen talking to Rod and Kurt."

"Ok, you are right. They are probably behind all of it. You stay here. I'll go check it out, unofficially."

"I am not staying here. You are going to need help."

"Payton, this is police business. I will call for back up the second I see anything suspicious. Besides, if you got hurt, it would be my ass."

"Fine. I will go get my purse from Brad and wait there. He has a Police Scanner. I will be able to hear the play-by-play action."

"Don't tell Brad anything. He will rat me out to his dad if we are wrong."

"We're not wrong, Tim." I climbed out of Tim's police cruiser. Before I closed the door, I paused to look at Tim. "I guess I owe you big time for this?"

"Yes, you do. When I get back from Rod's, I am going to collect," he said with a smile.

"Name your poison?"

"A foot-long Philly cheese steak sandwich and a beer."

"That's it?"

"I'm hungry, not greedy," he said with a grin.

I smiled back and closed the door. He rolled up his window. Tim backed the police car up quickly with extreme precision. He drove down the road at a high rate of speed towards Rod's house. He left the lights and sirens off for stealth. His car disappeared over the hill. He was my knight in shiny blue steel on his way to save the day.

. . .

Was that a foot wedge?

CHAPTER TWENTY-SEVEN

I pulled up to Brad's house wondering how bad I really wanted my purse back. The case was pretty much solved. We had enough evidence to connect Rod and Kurt to the murders. They would be behind bars soon. I didn't really need the necklace to prove anything. Well that settles that. I'm out of here. My car clunked into reverse. A horrible thought popped into my head causing me to be perplexed. My foot hit the brake pedal. I certainly didn't want Brad to have it. More important than that, what if I still needed the necklace to barter my way out of this mess? What if I needed to trade it for Amber's life? Crap. I was going into Brad's whether I liked it, or not.

While I was weighing out my options, Brad unexpectedly appeared at my driver's window. He was wearing a stupid black and blue striped stocking hat. It was not a good look for him. "Coming in?" he asked.

"How about you just bring my purse out?"

"No can do, Payton. You have to pay the toll and have a beer with me."

Brad walked back inside his house. I sat in my car for about five minutes weighing out my options again. The desire for an ice-cold beer won over sitting in an ice-cold car. Who was I trying to fool anyway? I am Payton Marie Richardson. I never turn down a free drink.

I climbed out of my car, walked up the steps, and opened the door. It had been a while since I had seen the inside of Brad's country estate. He had bought it when we first started dating. It was a definite fixer-upper. You wouldn't know it now. The place looked great.

The kitchen had nice Bella hardwood floors. New, modern, oak cabinets replaced the old, white, wooden ones. Beautiful, sage green, high-definition countertops replaced the funky, outdated orange. Brad had recently painted the walls in the kitchen a pale yellow. His curtains actually matched his rug. I know, right? I was impressed. You don't see that every day. Brad had put a lot of time and money into the old house.

I walked through to the living room. That's where I found Brad sitting on his brand-new, brown, leather sofa. Next to him sat a second beer.

"You are such a shit, Brad."

"What? You think I don't know how you are, Payton. We dated for over a year. I knew I could lure you in here with a beer."

"Well, I prefer to remember it as we dated over a year ago."

"Congrats, Payton. You win round one. Now sit down and drink your beer."

"Ok," I said. "I call a truce for the next twenty minutes. Agreed?"

"Agreed," he said, staring at his new HDTV tuned into ESPN.

I sat awkwardly rigid at the far end of the couch. I nervously took a swig of my beer.

"Chips?" he asked, shoving the bowl down the coffee table in my direction.

"Sure," I said, to be cordial. I took a large handful. I was hungry. "So the house looks nice."

"Thanks. Julie helped me pick out all the stuff in the kitchen."

Ugh! Burn! I hated to admit it, but that one stung a little

bit. Maybe it stung a lot. This was supposed to be our fixer-upper. "Where is the magnificent Julie?"

"She is at the shooting range."

I was shocked. "Julie has a gun?"

"Yeah, she has this whole other side to her that I never would have expected. I used to think she was just one of your chunky, nerdy friends. Who knew that under that baby fat there was a smokin' hot kindergarten teacher with a gun?"

"Ugh." Plus an eye roll. "Well, I hope she doesn't accidentally shoot the kids who can't color within the lines," I said with a super sassy tone.

"Very funny, Payton. Sounds like someone is jealous?"

"Sounds like someone needs to get over himself. I have moved on. I have a boyfriend now."

"That is what I wanted to talk to you about, your boyfriend, Dylan."

"You want to talk to me about Dylan? Thank God. I thought you had me come over here because you wanted to have sex with me."

"Sex with you?" Brad laughed. "Sounds like someone needs to get over herself." Brad paused. "Wait a minute. You came in here." Brad looked at me and laughed again. There was an awkward silence. Record-breaking sexual tension filled the air.

"Don't flatter yourself, Brad. I just want my purse back." I slammed the rest of my beer attempting to put out the fire that was smoldering. My phone rang. It was Teagan. I was saved by her obnoxious ringtone. I walked away from Brad to get some privacy. I moved down the hall so that Brad couldn't hear our conversation.

"Did you find Amber yet?" asked Teagan desperately.

"No. Tim is over at Rod's right now looking for her."

"Where are you?"

"I'm at Brad's getting my purse back."

"How did Brad get your purse last night? You left with Dylan, right? I'm confused."

"It's a long story. I will call you as soon as I hear from Tim.

He should let me know something soon."

"Payton, I am freaking out. I cannot just sit here and wait."

"I know. I'm freaked out too. We need to keep it together for Amber."

"As soon as Lisa gets back from her run, we are heading to River Bend."

"Whatever you do, do not go to Rod's house. Go to my house and wait. I will call you as soon as I hear something."

"Ok, sounds good." She disconnected.

I walked back down the hall towards the kitchen. While I passed by one of the closed doors, I heard a voice. "Hello, is someone there?" There was no answer from behind the door. "Hey, Brad, is there someone else here?" I heard the voice again. It was coming from behind the closed door of Brad's office.

I slowly turned the knob, pushed the door open, and turned on the light. Brad's office was a small ten by twelve foot room. Inside, I found a small desk, two couches against adjacent walls, and a television in the corner. I heard the voice again. It was coming from the TV.

"Warlock, Warlock, come in, Warlock. Ready for a re-match, ass face?"

I stood in front of the TV with my mouth hanging open. I was speechless.

Brad burst into the room. "Payton, what are you doing in here? This is my private office."

I turned and faced Brad. "You're Warlock?" I pulled Brad's stupid stocking hat off his head before he could stop me. I was speechless again because he wasn't bald.

"What is your problem?" demanded Brad, obviously upset that I invaded his privacy.

"You're Warlock, the creepy old guy the kids play against."

"No, I'm not. It's an online game. You can hear all of the gamers talk to each other. And what did you mean by creepy old man? I'm not creepy, or old."

"Oh. Sorry. My bad. Since when do you play video games?"

"What? The whole force has been over to play. Even my

dad plays with us. We're cops. We like to shoot stuff. Is that such a big secret?"

"No. I guess not."

"But seriously, don't tell anyone. We have a serve and protect image to uphold around town."

"Ok. Ok. Your secret is safe with me." I walked out of the room. It was time to turn my focus back to something that actually mattered. "Where is your police scanner? I haven't heard it since I got here."

Brad followed me out of the office, closing the door. "The scanner is still in the kitchen. I don't turn it on when I am off duty. I can't relax and get away from 'the job' if I have it on."

"But what if you miss an important emergency?" I walked into the kitchen. The scanner was on the counter next to the coffee maker. The scanner squawked when I turned it on.

"Be advised. I'm taking my supper break. I'll be back on duty at 17:30," stated the officer.

"Roger that," answered the dispatcher.

Brad followed me into the kitchen. He leaned on the counter next to the stove, his arms crossing his chest. I was in another kitchen with Brad. Déjà vu was in the air.

"What are you up to, Payton?"

"Nothing. Didn't you want to talk to me about Dylan?" I said nervously, to change the subject.

"Yes, I do. I don't think he's the right one for you."

"Why is that?"

"For one, he stole a car."

"He borrowed it from his ex-girlfriend. She reported it stolen to get back at him. Besides, she decided to drop the charges, so it doesn't count." I said in his defense.

"That doesn't make it any better. Sounds like a bunch of unnecessary drama to me."

"Well, if you ask me, I think Julie has been acting odd lately. Maybe she isn't the right one for you either."

"How so?" Brad raised an eyebrow. He was obviously interested in my opinion.

"Besides her sudden gun toting makeover, she snuck into

the restaurant once and my house twice. All three times, she scared the hell out of me, Brad. At the restaurant, she appeared out of nowhere with a knife in her hand, acting like a PMSing psycho. Then, without any warning, she just disappeared. Who does that?"

"Relax, Payton. It's not like she was trying to kill you. If she wanted to do that, she would have just shot you. She was just trying to tell you about our relationship."

"That doesn't make her weird behavior any better. It was creepy, I tell you. She has definitely changed."

"Payton, she was just having some fun with you. She knows how easy it is to scare you. Wait. Let me rephrase that. Everyone knows how easy it is to scare you."

"Haha, you are hilarious. Well, you won't think this is very funny. I never told anyone this before. I wouldn't have found Streak's body that morning if Julie wouldn't have shown up unannounced, practically demanding that we go for a walk. It was her idea to go down by the river."

Brad took a few steps closer towards me. He put one hand on the counter and his other hand on his hip in a confrontational manner. "Are you suggesting that Julie had something to do with what happened to that boy?"

"You have to admit that it is a really weird coincidence."

"Not as weird as your boyfriend showing up in town around the time we started finding boys floating in the river."

"So we're picking sides now?"

"I am just defending Julie."

"And I am just defending Dylan. It can't be Dylan anyway. He almost died last night. Lily and I found him on the bank of Half Moon Lake this morning. If the lake wasn't still frozen he would have drowned."

"He almost died. That's convenient," scoffed Brad.

"Convenient? What do you mean by that?"

"It is basic police 101. Becoming a victim is the oldest trick in the book to hide your guilt."

"It's not Dylan. Someone left a note in Dylan's pocket addressed to me."

Brad raised his voice. "You never told me this. Why didn't you tell me about the note? What else aren't you telling me? And for the record, Dylan could have easily written that note himself."

"Brad, give it a rest. It's not Dylan. Tim and I are convinced that Rod Huntley and Kurt Meriwether are responsible for what is going on. I think your dad is looking at Rod as well. I saw him with Rod's file yesterday."

"That's crazy. My dad would have said something to me about it. Besides, Rod and Kurt are wannabe gangsters, not serial killers. They don't fit the profile. You need evidence against them."

"I have evidence." My phone rang. It was a number I didn't recognize, so I ignored it. "First of all, it has been brought to my attention that Hood Rat—the kid that died behind the college—and Streak—the kid found in my back yard—both worked for Huntley and Meriwether. Maybe they saw or did something Huntley didn't like."

Brad jumped up on the counter and took a seat.

"Ok, this should be good. What else do you have for proof? Convince me. Why would they try to kill Dylan?"

"Maybe they decided to get rid of him because of his cooking skills. Rod and Kurt are trying to turn their struggling topless bar into a legit restaurant. Dylan was their competition, so they tried to kill him."

"That's a stupid theory. You don't kill the competition. You hire them to work in your restaurant."

"Ok, smart guy. What do you think of this? Amber saw Rod and Kurt watching us through the window of Smiley's last night. Now she is missing."

"Are you serious? Payton for future reference, lead with the important facts and keep the bull shit to yourself."

"For future reference, it's not bull shit. I was building my case against them." I paused briefly before spilling the beans. "Would this be a good time, or a bad time, to tell you that Tim is over at Rod's right now looking for Amber?"

Brad jumped down from the counter.

"What? Tim isn't on duty."

"I know. He did it as a personal favor for me."

Brad's eyes bulged out of their sockets with anger. "He went over there without back up? Why would you drag Tim into this? How long ago was that?"

"It was just before I came over here. I only told you because he should have gotten back to me by now."

"Payton, Damn, #@$#&*! You have really done it this time. Mother*@$#$$%& on a biscuit. For Crissake! Bleeeeeep!"

Brad was beyond angry with me. He was such a control freak.

"Jeez, Brad. Calm down. It's all good. Everything will be fine." My phone rang again. It was the same number as last time. Under the circumstances, I decided to answer it. "Hello?"

"Payton," cried Amber with desperation in her voice.

"Oh my God, Amber. Are you ok? Where are you?"

Brad stopped cursing me out long enough to listen to our conversation.

"You have to help me. I am locked in a bathroom at your creepy neighbor's house."

"Is Tim there with you?" I asked.

"I don't know. Please send help right away. I heard gun shots."

"Gun shots?" I yelled. Panic ripped through my body.

Brad scrambled around his kitchen with great precision. He grabbed his gun and holster that hung on the back of a kitchen chair while he dialed the station for back up.

"Amber, stay in the bathroom. Brad and I will be right there."

She didn't answer me. On the other end of the line, I heard a loud pop that sounded like a gunshot. The line went dead.

"Amber? Amber?" I turned to Brad. "She's not answering me. We need to get over to Rod's ASAP."

"There is no we, Payton. I am going to Rod's. You are staying here."

"The hell I am." I headed for the door.

223

Brad grabbed me around the waist, pulling me back into the kitchen. I put up a solid fight of flailing slaps and punches. Brad was too strong for me. He pulled me over to the refrigerator and handcuffed me to the stainless steel handle.

"What is it with you cops and your handcuffs?" I had another quick flashback of Tim, Dylan, and I in the ER. It was not a good memory.

Brad pointed his index finger just inches from my nose, a trait he undoubtedly inherited from his father. "You stay here, and you stay out of trouble. I will deal with you when I get back."

"I can't guarantee I'll be here," I said super sassy.

Brad shook his finger at me and grimaced under his breath.

"Damn it, Brad. I need to come with you," I begged. "I'm the one who sent Tim over there. This is all my fault. I need to try to fix it."

"Yes, it is your fault. So stay put. Do not make this any worse."

"What if I have to pee? You know I can't hold my beer."

Brad reached into one of the lower cabinets in the kitchen and pulled out an empty plastic ice cream bucket. He sat the bucket down on the counter in front of me. "There you go, sweet cheeks. Don't get any on my new hardwood floor."

"Brad, you asshole."

"What do you mean? I am being a fabulous host. If you get hungry, make yourself a sandwich," he said with a smile. "Help yourself to another beer, if you want."

I glared at him. He knew I was not happy.

"I almost forgot." Brad reached in the microwave and pulled out Prada number two. He tossed it to me. It landed at my feet.

"Thanks," I said, with a corrosive tone. I quickly rummaged through the purse with one hand looking for the necklace. It was gone and so was my candy bar. "Shit!"

"Something wrong?"

"Brad, were you in my purse?"

"Why? Is something missing?"

I looked at him, trying to decipher his grin. Which did he have? To me, it looked like a chocolate eating grin, nothing more. There wasn't time, and I wasn't about to tell him about the missing necklace. I went with the smart-ass approach to answer his question. "Yeah, someone ate my Snickers." That still didn't answer the big question. Where the hell was the necklace?

"Bummer," he said. "Sucks for you."

"You are such a dick, Brad," I said as he walked away.

"Well, I am my father's son." He stopped by the door. Brad turned to look at me. "You know all of this is because I still care about what happens to you."

Our eyes met. I knew he meant it. "Shut up, already, would ya. Go save Tim and Amber," I said, giving in. Don't get me wrong. I was still plenty pissed off. He just has a way of wearing down the edges of my fury.

He closed the door behind him as he exited the house. I quickly started working on my escape plan. I was going to Rod's. No one was going to stop me. Lucky for me, I knew exactly where Brad kept his spare handcuff key and his spare gun. I opened up the refrigerator door. Bingo. Brad still kept them in the veggie drawer in a box of fake organic spinach. Every now and then, even I catch an incredible break and things go my way. This time was it fate or another test? I would surely find out soon.

I took off the handcuffs. Then I made myself a sandwich to go. It was more like a piece of ham and cheese shoved into a piece of stale bread. Don't judge me, but I took a roadie too. Like I said, I never turn down a free beer. I stuck Brad's spare gun in my wasteband and headed out the door. There was a party at Rod's house, and I was fashionably late.

. . .

It is moving day today, so I suggest you get a move on. Some of your friends have made the cut, while the others are about to fall out of the cart on the next sharp turn. Tuck and roll, Payton, lives depend on it.

The foursome and I are pushing you to step up your game. Are you going to pick up the pace, or do you mind if I play through?

CHAPTER TWENTY-EIGHT

It will come as no surprise that I exceeded the speed limit all the way to Rod's house. Don't worry. There were no laws broken. Everyone in the Northwoods knows that the speed limit doesn't really apply on the back roads, especially if you are having a personal emergency. I also drove occasionally with one knee while I ate my sandwich and drank my beer. I believe that too is legal in Wisconsin. I will have to check the Backwoods Driving Handbook and get back to you on that.

When I pulled up to Rod's, I parked along the road, attempting to be stealthy. I was not the only one. I immediately recognized Lisa's SUV and Lily's VW Bug parked by the bushes. Their cars were present. Their owners were not. Where the heck were the girls? I told them not to come here. Maybe Rod and Kurt kidnapped them too. As I walked by their cars, I drew little hearts in the dirt of their back windows. Please let them be all right.

The sun had set. Visibility was at a minimum. I found myself sneaking around in the shadows of the pine trees. The slivered moon held the night on the verge of total darkness. Leafless trees and bushes concealed my presence as I made my way around to the back of Rod's house. From my position in the twigs, I could see Brad, Rex, Matt, and the Chief huddled next to the squad cars in the driveway. They obviously hadn't worked through their plan of attack yet. I was nervous. There was no sign of Tim. He must still be inside.

Approximately thirty feet to my left, I heard a few twigs snap. I held perfectly still behind a thick tree trunk. They passed within ten feet of me without noticing I was there. It was Teagan and Lisa. I was definitely pissed. Teagan hadn't listened to me, but I was relieved that they were safe. That still left unanswered questions. What were they doing here? Where was Lily? Was Luke with her? I didn't move from my spot and listened in silence.

"What do we do now? We can't find her anywhere," whispered Lisa.

"We should leave before someone sees us. Things are about to get ugly. Let's go back to Payton's and wait," said Teagan.

"Ok. We can watch everything unfold from the telescope in her parents' bedroom," said Lisa.

"Good idea," said Teagan.

Every muscle in my body held fast. If the girls knew I was here, they might give away my location to Brad and the boys. I continued acting like a tree until the girls were safely to Lisa's SUV. There were a few seconds of eerie silence. I was about to step out from behind the tree when I heard the snow crunch in the darkness. I was not alone. Someone else was out here.

My eyes darted and followed the movement on the other side of the yard. I saw the reflection of the moonlight dance across his head. It was my buddy, the Bald-headed Man.

He moved towards the backside of the house. As soon as he disappeared around the corner, I followed. What was he doing here? I knew he was mixed up in this mess somehow. For all I knew, he could be the mastermind behind all of it.

The landscaping gods were on my side today. The backyard had enough established trees and scrub covered berms for me to perfect my skills. I crawled, rolled, and dove my way across the yard to the corner of the house. I managed to do so without giving myself a Smith and Wesson wedgie. My newfound stealth and agility gave me the self-esteem boost I needed to think I could actually pull off this dangerous mission.

I stood up against the siding like a secret agent. Then I rolled around the corner of the house ready to claim my Double-O status. I was basking in my own glory until I found myself face to face with Rod Huntley. Before I could scream for help, he grabbed me and pulled me inside the sliding glass door of his walkout basement. During the struggle, I heard the metal on stone clank of Brad's spare gun. It had landed on the brick patio outside. I was now unarmed, facing Rod alone. The Bald-headed Man had vanished.

"I warned you," said Rod. "You bitches couldn't stay out of my business."

I was temporarily speechless. He was absolutely right. He had warned me. And once again, I hadn't listened. Rod held on-to me tight in the dimly lit basement. His left arm was wrapped around my waist. I knew better than to try to squirm or run away because his actual gun was digging into my hip. Rod would surely use it if I tried anything.

A small amount of moon light came in through the patio door and basement windows. After my eyes adjusted, I could see an outline of a body face down next to the couch. It was dark, but I could still tell it was one of my friends by what she was wearing. Her long, dark coat gave away her identity. It was Lily. She wasn't moving.

"Oh my God, is she dead?" I asked.

"How should I know?" snapped Rod.

I tried to go to her. Rod pulled me back. My attention shifted to the unmistakable sound of doors being kicked in upstairs. The police officers' shouts echoed in the darkness as they made their way through the house.

"Clear."

"Clear."

"Clear."

The echoed shouts became louder. It was obvious to Rod and I that the men in blue were at the top of the stairs. They were right behind the closed basement door. Rod removed the gun from my side. He pulled me closer, pressing the barrel against my right temple. I just went from a Double-O status reject to a human shield.

One of the officers kicked in the basement door. The light flicked on. I closed my eyes and prayed. A gun battle was about to begin. Footsteps rushed down the stairs.

"Wait! Don't shoot," I screamed.

"Payton? Is that you?" asked Brad, obviously shocked to see me. "How the hell did you get here? You were handcuffed to my refrigerator."

"It's kind of a long story. How about we discuss it after a nice game of Splinter Cell . . . or COD . . . or . . . Zero Dark Thirty? Do you boys understand the words that are coming out of my mouth?" I hoped they picked up on my less than subtle video game reference to shoot the bastard.

"Shut up, you stupid bitch," said Rod.

Rod cocked his gun. It wasn't looking good for me. I heard a noise to my right. Out of the corner of my eye, I saw the shine of his bald head by the patio door. Then I heard and felt the blast of the gunshot. The blast carried Rod and I backward into the couch. Before I could blink, there were four cops and four guns in my face.

I looked down. Brains and blood covered my shirt and pants. "That's not mine, right?" I asked, feeling my head for holes. When I looked over at Rod, he didn't look so good with half of his face missing. "Nice shot," I said.

"What do you mean?" asked the Chief. "I was aiming at you."

I laughed.

He didn't.

I let the Chief have his moment of glory, but I knew the truth. The Bald-headed Man had just saved my life. And for that very reason, I let him escape into the darkness. I was confused, unsure of his motives. Was he friend, or foe?

Brad and the boys were still in their super serious cop search mode. Once they saw that Rod was no longer a threat, they moved on.

"What is going on?" I asked Brad.

"We haven't found Kurt yet. He might still be in the house, so stay put," said Brad, with extreme seriousness.

"Have you found Tim or Amber yet?" I whispered.

"No," he mouthed back, shaking his head.

"Can I at least check on Lily?"

"Yes. Then stay put and stay down."

Brad and the boys moved out the recreation room. They slowly began searching down the hall. A chunk of Rod's brain was on my thigh, so I flicked it off with my hand. I moved to Lily's side and rolled her over. She had a gash on her head where someone had pistol whipped her. I checked her for a pulse. Lily was unconscious, but she was still breathing. That was the good news. The bad news was that when I checked her for a pulse, I found the missing key around her neck.

I removed the key from Lily's neck. Then I placed it around mine. The key would be safe for now tucked behind my sweater and turtleneck. I gave Lily a firm nudge, then a shake, trying to revive her. She had questions to answer. I needed to know what side she was on.

Lily's eyes opened slowly. "Ow, my head hurts."

She reached up and felt her forehead. Our eyes met. She looked surprised to see me. "Payton, where are we?"

"You don't know?" I was puzzled. Her car was parked outside.

"No." She shook her head. "The last thing I remember, I was hiding in the bushes from the Bald Guy. I think someone hit me from behind when I made a run for my car. Now, I am here with you."

"Well, to save on time, I will give you the highlight reel version of what you missed. First, we are in Rod's basement. Second, Rod is dead. Third, the police are here looking for Tim, Amber, and Kurt who are still missing. Any questions?"

Lily didn't get a chance to answer me. We heard Rex on his police radio calling dispatch. "I repeat—we have a female down in the bathroom from an apparent gunshot wound. We are requesting an ambulance to the Huntley residence at 1313 River View Circle."

. . .

You thought this was going to be an easy up and down. Think again. There are holes in your friends and their alibis. Watch out. There will be another hole in one before I am done. Four!

CHAPTER TWENTY-NINE

Lily and I ran to the doorway of the bathroom. We tried to push our way inside. Brad pulled us both back. It was an intense scene. Amber was lying on the floor of the bathroom in a pool of blood with a gunshot wound to her shoulder area. Lily and I stood in the doorway gawking. We watched the Chief and Matt as they checked her for a pulse.

I ran my fingers over the bullet holes in the bathroom door. Was this a stray bullet or a blindsided ambush? My jaw dropped. Not because of the sight of Amber lying on the floor bleeding, but because of what was lying next to her. It was a periwinkle purse and pump. The shoe was an exact match to the one found in the area of Streak's body.

Brad looked at me. "I told you to stay put. Do you ever do as you are told?" he asked.

"That's a rhetorical question, right?" He didn't answer me.

From down the hall, Rex shouted, "Officer down!"

Lily gave me the look. "Go. I will stay with Amber," she said.

Brad didn't try to stop me. Instead, we both raced down the hall. Rex found Tim in a storage room filled with cardboard boxes. No doubt filled with stolen merchandise, not

Christmas decorations. We both stopped dead in our tracks.

Tim sat on the cement floor in a pool of his own blood. His head and torso leaned against a stack of boxes. Tim's eyes were open. He had taken two to the chest and one in the thigh. Brad and I ran to his side.

Brad ripped open Tim's shirt. Tim was a smart cop. He wore his vest today. We both breathed a sigh of relief. Two bullets lodged in his vest. The other entered his leg. Tim had taken off his belt, using it as a tourniquet. He attempted to stop the bleeding.

Tim looked at me mysteriously. He couldn't help but notice the abundance of blood spatter on my face, hair, and clothes. "Payton, you look like hell," whimpered Tim.

"You should see the other guy. Rod is half the man he used to be."

Tim tried to chuckle at my joke. He was just too weak. Tim had lost a dangerous amount of blood. Tim closed his eyes out of sheer exhaustion.

"Hang on buddy. The ambulance is on its way," said Rex.

"Do you think we should call a Priest or a Rabbi?" I whispered to Brad.

"I don't know. Maybe?" Brad whispered back. "What religion is he?"

"I don't know. Lutheran?" I whispered back.

"Yeah, he looks Lutheran," added Rex.

Tim's eyes opened. "Just in case I'm not dying, could someone go find some towels to help stop the bleeding?"

"I'll go." I volunteered. I ran down the hall to the bathroom. There was no sign of Lily anywhere. Matt and the Chief were tending to Amber. They had already mastered the art of EMTism. Matt was applying pressure to her wounded shoulder. The Chief was busy asking her questions. I had a few questions for her. Like who shot you? And where the heck is Crystal? The questions would have to wait. I had more pressing matters. I grabbed some towels from the bathroom cupboard and ran back to the storeroom at the end of the hall.

"How is he?" I asked, handing the towels to Brad.

"He is in and out of consciousness," said Rex.

I knelt at Tim's side. "Did either of you ask him what happened?"

"Tim told us that Kurt shot him," said Brad. "Tim fired back and is sure that he hit Kurt. I just put out an A.P.B. on Kurt and his car."

"Are you sure Kurt is gone?"

"Payton, we secured the whole house," said Brad. "He's not here."

One of the large boxes behind us started moving. Brad shoved me to the ground, landing on top of me. Brad, Tim, and Rex simultaneously drew their weapons on reflex.

"Come out with your hands up," demanded Brad.

"Don't shoot. Brad it's me," said a familiar girl's voice. The flaps of the lid opened. She stood up with her hands in the air. The boys lowered their guns. It was Julie, Brad's fiancée.

"Julie, what the hell are you doing here?" asked Brad.

Julie immediately started crying. "I don't know. I was at the range shooting targets. Someone hit me on the head. I just woke up now."

I pulled myself to my feet. "That's convenient," I muttered under my breath.

"Payton, knock it off," said Brad. He went over to console her and help her out of the box.

Eye roll, plus I added head shakes this time. Julie was milking the damsel in distress a little too well.

I went over to Tim and helped Rex apply pressure to his wound again. He winced. The ambulance crew wheeled a gurney into the storeroom. They took over our job. The EMTs quickly checked his vitals, started an IV, and loaded him on the gurney. At the moment, Tim was conscious.

I took Tim's hand in mine. "Thanks for saving my friends," I told him.

"You were right about Rod and Kurt, Payton. You are one heck of a detective. Maybe the Chief should put you on the payroll."

"Good one, Tim, but I won't hold my breath."

The EMTs started wheeling Tim out of the storeroom.

"Wait," Tim insisted. He held up his hand. "I have something for Payton."

The ambulance crew stopped at the doorway. Tim reached under the blanket. He pulled out a black handled stiletto knife and handed it to me.

"Payton, you get into more trouble than anyone I have ever met. The Chief would have my badge if I gave you my gun. I hope this knife will help keep you safe when I am not around."

"Aw, thanks, Tim. That is so sweet and so disturbing that you think I need to be armed. I promise to have it with me every day."

"Don't forget, you still owe me a sandwich." Tim smiled at me. Then he closed his eyes.

"We need to move people," said one of the EMTs. "His blood pressure is dropping." They swiftly wheeled Tim away.

Brad had his arm around Julie. They walked over to me. "Do you think Tim will be ok?" I asked Brad. "He didn't look so great."

"Sure. They will dig the bullet out and pump him full of blood. He will be fine."

"That's good, because I kind of feel responsible."

Brad could have started in on me, but he didn't. "What's the deal with you and Tim? You two are getting chummy."

"What? Don't be weird, Brad. We are just friends."

"Ok. Sorry, I asked."

When we got outside to the garage, Tim's ambulance pulled out of the driveway. The lights were on and the siren was blaring. They were loading Amber and Lily into the other ambulance. I ran over to the second ambulance as they were closing the doors. I had so many questions to ask my friends.

"Wait. I'm riding with," I demanded.

"Are you family?" asked the female EMT.

"No. They're my friends."

"Sorry, only family." She slammed the door in my face. I attempted to open the door again. Brad stopped me. The ambulance pulled away.

"Haven't you had enough for one day, Payton?" said Brad.

"I just wanted to go to the hospital with my friends."

"They'll be fine. They're in good hands. Do me and everyone else a favor. Go home, lock your doors, and stay put."

"By myself? Are you crazy? Kurt is still out there somewhere."

"Payton, I'm sure he left town as fast as he could. Kurt did the unthinkable tonight when he shot a police officer. Every cop in the county is looking for him. My dad has the State Troopers setting up roadblocks for him and his car. I'm sure we will have him behind bars within the hour."

"I hate to break it to you, Brad, but you boys don't have a clue on how to find Kurt." I pointed to the garage behind us. "Isn't that Kurt's Cadillac neatly parked next to Rod's red Chevy pickup?"

"Oh, shit. How did we miss that?" Brad left Julie's side to go talk to his father. I couldn't hear what was being said. The Chief did not look happy.

I turned to Julie. I wasn't about to admit to her that I was scared after the stupid pranks she had played on me. I would never give her the satisfaction. Hell, I'm not sure how much I even trusted her at the moment. Keeping your friends close and your enemies closer, actually applies here. I was also desperate for companionship on my way home. That safety in numbers thing is also a good idea. Kurt still had me spooked. It was time to put on a brave face. "I'm about to leave. Do you want me to drop you off at home or at the hospital?"

"No, thanks. I'm good. I called my mom. She should be here soon."

"Ok," I said. "I just thought I would ask."

Julie turned and walked back to Brad when she saw Teagan and Lisa running up the driveway. They were out of breath. The two of them cringed when they saw me covered in blood, but they never asked why. Apparently, it was now the norm for me to be drenched in bodily fluids.

"Payton, did they find Amber?" asked Teagan. "We saw all the lights and sirens from across the river."

"We found Amber downstairs with a gunshot wound to her shoulder area. She is on her way to the hospital."

"Is she ok?" asked Lisa.

"Oh God, who shot her?" asked Teagan.

"I don't know for sure. I haven't talked to her yet. We think it was Kurt."

"Come on, Payton. We need to get to the hospital," said Lisa. The girls started jogging back down the driveway in the dark to Lisa's SUV.

"Can you guys wait for me? I need to go home and change clothes first."

"We'll meet you there," Teagan shouted back.

"You guys be careful. Kurt is still on the loose. He is armed and dangerous."

Their jog to Lisa's SUV turned into a flailing, flat-out sprint for their lives. They were not the only ones who were scared shitless. The thought of walking to my car alone right now made my skin crawl. As the girls drove away, I realized that I should have insisted that I go with them.

I turned to walk back up to the garage to ask Brad to walk me to my car. He was too busy playing kissy-face with Julie. Yuck, permanent eye roll. Matt was on his police radio arguing with dispatch. Rex was busy helping the coroner with the bag and tag paper work. That left the Chief. He was busy standing with his hands on his hips scowling at me. I decided at this moment that I would rather die, than listen to what the Chief had to say to me. I headed down the long, dark driveway alone. Wait a second. I have Tim's knife. I can totally do this, right?

I held the knife awkwardly in my hand, blade out, trying to be ready for anything. My slow steady steps echoed in the cold, crisp night air. With every leaf that blew, with every twig that snapped in the woods, I twitched and jumped with fear like a crazed cat. My nerves and adrenaline pushed me forward.

The Escape was in sight, yet it seemed like it was parked so far away from the house. My earlier attempt to be stealthy could have just put my life in danger. Was Kurt hiding out there in the woods somewhere waiting for me to be alone?

When I turned to run back to the safety of Rod's house, I saw a car on the road turn its lights on. It was moving towards me. I changed direction. I ran to my Escape. As I tried to unlock my car door, my keys fumbled in my hands imitating every horror movie ever made. The keys and knife slipped out of my hand and hit the pavement. I had no time to pick them up. I started punching in my five-digit access code when I noticed that my car door was already unlocked. I climbed inside and swiftly slammed the door shut.

The burgundy sedan stopped even with my car. My heart raced when I heard their car doors open. I tried to duck down below the steering wheel. They knocked on the glass. I reached up and flicked the door lock. The clunk echoed in the night air. I held my breath. I just wanted them to go away. They knocked on the glass again.

"Hey, Payton. Open up. It's us."

That voice, I recognized it. I sat upright. My own stupidity turned my face red. I rolled down my window to find six bald-headed boys and one hairy Wolfman staring back at me.

"Bad night?" ask Chameleon.

"Bad week," I replied. "What are you boys doing here?"

"We heard it on the police scanner in my car," said Blond Ambition.

"We came to watch," said The Singe, taking a bite of pizza.

"You guys have pizza?"

"We sure do, Payton," said Feed Bag. "We have meat lovers and pepperoni."

"Yeah, but we told you to get two cheese pizzas," said Blond Ambition, jabbing at his incompetence.

"I couldn't help it. I was hungry," said Feed Bag. He handed me a slice of meat lovers.

"We have beer too!" said Pump Up the Volume, loud enough for Brad and the boys to hear. He tossed one in my car.

"Thanks for the suds," I said, taking a huge bite of my pizza.

"I told you to put the beer in the trunk," said Wolfman, still trying to be the gatekeeper. "You're not supposed to bring beer to a crime scene, dumb ass."

"Blond Ambition wouldn't let me put the beer in the trunk," argued Fourteen as he played with his piece of meat lovers pizza. We all watched intently as he organized his meat into their separate groups before he took a bite.

I gave my head a few quick shakes and blinked my eyes, regaining my focus. "You boys should really go home. There's nothing else to see."

Chameleon bent down and picked up my knife and keys for me. "On the contrary, Payton, I think things are just getting started," he said. I watched him handle Tim's knife. It wasn't his first rodeo. He flipped it in the air, caught it, then pushed the retract button. The blade disappeared back into the handle.

"What do you mean by that?" I asked, taking my belongings back from his outstretched hand.

"Kurt Meriwether is still on the loose. I think there's more carnage to come," said Chameleon.

"I hope not. I've had just about all the carnage I can take for one day, thank you."

"Can we go now?" yelled Pump Up the Volume. "I gotta take a piss."

If there was ever a cue for me to leave, that was it. "You boys behave," I said as I pulled away. I grabbed the beer from the passenger seat and cracked it open. It was a Red Dog. Yummy.

On my way home, I caught a glimpse of myself in my rear-view mirror. My reflection was scary, bordering on undateable. Not as bad as the night of the Prada puke, but a definite runner up. A shower was the clear choice before I checked in on Dylan or went to the hospital to check on my friends. Later, my plan was to show up calm, cool, and collected.

. . .

I thought I was going to knock it in for an easy par. Now, there has to be a sudden death playoff because of your interference. I hear about everything that is going on Payton, so watch yourself.

CHAPTER THIRTY

I pulled up to my parents' house. It was like a lighthouse beacon in a storm. You could see it for miles. In their haste, Teagan and Lisa had left every light on in the entire house, and of course, the door unlocked. I guess it was better than coming home to a dark, spooky mansion. Just to be on the safe side, my new knife and I checked out every closet and under every bed for Kurt. The good news: I didn't find Kurt. The bad news: We have so many closets and beds, I wasted half an hour looking for him.

After my shower, I was squeaky clean and OSHA certified. I was no longer a biohazard or a disaster waiting to happen. Well, maybe that last one was a stretch. Anyhow, I felt revitalized and ready to take on the world. Before I left the house, I tried to check my phone for messages. I couldn't. It was completely dead. My car charger would have to suffice on my way into town.

When I stepped outside, I spotted a dark vehicle parked behind my Escape. My driver's door was open. Someone was crouched down digging under the dash. With my knife in hand, I walked around to the driver's side of my car. I pressed the raised silver button on the handle. The razor-sharp, silver blade slid straight out of the handle ready for action.

I quietly rolled around the back bumper of my SUV, ready to sneak up behind my visitor. Seriously, my bravery today continues to shock even me. At this point, it could have easily been Kurt or my Bald Friend. It wasn't. I was more than relieved. I was ecstatic. It was Dylan.

"Hey, I see you survived the wrath of Vivian."

He turned and looked at me with fire in his eyes. "Where is my book, Payton?" he yelled. "It's not where I left it."

Wow, I had never seen Dylan angry. "Relax. I hid the book just like you told me to. I put it—"

"No." He glanced down at the knife in my hand. "Don't tell me. You just hang on to it. It's better if I don't know where it is," he said in a calmer voice. "Don't tell anyone you have it."

I pressed the silver button. The blade retracted into the handle. I placed the knife back in my pocket. "What's going on? You are not making any sense."

"Just trust me. I was never here." He turned away from me. Dylan started walking back to the dark sedan.

"Wait. Where are you going? Do you want to come to the hospital with me to see my friends?"

He didn't turn around to look at me. He stopped, staring into the darkness. "I have to go." He continued on to the sedan.

"What about tomorrow?" I caught up to Dylan, walking behind him.

"That's not going to work for me," he said in an emotionless tone.

"What about the day after tomorrow?" I pleaded.

"That's no good for me either." He opened up the car door.

I stood directly behind him. "So when is it going to work, Dylan?"

He didn't turn around. "Payton, it's not safe for us to be around each other."

"But it's almost over." I could feel a tear forming in the corner of my eye.

"Forget you know me." Dylan slid behind the wheel of the sedan.

I stood next to the driver's door. "Are you breaking up with me?"

Dylan still wouldn't look at me. He started the engine. He grabbed the door handle to pull it closed. I jerked the door back open. He glanced up at me out of reflex.

"Talk to me, Dylan. Tell me what is going on," I demanded. "You can't just leave."

Dylan manned up. He continued to look me in the eye as he ripped my heart in two. "Look, Payton, I don't know how to make this any clearer. So here it goes—It's not you—it's me. Ok? This you and me thing—it's not going to happen—so just drop it and leave it alone."

I could see the pain in his eyes. His eyes said one thing and his words another. I reached out to touch him.

He pushed my hand away. The tear rolled down my cheek.

"This time, I can't drag you into my wake of destruction," he said. Dylan looked away. "I'm sorry. I need to go." He reached out and grabbed the door handle. I took a step back as the door swung to close. "I don't want us to die, Payton." The door clicked shut. He threw the sedan into reverse. Dylan turned around in the driveway and drove out of my life.

I ran halfway down the driveway after his car. "Stop! Please! I don't want to lose you, Dylan," I screamed at his taillights as they disappeared into the darkness. I couldn't blame him for feeling that way. I didn't want to die either. But now, what did I have to live for? I loved him. I really loved him.

. . .

He really got a hold of that one. What incredibly stupid thing is Payton going to do to repair this devastating divot?

. . .

The hospital was about six miles away. The snow fell fast and heavy as I made my way into town. I took a big swig from my bottle of wine. This was not a celebratory Chardonnay. It was more like my life is a puddle of piss Pinot Grigio. I wiped back my tears with one of my hand-knitted mittens from my grandma. Then I dialed Teagan to let her know I was on my way.

"Hi, how is everyone?" I whimpered.

"There isn't any new news yet. Tim and Amber are still in surgery," said Teagan.

"That's nice." I started blubbering like a baby.

"Payton, what's wrong with you? Are you getting your period?"

"Dylan dumped me."

"Do you want to talk about it?"

"No," I whined. There was no holding it together. I sobbed harder. Teagan would understand. She was my friend.

"Are you drinking?"

"Yeah." I wiped my nose with my other mitten. I drank more wine.

"Good girl. Hurry up and get here."

I let out a weak, whimpering sigh. "Ok . . . I should be there in about five minutes." I used my mitten again to remove the tears from my cheeks. "How is Lily?"

"She's not here. She jumped out of the ambulance at the hospital and took off."

"Seriously? Where did she go?"

"Nobody knows. Just hurry up and get here. I am having a hard time keeping Lisa calm by myself. She has this crazy idea in her head that something horrible is going to happen."

I had the same darn feeling. This was far from over. "I will be there as fast as I can."

I hung up and dialed Lily. She didn't answer. I dialed Luke. He didn't answer. I left them both anxious call me back immediately voicemails. I glanced in my rearview mirror. There was a set of headlights behind me. I took a big guzzle of wine, continuing to glance in the mirror periodically until the car turned off. It was a relief that I wasn't being followed. I was just on edge, being paranoid.

I took another big pull off of my bottle of wine. Then I turned on the radio. Maybe some music would cheer me up. The radio blasted an oldies song. I quickly turned it down. I was expecting my hard rock radio station.

My hand was on the knob, scrolling up and down the dial. I was searching for some age appropriate blastable music when I heard a noise behind the back seat. My eyes rolled up to check out my rearview mirror again. I looked up just in time to see a person attempting to climb over the back seat from the cargo compartment. My foot pressed down hard on the gas pedal, which caused my traveling companion to fly backwards, slamming into the hatchback.

My Escape slid around the corner in the new fallen snow. I almost hit a mailbox. Their head popped up again. I slammed on my brakes. This time, the person flew over the rear seat and slammed into the back of my seat. They groaned with pain in their voice. My blood went cold. I knew that creepy groan. I was in for the ride of my life.

I stomped on the gas trying anything to stop him from getting his slimy paws on me. He groaned again and swore at me. My car drifted around the next corner on the icy snow. I was in control of my car until the back end slid off the road. I cranked the wheel trying to stop the car from going in the ditch. The tires bit on the snowy gravel. The car spun in a continual 360-degree virtual tour down the highway. By the time I could safely reach for the knife in my pocket, we had come to a sliding stop in the middle of the road. The cold, steel barrel of his gun rested against my skull.

"Drive," said a very distraught and wounded Kurt Meriwether.

He continued to sit on the edge of the backseat while holding his handgun to my temple. At this point, all I could do was follow his wishes. I took my foot off the brake. There was absolutely no traffic, not a single person to flick my lights at or flag down for help. I turned the car around, heading towards town.

"Where were you taking me?" asked Kurt impatiently.

"Last time I checked, you were the one with the gun barking out orders. Where would you like to go? I suggest the hospital. You don't look so good, Kurt."

"No shit, Payton. I've been shot. How did I get in your car?" he demanded.

"Don't look at me. I'm just as surprised as you are."

"Cut the crap, Payton. What is your game?"

"I don't play games, but you do. Why did you and Rod kill those boys? Why did you try to kill Dylan? He just broke up with me because of you, you know."

"I had nothing to do with that."

"Then how did you get my purse last night if you're not involved?"

"I found it."

"Bullshit!" I said. "Try again. I don't believe you."

"I don't give a rat's ass what you believe, bitch. I found it on the hood of my car this morning along with a note. The note said, 'Want 500 bucks? Bring the purse into the police station. Give it to the officer at the front desk.' "

"Who paid you the money?"

"I don't know. The money was in an envelope under my wiper blade when I came out of the cop shop."

"I don't understand. Why would you do it?"

"I'm not rich like you. I have bad habits to pay for."

"Trust me. Having money doesn't make your life any easier. People resent you for having it."

"Well, boo-frigging-hoo. Is the rich bitch having a bad day?" he asked, with great sarcasm.

I wrinkled up my nose at his comment. I was sure that he saw my reflection in the mirror because he sneered back. We came to a stop sign. I carefully pumped on the brakes because of the icy conditions. The brakes reacted at first, then my car slid past the stop sign. "Which way should I go?"

He motioned to the right. We were still heading in the direction of town. I was relieved. Maybe he wasn't going to leave me for dead in the middle of nowhere. This was excellent, seeing as how I still had questions for him. I held up the necklace for Kurt to see. "What can you tell me about this?"

"I've never seen that ugly hunk of junk before."

"Well, Kurt, I hate to tell you this, but it sounds to me like you were set up. Someone is using both of us as pawns in their sick little game. Welcome to the party."

"Who's doing this?"

"Don't ask me. I have no idea. You need to come to the hospital with me. I need you alive so you can tell the police your story. They will never believe me."

He pressed the barrel of the gun harder against my head. I was sure he was about to blow my brains out.

"No way. No cops."

"They already found your stolen merchandise in the storeroom. Do you really want to be charged with murder too?"

"Hell no. Didn't Rod explain everything to them?"

"No. He didn't get a chance to explain anything. Rod is dead."

"The freaking cops shot him?" he asked, severely agitated.

"No. It wasn't the cops. It was the big Bald-headed Man. Does he work for you?"

"No. He doesn't work for us. What kind of goddamn mess have you gotten us involved in, Payton? Because of you, Rod is dead, and I'm going to end up in prison."

"You are not blaming me for this. If you ask me, you and Rod had this coming for all of your criminal activity." I know it was not a smart thing to say with a gun pointed at my head. I didn't care anymore. I was pissed.

"Screw you, you spoiled rotten, uptight, little bitch," he snapped back at me.

"Really? I would tell you to go screw yourself Kurt, but knowing you, you probably already took care of business."

He smacked me on the side of my head with the barrel of the gun. "I have something else in mind," he said, with a sadistic grin. Kurt motioned with his gun hand. "Pull down the road up there to the right."

I was confused. "Don't you want to go to the hospital? You need medical attention."

"It's more of a flesh wound really," he said, checking the wound on his upper abdomen. "There is something I need to take care of first." He stroked my hair. "Then I will drive myself to the hospital."

I was no longer confused. Creepy Kurt was going to do unspeakable things to me, then kill me. Or he was going to kill me and then do unspeakable things to my dead body. Neither option worked for me. With the gun temporarily pointed away from my head, I slowly reached in my pocket for my knife. It was life or death . . . him or me. The old lady deep down inside chose me again.

I didn't slow down to make the turn. It was not my time to die. My right foot pushed down hard on the gas pedal. I pulled the knife out of my pocket. Without hesitation or aim, I hit the button and jabbed my hand backwards. The spring-loaded four-inch silver blade entered Kurt's chest cavity. His gun discharged. The bullet shattered the glass of the passenger window.

Out of nowhere, I felt a nudge that caused me to crossover to the other side of the road. I immediately lost control of my Escape. My foot stomped on the brake pedal. Nothing happened. The Escape left the highway, slamming into a grove of large pine trees. My face hit the air bag. Kurt's face hit the front windshield.

. . .

Mashed Potatoes! That was outstanding, but I think I hit that one a little fat.

You disappoint me, Payton. Kurt is in your car to test your survival skills. You are failing miserably, so I gave you a push in the right direction. You recover with a knife. Nice. Not bad, but we will have to work on your aim. The Pro tour should be on your bucket list.

As for Kurt, everyone knows he is a pig with impure thoughts. It would not take a rocket scientist to figure out what was on his mind. I would never let that happen to you. You will only play my games by my rules. Kurt will have to take a penalty stroke for his Mulligan. I am afraid he will not be making the cut to play the next round.

Fortunately, for me, the crash did not break Kurt's neck. I will get to break it for him. First, he will need to suffer. ☺

Too bad you are missing this, Payton. I am letting everyone else watch. There is blood everywhere. I have Kurt by the hair, and I am raking his neck across the edge of the broken windshield. Fixing Kurt's wicked slice is no longer an option. He is gurgling for mercy. Do not look away. This is what you want, right? The sadistic asshole dies an agonizing death—I thought so.

It is time to grant him his final wish. I grab him by the neck. There is the snap—and then the follow through. Magnificent. Right down the middle of the fairway. The crowd goes wild.

You are welcome. Now, get ready for the final round this evening. I call a game of skins.

CHAPTER THIRTY-ONE

Shhh! Quiet please. I am about to pull the pin.

. . .

My eyes opened from my crash induced catnap. I found myself lying in the snow next to my Escape. A thin blanket of snow covered me as I slept. From the amount of snow on my clothes, I would guess that I had been unconscious for about ten minutes.

I pulled myself to my feet. This was weird. I had zero recollection of leaving my car. Even more disturbing, I had no idea what I had done during that time.

When I looked down at my hands, I found my mittens drenched in blood. I pulled them off, dropping them in the snow. Instinctively, I felt my head and neck for cuts and abrasions. Where had all the blood come from? The process of checking myself over for bodily injuries was interrupted as soon as I saw him. When I glanced over at my car, I spotted Kurt's lifeless body on the hood. It didn't take me long to come to the awkward conclusion that it probably wasn't my blood on my mittens. I felt sick and confused.

I looked over at my blood-soaked mittens on the ground and then back at Kurt. I must be losing it. There was no way that I had done that to him even though I was battling for my life. Pushing that thought out of my brain, I moved towards my SUV to take a closer look at Kurt.

Because of my air bag and seat belt, I survived this horrific ordeal with only minor scrapes and bruises. Kurt didn't have the luxury of either. He ended up a mangled bloody mess on the hood of my car. Protruding bone, ripped flesh, it was disgusting. There was no need to check his pulse. His neck looked like a pulled pork sandwich. Yuck. He had bled out all over the hood of my Escape.

My knife stuck out of Kurt's right shoulder area just below his clavicle. With the handle of the knife in my hand, I closed my eyes and pulled. The sound I heard when the metal left the muscle was unforgettable. It will haunt my thoughts forever. I wiped the blade in the snow and then on my pant leg to remove Kurt's blood. I put the knife back in my pocket. I took a few seconds to thank Tim mentally for his gift.

I also paused for a second of silence for Kurt. Is it immoral of me to smirk on the inside just a little? After all, he was the one who tried to take our relationship to an unhealthy level. Then I punched him in the nose for wanting to violate me. He stared back at me with his gray fixed eyes. His mouth twisted from pain and agony. He had died a gruesome death. That was for sure. The creepy bastard got exactly what he deserved . . . and then some.

Not to sound disrespectful, but there was a bright side to all of this. It looked like my car was going to pull through. It still had a pulse. The tree caused a fair amount of damage to the grill and right headlight. From my limited motor head knowledge, it appeared to be drivable. I hoped it could hobble the mile and a half to the hospital with me behind the wheel and Kurt on the hood.

I located The Prada and my phone on the floor of the front seat of my car. My wallet and second bottle of wine were unscathed in my purse. However, my phone was toast, obviously smashed during the crash. I wanted to call Brad and the Chief, so I could gloat. The fact that I had located and single-handedly apprehended Kurt was phenomenal. Was it wrong of me to be proud of myself? I don't think so. Now I was even more determined to show them that I wasn't a helpless screw up. I could take care of myself.

I punctured the air bag with my knife. With a sawing motion, I removed it from the steering column. I slid behind the wheel. The Escape clunked into reverse. I revved the engine. When I backed out of the snow bank, Kurt nearly slid off the front of my hood. I stomped on the brake pedal. Nothing happened. Was it my bad luck again, or did someone tamper with my brakes?

I immediately grabbed the emergency brake lever and pulled up as hard as I could. My car jerked to a stop. Kurt slid back across the hood. This time, Kurt's size eleven shoes slammed into my face, giving me a bloody nose. This was impossible. I desperately needed a new plan. I closed my eyes and took a deep, cleansing breath. "I got this," I said to pump up my confidence.

While plugging my nose to stop the bleeding, I dug through the middle console of my car, hoping to spark an idea. Inside, I found an old pack of stale crackers, a pack of wet naps, an unused tampon, a corkscrew, a flashlight, and a set of bungee cords. Bingo. I could use all of these. "I seriously got this."

First things first, I unwrapped the tampon and shoved it up my nose to stop the bleeding. Second, I used the flashlight to knock off the loose remnants of glass from the windshield. Third, I used the wet naps to wipe the blood off my hands and the steering wheel. Next, I used the flashlight again to shine light on the front of my car. That way, I could see well enough to bungee Kurt's ass to the hood. Finally, I used the corkscrew to remove the cork on my last bottle of man my life sucks Moscato. I only wished I had some cheese to go with my stale crackers. I took a brief moment to toast my success and wash down the last of my snack. Then it was off to the hospital. Nothing was going to stop me from delivering Kurt to Brad and the Chief.

As you can imagine, my drive to the hospital was anything but uneventful. I had to drive fifteen in a forty-five. People honked and yelled at me until they saw Kurt strapped to my hood like a buck during deer camp. They blew by me on their phones, no doubt dialing 911. The sight of Kurt on my hood, and the bloody tampon string hanging out of my nose equally horrified my fellow travelers. I didn't care, 'cause I got this. I was in control of the situation.

My Escape glided up to the emergency entrance. If this wasn't an emergency, I don't know what would be. Two wheels of my car jumped the curb. I wrenched on the emergency brake just in time, abruptly stopping just short of creaming a big blue mailbox in front of the door.

When I reached down to grab my purse, I saw Kurt's gun on the floor of the passenger side. It must have slid out from under the seat when I stopped. I grabbed the Prada, threw the gun inside it, and automatically locked my car. As if anyone would try to steal it with a dead body strapped to the hood, but whatever.

On the way into the ER, I thought it was in my best interest to remove the used tampon from my nose. I threw it in the garbage receptacle by the entrance. Inside the ER waiting room, I found almost the entire River Bend Police Force: Brad, the Chief, Rex, Matt, Joe, Kiel, and Nick who just entered the room from down the hall. It made me wonder who was out protecting and serving our great city.

All the police officers had very sullen expressions on their faces. "Cheer up, guys. I found Kurt for you." I announced to the entire waiting room.

Brad walked over to me. "Where is he?"

I pointed out the window. "He's strapped to the hood of my car."

"This is no time for jokes, Payton," said the Chief. "Tim just died."

It took a second or two for me to process what the Chief had said. I fell to my knees. It felt like someone punched me in the gut. I looked up at Brad. "You told me that Tim was gonna be fine."

"There were complications," said Brad. "He lost a lot of blood. Doctor Von Hohberg told us that he had a blood clot in his leg that traveled to his brain. He had a massive stroke and died suddenly."

"Oh my God, this is all my fault," I said, clearly distraught.

"Yes—it—is." The Chief walked over to me. His voice inflamed. "You just couldn't keep your damn nose out of other people's business. Now, one of my police officers is dead. Tim paid the ultimate sacrifice for you, Payton. What do you have to say for yourself?"

"I'm sorry. I obviously feel horrible," I said to the Chief. I directed my attention back to Brad. "Where is he? I want to see Tim. I need to say good-bye to my friend." I picked myself off the floor and headed towards the double doors that lead to the patient rooms.

Brad stopped me. He held me back. "Payton, I don't think that is such a good idea. You don't want to remember him like that."

I nodded in agreement. It was better to remember him in the land of the living. I didn't need to see Tim's fixed gray eyes to get my closure. It would probably make me feel worse.

"I propose a moment of silence in Tim's honor," said Nick. All seven officers removed their hats, bowing their heads. Joe, Nick, and Kiel were bald. I didn't need to ask. I already knew why. I bowed my head out of respect for Tim. I put my hand in my pocket, holding the knife Tim had given me tight in my right hand. While his gift was saving my life, he had lost his. It was almost poetic.

A woman screaming outside broke our moment of silence. Everyone in the waiting area directed their attention to the door. A panic-stricken, well-dressed, middle-aged woman appeared in the doorway of the ER.

"Somebody help! There is a dead man out here strapped to the hood of a black Ford Escape."

The entire police force turned to me with a raised eyebrow.

"I don't know why you all look so surprised. I told you I found Kurt."

The waiting room full of people emptied into the parking lot. Brad groaned under his breath. Then he kindly escorted me outside.

Just as we got outside, Blond Ambition and the other six boys pulled up next to my Escape. "What did we miss?" asked Blond Ambition.

"Are you guys following me?" I asked.

"No. We heard it on the police scanner," said Feed Bag.

"We heard that a girl was driving down the road with a dead guy on her hood. I figured it had to be you, Payton," said Chameleon. He directed his attention back to his friends. "Ha, all you guys owe me ten bucks."

"Thanks for your vote of confidence. I think?"

"Payton, this is the part where you start explaining what happened to Kurt," ordered the Chief.

"Do you want the long or the short version?" I asked.

The whole crowd of spectators looked a little judgmental. I decided to give the Chief the tampon-free version without the blubbering, wine guzzling, nose punching, and cracker snacking.

"Today, Payton," yelled the Chief.

"Ok. I was on my way to the hospital when Kurt kidnapped me and held me at gunpoint in my car. He was about to have me turn down a deserted road, so he could violate me and then murder me. Somehow, I lost control of my car. It sailed through the ditch and rammed into a huge tree. Kurt flew through the windshield, landing on my hood. I guess the bastard should have been wearing his seat belt. Any questions?"

"Why didn't you call me for help?" asked Brad.

"Because my phone was smashed in the accident. I just wanted to get to the hospital to check on my friends. The only thing I could think of doing was to bungee Kurt to the hood, so he wouldn't fall off. I couldn't just leave him in the snow bank all mangled. Some kids might have found him."

The Chief blew out a huge sigh of exasperation. "Is there anything else you would like to add to your statement?" asked the Chief.

"Actually, there is. Before the accident, Kurt told me that

he and Rod had nothing to do with the deaths of those boys."

"Let me get this straight, Payton. You would believe the word of a raging psychopath that was about to rape and murder you?"

"Yeah, I guess you had to be there. We kinda had a moment before he tried to kill me."

The Chief let out another huge exasperated breath in my face. It stunk of coffee and cigarettes. I cringed. He leaned over and whispered in my ear. "Follow me." He looked over at his crew of officers. "Someone take Kurt down to the morgue. I don't want to see that S.O.B.'s face ever again."

I followed the Chief back inside the ER doors. As soon as we were out of ear and eye shot of the crowd, the Chief went off on me. Big surprise there.

The Chief grabbed me by both shoulders. "Listen to me good, Payton. Rod and Kurt were responsible for their deaths. I did not shoot an innocent man today. Is that clear?"

"Actually, Chief, you didn't shoot Rod. The big Bald-headed Man did."

Apparently, that was the wrong thing to say to a veteran cop with his credentials. Dick pointed his index finger at me. Just to let you know, when Dick gives you the index finger, it is ten times worse than getting the actual middle finger from him. I was in big trouble.

"You listen to me, Payton Marie Richardson. There is no Bald-headed Man. There is no more investigation. Rod and Kurt are dead. The End."

Here comes another one of my serious personality flaws. When I am right, I need to point it out no matter what. I pulled the key out from my shirt and showed it to the Chief. "I found this last night when Amber and Dylan went missing. I believe it belongs to the killer."

"What makes you believe that?" The Chief asked with curiosity.

"The killer left a note in Dylan's pocket that said, 'you have something of mine, and I want it back.' Blah, blah, blah."

"Why would Rod or Kurt want that old hunk of junk back?

I doubt it's theirs. It looks like it belongs to a woman."

"Exactly. I thought the same thing. So I asked Kurt about it. He swore he had never seen it before."

"Maybe it belongs to Rod's grandmother. Maybe the necklace has nothing to do with this at all. I don't really give a shit, Payton. The killers are dead."

"Don't loose ends bother you?" I asked the Chief.

He got in my face again. "Nope. When I find them, I cut them off."

The doors burst open, letting in the cold night air. Two orderlies escorted a very combative and irate Miss Gilbert back into the building.

"I can't believe she got out again," said Dave, the taller orderly.

"Where do you think she goes?" asked Paul, the shorter, stockier orderly.

Dave shrugged. "Who knows?"

"At least she had a few hours of fun," commented Paul. They both chuckled.

When Miss Gilbert saw me, she reached for the necklace. "Mine," she screamed.

The orderlies pulled her away from me. "Sorry, Miss," said Paul.

"It's ok. We know each other." I told them.

The orderlies pulled Miss Gilbert to the elevator kicking and screaming. They disappeared inside. Just before the door closed, she smiled an all-knowing smile and winked at me. It was weird to say the very least.

"Now I suppose you are going to tell me that crazy old lady is the killer," mocked the Chief.

I tucked the necklace back behind my sweater. "No, that would be impossible."

"Finally, you are making sense. Do us both a favor, Payton. Go see Dr. Parks. Get some new meds. Take a long vacation. Get the hell away from River Bend. If I find you anywhere near another dead body, I'm going to assume that you're the killer and lock you up forever. Understand?"

"Gotcha, Chief. Beach, sand, umbrella drinks. I could definitely use a vacation."

"Good. Now get the hell away from me," he demanded.

I knew it was time for me to give up and walk away before I spent the rest of my childbearing years behind bars.

. . .

It is time to tally up the score. I will give you the skin for the police officer, seeing as how that was all your fault. I will let you have the skin for Kurt too, even though I finished him off. As for Rod, Rod was a group effort. We will split Rod's skin right down the middle, like his skull. That makes two and a half skins for you, and two and a half for me. We have ourselves a tie.

If we include the death of your relationship with your boyfriend, we end up with three apiece. It is still a tie because we both need to claim responsibility for that demise. Keeping him alive turned out to be more painful for you, more fun for me. That means I win on that one, but I will not be taking any extra credit. Last, but not least, if we add the death of the boy from Twin Valley, one of us comes out on top with today's magic number four. How miraculous!

Riddle: Was his death Payton's fault? Answer: Yes. Why? Always have a back-up plan.

We can settle-up in the clubhouse when you are ready, Payton. You owe me the customary beer or the customary life. It is time to flip the proverbial coin again. It is heads. Nice. See you soon.

CHAPTER THIRTY-TWO

Teagan and Lisa were sitting at Amber's bedside when I entered her room. "How is she?" I asked.

"She is going to be ok," answered Lisa. "How are you?"

There was no sense lying about it. They obviously could tell I was unraveling at the seams like a cheaply made, hand-knitted sweater. I plopped down in the spare chair. "Not good. Tim is dead. Kurt is dead. My relationship with Dylan . . . done."

The girls gave me a sympathetic look. "We heard about Tim. We are so sorry, sweetie," said Teagan.

"Tim died a hero," added Lisa.

"That he did," I agreed. "I just stopped by quick to check on Amber and to let you guys know that I'm leaving town tonight."

"Where are you going?" asked Lisa.

"I'm not sure. I just need to get away. I seriously need to clear my head. Can you please explain that to Amber when she wakes up? Can you also tell her to stop flexing her beer muscles for a while?"

"Don't worry, Payton. We will do that for you," said Teagan.

The girls said good-bye. I was about to walk out the door

when idle curiosity took over. I had some loose ends. I needed to check them out before I could amputate the questions from my brain. I stood in the doorway to Amber's room and paused. There was no roundabout way to ask them, so I went right for their jugulars. "I saw you two in the woods outside Rod's house tonight. Teagan, I told you to go to my house and wait. What were you doing there? Who were you looking for?"

The girls looked at each other. "Payton, you left us a note at your house to meet you at Rod's," explained Lisa. "We were looking for you."

"Yeah," said Teagan. "If you saw us, Payton, why didn't you say something?"

I came back inside the room. This was not a conversation I wanted anyone else to hear. "Guys, I never left you a note."

"Well, somebody did," commented Lisa.

"What did the writing look like? Was it male or female?"

"I don't know. It was written in all capital letters," said Teagan.

I had a knot in the chest. It was hard to breath. The writing was the same as the note in Dylan's pocket. It was probably the same writing as the note left on Kurt's car. Someone was playing a dirty game. This sucked. It could be anyone. Well, anyone except Rod and Kurt. They were dead.

"Payton, is anything wrong?" asked Teagan. "You have been quiet for a while."

"Sorry, I was deep in thought. Did Amber say anything to you two about what happened?"

The girls looked at each other. "No, not really," commented Teagan. "She has been sleeping a lot since she came back from surgery."

"She didn't mention seeing a big Bald-headed Man at Rod's house?"

"No, she didn't," answered Lisa.

"What is it with you and this Bald-headed Guy?" asked Teagan.

"He is behind this somehow. Every time I see him, something bad happens. You two didn't see him in the woods tonight or last night at the bar?"

Both the girls shook their heads no.

"Why am I the only person that ever sees him?"

The girls shrugged.

"Maybe I should talk to Levi. He saw him last night in the bar. He told me the Bald Guy was looking for Dylan before he went missing."

"Payton, Levi was wasted last night," said Teagan. "The bald guy that was looking for Dylan was Ted the bouncer. Last night, I heard that when Dylan worked at Smiley's there was an issue of money missing from the till. He never showed up for work again and never paid his bar tab. Now that you guys aren't together anymore, I figured I could tell you."

"Oh, I guess that explains that." I suspected Dylan wasn't the person I thought he was. Maybe it's a good thing that he was out of my life. Don't get me wrong. It still hurts like hell. My heart was shattered. One more question before I go. "Did Amber say anything else to you two about what happened tonight?"

The girls paused before speaking. They were thinking so hard I could see the presence of premature wrinkles forming. Lisa finally spoke. "Amber mentioned that she heard a woman's voice before she was shot through the bathroom door."

"Does that help?" asked Teagan.

"Actually, it does. Thanks, guys. See ya." I felt like I was walking out of Amber's room one-step closer to the truth. Before I could leave town, I had questions for Brad.

Next on my bucket list was talking to Dr. Parks. I went downstairs to the front desk to ask if Dr. Parks was still in the building. It was my lucky day. The hospital called her in to deal with runaway Rose.

Dr. Parks gave the front desk attendant the permission to send me up to the fifth floor. Apparently, it is harder to sneak onto the fifth floor than it is to sneak out.

The elevator door opened. Dr. Parks was waiting for me at

the Nurses Station. Even on call, Dr. Parks looked like she had just stepped out of a magazine. Designer clothes, designer shoes, designer hair, she had it all working for her. Even with my monthly allowance, I would never measure up to her grace and poise.

"Should we step down to my office?" she asked.

"That's ok. Here is fine. This shouldn't take long."

She motioned for me to take a seat.

I declined.

"But, Payton, you have been through a ghastly experience today. Do you want to talk about it?"

"You know what? I really don't. I have come to realize that my life sucks and I'm just going to roll with it. I thought I should tell you face-to-face that I am leaving town for a while."

"Where are you going to go?"

"I'm not sure yet. Somewhere with sand and water, I think."

"Are you taking a family vacation?"

"No. I am going by myself."

"Do you think that is wise?" She looked at me with professional and personal concern.

"Look, Dr. Parks, I need to get out of town and clear my head. I might stop and see my parents in Texas on my way to some exotic island. I think it would be best if no one knew where I was going. The best thing for my mental health is for me to disappear for a while and forget this week ever happened."

"As your psychiatrist, I cannot condone your choice to be alone. Locking you up here on the fifth floor for a month is not the answer either."

"Thank you for understanding, Dr. Parks."

"Before you go, let me write you out a prescription for your anxiety medicine. That way, if you are struggling, you can refill it while you are away."

"That would be great." This was easier than I thought it would be. I could feel my epic downward spiral change to a very slight temporary incline.

"My prescription pad is down the hall in my office. I will be right back."

"Ok, I will wait right here."

I stood alone at the Nurses Station until a short dark-haired nursing assistant named Pam appeared. She had just come out of Miss Gilbert's room across the hall.

"That damn grumpy old bat won't take her medicine again," said Pam, under her breath.

Miss Gilbert appeared in the doorway of her room. She flipped Pam off and went back inside.

That just totally made my day a little brighter. I walked over by Pam and put my purse down on the counter. "So what's her story?" I asked, gesturing to Miss Gilbert's room.

"She has Alzheimer's."

It was time to troll for more answers. "Any idea why she sneaks out or where she goes?"

Pam continued to work on her charting while we gossiped. "They usually find her up by the high school."

I leaned against the counter. "Why the high school?"

Pam leaned in as if she was telling me a secret. "We all joke around that she is going to Prom."

"Oh, that would explain the gown, flowers, and the crown."

"Yeah, can you imagine what she must go through in her mind with her dementia? Miss Gilbert goes to the dance over and over again, but her date never shows."

"Wow, no wonder she's cranky. The poor woman. Does anyone ever come visit her?"

"No, not that I know of," said Pam, with a sorrowful look.

"That is so sad."

"Yes, it is. To be old and all alone." Pam closed the chart she was working on. "Nice talking to you. I should probably deliver the rest of my patients' medication." Pam walked down the hall, stopping at the med cart.

Miss Gilbert popped her head out of her room. She smiled at me. I waved and she waved back. Dr. Parks was still nowhere in sight, so I walked over to Rose's room. I suddenly had a fabulous idea on how to make us both feel better.

When I was inside Rose's room, I took off the necklace and handed it to her. "This is for you to wear to Prom."

I could tell by her excitement that she was seventeen again. Well, at least on the inside she was.

"You have to promise to take good care of it. Don't let anyone see it, or they will take it away from you. Ok? It will be our little secret. Keep it somewhere safe."

Miss Gilbert crawled under her bed. She came back out with a small box. The three by four inch wooden box had three mutually intersecting circles carved into its lid. Rose opened the lid and placed the necklace inside. She removed a pair of dangly, silver, wing-shaped earrings embossed with diamonds from the box. Rose handed them to me.

"A trade? That seems fair." I accepted her gift with a smile. Right after our swap, she crawled back underneath her bed and put the box back where she found it.

"Don't worry, I won't tell anyone about your secret stash spot. I have one too in the back of my closet."

"You should go. My daughter will be here soon." She pulled me to her doorway by my arm.

Poor Miss Gilbert, she is so delusional. As I left her room, she smiled at me. I had lost a friend and gained a friend today. They say, when one door closes, another door opens. Clearly, it was true. Hey, maybe I should give the earrings to my mother to replace the ones I lost to the tow truck driver. Apparently, that door works for jewelry as well.

I collected my purse from the counter and waited at the Nurses Station for Dr. Parks. After about five minutes, she appeared from down the hall.

"Sorry, Payton. I had to take an urgent phone call." She held out the prescription in her hand. "You can have this under one condition."

"What is that?" I asked.

"You must send me a weekly post card so I know you are ok."

"I can do that." I took the slip of paper from her hand.

"See you later, Dr. Parks."

"Get some rest, Payton."

"You can count on it." I left the fifth floor once again a free woman. Next on my bucket list was retrieving my car.

. . .

Nice double eagle. You just knocked strokes off your scorecard.

CHAPTER THIRTY-THREE

The front doors of the hospital opened. I looked around. The Chief and the spectators were gone. Kurt's dead body had vanished from the hood of my car. My life was an inclined plane. I was ecstatic until I saw my SUV hooked up to a tow truck. Ugh! This was a complete downer. My inclined plane just flew right into the side of a mountain.

I needed to think quick before I crashed and burned. Bribery was not an option this time. The rest of my allowance was necessary for my escape plan. I reached into my pocket and stopped myself. He wasn't getting Rose's earrings either.

"Where are you taking my car?" I asked the lone tow truck driver.

"To the police impound lot."

"You can't do that. How am I supposed to get home?"

"That's not my problem, lady. Your car is an official crime scene."

"That's just great." Before he drove away, I sighed, shrugged, stomped, and rolled my eyes just to make sure I got my point across. I was definitely a fiery wreck.

My new car-free lifestyle sucked. I was about to go back into the hospital to see if I could catch a ride home from someone, when I noticed a truck in the parking lot. Someone was sitting in the driver's seat in the dark watching me. The lights of the truck flicked on. The truck moved forward slowly in my direction. I didn't recognize the vehicle or the driver. The parking lot was too dark to make out any details.

As the truck moved closer, I noticed the smashed in front bumper. I'm not going to lie. A flash of impending doom crossed my mind. After everything that has happened lately, I should have run back inside the hospital. I completely understood that line of thinking. If you run away, you get to live to fight another day. Not this time, curiosity froze my feet to the sidewalk. If I had decided to run, when would I stop? You can call me crazy if you want, but I was ready to make a stand.

The dark colored, late-model pick-up truck pulled up next to me at the edge of the sidewalk. The passenger window rolled down. Adrenaline surged through my chest. I wished I had filled my prescription from Dr. Parks. I could be popping my anti-anxiety pills like Skittles and feeling the rainbow. Instead, I was a live wire. I stuck my hand in my purse, touching the gun.

The driver leaned forward. Her face appeared out of the shadows. "Payton, hurry up and get in before someone sees us." She seemed visibly shaken and nervous.

"Lily, where have you been?"

"Just get in. We need to go talk to a friend of mine. You need to hear what he has to say. It could save your life."

With that last phrase, I was hooked. I dove onto the passenger seat. Lily quickly maneuvered the truck out of the parking lot before anyone saw us. We headed down Main Street.

"Where did you get this truck?" I asked.

Lily continued looking over her shoulder periodically to see if anyone was following us. "I borrowed it," she commented.

"From your friend?"

"Not exactly." Lily paused. "I stole it from the hospital parking lot."

I shot her a look.

"What? It's not like it was grand theft auto. The keys were in it, and the engine was running."

"That doesn't make it any better," I argued.

"I'll bring it back when we're done. I promise."

I buckled up anticipating a bumpy ride. "Why did you borrow it?"

"Desperate times call for desperate measures. I figured it was up to me to save your ass." Lily looked in the rearview mirror again.

"I have been doing just fine saving my own ass, thank you."

"Yeah, I saw your handy work on Kurt. Nice job, Payton."

"What can I say? The world is a better place with one less demented pervert in it. By the way, where are we going?"

"We are headed to the tattoo parlor to talk to my buddy, Brent."

I grabbed the lever, turning up the heat. "How can a tattoo artist help me?"

"Brent knows what the symbols mean." Lily looked at the lever I just touched. "Please wipe your prints off of that. You don't want to be linked to this truck in any way."

I did as I was told. It made me wonder if this wasn't Lily's first borrowed vehicle. "You have my permission to drive faster to Brent's shop." I was pumped to finally get some answers.

"Payton, how about I just drive the speed limit in the stolen truck, so we don't get busted?"

"Good call. How about we do that instead?"

We turned left off Main Street. Then we parked in the alley behind the Adult Bookstore. The alley came complete with the typical dumpster, a stray cat, and creepy shadowy places for the criminal element to hide. I had that bad feeling again. Nothing good ever happens in a dark alley, in a stolen vehicle, this close to midnight.

"What are we doing here?" I asked.

"This is Brent's shop."

I looked up at the Adult Book Store sign. "Brent isn't a big fat pervert is he? I don't think I can stomach another one tonight."

"Relax, Payton. Brent rents space in the back of the book store for his tattoo business."

"Oh. That makes me feel better. So how do you know him? Did he do your tattoos?"

"Some of them." Lily pulled a pack of cigarettes and a lighter from the pocket of her coat. She rolled down the window and lit one. "I actually met him online a few years ago."

"Does my brother know?"

"It's not a dating website. It is more like a chat room."

"Potato, pototo," I said sarcastically.

"Seriously, I am not cheating on your brother."

"Ok. Good to know." I decided to believe her. We sat in the dark waiting for Brent. "Speaking of my brother, does he know what is going on?"

"No. I don't think we should tell him."

"Why not?" I don't like keeping secrets."

"We can't tell him. He will tell your parents. I am already on shaky ground with your mother."

"Believe me, they already know."

"How would they find out? They're in Texas."

"I drove to the hospital with Kurt strapped to the hood of my car. I am already front page news," I said laughing.

Lily laughed with me. "You're right. The You Tube video has probably gone viral by now."

"No doubt about it. If I know my little nerds, I am the latest You Tube sensation." Thank God my phone is broken. I was not up to that conversation with my mother.

"Can I count on you, Payton, to keep this secret from everyone?"

"Sure. As far as I am concerned, I'm not here and neither are you."

"Fabulous," said Lily, with a relieved smile.

The back light of the store flicked on and off three times quickly. Lily flicked the truck lights on and off four times.

"Ok, he's here. Let's go," instructed Lily.

Great, my life has just turned into a cheesy spy novel. This was weird even for me. I opened the truck door and hopped out. Lily was already at the back door. She signaled me inside. It was hard to see. A Space World nightlight dimly lit the back entryway. Oh brother, my hero has the maturity of a twelve-year-old.

"I thought you said Brent was here," I said being skeptical.

"He is. He must be downstairs."

I motioned to her to lead the way. I was kind of freaked out, but I tried to not make it a big deal. Lily and I followed the nightlights through the dark tattoo parlor. We took a left at a well-known droid, a right at a legendary spacewalker, before coming to a complete stop at the basement stairs next to an annoying robot.

"Who is this guy, a short, green, backwards talking midget?" I asked.

"Better," Lily whispered back. She turned on the flashlight App on her smart phone. "Watch your step," Lily said, swinging the basement door open.

The steps were severely steep and narrow. I grabbed the wooden railing with both hands. She closed the door behind us and turned off her flashlight. We were cloaked in darkness until she flicked on the light. The basement wasn't any less scary with the lights on. Everything I imagined in the dark was there in the light. Old walls made of stone, an abundance of dirt and dust, and plenty of cobwebs containing eight legged cobs.

At the bottom of the stairs, Lily turned on another light that revealed nothing but a storeroom filled with boxes of tattoo supplies.

"Where is he? No one's here."

"He's a bit eccentric." Lily walked over to a shelving unit. She reached under the third shelf from the top. I heard the clunk. She had unlocked something. The shelving unit swung open on a hinge like a door. Behind it was another camouflaged door that matched the other walls of stone. It was barely detectible. Lily reached out with her left hand, pressing on a reddish rock. The door unlatched and opened from the top like a wooden drawbridge. Yes, I am serious. I checked for a moat and alligators before I followed Lily across the threshold.

271

We stepped into the mini man cave or should I say man castle. Tapestry type rugs covered the cement floors. Red velvet fabric covered the overstuffed furniture. Medieval weapons filled a glass display cabinet. Space Battle figurines and memorabilia filled another. There was even a suit of amour standing in the corner.

The sheet-rocked walls were faux painted from floor to ceiling to look like castle stone. Brent used the walls to showcase his artistic ability. We were completely surrounded by life-sized murals of the Space Battle gang and the Lord of the Wizards characters. Brent wasn't a pervert. Brent was a straight-up nerd boy.

. . .

There is nowhere you can hide from me.

CHAPTER THRITY-FOUR

We found a bald-headed Brent in his reclining La-Z-Boy throne in full-on gamer mode.

"Die, you resilient intergalactic bitch!" he shouted.

"Wow," I said, completely taken in by his commitment to a video game and his posh, yet tastefully decorated digs.

Lily stood next to me. It was clear that Brent was completely zoned-out on his game. He didn't realize we were standing there. "Yeah, his mom won't let him play video games at home, so he hides out here," she said, answering my question before I could ask it.

"But he's like twenty-five."

"And still lives at home," she whispered in my ear.

This was my savior? This skinny, mid-twenties, hairless, nerd boy with glasses, sporting a wicked case of acne was about to enlighten me and save my life. It was definitely a stretch of reality. I would feel more confident if he had big pointy ears. Impressed I would be.

Brent finally noticed us. He immediately paused his video game and set his controller down on the heavy wooden end table. "Lily," he shouted. "I can't believe you brought a mere mortal into my secret lair."

Is this guy for real? "Relax, nerd boy, no one is going to rat you out to your mommy," I said, clearly upset by his horrible attempt at reliving the days of yore.

"Lily, remove her from my presence at once."

"Lily, tell his Highness he doesn't need to get his royal jewels in a bunch. Payton the peasant is leaving." I spun around and headed towards the door.

He stood up. "Payton?" he asked. "Payton Richardson?"

I stopped in my tracks. Curiosity made me turn around. "Yeah?"

"You are thee Payton Richardson?"

"The one and only." I was now famous or was it infamous?

"This is so cool that I finally get to meet you. My mom totally hates your guts. I'm your biggest fan," Brent gushed.

I was glad to see the king drop his medieval superiority complex. "And who might your mother be?"

"Everyone knows my mom, Big Bad Nancy Biggerton."

Wow, I thought I was the only one who called her that. "My condolences. I pity your hardship, my Lord." We had something in common. We both despised his mother. I decided to call a truce.

I walked over to the loveseat next to the mural of The Great White Wizard and took a seat. Lily followed. She took a seat next to me.

"What brings you to my castle, m'lady Payton?"

Lily nudged me. "Show him the necklace."

Was this a test? Did she know that I took the necklace from her while she was unconscious? Maybe she was just guessing. I will play dumb and troll for the truth. "I don't have it. You had it last."

Lily gave me a surprised look. "Payton, I don't have it."

Brent budded in. "Ladies is there a problem? If you don't have the necklace, I suggest you stop wasting my time and let me get back to my—"

"I have pictures of it on my phone." She pulled her phone out of her pocket. Lily scrolled through her gallery until she found them.

Now, I was surprised. "When did you do that?"

"While you were making out with Dylan on the dance floor, I took the necklace out of your purse. I went into the bathroom to take a closer look at it. I snapped a couple quick pictures, so I could research the markings without you knowing. Sorry. When I came out of the bathroom, you were back having an emotional breakdown because Dylan was missing. I never got a chance to slip the necklace back into your purse."

I believed her. "Lily, you don't have to keep secrets from me."

"I know. I just wasn't sure how you would feel about me rummaging through your purse without permission. And for the record, I didn't steal the necklace. I borrowed it."

"It's ok. It all worked out for the best," I told her. "It is in a safe place."

Lily grabbed my purse and reached inside. She didn't believe me. She was looking for the key. Instead, Lily pulled out Kurt's gun.

"Seriously, Payton?" asked Lily. "Where did you get this?" She pointed it in my general direction.

"I confiscated it from Kurt." I said, with my hands raised over my head.

"I'm seriously impressed," added Lily.

Brent stepped in between us, skillfully taking the gun from Lily. "My lair. My rules. No weapons unless they are from the correct period. That means no guns." Brent grabbed a Bible from his bookshelf. He opened it. I expected a sermon. Instead, I got schooled by Brent's stealthiness. The Bible was empty. It was a stash spot for valuables. Apparently, everyone has one. He placed the gun inside and put it back on the shelf. "The Good Book. It will be safe in there," he scoffed. "Now, where were we?"

Lily narrowed her eyes at me as she handed her phone to Brent. He carefully scrolled through the snap shots. Brent zoomed in on a few of the pictures to take a closer look at the detailed artistry. His mood and mannerism changed from mad to manic. "Where did you get this?"

Lily and I looked at each other. Brent was on a need to know basis.

"We found it," I blurted, before Lily could tell him anything more. That was all he needed to know.

"I have heard stories that it existed," said Brent. "I never thought I would actually get to see it in my life time. Do you two have any idea what this is?"

Lily and I shook our heads no. We knew it might help catch a killer. We had no idea it was a renowned treasure.

Brent jumped on top of the couch. He continued bouncing with excitement of the find. Or maybe it was the five Mountain Dews he drank before we arrived. The empty cans were still sitting on the table. "Guys, this is the Key to Immortality. He who possesses it and understands its secrets is guaranteed everlasting life."

"You are shitting me," I said.

"No, I shit you not. I take my history of medieval occultism very seriously." Brent stopped bouncing and jumped off the couch.

"I thought it was just an old family heirloom." I was shocked at its significance.

"Oh, it is a family heirloom from a very old, very famous family. Let me explain."

We moved closer to Brent. He took a seat on the massive oak coffee table in front of the couch. Lily and I plopped down in front of him like eager students ready to cram for an exam. We hung on his every word. We stared at the pictures on Lily's phone while Brent explained to us what he knew about the necklace.

"First, I will start with the symbolism on the front of the key. These four colored stones represent the four royal stars, which are the supporters of the heavens. They are considered the sentinels, watching over the other stars in the sky."

"They are birthstones, aren't they?" I asked Brent.

"Yes, they are. You are very observant, m'lady. You get an apple for your effort."

"Why, thank you, Sire."

Brent smiled. Lily mentally palmed herself. We had this conversation already.

"Can you two cut the medieval crap and focus?" pleaded Lily.

"Sorry," I said. "I recognized my birthstone. The light green one is a peridot."

Brent continued. "Yes, the royal stars coincide with the fixed signs of the zodiac. The peridot, found at the bottom of the head of the key, represents the royal star Regulus. It is the brightest star found in the constellation Leo the Lion. Regulus is the watcher of the North."

"The purple amethyst, found at the top directly across from the peridot, represents the royal star Fomalhaut, found in the constellation Pisces Austrinus. It falls under the zodiac sign Aquarius and is the watcher of the South."

"The emerald stone, located down and to the left, represents the royal star Aldebaran, found in the constellation Taurus the Bull. The star is actually the bull's eye. It is the watcher of the East."

"The golden citrine stone, located directly across from the emerald, represents the royal star Antares, found in the constellation Scorpius the Scorpion. It is the watcher of the West. The four stones are set just like the royal stars appear in the sky. They are at a 90-degree angle to each other. It is called the fixed cross. Isn't that interesting?"

"Not really," I said. "You are losing me. Why is all this star mumbo-jumbo important?"

"It is important, Payton, because it means that the owner of the key obviously is interested in Astrology," said Lily. "They might even worship the stars as well as the sun and the moon."

"That is correct," said Brent. "Astronomy is important as well. The science that studies the origin, size, and motion of the stars, sun, and the planets is relevant."

I had to admit Brent was as smart as that little, green guy. He knew a lot of stuff that most people never knew existed. "What is the significance of the blooming rose in the middle?" I asked.

"The rose could represent several different things. It could represent duality, the soul perhaps, or last, but not least, death."

"Couldn't it just be pretty?" I asked, trying to lighten the mood.

"I don't think so, Payton," said Brent.

"Maybe it represents New York. The rose is its state flower."

Brent sighed. "I don't think so, Payton."

"It was worth a shot. New York sounds better than death to me."

"Apparently, you have never been homeless there in July without money for cigarettes," stated Lily.

I looked at her. Lily had so many levels to her darkness that I just could not comprehend. On a rare occasion, it was ok to be me.

Lily was anxious to change the subject from herself. Lily pointed to the screen. "Tell us more about the clear stone in the middle of the rose?" she asked.

"It looks like a diamond, but it is hard to tell from just a photograph. It could symbolize infinity," said Brent.

"Maybe it's a birthstone," I commented.

"Maybe it's just pretty," said Lily, being a smart-ass.

"Maybe," I snickered, shoving her gothic ass off the couch.

Brent cleared his throat. Which everyone knows is the universal sign for you are annoying me, please pay attention.

I got serious again because I desperately needed his help. "What is the significance of the seven vines, each with seven leaves that surround the rose?"

"Sorry, Payton, that one eludes me. I will have to do some research and get back to you on that."

"That is ok. Maybe it isn't important."

"Oh, I assure you that it is. We just have to figure out what it means."

He was right. Even the smallest detail on the necklace meant something. It was time to dive in deeper. "What are the four triangular symbols near the scalloped edges?" I asked with anticipation.

Brent was ready to get back on track. "They represent the four elements: Earth, Air, Fire, and Water. Does either one of you know what the fifth element is?"

I shook my head. Lily raised her hand.

"The fifth element is the spirit of man. A pure ethereal worth spirit," Lily said with confidence. "It is also known as the Quintessence." She smirked at me. "The symbol of the five elements is the pentacle."

"Brown-noser," I coughed under my breath.

Brent cleared his throat again. Then he continued. "The four elements also coincide with the signs of the zodiac, but I will not bore you with the details at this time." He pointed to the triangle between the peridot and the emerald. "The equilateral triangle that sits on its base without a horizontal line through it represents Fire." Next, he pointed to the triangle between the emerald and the amethyst. "The equilateral triangle that points downward without a horizontal line represents Water." Now, he pointed to the triangle between the amethyst and the citrine. "The equilateral triangle that points downward with a horizontal line running through the bottom third of it represents Earth." Finally, he pointed to the triangle between the citrine and the peridot. "This equilateral triangle that sits on its base with a line through its top third represents Air."

"Brent what does it mean when the symbols are carved into trees?" I asked.

Brent's eyes widened. "Were the carvings on the trees set up in a north, south, east, west pattern?"

I had to think back to what Crystal had told me. "Yes, I think so," I answered. "Hey, look at that. So is the necklace."

Lily and Brent's eyes met. I knew it was something important by the look they shared. They smiled and nodded at each other.

"What? I'm not stupid. This means something big, doesn't it?"

"Yes, it means we have a Wiccan in the neighborhood," said Lily.

"A whatan?" I asked. I was confused.

"A witch," said Brent calmly.

"Why do we have a witch in my neighborhood?" I shouted, clearly distressed.

"Relax, Payton." said Lily. "Wiccans are a peaceful group that worships nature."

I stood up. My voice went supersonic. "There is more than one?" It was suddenly hard to breath. The room was spinning. "Have you two seen the movie with the brick road and the flying monkeys?"

"Calm down, Payton," said Brent. "That was Hollywood. Witches are not green, and they don't have flying monkeys for pets."

I sat back down. My head went between my knees. "How and when did I become Dorothy?" I definitely wasn't in Kansas anymore. Too bad I couldn't click my heels together to make this whole mess disappear. "Next, I suppose you two are going to tell me that vampires are real."

"Seriously, Payton, we don't joke about that ever," said Lily.

I popped my head up for a second, giving her a weird look.

After a few minutes of deep breathing exercises, I felt a nudge. It was Lily. "Here, I found this bottle of wine in your purse."

I pulled out the cork. "To the frickin' Wiccans," I toasted, raising my bottle. I downed a healthy portion without feeling any guilt or remorse.

Brent looked at Lily. He was concerned. "Is she going to be all right?"

"She will be fine. Payton is like a machine. You can continue."

The wine helped my gears click back into place. "Wait, go back. Why did they mark the trees with symbols?"

"They were calling the quarters," answered Brent.

I set the bottle down on the table. "Come again?"

"They were calling the watchtowers, also known as the guardians, or the supporters of the heavens," said Brent, attempting to help me make sense of it all.

"What is the purpose of that?" I asked.

"To erect a circle to conduct their magic," explained Lily.

My head went back between my knees. "I've changed my mind. I've heard enough."

"Payton, relax. There are rules to their magic. They have a rede they must abide by," explained Brent.

"Harm none and do as ye will," stated Lily.

I popped my head back up. "Well, tell that to Streak, Hood Rat, and Tim. Oh yeah, I guess you can't—because they're dead," I said, sarcastically to get my point across. I put my head back down, trying not to hyperventilate.

Brent paced around his man cave. "This is about the boys that drowned in the river isn't it?" he asked nervously.

My head popped back up. I had his attention and he had mine. "Continue," I said.

"See, she's a machine," said Lily. "You just have to give her the right fuel. Payton, take a drink and then pass the bottle to Brent. I think he might need it."

Brent sat back down, passing on the wine. He didn't want any, so I drank his share. Brent scrolled to a picture of the back of the key. He looked at me. "Are you sure you want me to continue, Payton? Are you sure you can handle this? What I am about to tell you is deep, dark, and downright sinister."

"Worse than witches?"

"I am afraid so. It involves Old World Magic, Science, and the Dark Arts."

I nodded, crossed my fingers, and then I did a sign of the cross. I might be just an Easter-Christmas Catholic, but I knew I was going to need some extra spiritual guidance to get through this. Brent was about to explain to me what the horned stick figure on the back of the key represented.

CHAPTER THIRTY-FIVE

The three of us stared at the screen of Lily's phone. Brent once again impressed me and scared the heck out of me with his knowledge.

"The horned symbol in the middle of the back of the key is an Alchemy symbol."

"What is Alchemy?" I asked.

"Alchemy is the chemistry of the Middle Ages."

"Cool. I got an A in college chemistry."

"Excellent, then I shouldn't have to repeat myself. Some of this might get a little deep."

I gave Brent a sour look. "Don't worry. I can keep up."

"Then I shall continue. That symbol can be broken down into three separate symbols. The first one is salt. Do you see the diamond-like stone in the middle?"

Lily and I nodded.

"The silver circle around the diamond, including the silver horizontal line through the middle of the diamond, represents salt. The second one is sulphur. In this symbol, the triangle drawn around the circle represents sulphur." As Brent spoke, he followed the lines with his finger. "The rest of the sulphur symbol is the plus sign coming out of the base of the triangle. The third one is mercury. In this symbol, the circle from the salt, the curved line at the top of the circle that looks like horns, and the before mentioned plus sign coming out of the bottom of the circle, all represents mercury."

"Do you see how the three symbols are superimposed on top of each other to form a single glyph? Throughout history, this technique was used to conceal the true meaning of things that were meant to stay hidden. The Alchemists like their secrets."

"Why was that?" I asked.

"Because their beliefs and practices were forbidden by the Church. This actually caused the Alchemists to take their love of Science underground to form secret societies. This was probably the start of the age-old debate of who is right, Science or the Church?"

"Really," I said. "It's a good thing that my mother isn't here right now to hear this. She would give you an ear full that you would never forget."

"I look forward to opening Pandora's Box with your mother sometime," said Brent.

"Don't bother," commented Lily. "Trust me, you would lose that debate. Her mother is relentless when it comes to her religion."

Brent still seemed intrigued by the challenge.

"When do we get to the sinister part?" I asked.

"I will get to it, all in due time. Patience is a virtue, Payton. First, I need to explain a little more of their philosophy. The early Alchemist believed that salt, sulphur, and mercury were the Earth's three primary substances. They also call them the three essentials or body, spirit, and soul. These three substances had to do with spiritual refinement and purification. In Alchemy imagery, the body, the spirit, and the soul represent the divisions of the world. It is called the Secret Fire."

"They sure seem to like the number three," I said.

"I see you noticed that, Payton?" said Brent. "The sacred number three is the most positive number not only in symbolism, but also in religion, thought, and mythology. It has magical powers."

"Excuse me," said Lily, getting in Brent's face. "The number four is much more important. There are the obvious four classical elements: Earth, Air, Fire, and Water. There are the four Horsemen that support the heavens. And let us not forget, the four basic directions: North, South, East, and West to aid with navigation. There are the four levels of the sky in the Indian Philosophy. And last, but not least, the four major phases of the moon."

"Is that all you've got?" asked Brent.

"No, my square can kick your triangle's ass any day."

"That's it?" Brent laughed.

"Listen here, the four fundamental aspects of Jungian Psychology are far superior to your three Secret Fire theory," explained Lily, poking Brent's chest with her index finger.

"Seriously, guys, stop it," I said, pushing them apart. "I don't have nearly enough wine left to listen to you two fight over the coolness of your favorite number. This is like watching a bad episode on the Kid's Network. The program was brought to you today, by the number three, the number four, and the letter S. Good grief, remind me never to talk politics with you two."

Brent and Lily settled down after my display of feistiness. They looked embarrassed by their actions. Brent cleared his throat and continued.

"Other Alchemists back in the day believed that all matter was composed of the four elements: Earth, Air, Fire, and Water. They also dabbled around the edges of mysticism and magic."

"They sound a lot like the Wiccans. How are they different?" I asked.

"Well for one, witches don't like salt," blurted Lily.

Brent ignored her comment. "The Alchemists have three intertwined goals." Brent smiled as he held up three fingers.

Lily stood up. She walked across the room, giving Brent a chilling glare.

"Lily, do I need to remind you of the rule of three?" asked Brent. "What you send out comes back threefold."

Lily stuck her tongue out at him behind his back. "Can you

guess which one of my fingers I am holding up?" Lily asked Brent.

"The third one," popped out of his mouth without any hesitation.

Lily cursed something under her breath.

I looked at my hand. He was right. No matter if you started counting from your thumb or your pinky, it was the third or the middle finger. I smiled on the inside. He was always one-step ahead of her with his wit and his knowledge.

Brent directed his attention back to me. I hung on Brent's every word. "The first goal is the Philosopher's Stone. It is a mythical substance that would enable the transmutation of a base metal like lead, into gold and silver. A red stone represents gold. A white stone represents silver."

"Hey, the key is made out of lead and silver with a white stone. I bet that is not a coincidence," I said.

"You are correct, Payton. I believe that this key or talisman is for doing just that, trying to turn lead into silver."

"What is a talisman?" I asked.

"A talisman is a man-made object endowed with magical powers. According to the Hermetic societies, it is charged with the force it is intended to represent. In this case, I have a theory that the silver may also represent the moon and the lead may represent Saturday."

I felt my neck where the key had hung earlier. Magic powers? I was psychologically getting itchy. Now I had to deal with the prospect of magic cooties. I wondered if they were as hard to remove as the death cootie.

"I think you're right," said Lily, deciding to rejoin the party. "In the ancient teachings, silver is referred to as the milk of the moon. In Astrology and Magic, certain phases of the moon dictate the action and the time to perform different types of spell work."

"Anyone who knows anything about Astrology knows that the days of the week are named after the planets and are ruled by a metal. Sunday-Sun; gold, Monday-moon; silver, Tuesday-Mars; Iron, Wednesday-Mercury; Mercury, Thursday-Jupiter;

Tin, Friday-Venus; Copper, and Saturday-Saturn; Lead," said Brent.

"There was one Alchemist that claimed he had found the Philosopher's Stone. Do you know who that was, Payton?" asked Brent.

"Let me guess, that magic kid with the broom?"

Brent looked disappointed with my answer. "No, Payton. That is not the correct answer. The correct answer is Nicholas Flamel."

I gave Brent an exasperated look. "How was I supposed to know that?"

"Nicholas Flamel was an Alchemist in the late 1300s to early 1400s. This talisman could have belonged to him or his family," said Brent.

"Wow, I knew it was old. I just didn't think it was that old."

"And priceless," added Lily, reclaiming her seat next to me.

Brent got back on track. "The Alchemists' second goal is a universal cure for all diseases called Panacea."

"That would be cool," I said. "So far the Alchemists sound like ok people."

"Their third goal is Immortality," said Brent. "A substance believed to maintain life indefinitely."

"Well, as long as they don't try to turn anyone into a vampire, I'm ok with it."

"Seriously, Payton, we don't joke about that—ever," instructed Lily for the second time.

Brent let Lily have her moment. Then he continued. "Just wait, Payton. This is where Alchemy was taken down a dark path by a select few in their quest for immortality."

"So this is the sinister part you were talking about?" I asked.

"Yes. These three mystical substances are regarded as one. They refer to all three as the Philosopher's Stone. In the ancient teachings there are claims that the stone can be found within man himself."

"What does the quest for the Philosopher's Stone have to

do with the boys who drowned in the river?" I asked.

"I was just about to address that, Payton. The stone is rumored to be removed only by one of two ways. The first is mortification embalming. Trust me. This is messy decapitating process that I will not go into because it does not apply here."

"Thank you, Brent, for sparing me the gruesome details," I said.

"The second process requires the person to drown. The stone is released, exhibiting its magical properties when the Hermetic seal is broken and the soul is allowed to escape the body."

"Holy Shit," I said. It all sadly fell into place and made sense.

"Yes, I agree. Holy Shit," said Brent.

"Wait a minute," I said. "Didn't a lot of the boys drown or go missing on Saturdays?"

"And during certain phases of the moon," added Lily.

"What does it mean when they remove a piece of jewelry from the boys' bodies?" I asked Brent, trolling for more answers.

"What kind of jewelry?" he asked me, with intense interest.

"A cross necklace. Sometimes they are gold. Sometimes they are silver."

"The cross is a symbol for the stone of Alchemy. When they remove the cross necklace, they are symbolically removing the stone from the body. It is part of the ritual. How do you know about the removal of the cross?"

"Let's just say that I have an inside source. A few of the dead boys were missing their cross necklaces."

"Bingo," said Brent. "My theory now has substantial supportive data."

He was happy. I was sick to my stomach. "The boys all made the ultimate sacrifice for the quest of immortality."

"They were the ultimate sacrifice," commented Lily.

After a moment of silence for the boys, I looked at Brent. "Any idea where we should start?"

"I have always thought that a lot of the answers we are

searching for could be found with the first few victims. Many of the missing boys were from the same area. I think if I look around, I will find some answers," said Brent.

"That sounds like a waste of time to me," commented Lily. "That was so long ago. No one will remember anything."

"Brent, how do you know all of this stuff?" I asked, changing the subject.

"In college, I studied Religious/Medieval History, Art, and Philosophy, but a lot of it I learned on the internet."

Lily pointed to the screen of her phone. "What are these markings surrounding the Alchemy symbol?"

"They look like an ancient form of writing called runes," said Brent. "I will have to do research before I can tell you which ancient language this is or what it says."

"I bet if we figure out what it says, we will unlock the secret to immortality," said Lily. "This is exciting."

"Some things you just shouldn't have a key for," I said. "I don't think I like these Alchemists anymore."

"Payton, most Alchemists are the world's scientists. They have made amazing discoveries in the field of medicine. Other Alchemists pursue ways to refine the soul to make the world a better place. They are harmless."

"Well, I don't like the other kind. The other kind scares me," I said. "That is why I am leaving town tonight."

"You're just going to leave without finding out who it is?" asked Lily.

"Yeah, at best I am being followed by a Wicked Witch or an Evil Scientist, or both. I need to leave town, pronto."

Brent got a panicked look on his face. "You weren't followed here were you?"

"No, but they always seem to find me."

"Have you had that purse long?" asked Brent. He took it from me.

"No, not really. It was a gift." I looked at him with concern for the well-being of my Prada.

"Has it ever been out of your possession?" he asked impatiently.

"Yeah. Why does that matter?"

Brent turned the Prada 2 upside down. He dumped the contents on the floor. Before I could stop him, he reached inside the purse, grabbed the red satin lining, and pulled. Rrrrip. Out came the lining.

I gasped in horror. "Oh my God, what are you doing?"

"I am playing a hunch." Brent reached in every small zippered pocket on the outside of my purse, totally violating my privacy. Tampons, makeup, and my birth control pills flew everywhere. So much for Prada 2 and my dignity, my life was now on display.

"Aha," Brent yelled, holding up a tiny, black chip.

"What is that?" I ask, as I crawled around the floor stuffing my life back in my coat pockets.

"It is a locating device. The police call it LoJack. Shit! They know you are here."

"Relax, Brent. I have a sneaky suspicion that was the work of my ex fiancée, Brad. He is a control freak and a local cop. I am sure that he has an App for that chip on his phone. He is probably sitting in the alley right now trying to figure out where I am."

That seemed to calm Brent down a tad. He sat down in his La-Z-Boy throne. I could tell he was mentally working things out in his head. I excused myself briefly to use the bathroom. While I was alone, I tried to see if there was any hope of resuscitating the Prada. Thanks to Brent, it was DOA. I sighed and threw it in the trash. I paused. Then I retrieved it from the garbage can. For some reason, I felt great sentimental attachment. Yep, tragically pathetic I am. When I returned from the bathroom, Brent was on his laptop.

"Brent, what are you doing?" I asked.

Without taking his eyes off his screen, he said, "We need a plan."

I walked over by his desk. "What for?"

"We need a plan to catch the killer and save the day," answered Brent.

"What do you suggest?" Lily asked, excited about a possible adventure.

"I don't know," said Brent. He popped out of his chair. Brent nervously paced around the room. He flipped through his collection of books looking for a spark. He perked up as if he had an idea. Brent jumped back on his computer.

Lily and I gave him his space to work his computer genius. Brent hammered away on his keyboard. While he flipped through numerous web sites, Lily and I played with Brent's Space Battle action figures to pass the time. Brent allowed it until we made the mistake of crossing the line with his prized possessions. Lily pretended that the droid and the annoying robot were having sex. I made the mistake of having the spacewalker ask the Queen for her hand in marriage. Brent stopped what he was working on and took away the action figures. I forgot that they were actually brother and sister. Apparently, there are no rednecks in outer space.

Lily and I sat quietly in our timeout. I finished the rest of my wine while Lily smoked a cigarette. Lily thumbed through gaming magazines. I attempted to make sense of the books on medieval mythology and folklore. My eyelids were getting heavy as I started reading a story called Iron John.

Brent jumped out of his computer chair startling Lily and I. "I've got it," he yelled. "This is perfect. There is a Science Convention that overlaps a Wiccan Festival in March during the Super Moon and Pi Day."

"I like Pie," I said. "My favorite is strawberry rhubarb with a big scoop of vanilla ice cream."

"Sorry, Payton, this is a different kind of Pi," said Brent. "It is the 3.14159 version. Pi day is March 14."

Lily and I went over by Brent at his computer. "What is a Super Moon?" I asked.

"It is when a new or full moon occurs within ninety percent of its closest approach to Earth. In the case of a full moon, it will appear larger and brighter in the sky," said Lily.

"So let me get this straight. In March, there will be a town somewhere crawling with witches and mad scientists?"

"Yes," said Brent.

"I think I'll pass on the Pi. I would rather go to a galaxy far, far away."

"Payton, you can't just run forever," said Lily.

"I bet I can. That is the beauty of electronic banking. I can access my allowance from anywhere."

"That is silly, Payton. We will be there to help catch them," said Lily.

"Does anyone have a plan to flush out the killer?"

"I have one," said Brent. "Payton, how do you feel about getting a tattoo?"

I gave Brent a troublesome look. "Why? Where exactly is this convention?"

"Where else would they have it? Spring Break on Port Christibel Island, Texas. How do you look in a bikini?"

I did a double eye roll, topped off with a ginormous sigh. "That is where my parents are staying." Shit, now I knew I had to help. My parents were not going to be happy or safe with witches flying all over town. "All right, I will do it."

"This is perfect," said Lily. "Luke and I will meet you there. We will stay with your parents. It will be fun, like a family vacation."

"Seriously? Why do I suddenly feel like a worm dangling on a hook at a fishing contest? I will do this under one condition. Lily has to promise to get a tan at the beach. She has to wear a pink polka-dot swimming suit, absolutely no black."

"Deal," said Lily. "Now let's go upstairs to the tattoo parlor and pop Payton's tattoo cherry."

"Brent, what kind of tattoo are you thinking?" I asked as we climbed the narrow basement steps.

"I think we need to make it visible."

"How about a tramp stamp?" Lily suggested.

"I approve," said Brent.

"How about a rose tattoo for Tim, Hood Rat, and Streak?" I proposed. "We could put each rose inside the triangle sign for water."

"I like it," said Brent. "They do like the number three."

Lily painfully restrained herself from making any snide comments. "Can you add the date that each of them died? I think that would be a nice touch," said Lily.

We walked into one of Brent's workrooms upstairs. Brent had me lay face down on the table. I pulled my shirt up to expose my lower back.

Lily grabbed my purse off the table. She walked over to the garbage can, carelessly tossing it in with the other trash.

"Hey, what are you doing? That was a gift from my mother."

"Let the piece of pretentious crap go, Payton. It's ruined."

"I don't care. I want to keep it."

"Suit yourself." She retrieved my purse from the trash. Lily took a seat next to the table, grabbing my hand.

"This isn't going to be dabbed on by cute, little, fuzzy bunny tails, is it?"

They both laughed.

"This is going to hurt a bit," said Lily.

This was not a good time to be out of alcohol.

. . .

Is everyone ready for the oldest magic trick in the book? I know what you are thinking. No, I am not going to saw a woman in half, maybe later. This is better. Do not blink or you will miss it. The secret is to watch my right hand while I try to kill you with my left. Good luck with that. Curtain please.

CHAPTER THIRTY-SIX

I checked out my new artwork in the mirror. It looked awesome even though the tattoo was red and slightly swollen. I took one for the team. This one was for the boys.

"Brent, you do nice work," I said. "What does it say between the triangles?" It was backwards in the mirror.

Brent was diligently cleaning and sterilizing his equipment. "I have no idea. It was written on the back of the key."

"Holy crap! Isn't that dangerous? I could be insulting someone."

"That is the idea, Payton. You need to stir things up and get noticed," said Brent.

"Great," I said with skepticism. Who doesn't love being the bait. "But what if we're wrong? What if you are completely off track with your theory, Brent?"

"Then no harm done, I guess. The three of us will come back with a tan."

Lily grimaced while she moved in the direction of the door, shutting off lights as she walked. "There are other theories out there: like a group of gamers taking the online games to the next level, girls luring boys to their death, clergy killings, a serial killing gang, cult killings, murderous internet dating hookups, high-tech mind control, bouncers and fake cops, or just bad cops, and a numbers fanatic, but OURS is the right one. We'd better go. We still need to ditch the truck."

Wow. That gives me a lot to think about while my toes are in the sand. "How are we going to get home?" I asked Lily.

"I will take you guys. I have nothing better to do," said Brent as he locked the door. "Hey, Payton, just out of curiosity, where is the key now?"

"Don't worry. It is in a safe place."

"You're not going to tell us?" asked Lily angrily.

The three of us stepped into the alley.

"Trust me. You are safer not knowing. Hey, what do you guys think the key opens?" I asked.

Lily and Brent's eyes widened. They froze motionless. Something was wrong. I turned around to see why they looked like two deer in the headlights. There stood a disconcerted Brad, leaning on the borrowed pick-up truck.

I tried my best to act casual. Inside, I was a mess of brewing bodily functions. Once again, it was time to turn on the charm or pick out a room. This time the room was a cell at the River Bend P.D. That wasn't going to work for me. It was time to put our getaway plan into action. "Brent, it was nice to meet you," I said. "Thanks for the tat."

Now it was Brent's turn to play along. "It was a pleasure, m'lady."

I hugged Lily. It was awkward. We don't hug—ever. Lily and I were still physically attached to each other when she whispered, "What are you doing, Payton?"

"Follow my lead. I will lure Brad away. You two get rid of the truck," I whispered back.

Lily and I parted. When we separated, she ended up with my Prada. With great stealth, she slid it into the open dumpster next to the back door as she walked away. I couldn't ask why. There was no time for that. I am thinking spite and her hate of anything that screamed 'rich bitch.' I grimaced at her defiance.

"I will see you and Luke on Port Christibel Island in March," I said, loud enough for Brad to hear, making sure I had his undivided attention.

"Have a safe trip," said Lily.

I waved good-bye. Then I turned away from Lily and Brent. I headed towards Brad's truck.

"Where do you think you're going?" Brad asked me.

"Oh, hi, Brad. I am going home to pack. Can you give me a ride?"

Brad followed me. My plan was working like a charm. "What are you doing here, Payton?"

I stopped at the passenger door of Brad's truck and opened it.

"I was feeling blue, so I got a tattoo. Is that a crime?" I asked, staring at Brad as he opened his door.

"A tattoo? That doesn't sound like you. Are you drunk?"

I jumped in and closed the door. "No, but I am kind of horny. Can we go now?"

It wasn't a total lie. Obviously, my boarded-up lady parts were having a going out of business sale. It was the perfect distraction to fluster Brad, so Lily and Brent could escape.

Brad got in and closed his door. "You're bluffing."

"Try me," I said, with my best sexy bedroom eyes.

He leaned in and kissed me. I kissed him back long enough for Brent and Lily to pull away in the truck and his car. "Not here," I said. "I have a few questions for you first. Drive."

"Where are we going?"

"My house," I said with a wink. Apparently, the tramp stamp was working. I was now a slut in progress.

Brad drove slowly down the icy highway. He had one hand on the wheel and one roaming hand. It was weird. It felt like old times. I began to wonder if I was actually going to stop him when the time came.

"My first question to you is about my car. Will I ever get it back?"

"After what you went through in it today, do you really want it back?"

"No, I supposed not," I sighed.

"Daddy will just buy you a new one."

I could hear the same old anti-money tone rising in Brad's voice. I changed the subject, not wanting to spoil the mood. I still needed information. "So the case against Rod and Kurt is closed?"

"Thanks to you finding Kurt, the case is closed." Brad put his hand on my leg.

"There are no loose ends?"

"Nope, they are both dead. End of story." Brad slowed down and maneuvered a left turn out of town.

"What about Crystal Pierce's shoe and purse found in Rod's house?"

Brad pressed down on the gas. "I don't care about that." He took his hand off my leg and switched on the radio.

I turned it off. "She could be out there somewhere dead or dying." I was upset at his nonchalant attitude.

"Then she'll eventually turn up." He turned the radio back on.

I pushed in the knob, shutting it off again. "I watch crime shows, Brad. Girls don't just leave their purses behind."

"They do if they want everyone to believe something bad happened to them."

"That doesn't sound like Crystal."

"You would be surprised at what people will do when backed into a corner. For example, if I wanted to fake my own death and disappear. I would leave everything behind including my wallet and keys. If I wanted to get away with murder, I would make it look like an accident or a suicide. If that didn't work. I would frame someone else to take the fall."

I was silent for a few seconds before speaking. My voice trembled slightly. "Sounds like you have given this a lot of thought."

"Relax, Payton. It is police-training 101, getting in the mind of a murderer. That is how detectives solve crimes."

"Well, stop it. You are freaking me out."

Brad laughed at me. "You still scare too easy. After what

you have been through this week, I thought you would have toughened up."

"I have," I said, punching him in the arm. It made me feel much better. "According to your spidey sense for murder, why would Crystal want to fake her disappearance or demise?"

"That's easy. She's a reporter. They like to create the news or be the news. Sometimes they spin the details or make stuff up just to get a story."

I was shocked. "They do?"

"Payton, you have to stop believing everything you see on TV. They do it all the time to get the big scoop."

"Do you think she would go as far as to frame or kill innocent people to get a story?"

Brad took his eyes off the road to look at me. "What are you talking about? Is there something you're not telling me?"

"No. Never mind. Forget I said anything. It was a stupid thought."

"If you're so worried about Crystal, why don't you call her news station?"

"Tim already called the station for me."

"And . . . ?" He drew out the question for added drama. "Is there any chance you would like to elaborate?"

"They told Tim that she was out of town working on a story."

Brad slowed down as he turned into my driveway. "See, she is fine. Crystal already has her claws into another story. Payton, you are old news to her."

"Yah, I guess so."

Brad pulled the truck up by the back porch. He shut off the engine and the lights. I needed to keep the conversation going. "Speaking of Tim, I should really send some flowers to his funeral. Is it going to be at Saint Pat's or at Bethany?"

Brad's facial expression turned grim. "Neither. There isn't going to be a local funeral. The hospital is shipping his body to his family. That is what he wanted. It was written on his DNR request in his medical chart."

"I didn't even get to say good-bye." God, I felt horrible all over again. Tim could be dead because he was snooping around and running tests for me. The tears welled up in my eyes. They flowed down both of my cheeks. There was no stopping them. Brad put his arms around me. He silently held me tight until I finished crying. After the tears of grief subsided, Brad finally spoke. In a low calm tone, he made his confession to me.

"I suppose it would come as no surprise that this is all my fault."

I let go of him, pulling back just enough to look him in the eye. "What are you talking about, Brad?" I was trembling again, waiting for his explanation.

"If I wasn't such an overbearing ass, we would be married by now. This never would have happened because you would have been too busy chasing our first kid around, instead of doing what you do best . . . making everyone's life a living hell." He showed me an irresistible ear-to-ear smile.

To be honest, I should have smacked the shit out of him for giving me heart palpitations, but he did make a very excellent point. And the fact that he admitted to being a controlling ass was a huge step for all mankind. Maybe he had changed.

"Well, unfortunately, we can't undo the past," I said.

"True. But we can move forward in a new direction."

My emotions took over. I planted a long, hot, steamy one on his lips. Brad pulled me close. He kissed me with more passion than he had ever shown before. What can I say? I caved. My lady parts have a mind of their own. Even more enticing than the thought of getting some, was the thought of a normal life without murder, madness, and mayhem.

We continued kissing. Animal instincts took over. Brad shifted positions, pulling me on top of his lap. He started kissing my neck. We had history together. He knew it would drive me crazy. Brad and I were about to strip off our clothes faster than teenagers in heat, when a set of headlights appeared in the driveway behind Brad's truck. Seriously, can't I catch a break? All I needed was about thirty seconds more of adulterated fun to find my happy ending to my story.

I reluctantly rolled off Brad to find my place in the passenger

seat. We quickly buttoned and tucked to make ourselves present-
able. At this point, it could be anyone. As we secured our last
buttons, the car pulled up next to Brad's truck. The driver got
out and walked in our direction. For some unknown reason, the
hooded figure chose to come to my window and knock. Before
I rolled down the window, I recognized the car. It was Lily's
two-toned, blue and white Volkswagen Beetle.

Feeling completely safe, I rolled down my window. "Hey,
that was fast," I said. In that split second, I realized that I was
face to face with my brother Luke instead of Lily.

Luke looked like hell. The dark bags under his eyes along
with the intense look showed his stress. "Have you seen Lily?
She isn't answering her phone."

I know he is my brother, but I thought it was in everyone's
best interest if I chose my words wisely. I was going to do my
best to keep my promise to Lily. "I was just with her. She is
fine. She is on her way home." I just hoped that Brad had the
good sense not to mention Brent right now. I decided my best
bet was to control the conversation.

Luke seemed relieved with the news that Lily was on her
way home. He turned to walk back to Lily's car.

"Wait, Luke," I called out through the opened window.

He turned around. The pain was still present in his eyes.
Something was definitely eating at him.

"Luke, I need you to take over the restaurant for a while
when it reopens. I need to leave town tonight."

"Jeez, Payton, why does it always have to be about you? I
have classes." Luke picked up one our mother's four clay flow-
erpots that sat next to the deck steps. He smashed them one-by-
one on the icy blacktop.

Brad and I cringed repeatedly at each act of violence.

Luke laughed as he admired his handy work. This seemed
to calm him down. He stood in the cold. His breath wafted
clouds of icy vapor around his head.

Brad's phone rang. He ignored it. Luke's violent outburst
took us both by surprise and held our complete attention. I
opened the door to the truck. Brad tried to pull me back. "He's

my brother," I commanded, pushing Brad's arm away. I got out of the truck. Brad followed in a protective manner.

I stood next to my brother with Brad at my side. "What is going on with you, Luke? Talk to me," I pleaded.

He finally broke down and spilled his guts. "Lily has been lying to me. Sometimes, she disappears. When she comes back, she won't tell me where she's been. Other times, I catch her on her computer. If I ask her about it, she quickly exits out of the web page she was looking at. I'm not sure what is going on. I think she might be having an affair."

"Maybe she is screwing that nerdy guy she just left the tattoo parlor with," said Brad.

I looked at Brad. "Really? You are not helping. Go back to the truck," I ordered. Next, I turned my undivided attention to my emotional wounded brother.

I put my hand on his shoulder. He refused my attempt at compassion. Luke shrugged it off. "You knew about this and you didn't tell me?" Luke looked at me with disdain.

Here we go with the need to know basis again. All I could do was to sugar coat it for now until I could explain their relationship. Hell, I didn't even understand it. I wasn't even sure how much they even liked each other. "It isn't like what you think. She isn't having an affair with Brent Biggerton. They're just friends. They share similar interests. Brent is her tattoo artist. He just gave me a tattoo tonight. But don't tell Mom."

This seemed to help. He gave me a hug. "I should go home and talk to her."

"Yes, you should. Everything is fine. Trust me." As far as her disappearing act, I wasn't sure what to tell him. Lily had dark emotional demons she was dealing with. She needed her space. For now, I will let her have this secret.

Before he climbed into Lily's car, he paused and turned towards me. "I guess I will see you on Port Christibel, Payton."

"You can count on it. I just need some time to decompress before then."

"I get it," he said, with brotherly compassion. "It hasn't been easy being a Richardson lately." He drove out of the driveway and into the darkness.

I walked back to Brad's truck hoping to pick up where we left off. When I hopped into the cab, Brad was on his phone. He put his finger to his lips signaling me to be quiet. "I will be right there," he said, disconnecting the call.

My heart sank. My new semi-normal life was going to have to wait due to police business. I attempted to speak again. Brad got a serious look on his face.

"Someone else is dead, aren't they?"

"Not exactly sure what's up. Remember the big hole cut in the ice by your parents' restaurant?"

"Yeah, Tim went there to put up open water signs."

"Someone keeps calling the station about suspicious activity."

"Can't you assign someone else to take care of it?"

"I could. But I should really deal with this."

"Come on. You don't really want to leave?"

"Payton, I need to take this call."

"Ok, then I will come with. Then after the adventure, we can—"

"Payton!" Brad sat in silence.

He had that look again. I could tell there was something else. "What is it?"

"Julie called. The toilet in the master bath overflowed again. I need to go deal with that, too. It could stain the grout and flood the first floor."

"Call her back right now. Tell her to call a plumber. Then tell her, don't let the door hit you in the ass on your way out," I snapped.

"Payton, I can't do that. It's all very complicated."

"Well, I will make it easy for you, Brad." I quickly put my coat on. I opened the door to the truck to get out. "I can't believe I was going to ask you to run away with me."

"You were?" Brad was shocked. Then he smirked.

He knew he had me again. "Damn you." I scowled at him. This was payback for leaving him at the altar. "Bye, Bradley." I was infuriated. I was about to slam the truck door shut.

"Don't forget your purse."

I frowned at him with the door handle in my hand. "Really? I don't have my purse anymore."

"I thought girls didn't leave their purses behind," he said sarcastically. "Planning on faking your demise?"

"No. My Prada was destroyed looking for the locator chip you planted in it."

"I didn't put a chip in your purse."

"Yeah, right." I slammed the truck door.

Brad jumped down from the driver's side. He followed me up the deck steps. "Seriously, it wasn't me," he pleaded.

"Then how did you find me at the tattoo parlor?" I yelled back at him as I walked.

"I followed you from the hospital. I saw you get into that pick-up truck."

I turned and faced him. "You were watching me?"

"I didn't recognize the vehicle. I just wanted to make sure you were ok."

"Well, your services are no longer needed." I turned away. "Good-Bye, Brad." I had one hand on the doorknob when Brad grabbed my arm.

"Payton, I saw the stab wound in Kurt's chest."

"Good. Then you know I can take care of myself. I don't need you to protect me and save me anymore." I cracked opened the door to the house. I glared at Brad's hand on my arm. Then I gave him a daggered look straight in the eyes. He let go.

"You are not going to tell Julie about what happened between us, are you?"

"That is up to you, Brad. I wasn't planning on telling her anything about this." I paused briefly and then decided to share my theory on Julie with him for his own good. "By the way, from now on, I would sleep with one eye open. Amber said, 'she heard a woman's voice through the door before she was shot.' "

Brad didn't like my comment about his beloved Julie. He shook his head. "Payton, you are the one that I'm concerned about. You are the one claiming to have seen a mysterious Bald-headed Man and knives that aren't there. You are the one stab-bing people, blacking out, and finding dead bodies. As a police officer, I don't know if I can keep ignoring these coincidences. It looks a lot like paranoid, delusional, psychotic behavior to me."

My jaw dropped.

"What if there's another investigation? I might not be able to guarantee a good outcome for you, Payton. I think you are keeping secrets from me."

"What? Me? So this is how it's going to be? I'm not the problem and you know it. Don't trust her, Brad." I was furious. I turned away.

"Is this a bad time to tell you that it was me under the sheet outside the morgue?" Without saying another word, he turned and walked down the steps.

"I knew it was you. I'm done, Brad."

"I've heard that before."

I could feel my entire body tighten up with rage. I grabbed an icy ball of snow from the deck railing and threw it as hard as I could at his back. It hit him square between the shoulder blades. "What about your other secret?"

He barely flinched. Brad continued to walk to his truck. "By the way, I ate your Snickers, too," he added as he walked away. "Glad I got that off my chest. I feel better now."

"Asshole!" I shouted to get in the last word. "You know that's not what I'm talking about."

My comment made Brad glance in my direction as he climbed into his truck. I expected a glare out of him, not an empathic look.

Once again, I didn't feel any better. I was back to undate-able.

I was about to go inside when I spotted a box on the deck next to the door. I bent over to pick it up. It was probably an-other present from my mother. I went inside and set the box on the kitchen counter.

Lisa and Teagan must have left all the lights on again. "Hello,"

I called out just in case. I climbed the stairs with as much dignity as I could muster. At least I wasn't bare-assed this time.

I went to my room to pack. I decided to hose off quick in the shower to wake up and to remove the remnants of the magic cootie. The taxi service that Lily called would be here soon to pick me up and take me to the airport. The faster I left River Bend, the better off I would be. A red-eye flight to some tropical paradise was exactly what I needed.

. . .

Just so there is no confusion—what is in the box is from me.

CHAPTER THIRTY-SEVEN

You know you're kinda out-of-it when you accidentally put conditioner on your shower puff, and it takes a solid thirty seconds for your brain to register why there's no bubbles. Don't feel bad for me. It's nothing a nap on the plane won't cure. It could be worse. I could have accidentally knocked my bottle of expensive lotion into the toilet. Yep, we've all been there. It wrecks your whole morning pondering that five-second rule.

I opened the shower door and peeked out. It was in my best interest to check for Brad's soon to be pissed off, gun toting, fiancée, Julie. So far, the coast was clear. My toilet seat was just how I left it, down and unoccupied.

Even if Brad had confessed, I don't think Julie should have the right to be mad at me. According to girl logic, he was mine first. Therefore, he was still sort of my property until I decided otherwise. As messed up as it seems, that was my unspoken rule.

On the other hand, she might have a teeny-tiny reason to be pissed. I did tell Brad that I thought she might have shot Amber and could quite possibly be behind the mysterious deaths. Julie is not going to be happy to see me if Brad spilled his guts.

Wrapped in a towel with my beer in my hand, I stepped out onto the rug. I put the bottle to my lips, tipping it back to drain its contents. The last swig of my beer went down as smoothly as the first. No doubt when the beer industry invented the plastic beer bottle with the screw top cap, the shower beer was born. Who wants soap in their suds, broken bottles creating hazardous circumstances, or water diluting out the perfect balance of barley and hops? Certainly not me. Truly, the shower beer is almost as innovating as frozen pizza and sliced bread. Oops. Sorry. Beer mixed with shower steam made my mind creatively wander.

I got dressed in comfy travel attire, jeans and a sweatshirt. After that, I threw on a light coat of makeup and dried my hair. The second I shut off my hair dryer, I knew I was no longer alone. Someone was rummaging around in my closet.

"Brad, is that you?" I called out.

The rummaging stopped briefly. "Julie? You're not mad, are you?" Still, no one answered.

A thought popped into my head like a blinking, bright orange, neon sign. WEAPON. You need to protect yourself. The knife Tim had given me wasn't an option. It was in the bedroom packed in my suitcase. I scanned the bathroom for ideas. There was nothing in the draws but beauty products. Cardboard nail files and blackhead strips weren't going to get the job done. It was time to improvise.

I inched my way to my closet armed with a hot curling iron in one hand and a can of hairspray in the other. Whoever was in my closet was going to be blinded by hairspray and then annoyed by small, random burns of my choosing. This was not a good start to my vacation.

When I reached my closet, I jumped out to create the element of surprise. Unfortunately, I was the only one surprised. I found my new BFF Rose in a full-length, flowered, flannel nightgown with her head buried in the wall of my closet. She was so busy digging in my secret stash spot, she didn't see me.

How did I know it was Rose? Her fancy, silver high-heels and old lady feet gave her away. Now it was up to me to decide

if she was going to be hazardous to my health. Rose didn't have
the thorny bouquet with her, so I returned the curling iron and
the hairspray to the bathroom counter.

"Hey, Rose, what are you doing here?"

She pulled her crowned head out of the hole in my wall.
"Here, take this." She handed me an object from the pocket of
her nightgown. "Use this to find your way."

I looked down at the standard nursing-home-issued, black
handled, three-inch circular magnifying glass that was now in
my hand. "All righty? Where am I going?"

"To the cemetery," she said as if it were the obvious
answer.

"I was thinking more along the lines of a tropical paradise
myself. But you can still go if you want to," I said, trying to be
cordial.

"Let the light reveal the darkness, when death is all around
you, Grimm holds the key. But beware of the horsemen. They
are the bringers of death," said Rose in a precarious tone.

"I thought they were the four pillars of the universe or
something like that."

Rose shot me an almost cross-eyed glare.

"Okay. Maybe not?"

"Boy froze, red nose. Boy froze, red nose. Boy froze, red
nose. Black, black, black, white, yellow, red." Rose went back to
digging in my closet.

Oh boy. Is this what happens when Rose doesn't take her
medicine. She gets . . . crazy. This was an excellent opportunity
for me to sneak away and call for help before she hits me with
something. I set the magnifying glass down on my dresser and
crept downstairs to the kitchen.

I used the portable phone on the kitchen counter to call the
hospital. The girl at the front desk informed me that Dr. Parks
had already left for the day. I was about to dial 911 when I
heard a noise behind me.

Someone was knocking on the window of the patio door. I
spun around. A man stared at me through the glass. It was Tim
in his full police uniform. The cordless phone dropped out of

my hand. It hit the hardwood floor. He waved. My blood stopped flowing. I instinctively waved back. It would have been impolite of me not to.

I bent down to retrieve the phone from the floor. When I looked back at the patio door, Tim was gone. I went over to the patio door to look for him. Was this Tim's attempt to say good-bye to me?

Suddenly, there was a knock on the kitchen door behind me. My body jerked out of reflex. I spun around. Through the curtains, I could see a police officer in full uniform standing in the cold. I ran over to the door and threw it open.

The light from the kitchen hit his face as he stepped inside. He removed his hat. I backed away completely in shock. It wasn't Tim. It was Officer Nick Burrell. Nick oddly looked a lot like Tim. Granted, he didn't have any hair at the moment, but the similarities were uncanny. They were roughly the same age, same height, same basic build, and had the same cop-certified mustache. I never noticed the similarity before. Nevertheless, I know what I saw. It had been Tim. I was sure of it.

"Sorry, Payton. I never meant to scare you," said Nick.

"That's ok. I am getting used to it. This might sound weird, but I thought you were Tim."

He smiled. "I get that . . . I mean . . . I got that a lot. Actually, this was supposed to be Tim's shift. I volunteered to take it."

There was the awkward moment of silence and sadness when you start referring to the deceased in the past tense. Tim was really gone.

"I'm so glad that you're here, Nick. I was just about to call the station. I have a visitor upstairs."

Nick seemed relieved. "So Rose is here."

I took a step back. "How did you know that?"

He took a few steps towards me, backing me up against the center island. "Dr. Parks called the station. She reported her missing again. The Doc should be here soon."

Nick made me feel uncomfortable. I couldn't quite put my finger on it. Let's just say that I won't be turning my back on him any time soon. I paused for a second to think about what Nick had said. He hadn't answered my question.

"No, that's not what I meant. How did you know where to find her? And better yet, how did Rose get here?" To increase the size of my space bubble, I took two sliding steps to my left to avoid the awkwardness.

Nick smirked ever so slightly from behind his mustache. He knew he had gotten under my skin. "The old black truck from the maintenance department of the hospital is parked outside," he said. "I noticed it while patrolling the area."

"Oh?"

"I told the maintenance crew they should stop leaving the keys in it. This isn't the first time that old truck has gone missing. The funny thing is, it always seems to find its way back to the hospital parking lot."

"Really? That is strange." Knowing what I know, I can only assume that Lily and Brent were able to return the truck without getting caught. "So you think Rose drove the truck here? How did she find me?" I asked.

"I think Rose knows more than we give her credit for."

"Maybe someone helped her," I insinuated.

"Maybe. But who?" he inquired, inching toward me again.

It was time to put some serious space between us. I made my way across the kitchen looking for another beer. As I approached the refrigerator to claim my well-deserved liquid prize, I glanced over at the counter. My mom's favorite celebrity knife was still missing from its spot in the wooden butcher block holder. Honestly, I was done trying to figure that out. It would surely turn up eventually.

"Sorry. Where are my manners? Would you care for a beer?" I asked. "It has been one hell of a day."

"No, thanks, Payton. I am on duty. I will have to take you up on that beer some other time."

"Ok. Well, I hope you don't mind if I have one?" I opened up the door to the refrigerator. With one fluid motion, I grabbed the bottle, twisted the top, and took a drink. "Hey, Nick, can you grab me a beer mug out of the dishwasher?"

I heard him open up the dishwasher that was next to him and grab a clean mug from inside.

I closed the refrigerator door. When I turned around, Nick was back in my space bubble. He held out the mug to me with an outstretched arm.

"Thanks." I was grabbing the mug from his left hand, when I noticed the knife in his right.

"Payton, you never answered my question. Who do you think is helping her?"

I was too busy sweating profusely and running names of possible suspects through my head to notice that someone had walked up behind us.

"Nicholi?" asked Rose.

We both turned around.

"Do you two know each other?" I asked.

"No," said Nick. "Definitely not." Nick slid the six-inch, celebrity knife into the one open slot of the wooden butcher block. "The alleged missing knife, I presume," he said. "I found it in the dishwasher."

"Thanks. Mystery solved . . . I guess?"

"I will make sure it gets in the report and the Chief is notified."

"And I'll make sure Vivian gets a spa vacation in her brand-new convertible."

Nick laughed, thinking I was making a joke. I was never more serious.

As I joined in with my own nervous laughter, Dr. Parks burst through the kitchen door. "Thank goodness you are okay, Rose." Dr. Parks gave Rose a big hug. "You had us all so worried."

"Dr. Parks, how does Rose keep getting out?" I asked.

Dr. Parks pulled me aside. She lowered her tone too slightly above a whisper. "We are not entirely sure yet. It is a delicate process trying to extract information from her without causing her a mental break or any kind of a setback."

"Any idea on how or why she found me?" I asked.

"Unfortunately, I cannot answer that either. That is why I must ask you to please keep this quiet."

I had to ask her the dreaded question. "You want me to keep this a secret?"

"If you do not mind, Payton, it would be appreciated. My reputation, as well as the reputations of the hospital and the entire staff are on the line."

"Sure. Why not?" I asked, throwing my hands in the air. I was leaving town within the hour. What was one more secret rattling around in my brain anyway? After a dozen or so umbrella drinks, the secret was bound to fall right out of my head and be lost forever.

"Thank you so much for your discretion, Payton."

"Don't mention it," I said, taking a drink of my beer.

"Do you think that is wise?" asked Dr. Parks, motioning to the beer in my hand. "Self-medication is not the answer, Payton."

"Well, it's a darn good place to start until I find a better one. I thought I saw Tim outside a few minutes ago."

"Really?" asked Dr. Parks, raising her eyebrows at my statement. "Maybe we should discuss this before I go?"

"Sure," I said, taking a seat at the table.

"Nick, could you give us some privacy?" asked Dr. Parks. He nodded.

"Take Rose outside, please. Put her in the back of your squad car. I will be out shortly."

Nick took Rose by the arm, leading her to the door. Rose didn't put up a fight. She smiled and waved at me. With her left hand, she showed me a strand of pearls that hung around her neck. They looked a lot like the strand that belonged to my great grandmother, which my mother kept hidden somewhere in her bedroom. Rose winked at me when Nick and Dr. Parks weren't paying attention. As she passed by, I noticed her tan winter boots and long blue down jacket. They were oddly similar to a jacket and boots my mother has/had in her closet. It made me wonder if Rose had been here before. She seemed to know her way around pretty well. But that would be crazy and highly unlikely, right?

As soon as we were alone, Dr. Parks took a seat across from me at the table. "Payton, tell me about your visions of Tim?"

I told her what happened. She nodded and smiled.

"Payton, this is very common when someone close to us dies."

"It is?"

"Yes. Our subconscious remembers them. We want to see them again. The slightest similarity to the deceased can trigger a response."

"It can?" I took a sip of my beer. Dr. Parks moved the mug out of my reach.

"Sure. A similar hat, coat, or uniform that was worn by the deceased can make our mind play tricks on us."

"That makes me feel better, Dr. Parks. How long will this last?"

"It differs from person to person. I would say a few weeks to a couple months. Time and a change of scenery will help. That is why I think you should still go on your trip."

"Great. I was hoping you were going to say that."

Dr. Parks stood up. "I should leave now, Payton. I need to get Rose back to the hospital." She walked to the door and turned around. "There is one more thing. Could you write down your parents' address in Texas for me?"

"Sure. Why do you need that?" I asked, grabbing a pen and paper from the kitchen counter.

"Do you still want me to send your mother those shoes for her birthday?"

I gave her a blank stare.

"Do you remember our conversation, Payton?" Dr. Parks snapped her fingers twice. "We discussed this at the hospital."

"What? Oh yeah, of course, I forgot. That would be great. Sorry. I am completely out of cash. Can you just add the shoes to my weekly tab? I'm good for it." I made a mental note to stop at an ATM on the way to the airport. Umbrella drinks and white sand beaches do not come cheap. I handed her the address.

She smiled. "Have a safe trip. See you soon, Payton." She closed the door.

The rest of my beer was still on the table. I waited for their taillights to fade into the darkness. Then I slammed the rest of my beer against doctor's orders.

There was only thirty minutes until my taxi would arrive. I ran upstairs to brush my teeth and grab my suitcases. While I was upstairs, I could check on the status of my closet.

When I entered my bedroom, I could tell that Rose had been in my suitcase. My larger suitcase was open and my clothes were all messed up. She had went through my suitcase and found the earrings she had given me. For some reason, Rose placed them on my dresser next to the magnifying glass.

I didn't have time to dwell on her odd behavior. I had a plane to catch. I threw them both in my suitcase and did a quick closet inspection. Rose had left it just as she had found it. Rose carefully and methodically tucked all my belongings back into my secret stash spot before coming downstairs. What was she doing here? And better yet, what was she looking for in my closet? When I get back, I will have to sneak onto the fifth floor and ask her. Right now, I had one mission and one mission only. I was getting the heck out of River Bend.

I grabbed an old purse from my closet. I sighed. It would have to do until I could shop for a new one. Don't laugh. I miss Prada number two. The hot red color made me feel spunky.

I unzipped my old denim purse for a quick inspection. Inside one of the pockets, I found an unopened pack of cigarettes and a lighter. Yes, even I, the Great Payton Richardson have my secrets. I looked at the clock to see if I had time for a quick smoke. It had been months since I caved to my old habit that I acquired at college. Should I do it? Why the heck not? This week has been beyond mind-blowing. I'll just have a couple puffs and throw the rest away. I promise.

To avoid a lecture from my mother, I opened up my bedroom window and sat on the sill. Seriously, the woman is like a shark. She could smell a drop of blood in a swimming pool. I put the cigarette to my lips and flicked the lighter. Just as it sparked, I huge gust of wind blew my hair across my face. I dropped the cigarette and lighter out of fear of spontaneous hairspray combustion. While I frantically checked my hair for melted ends, I watched the lighter and cigarette slide down the icy roof. The cigarette rolled out of sight, but the lighter stopped just short of the edge. Holy crap, that was close. I almost made a trip to the burn unit instead of the beach.

This damn roof was not going to beat me, again. Out I went to retrieve my lighter. This time I was better prepared. I tied eight shirts, six pairs of sweat pants, and the belt from my bathrobe together. Before I climbed out the window, I secured one end to the leg of my bed. No more gold metal Olympic luge runs for me. I had learned my lesson. I carefully lowered myself down to my lighter in a responsible manner.

Just as I was inches from my prize, the snow around my feet moved, causing a small avalanche. My lighter slid off the edge. I let out a "Nooooo!" Then realized that it didn't fall off the roof. It had just fallen into the rain gutter.

I was now at the end of my pitiful rope. Seriously, one more pair of sweat pants and I would have totally nailed it. To reach my lighter, I was now going to have to let go of the rope with one hand and blindly dig in the gutter for it. First try—nothing. Second try—nothing. Third try—nothing. Fourth try—bingo! Huh, four does have its attributes. Lily would be happy.

I pulled the object that was in my fingers out of the gutter. I looked at it in complete outrage. How could I have been so stupid? It wasn't my lighter. I had found something much more important. I climbed back up the roof to my window. I no longer had a desire for a cigarette. I had a bigger monkey on my back.

Once I was safely inside my room, I closed the window. I sat on my bed staring at the object in my hand. I thought about Brad's disparaging remarks, 'You're delusional, Payton.' "Delusional and paranoid my ass, Bradley!"

The object I found was a silver, six-inch, double-edged, knife with a wooden handle. It had odd markings carved into the blade and the handle. The word "Red" boldly stood out. I immediately grew angrier and was able to piece my latest adventure together with the utmost clarity. This changed everything.

I thought about Rose's insane rambling nonsense, her beating me with her dead flowers, and earlier that night, my encounter with Vivian on my roof. Holy Crap! Maybe Rose isn't crazy. What if Rose didn't mean, 'Boy froze, red nose?' What if she meant, 'Boy froze, Red knows?'

Good grief. You need to calm down, Payton. That is about the stupidest thing that could have popped into your brain. You are tired, wired, and liquored up. What a crazy and highly unlikely hypothesis. My head was spinning with possibilities. This new information was beyond troubling. I couldn't tell anyone. No one would ever believe me, especially the police. One thing was for sure. Vivian was NOT getting a convertible or a spa vacation. She was back on my shit list, and this time, I'm talking about the laminated version.

I needed to think seriously about how I was going to handle her. But first, I must put distance between us. Better yet, at least for a while, I should distance myself from everyone. I had no idea who I could trust. It was time to get the hell out of River Bend. I could sort out this secret with my toes in the sand on a beach far, far from here.

Before I left my bedroom, I threw the knife in my suitcase, changed my wet socks, and snagged my passport from my top dresser drawer. I was headed for some fabulous faraway land, where hot guys and cold drinks would surely help me forget the past few days.

Should I go to the French Riviera and bask naked on the beach? Maybe I should go native in Bora Bora with a hot young stud. Take surfing lessons from the local hotties in Hawaii. Go down under in Australia. Come up for some air and parasail in Belize. Or just get down and dirty in Mexico with a bottle of tequila and a Latin lover. I decided to add them all to my bucket list. Why? Because I frickin' deserve it.

I was in my faraway daydream state, thinking about my endless possibilities, when I heard a horn honk. I glanced at the clock. The taxi was early. Like a flash, I grabbed my suitcases, shut off the light, and frantically bungled my way down the stairs. When I reached the kitchen, I stopped in my tracks. The box I found outside on the deck was still on the counter. The taxi driver would have to wait. I tore into it like a six-year-old on Christmas morning.

I know what you're thinking. Maybe because of my recent history of horrible events, I should have called the Bomb Squad or the Swat Team. I didn't. Shame on me. I couldn't help myself. I smelled leather, very expensive leather. So I ripped the box open. I peeled back the brown cardboard lid, exposing the treasure inside. I gasped. It was absolutely gorgeous. Inside the box was a brand-new, periwinkle blue Prada purse. I shall call her . . . Prada number three.

The horn honked again. I pulled the new purse from the box and ditched the denim. It was time to say a quick good-bye to the Richardson mansion and hit the road. Believe it or not, after I grabbed a roadie from the refrigerator, I actually shut off all the lights and locked the door. As I made my way down the steps, I made another mental note to buy a phone to call my parents. They needed to know that I was all right.

When I reached the taxi, the driver popped the trunk lid from inside the car. I waited for a minute for the driver to get out and help me. He didn't. I loaded my bags inside the trunk myself. I opened up the left rear passenger door. Then I climbed inside the cab. Soon, I would say good-bye to River Bend and all who resided here. I was off on a fabulous new adventure. I cracked open my beer in celebration, taking a long well-deserved drink. Vacation at last.

"To the Twin Valley Airport please," I commanded.

The door locks clunked into the locked position. Something didn't feel right. The driver turned around and looked at me. "Payton, we need to talk." Even in the darkness, I knew who it was by his massive silhouette. It was my mysterious Baldheaded Friend.

A second figure rose up in the front passenger seat. It was a woman. The shadowy face of the news anchor appeared over the front seat. "Nice to see you again, Paylula," said Crystal Pierce.

"I thought you were dead," I said.

"That seems to be the rumor floating around," stated Crystal. "I guess you can't believe everything you hear."

"And only half of what you see," I said, directing my comment to my Bald Friend.

They both had an interesting story to tell. Apparently, they met the night Streak died. Crystal ran into Secret Agent Smith of the FBI while checking out the crime scene behind the college. Agent Smith was assigned to follow me to see if I could lead the FBI to the killer. I would have to say there was still an excellent chance of that plan panning out. So I need to stay focused.

Crystal decided to join Agent Smith in the quest for justice. She is helping solve the case while getting the ultimate exclusive to the story. It is a win, win situation for her. As Crystal always says, 'Awareness equals answers.' Damn. She's got that right. I'm aware I need some frigging answers fast.

I learned a lot from our chat. The icing was slathered on the conversational cupcake when Crystal was kind enough to divulge the name of the first victim. I am talking about the victim from Twin Valley that didn't seem to fit in with the other three. Guess what? He does. And it's just a matter of time before the dots are connected. Everything is pointing in a bad direction. This could get complicated.

On a tragically pathetic note, Crystal and Agent Smith have also informed me that my life was still in danger. Duh. That is why they are personally escorting me to the airport for my own safety. They have informed me to trust no one, so that is what I must do.

I, in turn, informed them of my plans in Texas. On our way to the airport, we will devise a backup plan to lure the killer out of the shadows. My mission, if I chose to accept it, is to shake the tree to see who falls out. Packing my own chute and keeping my own secrets are my safety net for survival. How great will this look on my resume for the FBI when I help solve the case and catch a killer? Sadly, the rest of the mission has to remain under wraps for now. Wish me luck. I'm going to need it.

With great secrets comes even greater responsibility. Then the lies start and the whole thing blows up in your face. Everyone you know, and everything you thought you knew, can change in a split second. Your life can suddenly turn into a huge pile of crap. Fortunately, for me, my life is hopelessly already there. I cannot wait to see how this whole thing turns out.

SNEAK PEEK INTO THE ULTIMATE SECRETS

I dared you to look away and here we are. You are right where I want you to be—on the edge of your seat wanting more. And you shall have it. More death, more gore, more secrets, and more fun and games for me. I will not disappoint. And the answers you are begging for? You shall have them all soon enough. No matter who has to be sacrificed.

As far as Payton is concerned, I predict trouble for her. Why? Because I will be the tour guide. First stop, the inevitable beach of a party where someone will be dying to get in. Heads are going to roll. Want a front row seat? Want to know who is getting the axe? I thought so. Your dark side is showing.

This time, you will be the one dying to get in. I knew I had you at hello, and now, you are the one lining up with the demented and the corrupt. Nice. My advice to you: They are a rough bunch, so watch yourself. No budgies or savies, or you will never make it past the ropes to get inside.

For those of you who are already rocking your 'In Crowd' status, grab your suntan lotion, cloak, candles, and a dish to pass, and hit the beach. Remember, this party is by invitation only and B.Y.O.B. Please select your plus one wisely. No unwanted guests will be tolerated. Party crashers will pay the ULTIMATE price.

For the poor souls who will never make it inside the coveted circle, you are in for a treat. A few secrets will spill out. As always, I will leave it up to Payton to clean up the mess.

If you are one of the slower wannabes who are still a little dazed and confused by it all, pay closer attention this time. Trust me. You will get the answers you are looking for. I promise. But I will only say things once, and I will not be holding your hand while you try to figure it out.

Dangling clues and watching you chase them gives me a mental hard on. Knowing that you are struggling gets me off. Let me guess, last time you thought you had it all figured out and then someone died. Congratulations! You fell for the oldest magic trick in the book—misdirection. Can I get that standing ovation now? I am the master.

Since I am in such a good mood, I will give you another shot at cracking the case wide open. If you are not a complete numbskull you have

319

probably figured out that I am not in this alone. Someone is helping me. What can I say? Every good magician has an assistant. Good luck to you figuring out who it is. Good luck to you ever stopping us. See you in the winner's circle. I will be the one waiting under the full moon with my piece of cake.

One last thing to dangle in front of you before I go; here is the bait to reel you back in. Riddle: Who or what is down under the ice? Answer: Not quite yet. This secret needs to simmer under the surface for optimum impact. What a tangled, twisted, deceitful, little web I have woven. My new game will be fun. Would you like to watch?

S.K. Lundberg started her career off in the medical field before switching gears later in life to follow her passion for writing. Currently, she and her husband enjoy their quiet, small town lifestyle that allows them to spend time on their favorite hobbies. Most of her spare time revolves around family, friends, food, sports, good cheer, and of course, a great book to read.

77268523R00198

Made in the USA
Columbia, SC
30 September 2019